TIN GOD

Brigid Connor is a vampire familiar with ghosts. The ghosts of her past, the ghosts of her victims, and the ghosts of those she couldn't save. Now in the wilds of America's most remote frontier, she'll face a specter who has haunted her steps, a fire vampire with a baffling connection to Brigid's mate, her clan, and those she holds most dear.

Tenzin is an immortal who has lived a hundred lives. She's been a daughter, a sister, a villain, and a hero. With every millennium, she has evolved, cutting ties with the past and moving forward with relentless focus, a survivor among the fiercest predators in history.

But history has a way of finding those who flee from it.

Tin God is a crossover between the Elemental Covenant and the Elemental Legacy novels. It is the final book in the Elemental Covenant series by eleven-time USA Today bestselling author Elizabeth Hunter.

As usual with Hunter's writing, there's lots of world-building and dynamic characters. The final showdown is pretty epic.

TIN GOD by E. Hunter is the spectacular finale to an awesome series.

TIN GOD

AN ELEMENTAL COVENANT NOVEL

AN ELEMENTAL LEGACY NOVEL

ELIZABETH HUNTER

FOREWORD

This book is a crossover novel between the Elemental Legacy series featuring Ben and Tenzin, and the Elemental Covenant series, featuring Carwyn and Brigid.

For more information about both series, please visit:

ElizabethHunter.com

THE ELEMENTAL UNIVERSE

THE ELEMENTAL MYSTERIES

GIOVANNI AND BEATRICE

A Hidden Fire
This Same Earth
The Force of Wind
A Fall of Water

ELEMENTAL WORLD

VARIOUS SIDE CHARACTERS

Building From Ashes
Blood and Sand
The Scarlet Deep
A Stone-Kissed Sea

Waterlocked
The Bronze Blade
A Very Proper Monster
Valley of the Shadow

ELEMENTAL LEGACY

BEN AND TENZIN

Midnight Labyrinth
Blood Apprentice
Night's Reckoning
Dawn Caravan
The Bone Scroll
Pearl Sky

ELEMENTAL COVENANT

CARWYN AND BRIGID

Saint's Passage
Martyr's Promise
Paladin's Kiss
Bishop's Flight

TIN GOD

Place me like a seal over your heart,
    like a seal on your arm;
    for love is as strong as death,
    its jealousy unyielding as the grave.
    It burns like blazing fire,
    like a mighty flame.

SONG OF SOLOMON

PROLOGUE

The wind vampire flew over the frozen plateau, hunting for signs of life in the clear night. The sky was lit by a newly waning moon, and the earth beneath her was threaded with river valleys so fine and numerous that they reminded the hunter of the unfurled leaf of an ancient fern.

She smelled smoke in the distance and turned toward it.

The small wooden house was surrounded by dense forest, nestled in a narrow river valley flanked by snowy peaks. There was nothing for miles except trees, wild animals, and a drifting group of human pastoralists she could easily avoid.

She'd found him. A thrill hummed in her blood.

Finally.

She had been hunting her quarry for centuries.

The isolation was impressive. There was nothing permanent in the vast landscape save for a tiny human village on the banks of a lake on the other side of the plateau.

The wind vampire she hunted was the last of his immortal bloodline.

His brothers were dead. His sire was dead, and she'd killed his grandsire thousands of years before he'd been born.

But flowing through this vampire's veins was immortal blood that the hunter had sworn an oath to destroy.

She perched in the branch of a pine tree, watching the cabin where glowing gold light flickered through small glass windows. Snow fell through the branches of the pine, drifting and dancing in the air, triggering a faint memory of sunlight and laughter she had nearly forgotten after endless years.

The house in the valley was built in the traditional manner of the Russians who had come into these lands, made of stacked logs with a steep roof to channel falling snow to the sides of the dwelling. There was a spiked wooden fence that surrounded the compound to keep predators away from the frozen meat hanging from the eaves.

Humans would see that as a barrier, but it wouldn't stop her.

Humans also wouldn't detect the faint scent of frozen human blood from the bodies hidden in the snowdrifts, but she could smell it through the ice and the snow.

It was too cold in the winter to bury human bodies, but the ground around her was thick with bones. She could hear them whispering as they moldered in the earth. These immortals had been hunting in this area for many seasons.

From the house, the faint sound of music drifted in the air, interspersed with affectionate endearments in the Russian tongue. She'd spent two years learning it so she could stalk this prey. When she had killed him, she would do her best to forget.

Rumors that her old enemy's blood still lived had reached her in Tibet, centuries after she had believed Temur's line to be extinguished.

This vampire had done his best to hide from her; he knew fate would find him should she discover his existence.

She floated from the pine branch down to the ground, dislodging flurries of snow like flower petals swept into the night air and snatched away by a breeze.

Her legs were wrapped in heavy wool and fur, her feet in thick leather boots. From a distance, she probably looked like an animal.

She *was* an animal.

Her feet landed in the snow, and the crunch of ice that reached her ears sounded loud as a gunshot.

The hunter lifted from the ground again, floating over the blue-lit surface of the frozen landscape. The sky was clear, and the stars shone in cold judgment.

There would be no mercy from the sky, just as there had been no mercy in Temur's blood.

It would end tonight. Finally it would end.

She flew around the house, looking for an entry point, searching for anything that would allow her silence. She hated noise. She hated all this, but it needed to be done.

Some blood needed to die. She would never sire a child, so her own sire's blood would die with her. It was the best. It was necessary.

She spotted a blackened window at the back of the house and arrowed toward it. The weight of the bronze blade was heavy at her side, bound to her thigh next to a dagger and a thin, short rapier she'd paid a smith in Kashgar to forge. It was carefully designed to pierce between ribs and precisely reach the heart where a swift flick of her wrist would end a human life in seconds.

She had no need for the rapier that night, but the blade brought her delight. It was the only satisfaction the hunter took from life, the ability to end it with such swiftness that suffering was barely a thought in the mind of her victims before they were gone.

She was a merciful and efficient killer.

The vampire looked at the window, searching for a way inside the house, but the darkened window was sealed against frost and wind.

There was no helping it. The death wouldn't be as silent as she'd hoped.

She reached out with her senses and located the two vampires in the largest room of the house. She was a creature of air, and the void whispered to her.

Two creatures of her kind, both larger than she was. One who called to the wind and the other...

Interesting.

The other had been born to fire.

She knew of few vampires in that area who claimed fire as their element, and all of them were dangerous. She wondered if this vampire was one she knew.

But no. This was a newer immortal. Their blood was fresh and rich with human life. This was the predator who fed on the bodies in the ground, a hungry, grasping immortal still in the first years of life.

Young, erratic, and capable of bursting into flames.

The hunter would have to eliminate the young vampire first, which annoyed her. The young vampire was not her quarry, but they could prove too dangerous to allow them to their fate.

Unless...

She listened to the affectionate words flowing between Temur's Blood and the new vampire. They were tender and teasing. These vampires were lovers. Perhaps there was some loyalty between them. In that case, the young fire vampire could be an advantage.

Without another thought, she took her blade from her thigh and smashed the hilt through the heavy glass window.

All sound stopped, and there was a rush of feet and a whisper of metal. She flew into the rafters and curled into a corner of the room, waiting for her quarry. She pulled her amnis in, throwing a shield over the immortal magic that gave her life.

And waited.

Her quarry came first, but she did not move.

She hadn't seen him before, but she had smelled his blood. Smelled the blood that had betrayed her. He bore the same eyes she did, eyes from the east that swiftly searched the shadows, looking for whatever had broken into their hidden sanctuary.

He was hoping for the body of a bird or the clawed fury of a wolverine.

Her quarry was foolish. He didn't look up.

"Purev?" The new vampire walked into the dark storeroom. "What is—?"

"Zasha, no!"

Too late.

The hunter fell on the woman, her arms and legs wrapping around the young fire vampire as the bronze blade came to her neck, the tip pressing against the spine.

The young one panicked. "Purev!"

"Calm." Her quarry held up his hands. "I know you. You have no quarrel with her. Your fight is with me, Saraal."

"Sida." She spoke for the first time in a year, and her voice was rasping. "I do not know that name."

Sida, the tribe of ancient wind vampires who had ravaged the eastern plains where her human life had ended. Sida, the sons of her immortal sire who had treated her worse than the human women they captured.

A vampire slave would not break as human captives did.

"Please, Purev," the fire vampire whispered. "Make her stop."

The hunter did not care to know their names, and the moment she left, she would do her best to forget them. After all, memory was a kind of life, and she wanted all of them dead.

To her, all of Temur's blood were Sida. She felt the heat building on the vampire's skin and knew that with a fire element so young, control was tenuous.

Her blood was different, bearing the scent of both male and female. Curious.

But the new vampire's blood was interesting, not important.

Her fire, on the other hand...

"Her name is Zasha." Her quarry spoke, looking into her eyes. "She has nothing to do with us."

The hunter stared back. "You know why I am here."

"I am not my sire," the wind vampire said. "I live peacefully. I don't hurt anyone."

"I smell the bodies outside. Blood does not lie."

The man gestured at his woman. "I... I have to feed her. She's new, and she needs blood."

"And I need *your* blood. Temur's Blood."

The fire vampire was motionless but getting hotter under her hands.

"She will lose control unless you let her go." The wind vampire held out his hands. "Please let her—"

"Fine." The hunter gripped the head of the new vampire and snapped her neck to the side. "Now she won't burn."

The fire vampire fell to the ground with a heavy thud.

"No!" His mouth dropped open. "Zasha?"

"She will be fine." The hunter floated to the ground and stepped over the fire vampire's body as she walked toward Temur's Blood with her blade held out.

"Purev?" The voice was weak, and sobs caught in the young one's throat. "Purev?"

"See?" She kept her eyes on her quarry. "She's not dead."

Temur's Blood glanced at his lover, then back to the hunter. "My love, be calm. She will not hurt you." He whispered in a language long dead, "She only wants me."

"Don't you remember? This was how the Sida controlled me. You snapped my neck every night when I woke, leaving me defenseless." She stepped closer. "Then you did whatever you wanted to my body and buried me in the ground like an animal storing a carcass. That's all I was to you, remember? Another carcass to feed on."

He shook his head. "But I didn't do those things. I wasn't even born when those things—"

"You bear his blood."

"I bear the same blood as you!"

"Please." A tortured sob from the vampire on the floor. "Just leave us alone."

"Be quiet or I will kill you too," the hunter said. "Do you know how I found you, Temur's Blood?"

He shook his head. "I have lived my life knowing that you would kill me the moment you found me. My sire—"

"Your sire should have never passed this wretched blood to anyone else," she said quietly. "I *am* sorry for that. It is not your fault, but the blood is true, is it not? I found you because there were rumors of an Eastern wind vampire who was stealing children from the trade routes."

"Orphans," he said. "Beggars. Children who had already been thrown away. No one would miss them."

"*I* miss them." The hunter blinked. "My children were orphans after I was killed. And I missed them. Did you know that?"

Temur's Blood slowly shook his head. "I was only trying to feed her. She was hurt; she needed to heal. She needed time to grow strong."

"A pity." The hunter never looked at the sobbing vampire on the floor. "Her protector revealed himself, and now he will die. If you had remained here, I might never have heard of you."

"No!" the weeping vampire shouted, her voice strong though her body was useless. "You can't! You can't take him from me!"

She cast one glance at the creature.

The young vampire was eye-catching. It was no wonder some

immortal had become fascinated by her. She was as tall as a man with broad shoulders and striking red hair the color of flickering flames. The planes of her face were as pale and sculpted as the snowcapped peaks around them, and her eyes were striking, a brown so dark it was nearly black, and rimmed with pale red lashes.

"What color were your eyes?" the hunter asked. "Before you turned."

"Wh-what?"

"Your eyes." It was a curious thing. The hunter's eyes were grey, but she didn't know what color they'd been before her turning. She didn't remember anyone ever noticing them or talking about them. Perhaps they'd always been a storm grey, but she didn't recall.

"Blue," the vampire whispered. "They were blue like the sea in summer."

"I am sorry for you." She turned back to look at Temur's Blood. "Say goodbye to her."

"No!" the woman begged. "Please. Please."

Temur's Blood stared at her; though he remained motionless, the wind picked up, battering the wooden house with angry gusts.

The hunter raised an eyebrow, but his element could not defend him, not when her power was so much stronger. She was old. Very, *very* old.

Temur's Blood whispered, "Promise me that you will not hurt her. I will not fight you. I know I cannot. Only promise me that she will be safe from your vengeance."

"I will only kill her if she tries to kill me," the hunter said. "I vow it on my children's blood."

"You will only kill her if she tries to kill you." He looked at the weeping vampire. "Zasha, remember. You cannot take revenge. However long you live, you must not. You must allow her this debt."

"No!" the fire vampire screamed. "*Purev, no!*"

She smelled the smoke and knew that the young vampire's magic was already reaching out, repairing the strands of energy the hunter had broken. It would only be a matter of moments before she was a danger again.

Temur's Blood closed his eyes, put his hands together at his chest, and bowed deeply. "Am I the last?"

"Yes."

"Will it be enough for you when I am no more?"

The hunter cocked her head. "I do not know."

He kept his head bowed, but his eyes looked up. "Let it be enough."

The hunter lifted her blade, struck the neck of Temur's last child, and sliced his head from his neck while the young vampire on the floor lay screaming at her to stop. The body collapsed like a pile of flimsy sticks, and the head rolled to rest against the stacked firewood under the broken window.

Screams turned to choked sobs, and the smell of smoke filled the air. The woman's clothes were starting to burn.

Wind and snow were gusting into the storage room through the broken window, but neither of those would kill the young fire vampire. In fact, they might just save her.

The hunter turned to look at the sobbing vampire. "I made a vow not to kill you, and I will not."

"I don't care," she choked out. "Kill me. *Kill me!* Please, I don't want to live without him."

She shook her head. "Then your suffering is at his hand because I made a vow." She walked down the hallway, through the cozy front room where a fire burned in a stone hearth and a pot of something savory was slowly burning where it hung by the fire.

The hunter moved the pot away from the flames, the acrid smell of burned food almost covering the smell of burning wool that came from the back of the house.

She cleaned her blade on a blanket near the fire, then put it back in its leather scabbard and walked out of the house.

The wind was gusting more wildly, her magic churning it though she remained calm on the surface. Her blood was jumping, and her fangs ached in her mouth, but she searched for satisfaction. For peace.

Temur's blood was no more. Finally it was no more.

The hunter took to the air and barely noticed when the wooden house behind her burst into flames. She paused, glanced over her shoulder, and watched the flames engulf the house, the fence, and melt the snow where the bodies of stolen children had been hidden.

Fire vampires. So volatile.

She disappeared into the night and rid the last drop of Temur's blood from her memory.

He was dead. Finally he was dead.

CHAPTER ONE

B rigid Connor bumped over the snow, huddled in the fur-covered sled that a team of yapping sled dogs pulled through the dark, frozen woods of Alaska. The driver, a silent human who had introduced himself as Andre and then said nothing else, barked commands at them from time to time, but if he'd said another word to Brigid, the driving wind had blown it into the darkness.

Overhead, a glowing green-and-purple aurora borealis lit a clear night sky, dancing over the tips of evergreen trees. The northern lights were more vivid than she'd ever seen before, doubly vivid with vampire vision that turned them so bright she nearly remembered what it felt like to stand in daylight.

She pulled an old pocket watch from the folds of her winter coat. Her husband had bought it for her last birthday, the only timepiece that could withstand the pull of her amnis, the elemental energy that kept her vampire blood moving and connected her to her element.

Brigid's element was fire, but she wasn't very good at using it, and it didn't seem very helpful in a land surrounded by sea and covered with snow, ice, frost, and fog.

It was six in the evening, and the sky was black pitch. Stars sparkled through the lights, and the moon was visible on the horizon, peeking through the dense forests of the Alaskan wilderness. She was traveling to a remote station run by Oleg, a Russian fire vampire whom Brigid now owed several favors.

Oleg wasn't going to be at the station, which was a good thing. Under the archaic territorial rules that governed immortals, the Russian was trespassing. The area Andre's dogs were drawing them toward was the territory of Katya Grigorieva, who was based in Seattle. She ruled the Pacific Northwest with canny intelligence, keen strategic thinking, and the convenient ability to look the other way when she didn't really give a shit.

"So this used to be Oleg's territory?" she tried to ask Andre, but she had no idea if the man heard her. Brigid turned back to face the wind, crouching down so the tearing cold wouldn't lash her.

She was bundled from the tip of her nose to her carefully wrapped feet. Alaska in winter was no joke, and they weren't even in the coldest part of it.

Oleg's station was on the coast, a relatively reachable outpost on the Kenai Peninsula, only a few hours from Anchorage. The scope of the landscape was hard for Brigid to wrap her mind around.

This was "relatively close" to the city. This was "not far." This place, where she hadn't seen a sign of civilization other than a bright red stick coming out of the snow every now and then, was the "accessible" part of Alaska in the wintertime.

Brigid had been born in Ireland, a place where a person could drive across the entire island in the time it had taken them to drive from one city to the next in Alaska. She'd met Oleg's people at the airport the night before, found shelter during the very short day, then taken four-wheel-drive vehicles over frosty roads as far as they could before switching to the dogsled to get to the station.

She glanced at her watch again, guessing they were only about forty minutes away from the destination where she would start her search for the vampire who had stalked her for years.

She gripped the cold metal in her hand and remembered Carwyn giving it to her.

Gold, darling girl. It's the only thing that might keep this old thing running with your energy.

She'd protested that it was too extravagant to have a watch with a casing made entirely of gold, and he'd ignored her. He was old, much older than Brigid, and he'd had time to save money he rarely used.

"Aloha shirts and beer don't cost much, Brigid."

She thought of him constantly. His voice. His touch. The scent of his skin and his blood.

He was furious with her, and she deserved it.

There was a tapping on her shoulder, and she looked up to see Andre pointing at something in the distance.

A moose was tearing bark from a tree, shaking the branches with the force of his bite. She smiled up at Andre and gave him a thumbs-up to indicate she'd seen it.

Moose. Caribou. Birds of surprising variety.

No bears according to the locals. They would all be hibernating.

The world around her was cold and silent save for the barking dogs and the frosty shush of sled tracks on snow. The white blanket that covered the landscape devoured sound whole, leaving Brigid to her thoughts in the cocoon of fur that Andre had thrown around her.

No music. No news programs. No virtual assistant chirping at her.

Brigid was alone with her thoughts, and all she could think was that she missed her husband, her feet were very cold, and she had no idea how, in the vastness of the Alaskan wilderness, she was supposed to find the vampire who had caused so much chaos in her life.

Because she wasn't in Alaska for a holiday or a *vacation* as her US friends called it. She wasn't there for research. She'd come to the frozen darkness with one goal alone.

She was there to kill Zasha Sokholov.

———

THE DOGS RAISED a hail as they approached a low-slung building that curved along the rise of the hill. It looked like an old Quonset hut save for the snow-covered roof and the height. It appeared to meld into the hill behind it, forming the head of something that looked like a turtle while the tree-covered hill was the shell.

Flickering yellow lights surrounded the compound, and as they approached the guardhouse, Brigid saw the chain-link fence topped with barbed wire. There were guards in white clothing stationed along the fence, and a guard tower beyond the gate rose over the trees.

The better to spot a wind vampire.

She'd be waiting for a wind vampire at Oleg's compound. She hoped Tenzin was already on her way, but with that ancient immortal, there was no way of knowing.

You know Zasha.

I know of them.

You know more than that.

Tenzin, wind vampire of old, retired assassin, treasure hunter, and mate of one of Brigid's closest friends was a mystery that few tried to solve. Brigid had no desire to delve into the vampire's past, but the situation had forced her hand.

"Andre!" The guard shouted at the dogsled as they pulled in, and Andre brought the sled to a stop. "You have the Irishwoman?"

Andre said nothing, but Brigid popped her head from the pile of fur and waved.

"I'm Brigid Connor," she said. "Mika said you'd be expecting me."

Mika Arakas was Oleg Sokolov's head of internal security, which mostly meant that when heads needed to be cut off and Oleg didn't want his hands dirty, he pointed at Mika.

"Brigid Connor." The guard squinted. "Your face, Miss Connor."

Brigid peeled off the scarf, which had frozen to her face, and tugged off the hat that was keeping her shaved head warm.

The guard looked at her, then a picture, then back to her. "I like the haircut."

She'd burned off a good chunk of her short black hair months ago and decided to buzz cut all of it. It made for quick evening preparations and frosty ears. "Thanks." She shoved the wool cap back on. "Is Mika here?"

"Oh no." The guard smiled. "Lev will introduce you to the guys." The man had a slight Russian accent, but his manner of speech sounded American.

It was an unusual area. Brigid had called an old friend before she came—one who would deny talking to her if anyone asked—to ask for insight into Oleg and into the politics of the region.

Coastal Alaska was still considered Eastern Russia by most immortals. Which was why technically Katya ruled it, but from what Brigid could tell, it was far more like the American Wild West of old.

Oleg Sokolov had interests. The Eight Immortals who ruled Eastern Asia had interests. The Athabaskan Confederation had the most financial interest and territorial control, but they didn't want to deal with anyone but Natives and mainly ignored human interests completely.

To outsiders, Katya was the vampire in charge.

It seemed to Brigid that the immortals of Alaska paid attention to their own and ignored everyone else. It was a big place, and big places lent themselves to laissez-faire vampire politics.

"Come inside," the guard said. "Let Andre put the dogs away. I'm Emil. Welcome to the fishing camp."

Supposedly the compound in Kenai was Oleg Sokolov's personal fishing retreat, but Brigid had a hard time imagining a fishing camp needed the kind of security that she was seeing.

She climbed out of the sled and gave Andre a polite nod before she grabbed her backpack and headed toward a narrow door set into the wood-sided building that crawled out of the hill. Just as she approached the door, a large vampire barreled out of it, his arms going wide.

"Brigid Connor!"

She blinked. "Are you Lev?"

"Who else could I be?" He walked over and gave her two smacking kisses, one on either cheek. "Forgive me—it's been a long time since we've had visitors."

The man was a giant with a slight Russian accent, a beard that covered half his chest, and brown hair that curled in a riot all over his head like someone had gone a little wild with pruning shears. He was wearing a short-sleeved shirt open at the neck, baring his hairy chest nearly to his waist.

"No visitors, huh?" Brigid looked up and blinked. She was pretty sure her eyelashes were frozen. "I can't imagine why."

"I know!" The man's face lit up as he looked around the snow-covered compound. "Can you imagine that? With weather like this? I will never understand my brother."

"Are you..." She frowned. "Is Oleg your brother?"

"Oh yeah, yeah. Big family." He shuffled her into the building as the dogs let out a howling chorus and Andre mushed them away. "Huge family. Our father was a bastard! Cruel old bastard, but he liked siring children." Lev shrugged. "So Zasha is my sister.

Sibling." He held up a hand. "When Zasha came to us, they were a girl, so sometimes I slip, but I mean no disrespect."

"No disrespect to *Zasha?*"

Zasha Sokolov was an immortal who had been tormenting Brigid, her mate, and her friends for years. A fellow fire vampire, they'd fixated on Brigid from a distance, picking off people she cared about, killing humans that Brigid would miss, and generally creating chaos.

"Oh, I don't want to disrespect anyone." Lev guided Brigid through another set of heavy double doors. "There is too much cruelty in the world, isn't there? It's easy to be kind." He turned to her. "Can I take your bag?"

Brigid clutched her backpack tightly. "No."

"Okay, good." Lev nodded. "Good, good. No problem for me. I run Oleg's fishing camp and I keep track of everyone, but I don't want to intrude."

He led her through a small entryway that was stuffed with clothing, muddy boots, and various weather-related accouterments. There were snowshoes hanging on the wall, a few skis propped up in the corner, and lots of dirty towels piled on an old washing machine. The room smelled of dirt, motor oil, and men.

She looked around at the mess. "Is Mika here?"

Mika preferred tailored suits to flannel shirts, and she was having a hard time picturing him in the wilderness.

"Mika?" Lev laughed. "No, but he *likes* you. I could tell. He called you the little barsuk." Lev chuckled. "That Mika, so funny."

Brigid reminded herself to find out what barsuk meant. "Did Mika tell ya I'm here to... find Zasha?"

Find was good enough. The killing part didn't need to be stated.

"Oh yeah." Lev seemed unconcerned. "Yeah, yeah. I don't blame you for wanting them dead." Lev opened the door to the next room past the muddy entryway. "They're not an easy person to like."

"Zasha?" Brigid frowned. "Yeah, not too likable." She muttered, "Probably a result of the rampant homicidal mania."

Lev nodded sadly. "Zasha gets that from our father."

Brigid didn't know whether to laugh or not.

Zasha Sokholov did not deserve a sad nod from a friendly vampire bear. They were aligned with no one but themself, hungry for power and an unabashed lover of chaos.

Because they were completely unpredictable, most of Zasha's own kin had long ago disowned them. The Sokholov crime syndicate wanted nothing to do with Zasha. It wasn't the murderous tendencies so much, but they didn't want to be associated with someone they couldn't control.

Oleg Sokolov—the least criminal but still morally questionable head of his own clan—had changed his name in an outward attempt to distance himself from both his criminal relatives and Zasha.

Not that Oleg wasn't shady, but Brigid's sources seemed to agree that Oleg's criminal enterprises were no longer as profitable as his legal ones, so he was moving away from the darker corners of the vampire world.

It was the only reason Brigid trusted him enough to ask for help.

Lev led her down a narrow hallway and into a large room that looked like a cross between a cafeteria and a living room. There was a large kitchen along the back wall where two humans were cooking something that smelled like game meat.

On the other side of the room, a massive fireplace dominated one wall. Around it there were at least a dozen humans and vampires. Roughly thirty percent vampires if Brigid guessed the flow of energy correctly, and the rest were human. Visually it was hard to tell them apart.

So much flannel.

"Boys! This is Brigid." Lev clapped her on the shoulder. "She's here to kill Zasha."

There were a few grunts, a couple of nonchalant waves, and a lot of nodding.

"Hello."

"Hi."

"Welcome."

"Good luck."

Then everyone returned to what they were doing before she and Lev had walked in.

"Come," Lev told her. "Let me show you to your room."

———

"HAS HE ASKED?"

Lee Whitehorn was tapping on his computer keyboard, which was the position she usually caught him in whenever she video-called.

"Your angry husband?" Lee didn't stop tapping. "Uh... no. I'm pretty sure he knows you're calling me, but he hasn't asked because if he asks he knows I won't lie to him—"

"Because you refuse to lie."

"Exactly. And if he knows for sure that I'm talking to you, he'll ask me where you are—"

"Which you would tell him." She rubbed a hand over her freshly washed head and contemplated keeping it shaved to a buzz cut indefinitely. It felt so good.

"Exactly. But then you'd find out that I told him where you were and you'd stop calling me for help."

And Carwyn wouldn't want to leave her stranded without Lee's resources because she'd be less safe. "Got it."

"So where are you?"

"A fishing camp in the back arse of Alaska."

"Huh." He glanced at the camera, which was streamed to the private virtual assistant he'd built for their house and electronic devices. "And how's that?"

"Cold and dark."

"Vampire heaven?"

"No, I prefer dark and warm. Think Jamaica at night." She'd been in Jamaica at night. It was marvelous.

"How's the tablet working?"

Lee, being their own resident computer genius, had taken their old Nocht-compatible mobile devices, hacked them, and inserted his own operating system since he didn't trust anyone, including her old boss, who had created the first vampire-compatible mobile operating system that could be worked entirely by voice command.

Elemental vampires destroyed electronics.

Earth vampires like her husband could handle things longer, but fire vampires like Brigid were especially prone to shorting things out just by touching them. She'd lost multiple mobile phones from keeping them in her pocket too long.

"The tablet is working fine." She watched the screen of the small tablet that was halfway between a mobile phone and a computer. "It survived the dogsledding trip with no damage."

"Seriously?" That had Lee looking up from his typing. "Dogsledding?"

"According to my host, humans 'round here use snowmobiles, but vampires break them, so we go by skis, boat, or dogsled to get around."

"Unless you can fly like some vampires." Lee glanced up again. "Any sign of her?"

"I have no idea who you're talking about."

"Of course you don't. By the way, the next time you go to

New York to meet with a vampire assassin, turn off your location services, okay?"

"Noted." Brigid retrieved a compact 9mm handgun from her backpack and started taking it apart.

So soothing.

"Is that your emotional-support firearm?" Lee asked. "Adorable."

"Shut up, Lee." Brigid looked at the shuttered window. "She'll be here. Lev is taking me tomorrow to see the raid."

"You're sure it's Zasha?"

Brigid looked back at the screen. "I'm sure."

He frowned down at his keyboard. "But others aren't?"

"Opinions are mixed. Accordin' to Mika, Zasha is the only one who would have dared inflict this kind of damage under Oleg's nose. *But* there's some debate if Zasha is working solo and just wants to piss off their brother or..."

Lee looked up. "Or?"

"Some folks in Oleg's organization think Zasha is working with Katya."

Lee's eyebrows went up. "Katya Grigorieva? Our Katya? The vampire who *runs* Alaska?"

"'Runs Alaska' is a very fluid idea." She thought about the wild country she'd passed on the dogsled. "I have a feelin' that Alaska mostly runs itself."

"What about the Ankers?"

The Ankers were a shadowy vampire clan that dealt in information, illegal data harvesting, and identity fraud. They also had some shipping interests that Oleg used to his advantage.

"Zasha's worked with the Ankers before," Lee continued. "They worked together in Las Vegas and in Louisiana. Oleg's people don't suspect that the Ankers are funding Zasha this time?"

"According to Mika, it's not likely. Oleg has some kinda deal with them about moving fuel out of Russia with their unregistered fleet, and they make a lot of money by not pissin' him off."

"Could they be right?" Lee asked. "Would Katya work with Zasha Sokholov?"

"I doubt it." Brigid shrugged. "I get the feelin' that Oleg's crew up here knee-jerk blame Katya for most stuff if it's aggressive. I'm gonna try to talk some sense into Mika when I see him. I'm with you—I think Zasha is probably working with the Ankers again, but I'm a nobody up here." She frowned. "Actually, I'm a barsuk. Any idea what that is?"

"No." Lee pursed his lips. "But I can try to find out. Don't rock the boat in the Wild Vampire West, boss."

"I'll try not to." She hunched forward and started lining up the pieces of her compact Hellcat from magazine on the left to frame on the right. "Any luck tracking the Ankers' money lately?"

"No. I'm pretty sure they're using cryptocurrency, because there was a gold exchange in Antwerp that received a sizable deposit a week ago—roughly two million dollars—and another one that popped a two million outlay to a client two days later in Vancouver. If Zasha is in Alaska and someone wanted to send them money, Vancouver is the closest gold exchange they could use."

"Vancouver?"

"Yep."

That was close. "Vancouver is Katya's territory."

Lee's voice dropped. "So you think there might be some truth to what Mika was saying?"

"No." Please, God, don't let Katya be working with Zasha. That would be a huge mess. "Even if it's in her territory, Katya can't interfere with the gold exchanges."

"She'd make a lot of people angry if she did." All vampires relied on the gold exchanges to move money around in the human-dominated modern age, and lately more and more of them were discovering cryptocurrency, which was even harder to trace than gold. "But that confirms that whatever Zasha is up to, the Ankers are probably involved."

Brigid nodded. "Yeah. That *is* that it looks like."

"But?"

She looked at Lee's face on the screen. "Zasha made a lot of money in Vegas when they were there. They don't need money right now." And she didn't think Zasha was truly motivated by money in the first place. "So why piss off your vampire brother in his backyard to make money you don't really need?" She started reassembling her 9mm. "I'll figure it out. Just need time and more information."

"She's going to come."

"Hmm?" Brigid had been thinking about Las Vegas and lost track of Lee. "Who?"

"Tenzin. She's going to come. She always does when things get bad."

She pushed the slide lever back into position. "How'd you like that to be your reputation, Lee? The one who shows up when things go to shit."

He shrugged. "I guess as long as I could help make things better, I'd be okay with it."

"Yeah. Fair point." She tested the function of her gun, then carefully checked the magazine, reinserted it, and clicked the safety into place.

Of course, Lee's point was only good as long as you ignored the very real likelihood that was starting to stare Brigid in the face the longer she looked at this problem.

Tenzin wasn't the solution to this tangled mess that had ensnared Brigid's life. She was probably the one who'd started it.

CHAPTER TWO

The corporate office of Katya Grigorieva was located in an old brick building in Seattle's Pioneer Square. It was connected to various other buildings and residences via underground tunnels that the water vampire maintained with the help of earth vampires in her employ.

Carwyn walked through the tunnels, his amnis spreading out into the walls, the old mud, the broken logs and living things beyond the visible.

He was a creature of the earth, as connected to the ground beneath his feet as a tree or a grub. His head nearly brushed the top of the tunnel in places, and he had to duck as he walked through the narrow corridor.

The skylights that would illuminate the tunnels during the day—thick glass set into the modern sidewalks of the city—were dark at night, and rain dripped through the seams, dropping to the muddy floor where he walked.

The darkness matched his mood.

Carwyn reached the door that was the underground entrance to Katya's building and lifted his head to face the vampire security guard, a broadly built man with light brown skin, close-cropped hair, and an angular jaw.

"Father." The man nodded.

"Not a priest anymore, my boy." He'd been one for a thousand years, so he didn't judge the young vampire. He'd made his connections in the immortal world as a priest, and vampires weren't exactly known for keeping up with current events.

"Mr. Bryn." The vampire corrected himself. "Katya is expecting you."

The young vampire's energy sparked the image of green and growing things. Despite the man's curt voice and stoic expression, Carwyn sensed a kindred spirit.

"What's your name?"

The guard looked at him and frowned. "Jerome, sir."

"You're good," Carwyn said. "Your amnis touched mine nearly as soon as I entered the tunnel."

A slight flinch. "Thank you, sir."

"I didn't take it as a threat." The corner of Carwyn's mouth turned up. "It was a warning. Like a... polite knock."

Jerome nodded. "Thank you, sir."

"After all" —Carwyn stared— "we both know I could pull this entire building down on top of us if I wanted to."

"Yes, sir." Jerome didn't flinch. "But doing that might ruin that kick-ass Soundgarden T-shirt you've got going on."

Carwyn looked down at the T-shirt that peeked out from his heavy leather jacket. "It's vintage."

The guard lifted one shoulder. "Probably not a good idea to mess it up."

"Good point." Carwyn looked at the brick foundation sunk into the earth. "I suppose I'll spare the building for now."

"Much appreciated, sir."

Despite his foul mood, Carwyn couldn't stop from smiling. "Keep up the good work, Jerome."

"Thank you, sir." He opened the door and held it for Carwyn. "Have a good night, Mr. Bryn."

That's my father's name. He didn't say it. Humans in twenty-first century North America expected surnames, so he let it pass.

Carwyn's full name was Carwyn son of Bryn, patriarch of his clan, sired to the earth, immortal son of Maelona of Gwynedd, daughter of Brennus the Celt.

His sire was dead. His grandsire slept in a hidden mound somewhere in Scotland, and ever since the night over a decade ago when he left the service of the Catholic Church, Carwyn owed his allegiance to no man, woman, or immortal.

Except one fucking woman who was determined to drive him mad.

Someone had recently described Brigid Connor as "a badger trapped in a barn" and it wasn't an inaccurate comparison. She was stubborn, destructive, and single-minded. It made her a fierce protector, an absolute firecracker in bed, and one of the best vampires he'd known in a thousand years.

Of course he'd married her.

He emerged from the basement entrance to the modern lobby of Grigor Limited, one of Katya's many companies that she used to rule the Pacific Northwest. Carwyn lived in her territory through Katya's goodwill. If he was any other vampire, he'd have to swear some kind of allegiance to her because that was how vampire aegis worked.

Immortal predators weren't to be trusted with self-determination. If their kind had any kind of government, it was closer to ancient city-state fiefdoms than modern human states.

The guards in the lobby had clearly been told to expect him, and since he was well over six feet, built like a brick wall, and sporting a shock of unruly red hair, Carwyn was hard to miss.

He took the escalators built next to the elevators since vampires avoided elevators on principle. Carwyn was more grounded than most, but he didn't brag about that fact and tried to keep his profile the same as others of his kind.

Katya's office was on the third floor, and he spotted her secretary as soon as he reached the top of the escalator.

"Carwyn." The friendly woman stepped forward. She didn't extend her hand—most vampires avoided skin-to-skin contact with humans if they were polite—but she gave him a respectful nod. "She's ready for you."

"Thank you."

The door to Katya's office was open, and when he walked in, he saw the immortal leader of Northern California, Oregon, Washington, British Columbia, and Alaska sitting by a fireplace, her stocking-clad feet tucked under her as she read a file.

"Hi." She glanced up. "I'm reading this incredibly boring business prospectus, so just have a seat." She motioned to the sofa across from her overstuffed chair. "Almost done."

"No problem."

Katya Grigorieva had been turned when she was barely an adult, but like Carwyn, she came from an age when humans matured faster. She looked like she was in her early twenties. She was blond, had large brown eyes, pale skin, and ruby-red lips. That night she was dressed in a pink fisherman's sweater and a pair of light blue jeans.

Carwyn stared at the fire, thinking about Brigid.

His mate was a fire vampire, sired during a heroin overdose. He tried not to think about the manner of his mate's turning because everything about it had been traumatic. She'd been a grieving human who made a massive lapse in her recovery and a horrid mistake that led to her mortal death and her immortal birth.

"Does the fire remind you of her?"

Carwyn looked over to Katya, who had set the file to the side. "Always."

"Fair enough." She sat up and crossed her legs in the wide

chair where she sat. "Let's talk about Brigid and why I need her to kill Zasha Sokholov. And maybe Oleg too."

———

THE SECRETARY BROUGHT a French press filled with coffee into the corner office and set it on the table where Katya proceeded to push the plunger down and began to serve. "Cream? Sugar?"

"Cream, no sugar."

She pursed her lips. "I would have guessed sugar."

"Too sweet."

She looked up and winked at him. "But you *are* so sweet, Carwyn."

He growled, "You know better."

"I do know better." Katya handed him a heavy mug of fragrant coffee and smiled. "She thinks she's doing the right thing, you know."

He sipped the coffee, welcoming the bitter taste on his tongue. It matched his mood. "I'm sure she believes that."

"You don't think she can kill Zasha?" Katya raised an eyebrow. "Quite disloyal."

"Not disloyal." He leaned forward, bracing his elbows on his knees. "Can we speak in confidence?"

"We *only* speak in confidence," she said. "Nothing I say to you leaves this office."

"Understood." He hesitated, still reluctant to question his mate in front of another vampire.

But Brigid was in Katya's territory, and she was hunting a vampire who had eluded immortals far older than his mate. "Zasha is stronger than Brigid."

Katya nodded. "Most likely, yes. They're much older, so that would make sense."

"They have better control of their element."

"Also likely, though Brigid's skills are impressive for a young vampire. On the other hand, I'd say Brigid is smarter and more clear-thinking than Zasha. *Thinking* wins battles. In my opinion, they are evenly matched."

Carwyn said nothing.

Katya continued. "You need to give her some credit. She's levelheaded and she has allies. That's more than Zasha has going for them."

Katya was probably thinking about Oleg. He was betting she didn't know that Tenzin was working with Brigid, and he wasn't going to tell her. He had no idea how Katya would react to a slightly sociopathic wind vampire flying around her territory—better not to bring it up.

Because Brigid needed Tenzin. As much faith as he had in his mate, Carwyn was terrified for her, and Tenzin was the one vampire he could think of who was as terrible as Zasha Sokholov.

Katya set her coffee to the side. "Since it's just the two of us, you know that I'm mated, correct?"

"I'd heard he's some vague relation to Leonora in Spain. Is that correct?"

"Very vague, very distant." She settled back into her chair. "Have you ever met him?"

"No."

"No, you have not." She smiled. "We prefer it that way. He hates events. Won't really participate in business. Doesn't like most vampires at all really."

Carwyn could almost feel his eyes glazing over. "That makes for a very boring eternity."

"And yet he is happy."

"How does he keep busy?"

"He's a remarkable artist who paints under various names that you've heard of, and he hires humans to take his place." She picked up her coffee. "Now you know more about my mate than ninety-nine percent of the world. You should be flattered."

"I am. Why are you telling me?"

"Because you didn't marry one like mine. You mated Brigid." Katya said. "You'd be bored if she was any different."

"She's trying to shield me from all this." His jaw twitched. "It's annoying."

"She's trying to shield everyone, not just you. So far over a dozen people that she interacted with personally have been killed by Zasha Sokholov. More injured. Dozens, maybe hundreds, traumatized. Everyone Brigid knows could be a target because for some reason this vampire has fixated on her. Why the hell do you think she went to the frozen north?"

"Because that's where Zasha is, according to rumors."

"Yes. And while normally one vampire killing another in my territory would be very much my business, I looked the other way when she went to Anchorage because I want Zasha dead, and I think she can kill them."

"*...I need her to kill Zasha Sokholov. And maybe Oleg too.*"

Carwyn looked at Katya through narrowed eyes. "What's your conflict with Oleg?"

Katya pursed her lips. "How much do you know about Alaska?"

"Not much. I don't like the cold. I know that it's your territory."

"Yes. I acquired it about a hundred years ago. Before that, it was Oleg's."

"Why did it change hands?"

"He got distracted."

Fair enough. Carwyn only nodded.

Katya took a deep breath and let it out slowly. "I don't spend much time in Alaska, but maybe that's been a mistake. The people who live there, mortal and immortal, they're... a different kind. Have you ever visited?"

"The only time the weather is tolerable in that place, the sun is out for twenty hours a day. What do you think?"

"I think that's the reason I don't go there much either."

"You'd think an environment like that would be a vampire wasteland."

"But it's not a vampire wasteland at all. This time of year, the place is practically crawling with our kind." She shrugged. "The lure of long nights, I suppose."

"And Oleg keeps men there. Even though it's your territory."

"He has several compounds that remain. *Supposedly* for his men. He calls them his fishing camps, and I let him keep them as a gesture of goodwill. It wasn't a violent handover."

"But you think they're outposts? Incursions?"

"Alaska may be a remote territory" —Katya's lips firmed into a line— "but it's a very profitable one."

"Is Oleg interfering in that profit?"

She leaned forward and refilled her coffee cup. "There have been some strange things going on. And Brigid may think Zasha is the root of all evil, but Zasha is a Sokholov. Just like Oleg."

Carwyn read between the lines immediately. "You think Oleg is working with *Zasha*?"

Katya shrugged.

"Why are you so suspicious of Oleg after a century of coexistence?"

"Because two of my fishing vessels and a private yacht owned by a very important vampire in my territory went missing in the Inside Passage this fall. That's the territory around Juneau that's a whole network of islands and inlets. Deepwater channels."

"Boats go missing sometimes." Carwyn shrugged. "Anything else?"

"Two immortal compounds have been attacked by unknown enemies—dozens of humans and vampire missing or dead."

That wasn't a missing boat. He could see Katya's barely hidden rage.

"And now Zasha Sokholov is rumored to be in the same territory as those thefts. I don't think this is a coincidence."

"I don't either, but why would you think Oleg and Zasha are working together? Oleg is the one who flew Brigid north so she could kill Zasha."

"Maybe Oleg means to let Brigid kill Zasha, then get rid of Brigid."

He wasn't a strategic mastermind, but that didn't make sense to Carwyn. At all. "What about the Athabaskan Confederation? Maybe the indigenous population wants the Russians out."

Her eyes turned hard. "If they did, I wouldn't fight them. If they expressed interest in the coast and the sea, I would hand over that real estate without a word. But they're earth vampires and they don't want the administrative hassle, so they leave it to me. They're part of the reason this territory is mine and not Oleg's. I offered them better terms."

"Fine," he said. "You mentioned attacks. Have the Athabaskans been attacked? Or coastal compounds only?"

"Only villages on the coast. And the ships. No one would be idiotic enough to harass the Athabaskan Confederation. Their people have survived in conditions that would kill ninety percent of our kind. If Oleg has a bigger obstacle than me, it's the Athabaskans."

"Don't mess with any vampire who hunts grizzlies for a light meal?"

"Exactly."

Carwyn asked the question he really wanted the answer to. "Do you know where Brigid is?"

Katya shook her head. "I have a rough idea of three places she could be around Seward and stretching down to Katmai, but those would only be starting points and it's a big territory, my friend."

He sat back and turned his eyes back to the fire.

"Maybe you're right about Oleg," Katya said. "Maybe I'm being too suspicious."

"I know I'm right about Oleg." That vampire was not working with Zasha. Carwyn didn't doubt Brigid's judgment even if he was angry with her. She wouldn't work with anyone who was allied with the enemy she'd vowed to kill.

Katya pursed her lips. "If you wanted to look into Oleg's activities for me, that would give you a very good reason to head north. I have a boat or two that could take you there."

"I don't need a reason to head north. I'm looking for my wife." But as much as he hated boats, they would be faster than driving through Canada. "I'll look into it if you want me to just to prove you wrong." *And to keep Brigid from being caught in the middle of a vampire war.*

"Fine. If you agree to look into these attacks and thefts, you have official permission to be in the territory."

He stood and carefully set his coffee mug on the table between them. "I'll look into it. But Katya, I wasn't really asking for permission."

AS SOON AS Carwyn reached the nondescript rental house outside city limits, he walked inside, locked and secured everything, then pulled out the tablet in the locked bedroom.

"Cara, call Brigid."

The program automatically popped open, the screen a blank as the electronic chime trilled in the background. He paced in front of the screen, tearing off the jacket he'd worn to blend in and kicking off the shoes that covered his feet.

The program rang and rang. He was nearly ready to shut it off when the ringing stopped.

He froze and turned to the screen, bending down so his face was in the camera.

A black-and-white image of Brigid flickered onto the tablet, and Carwyn had to stop himself from weeping and shouting at the same time.

"Hello, darling girl." He bit down so hard he tasted blood. His fangs were out, and they shredded the skin on the inside of his lower lip.

Her eyes flickered to the camera, then looked away.

"Brigid, talk to me."

He heard her take a shuddering breath. "You're angry."

"I'm fucking *furious*. Look at me."

She took a deep breath, closed her eyes, and turned her face to the camera.

"Open your eyes."

Shattered whiskey brown singed by ashes. He could picture the color in his mind even though the camera leached it away.

"I won't say I'm sorry."

"Of course you won't." He braced his arms on the table, staring at her, examining her face for any sign of change. Was it fear that lined her eyes? She looked tired. Was that a burn mark on her cheek? "Where are you?"

"I can't tell you that."

"You won't tell me."

"I promised Oleg if he helped me, I wouldn't reveal locations."

"That bloody Russian bastard—"

"He's helping me. He wants to take care of Zasha too."

"That's utter bollocks, Brigid. If Oleg wanted to kill Zasha, they would already be dead. He's a fire vampire too, and he's older than Zasha. He should be the one cleaning up his clan's mess, but instead, he wants to cover his ass with the others and let you do it." He had barely kept from shouting and throwing the tablet across the room. It was the first time she'd picked up his call since she'd left him in Las Vegas. It had been months since he'd seen her face.

"I want to do it." Her brilliant eyes turned hard. "For Lee. For Lucas. For Summer and Dani. And they're the ones who are still alive."

"Tell me where you are."

"I can't."

"Fuck!" he roared. "Brigid Connor, I am your mate!"

"I know." She was crying, and the tears dripped down her cheeks, turning to steam as they crossed her skin. "I'm sorry."

"Shhhh." He knelt down in front of the camera when he saw her skin starting to heat up. "Calm, darling girl. Be calm. I love you, Brigid. I love you so much."

"I love you so much it hurts." She nodded. "And I promise I'm not doing this alone. But I need to turn off the camera now."

"No no no no no." Carwyn pleaded with her. "I'm in Seattle. Give me a clue and I'll be—"

"I have to go." There was shouting in the background, and she looked flustered. "I think I heard a gunshot, and I have a feeling I know why. Don't worry—I'm not in danger." She dashed the tears away. "I love you."

The screen went dark, and Carwyn had to resist the urge to fling it across the room, because if he wrecked that one, he didn't have another chance of seeing her until he hunted her down.

He walked outside into the pouring rain, his feet bare, and loosed his rage in a violent scream of elemental power he shoved into the earth behind the isolated house.

The ground rocked below his feet, but he felt the earth resist his amnis, unsure of what it all meant. This wasn't a place like California where the terrain was fluid and the faults were many. He could feel the old cracks deep below the surface, but they were sleepy, and the upper layers of rock and soil were wary to rouse them.

Carwyn let his amnis scatter along the surface of the ground, and the green lawn rolled like waves lapping at the shoreline while he gradually calmed the churning anger in his chest.

At least he'd seen her.

At least she was safe.

A sound like thunder echoed overhead, and a familiar thread of amnis hit the ground next to him like a lightning bolt a moment before a dark shape came shooting through the clouds, arrowing down to Carwyn's house.

The wind vampire's black clothes were dripping with rain, his hair was plastered to his face, and his eyes shot bolts of fury at the face of his old friend.

"Carwyn?" Ben Vecchio's voice was iced in anger. "Where the fuck is my mate?"

CHAPTER THREE

Tenzin looked down at the blood pouring from her thigh. What an odd and unpleasant sensation. "Did they shoot me?"

She looked around for where the sound had originated.

The human was in the guard tower across from the building where she'd landed, the tip of his rifle shaking as he quickly pointed it to the sky with wide eyes.

He muttered something in Russian, a language Tenzin had done her best to forget.

She pointed at him. "Did you shoot me?"

She was already forcing the bullet from her body. She drew her strength from the air, and air was everywhere. It was even in the middle of matter. The air in her blood and body jumped at the manipulation of her amnis, pushing the projectile from the muscle to the surface of her skin.

How truly, horribly unpleasant. It felt like a burn.

"I can't remember if I've ever been shot," she muttered. Had she? She felt like she would have remembered, but then again, she had forgotten more of her very long life than she recalled.

"Tenzin!"

She heard her name from the ground and saw Brigid running toward the guard tower, waving her arms. "It's Tenzin! Oleg is expecting her."

A large man who looked a little like a bigfoot walked out of the low, round-roofed building that reminded Tenzin of a giant yurt.

He gave her a cheerful smile and wave. "Oh hi! I am Lev. Welcome. Sorry about that." He pointed to her. "We tell them to shoot wind vampires we're not expecting."

"That seems on par for Russian hospitality." She didn't shout, but the man heard her anyway.

"Ha!" He grinned. "A good joke. I like you."

"You shouldn't." She started walking toward the edge of the roof, enjoying the sensation of air in the snow. It was powdery and loose, freshly fallen through cold skies.

The wind in this place was crisp and smelled as much of the ocean as the forest. It reminded her of Penglai but with less bowing people.

Nice.

"Tenzin!" Brigid ran up, her head bare. "I'm so sorry about that. Come inside and get warmed up."

She floated down to the ground but only so that they wouldn't look at her strangely. It was dark and cold, and the air was nearly frozen. She adored weather like this; it was so clean. She could have floated in the cold air, soaking it in for hours.

She liked hot weather too, but it was often languid and full of water, which annoyed her. This frosty air, so biting, reminded her of Tibet.

The cold kissed her cheeks, bringing a rare flush to her pale skin. Her eyes were steel grey, the color of a winter storm, and her hair had grown out the last time she took blood from her mate, so it was a black curtain nearly past her shoulders again.

Truly, new blood was very odd.

"Hi." Brigid was waiting for her on the ground. "Thanks for coming."

Tenzin narrowed her eyes and read the young fire vampire's eyes. "You don't want to thank me. You're glad I'm here, but you're angry too." She leaned closer. "And you've been crying."

That immediately irritated Brigid, which Tenzin found satisfying.

"Shut up and come inside." Brigid stomped off, and Tenzin followed her, casting one last glance at the guard in the tower who had shot her.

She narrowed her eyes, squinted at him, and pointed.

A hint of urine spoiled the fresh smell of the air.

Ew. She ducked inside the round building and was immediately assaulted by the smell of too many men.

"This place smells foul." She looked up at Lev, who was standing by the door in a pair of blue denim overalls and a red T-shirt. "You should clean it."

"We do clean it."

"Not well enough."

Brigid frowned. "It's not *that* bad."

Ugh. These people were disgusting. "Where is my room?" She looked down. "I need to mend my pants."

"We'll get you a new pair," Brigid said. "They don't look very heavy."

"I don't need a new pair. I made these and I'll wear them. I just need to mend them." She didn't like most clothes. The only ones she liked were the ones she made and the ones that her designer friend Arthur made specifically for her.

Arthur had perfected the art of hiding dagger sheaths in formal dresses. He was a genius.

Tenzin took a dagger from her tunic and jabbed the tip into the wound in her thigh, prying the bullet the last inch out of her skin.

Brigid sucked in a breath. "Oh my God."

Tenzin showed the bullet to Lev. "I don't know what it's made of, but it itches." She reached over, wiped the tip of her dagger on his sleeve to clean it, and stuck it back in her tunic along with the spent bullet. "Where is my room?"

Brigid and Lev exchanged a look.

"Come with me," Brigid said. "I'll get you settled in."

Tenzin followed her, wishing there was some way to irritate the woman again.

She didn't like the way Brigid Connor had ambushed her in New York. She didn't like being pulled away from the very curated life she'd built with her new mate.

She didn't like thinking about Zasha Sokholov.

They walked down a long hallway that circled the outer wall of the building, and Tenzin realized it *was* a yurt, just a very large one with permanent rooms. There was a hallway that ran along the outside wall, which meant all the interior rooms were windowless and light safe. The ceilings were quite tall, and the floor was sunk three feet into the ground, meaning it was accessible for earth vampires too.

"This reminds me of something."

"One of Oleg's men said it was designed to mimic the houses the native people built here. That's why it's set into the ground and doesn't have windows."

"It will be easier to heat as well."

A low tent, vampires buried in the earth.

The taste of dirt in her mouth.

Tenzin blinked out of the reverie. "It's smart to build houses like native people do. They know the seasons best."

"I'm sure that was the thinking, yes." Brigid paused by one of the doors, then turned and handed Tenzin a key. "Old fashioned locks. Nothing electronic for us to mess up. Dead bolts inside."

"The nights are long here."

"And you don't sleep."

Tenzin leaned against the outer wall and examined her. "You should be glad to see me. These men are Oleg's. They are not your allies. They could be working with Zasha."

"I know that. I also know that you caused this. I don't know how or why, but somehow you did. Tell me I'm wrong."

The little fire vampire was smarter than Tenzin remembered.

Tenzin said nothing in response, and Brigid pushed away and started walking down the hall.

"I'll help you kill Zasha."

Brigid stopped and turned. "Why?"

"Why not? I'll teach you to hunt them, and then you can kill them and go home to your big, loud earth-vampire mate."

"Why not you?"

"I've never liked Carwyn. He smiles too much."

Brigid's eye twitched. "No. Why don't you go hunt and kill Zasha yourself? Since I'm gonna assume I'm right and you caused this somehow, why don't you take care of the mess you made?"

The smell of smoke and scorched stew burned to life in Tenzin's memory. "Because I made a vow."

———

SHE WAS DREAMING, and when she woke, her mirror image was sitting in a corner of the dark room, lit only by a single incandescent light bulb.

Aday smiled when Tenzin spotted her. "You're sleeping again."

"A little bit."

"I thought you trained yourself not to do that anymore."

"I didn't want to see you."

"Too bad." The mischievous vampire flew up and perched in

the wooden rafters over Tenzin's head. "Remember this? Remember when you killed them all?"

"Why are you here?"

"I come when I'm needed."

"I don't need you anymore. You can leave."

"Are you sure about that?" She spoke a name that Tenzin hadn't heard in centuries, a name that was dead to her. "*Saraal.*"

"I'm called Tenzin now."

"But that's not who you are." The vampire turned in slow circles in the air. "Is it?"

Tenzin wasn't sure if she was still dreaming. Sleep was foreign to her, and it had only come back to her when she and Ben had started exchanging blood. For thousands of years before that, she had not slept.

She'd slept at one time in her life; then she hadn't.

And now she was sleeping again.

Was the vision in her room only that? A vision? A memory best left on the ancient steppes of Central Asia? She had laid Aday to rest in a shrine in Tibet where the people worshiped her as a goddess and her sire had come to make amends.

She had buried her in the muddy banks of the Amur River, thrown her in the depths of Lake Baikal, and left her hanging in a deodar cedar, food for the carrion birds that nested in its great, dense branches.

"Why are you in this place?" the vision asked.

"Because I should have finished the job. I didn't know Temur's Blood had truly mated. That means his blood still lives."

Aday flew down to kiss her softly on the mouth. "And we can't have that, can we? Temur's blood must die. You should kill it."

"I made a vow."

"To the man?" Aday shook her head softly. "His blood has made you weak." She smiled slowly and ran soft fingers down

Tenzin's cheek. "Then again, he made you dream again, so I do not hate him. I missed you."

"You're not real."

"I'm real when you need me." She leaned forward and whispered, "You made that vow. I did not. Let me live and I will kill Zasha. I break no promises."

"You break everything."

Aday smiled. "As I said, I come when I am needed."

"You are no more. The vow is mine."

"Then flee this place and leave Zasha to the Russians. They belong together. Leave your little friend and fly away."

"Zasha needs to be stopped. I never should have let them live." She'd relived that night a hundred times since seeing Zasha's face through the smoke of a burning wheat field. "I should have killed them when I ended Temur's line."

"Why you? You've killed enough. What do you owe the world?"

New Year's resolutions. Tenzin closed her eyes. "I need to do this. I made a vow not to harm Zasha, but I can help Brigid kill them. That does not break my vow. So Aday, you need to leave."

"And you need to wake up."

———

TENZIN OPENED HER EYES, and the dream was gone. The room was empty, and so was her stomach. She needed to feed. She needed to meditate.

She needed to find Brigid and get this done.

The longer she was away from Benjamin, the more volatile she became. She hadn't dreamed of the small vampire in years, and now she was back?

This situation was tenuous. So was her mind.

She looked at the ruby ring on her left hand, the one she never took off even though she didn't wear jewelry. She collected it. She rarely wore it.

I don't believe in marriage.

Did I ask you? It's a ring. You like rubies. Wear the ring.

She wore the ring and gave him one of her own. It was made of gold taken from Solomon's mines, an ancient artifact of unspeakable value she'd bartered for in the second century after listening to a story from an Ethiopian merchant traveling through Arabia. He had enchanted her with his tales of war and love, and she'd given him one of her favorite swords in exchange for his gold ring just because she knew it would help her remember that night.

Ben had dropped that ring down the sink in the bathroom twice and had to take apart the plumbing to find it.

So normally Tenzin was fine with losing her grip on reality because Benjamin was with her. Benjamin grounded her. Their connection was the thin tether that anchored her to what was left of her humanity.

And then she'd left him in New York.

He was not going to be happy about that.

CHAPTER FOUR

"Careful, boy."

Ben glared at the old vampire standing in the rain. Carwyn was barefoot, strolling through the rain without a care in the world while Ben had just felt a punch through his amnis like fire. "Where the fuck is Tenzin?"

Carwyn snarled. "You think I know where she is?"

"You and Brigid are joined at the hip, old man."

"And you and your tiny sociopath aren't?"

"She's not a fucking—" He bit back his words, but nothing could stop the punch of air that blasted Carwyn in the chest as Ben tried to control his rage. His amnis was out of control.

The air shoved Carwyn back a few feet, and the earth vampire snarled, digging his feet into the ground.

Too late, Ben realized his mistake.

The old vampire didn't even move, but the earth opened up, grabbing Ben's legs and pulling him into the ground as Carwyn charged.

Ben's arm shot out and forced the larger man back, but the pull of the ground didn't stop. Ben tried to reach for the air within the soil, but he felt nothing. The ground was saturated with water, and while his amnis searched for something to grab, there was no purchase.

Ben lifted his arms, letting the air pull him from above, but the ground followed, crawling up his body as Carwyn braced himself, digging his hands into the earth.

"Fucking let me go!" Ben shouted at the behemoth covered in mud.

"Not until you learn some manners," Carwyn growled.

Ben's arm swiped down and the rain and wind followed, battering the vampire on the ground, buffeting him with the force of wind. The trees around the house shook, bending and creaking as Ben manipulated the air.

He might have been caught in the mud, but Ben gathered his element through the downpour and shoved his amnis at the earth vampire who had captured him.

The wind forced Carwyn's head back, but not before he'd sunk himself into the ground, drawing power from the rock, the soil, and the matter around him.

"You think you're strong." Despite the wind, the earth vampire stalked toward him, lifting his legs only to sink them up to the knees as he walked toward Ben. "And you are. But you're young, Benjamin."

Ben was six feet in the air at that point, but the earth holding him hadn't let go. He felt the ground holding him harden as Carwyn's amnis forced the water from the densely packed soil. Within seconds, the earth around Ben's legs felt more like stone than mud.

"Let me go!" Ben was angry and unfocused. He felt a burning pain in his thigh that pumped adrenaline through his body.

"Calm down." Carwyn reached him and rose, the ground beneath the vampire lifting him to meet Ben's eyes.

The moment he was within reach, Ben swung out, his fist

meeting Carwyn's rock-hard jaw with the force of a small hurricane.

Carwyn's head snapped back, and the scent of fresh blood filled the air when his jaw came down and his fang sliced through his lip. He snarled and reached out, closing his massive hand around Ben's neck.

The earth followed Carwyn's arm, closing around Ben's throat to choke off his words as Carwyn's element folded around the threat, cutting off his ability to breathe and speak.

Ben tried to force the air into his lungs, but the pressure grew and the mud turned solid around him.

He was slowly being choked by solid rock.

"Calm down," Carwyn said. "This isn't helping anyone."

Ben didn't need air to live. His amnis churned the wind around him, battering Carwyn, but it felt as effective as blowing bubbles at a brick wall. His amnis roused, angry and frustrated. The pain in his leg grew sharper. His rage built.

He will kill you, and she will have no one.

She will be alone.

The thought of his mate in pain and alone in the darkness flipped a switch in his brain. Ben closed his eyes and reached out with his senses.

The air was all around him, surrounding him, holding the water from the clouds, the air remaining in his lungs, but there was nothing in the rock that held him. The earth vampire had pushed everything out of the matter, leaving Ben nothing to manipulate.

Save for the air in his enemy's own body.

He opened his eyes, narrowed them, and watched as Carwyn slowly felt the air sucked from his lungs.

His blue eyes went wide, and he lifted the corner of his lip, baring a bloody fang.

"Bastard," the giant mouthed.

He felt a surge of satisfaction until the press of rock tightened around his neck. The earth vampire's element was slowly hardening around his body, no longer simply choking off the air but digging slowly and steadily into his spine.

His amnis raced in panic, and the air around him lost focus, swirling in spikes and erratic gusts that ripped at his hair and eyes.

What are you doing? Carwyn mouthed the words, his eyes streaming with bloody tears from the wind.

A jolt like a fist around his neck.

The shock of pain and panic snapped Ben back to awareness.

He stared at the man who had watched him grow up, the immortal who had been as much an uncle as a friend.

Carwyn's eyes and mouth were bloody from hurled debris; the air around them was churning with black mud, water, and gravel that sliced at his skin. Ben was bloody and his body was encased in rock.

He shoved his element away so hard that the churning mass of water and mud exploded out and the trees cracked from the force of his amnis.

As soon as he shoved the wind back, he released the air and Carwyn's lungs filled again.

"For fuck's sake, you lunatic, what do you think you're doing?"

Let me go, Ben mouthed, glaring at Carwyn.

"Are you calm?"

Ben looked around at the air that was now still, the rain falling in a light mist around them.

Carwyn eased his fingers back from around Ben's neck. "I'm letting you go."

Moments later, Ben could speak again and he felt the ground around him slowly crumbling away. "Where is she?"

"You think I know?" Carwyn shook his head. "They've done a runner on both of us, boy. Let's go inside and get you cleaned up."

BEN SAT at Carwyn's kitchen table, drinking the black tea the vampire had made for both of them. It wasn't the elegant loose tea that Tenzin enjoyed but two bags of cheap black tea dunked in mugs and heavily dosed with milk.

It tasted slightly of paper, but Ben drank it anyway.

"When did she leave?" Carwyn asked.

"Four days ago."

"Brigid left months ago. Right after we found that boy in Vegas that Zasha kidnapped."

"She went to New York. Tenzin didn't tell me. I found out from the O'Briens a couple of weeks after, but Tenzin wouldn't tell me what it was about. Then four days ago?" He flicked his fingers in the air. "Gone."

"It's not a coincidence. They're working together."

Ben sipped the paper-flavored tea. "I tracked her for the first day and then lost her trail. I went to your house in California but you were gone, so I came up here."

"How did you find this place?"

"Gavin's people tracked your stupid van, found the account you used to rent this place."

"Better talk to Lee about that," Carwyn muttered.

"Can't hide from traffic cameras," Ben said. "Get a more boring vehicle."

The earth vampire sat across from him, sliding a bottle of blood-wine across the table. "Drink that. You lost blood and expended a lot of energy."

Ben twisted off the top of the inexpensive variety. "You?"

Carwyn shook his head. "I went hunting at nightfall before I met with Katya."

"Does she know where they are?"

"No. Brigid didn't go through Katya—she got help from Oleg, and I don't know his people. She had better connections there."

"Why did she go to New York? Why did she rope Tenzin into this?"

Carwyn narrowed his eyes. "You know why."

The blood of Temur remembers who you were.

"Zasha Sokholov has some kind of grudge against Tenzin," Ben said. "So Brigid is using her to—"

"Brigid is using?" Carwyn leaned forward. "*Brigid* is using Tenzin? No, Benjamin. You've got it backward. *Brigid* is the one being used."

Ben kept silent because clearly the large, angry man wanted to vent. Carwyn didn't get angry very often. In fact, this was the most furious Ben had ever seen him.

"*Brigid* has been the one used for years now because somehow this fire vampire got it into their head that Brigid is connected to your mate." The earth vampire continued ranting. "Your mate is the one Zasha is after, and they've been using Brigid to attract her attention."

"Why not just go after Tenzin if she's Zasha's target?" Ben said. "She's not as secretive as she used to be. Everyone in the immortal world knows we're in New York. We don't keep it a secret."

Carwyn gave him a rueful laugh. "And what would this vampire do, Benjamin? Go after Tenzin and her newly turned and already-powerful mate in a frontal attack? Where? In the fortress of Manhattan where you have allies coming out of your ears? What leverage would Zasha have? How would they draw the two of you out? How could they make you vulnerable to attack?"

Ben narrowed his eyes. "We have family."

"You and Tenzin have a very small circle of people you care about, and those people are very well protected," Carwyn said. "Your sister is the child of two of the most powerful vampires in the world, including a fire vampire Zasha fears. Your friend Chloe is married to a vampire who has enormous power, influence, and protection. Zasha is not going to come after you directly."

"So what? Brigid is powerful, and she has your entire clan protecting her," Ben said. "She's not vulnerable."

"You think not?" His smile turned bitter. "The problem with my wife, Benjamin, is not that she's vulnerable. It's that she *cares* for the vulnerable."

Ben sat back and felt goose bumps rise along his arms.

"You know this," Carwyn said. "You know exactly why Zasha targeted Brigid. Because Brigid *cares*. What would Tenzin have done if Zasha had kidnapped a human under the O'Briens' aegis while they were in New York?"

"She'd have told them to deal with it." Ben's voice was soft.

"Tenzin would have wiped her hands of it," Carwyn said. "She wouldn't have even sent a sympathy card."

"The O'Briens are not Tenzin's people." He loved his mate, but her focus and protection were very, very narrow. "They have their own clan."

"Brigid's heart weeps for a wounded mouse, Benjamin. It's one of the reasons I love her and one of the reasons I hate her sometimes. Because every single person" —he jabbed his thumb on the table so hard it creaked— "who needs her has her. Give her a human in distress, and she'll cut her own vein and bleed to make them safe."

Ben swallowed hard because he knew Carwyn spoke the truth. Brigid had done the same for him. When he was an angry newborn, she was one of the few people he'd confided in and one of the only ones who'd put up with his shit.

"That's why she left you," he said quietly.

"Minimizing collateral damage." Carwyn set down his mug. "I'm furious with her, but I understand why. It's not a bad strategy."

Ben swallowed hard, setting aside the paper tea to drink the bottle of blood-wine. He tipped the bottle up, wiping the blood-enriched wine from his lips after he had finished. "So what do we do?"

"We fucking find them," Carwyn said. "They think they don't need us—"

"Bullshit," Ben blurted.

"Exactly." Carwyn leaned back and nodded. "So tell me, what do you know about Zasha? Why do they hate Tenzin so much?"

The blood of Temur remembers who you were.

"I don't know everything," Ben said, "but I know a little."

"Tell me. I'm not going into this blind."

What if Temur has other blood in the immortal world? What if he has descendants who don't even know who he was?

Then I will consider if their lives are worthy.

Should you be the judge of that?

I'm the only one with the right, and that right was born of the blood of my own children. I am not interested in justice.

Ben wasn't going to spill his mate's secrets, but he knew that Carwyn and Tenzin had very different worldviews. They got along because they both loved Ben's uncle, who considered the two old vampires his closest friends in the world.

Ben said quietly, "Tenzin comes from a different time."

"I come from a different time too."

"Yes, but I'm trying to tell you..." Ben frowned. "Our sire is even older than Tenzin. He's an ancient."

Carwyn nodded. "I know this."

"But until Zhang sired me, she was his only child," Ben said. "It's one of the reasons I can do..." He lifted a hand and stirred the air gently in the room. "All this."

Carwyn shrugged. "You're powerful, but you could work on your control."

Fine. He'd take that because it was true; Tenzin told him the same thing all the time.

"I'm so powerful because for about three thousand years, Zhang didn't have any other children than Tenzin." That wasn't a secret. Everyone who knew his sire knew that.

Carwyn narrowed his eyes. "But Zhang had an army once."

"Yes." Again, this was immortal lore. Nothing Ben was saying was a confidence his mate had shared.

"So an ancient immortal king has an army that dominated most of Asia." Carwyn tipped his chin up, considering. "And then one day your sire decides to give up his power and his army vanishes." Carwyn's fingers spread in the air. "Poof. Gone like the wind, no pun intended."

"Yes. Except for one child," Ben said. "One daughter."

"Who becomes his heir." Carwyn's eyes were steady on Ben. "And Zhang doesn't sire another child for thousands of years. Not until you."

Ben said nothing, but he kept his eyes steady on Carwyn.

Carwyn let out a slow breath. "Tenzin killed the others, didn't she? All of them."

"You know what life must have been for her, living with them," he said quietly. "You can guess."

Ben didn't know everything because Tenzin wouldn't tell him the details, but he wasn't an idiot. He had an idea of what kind of life Tenzin had survived, being the lone daughter in an army of immortal warriors in a time when women—even immortal ones—were property.

Carwyn stared at the table. "Was Zasha in Zhang's army?"

"I don't think so."

"No, of course not. The timing wouldn't fit," Carwyn muttered. "They're not that old. But there's something... *something* there. It goes back. I know it."

"We don't talk about it," Ben continued. "But you know her."

"I know she's a killer."

Ben flinched, but Carwyn pressed on.

"You have to know that," the old vampire said. "You have to understand that about her, Benjamin, or you will never understand Tenzin. I don't understand her and I never will, but you are her mate."

"She did what was necessary to survive."

"I don't doubt that." Carwyn's voice was harsh. "Any judgment for what she did is between her and her gods. But you and I are different. *Brigid* is different. We do have lines we won't cross. Tenzin does not."

"She's trying, Carwyn."

"I'm sure she is, but you need to realize that in many ways, Tenzin and Zasha are more alike than different."

The blood of Temur remembers who you were.

Were. Not are.

"She's changed," Ben said. "She's more human now."

"Oh no." Carwyn's eyes were sad. "It's possible she's changed, Benjamin, but she is anything but human. We will win this fight. Do not doubt it. Zasha and all her army could try to take on you and Tenzin, Brigid and me, but they will fail. I have no doubt." He leaned forward. "But make no mistake: there will be no winners when this is over."

CHAPTER FIVE

"There were attacks here" —Lev pointed to a red mark on a map near a place labeled Katmai Bay— "and here." He pointed to another red mark. "Small villages. Mostly human and a few of our kind."

They were talking in the great room where the fire still burned even though all the humans and most of the vampires had retreated to their rooms during the small hours of the night. Only Lev, Brigid, and Tenzin seemed to be awake.

"Were the vampires in these villages from the Athabaskan Confederation?" Brigid asked.

Lev said, "*Ath*abaskan."

"That's what I said." Her accent always betrayed her Irishness. The *th* in Athabaskan sounded like Atta-baskan.

Lev frowned, but he nodded along. "Okay, right."

Some mocked the Irish pronunciation of *th* —*three* sounded liked *tree*—but the Gaelic for three was *trí* and always had been. The Irish *th* lasted long after the English had nearly wiped out her native tongue under punishment of death.

The Irish persisted. Sometimes Brigid felt like she persisted just to annoy her enemies to their deaths, but it kept her going.

"So were they Athabaskan?" she asked again.

"No. Some of the humans might be Native, but most of the vampires in this area came during the Russian time, so they're not related to the Confederation." He gestured to the northern and inland parts of the map. "Confederation vampires are more inland and almost all earth vampires like me. This area attracts water and air vampires." He shrugged. "Mostly ones who want to hide but stay close enough to humans to... Well."

Hunt.

The area Lev was pointing to was along the coast, farther south and west of their location.

"It's remote and most of it is national park," Lev said. "It's only accessible from the air or the water. Tourists from the national park. Hunters and fisherman."

"Immortals love places like that," Tenzin said. "I love places like that."

Lev chuckled a little bit. "More than one vampire enjoys the humor of hunting humans who are hunting animals."

"Remote," Brigid said. "But with enough humans to keep a vampire fed."

"Exactly. It's a good area if you want to live quietly," Lev said. "Like you said, not busy but enough humans to keep you fed. Lots of wild game too."

"But too many missing people would be noticed," Tenzin said. "So you'd have to have the right sort of vampires."

Lev nodded. "Our kind in that place? Soft footprint. Enjoy the long nights, feed from the tourists, keep a low profile, and you can live very comfortably. It's all Katya's territory technically, but she can ignore it. Our kind who go there want to be anonymous. Many live on boats or in the woods near human villages."

"Even this time of year?"

"Eh..." Lev shrugged. "For a human? It's a bad idea to be isolated in the winter, but for a vampire, not too bad. There are enough islands that the big storms aren't too destructive, which is why we noticed when these villages were hit."

"By hit, you mean—"

"Hit." Lev's voice was low and lost all its usual humor. "No vampires left. No humans either. The houses were wrecked, the ground all torn up. Once the water warms up, the bodies might start washing ashore. Or they may be gone by then."

Brigid looked at the two small dots. "How many people?"

"Not many." Lev picked up a mug of heated blood-wine. "A few vampires and a few dozen humans. Old settlements, some of them family compounds."

"Human families or vampires?" Tenzin asked.

Lev nodded. "Probably some of that and some humans our kind gathered over time. Extended families in a way."

Brigid knew exactly the type of compound Lev was describing. She'd been raised among humans who were descended from her sire. Deirdre's human family lived on even after she was turned, leaving generations of humans who knew about their immortal ancestors and were alternately protectors and the protected.

It was a symbiotic relationship that more than one immortal had used to survive for centuries without losing their humanity. The fact that someone had violated that pact offended both Brigid's human and vampire sides. It was out of order in the immortal world where humans who "belonged" to other vampires were generally left in peace.

But Zasha was known for breaking immortal norms. They seemed to delight in it.

"Why do you think Zasha was involved?" Tenzin asked. "It's unfortunate, but there are immortal grudges, greed, any number of—"

"One of Oleg's informants spotted Zasha in Sitka," Lev said. "Deep in Katya's territory. It was some months ago, during tourist season. Then a few months later, there were reports of strange boats in the area, and then finally these two villages are destroyed."

"Destroyed is a strong word," Tenzin said.

"Destroyed how?" Brigid asked.

Lev threw some pictures down on the table. The photos showed exactly why Lev had used the word destroyed.

Houses were torn up like a giant storm had blown through. The ground was ripped as if an earthquake had hit. More than a little bit of the rubble was burned, tickling a purr of interest in Brigid's neck.

Fire was her element, but it wasn't always her friend. Just because she couldn't get high anymore didn't mean she didn't have an addictive personality, and her brain and amnis were wired for excess.

She needed fire, but she also knew it could destroy her. In the scorched earth of the destroyed villages, she saw something more than destruction.

She saw *delight*.

Tenzin picked up a picture. "It looks like a newborn had a tantrum. Or a lot of them had tantrums all at once."

Lev frowned. "What sire would let a newborn do something like this?"

"It's not a newborn." Brigid slowly looked through a stack of pictures. "If it was a newborn, there would be blood."

Newborn vampires weren't exactly known for delicate kills.

She tossed the photos to Tenzin. "There's no blood."

Tenzin picked up the pictures and looked through them, her head cocked at a curious angle. "I revise my previous statement. This was no newborn. There is no blood because they didn't want to waste it."

"What are you saying?" Lev asked. "This was some kind of attack, of course. Oleg suspects that Katya hired Zasha to clear out older vampire compounds who might be loyal to him."

"Katya?" Brigid blinked. "Absolutely not."

Lev shrugged. "She's no angel, and she hates that Oleg is here. On the surface, she may put up with us, but don't you think—"

"Katya would never work with Zasha Sokholov," Brigid said. "I know her."

"Do you?" Tenzin asked.

Brigid looked at Tenzin, who only shrugged, mimicking Lev.

"I'm only saying you don't amass a territory from the Bering Sea to San Francisco Bay by being a sweet little girl," Tenzin said. "No matter what she looks like."

Brigid found it impossible to imagine, but her main purpose was finding Zasha, not getting between Oleg and Katya.

"Maybe Zasha is movin' to create their own territory," she offered. "Maybe they're challenging Oleg for dominance or trying to rebuild your sire's empire."

"Doubtful," Lev said. "Zasha had no love or loyalty for our sire, and they have never wanted power the way other vampires do. They love..."

"What?" Brigid pressed him.

Lev stared at the map. "Chaos."

"So maybe the attack *was* the purpose," Tenzin muttered. "Maybe they were just having fun."

"Fun?" Lev's eyes went dark. "Yes, perhaps."

Brigid sat down and stared at the map, then delved into her memories. "Both the villages were like this?"

"Yes," Lev said. "The one was on the mainland, the other on Kodiak Island."

"Near a harbor?"

"They wouldn't need a harbor." Tenzin didn't look up from the pictures.

"We can't assume they're air vampires."

"Wind damage." Tenzin kept looking through the stack of photos.

"And earth." Brigid crossed her arms. "Fire too."

Lev frowned. "The vampires who lived there were quiet. Old immortals. Powerful ones who didn't bother anyone."

"That would add to the fun from their perspective," Tenzin said. "The older ones would have provided the amusement the humans couldn't."

"But still, a vampire's gotta eat," Brigid said, "so the humans are useful too."

Lev curled his lip. "What you're saying is—"

"Awful." Brigid kicked out her feet. "Disgusting. Abhorrent. And exactly something Zasha would do for fun."

"They've done it before," Tenzin said. "After all, Zasha learned it from your sire."

"Our sire ran human hunts, but Oleg put a stop to it when he killed him."

"And a few years back, Zasha's son was runnin', hunts in Northern California under Katya's nose," Brigid said.

"And before that, Ivan tried them down in the desert east of Los Angeles," Tenzin said. "Probably at Zasha's urging. This has always been their favorite amusement."

"Ivan made good money on the hunts," Brigid said. "Hundreds of thousands of dollars a night for the privilege of vampires letting their base instincts loose and thumbin' their nose at authority."

"So you think that is what Zasha is doing here?"

"Maybe." Brigid narrowed her eyes. "But that can't be the only reason."

"Probably not." Tenzin tossed the stack of pictures back on the table. "After all, you and I are here. Perhaps Zasha got another thing they wanted."

CHAPTER SIX

B en slept very little that day. He could feel Tenzin stirring in his blood, her restless energy reaching out to him while she daydreamed wherever she was. The throbbing in his thigh was long gone, and his mind was tormented by what Tenzin had done.

Tenzin and Zasha are more alike than different.

It wasn't true. He'd seen the kindness in her while Zasha was an empty vessel. Tenzin was a fury when the vulnerable were brutalized. He'd seen the flash of anger in her eyes when she witnessed casual cruelty.

She was more than what she had been.

Ben remembered a hospital room a very long time ago and a boy who had never been a boy sitting beside a woman he'd been trying to protect.

Was this the first?

He remembered the hot suck of the blade as it entered the man's belly, the force of it as he shoved it higher, under the ribs, so that his attacker would die quickly.

Just as he'd been taught.

You were defending Dez. You were protecting the baby. The

sound of hospital monitors and the slow beep of a heart monitor behind her quiet words. *You did well, Benjamin. You did right.*

She'd been the only one to see him cry after he'd killed the first time. The first but not the last. Life was brutal, and immortal life was even more so. He lived in a world of predators, but he'd known that ever since he could remember, and vampires weren't the predators who scared him the most.

One of Ben's earliest memories was blood on a shattered mirror and the way it glowed translucent when the morning light hit the reflection. It didn't stay translucent, of course. Blood dried hard and dark, not like in the movies.

Blood was almost black when it was dry.

Tenzin knew that. She saw that. She didn't judge him for being a killer. While Ben had tried his best during his years as a human in the vampire world and now as a vampire himself, he had killed again.

Sometimes there was no other choice.

She's a killer. You have to know that. You have to understand that about her, Benjamin, or you will never understand Tenzin.

Maybe he'd never understood Tenzin. She guarded her secrets more carefully than her gold. Was Carwyn right? Was all this violence—the attack on Chloe, the hikers taken in Northern California, the boy kidnapped in Las Vegas—was it all because of something Tenzin started?

Did he know her at all?

———

"I WANT ALL OF YOU."

"You have me. As no other has. Can you accept that without asking for more? When I tell you that the blood of Temur is part of a story you do not want and would never understand, can you accept that?"

———

THE FLASH of her smile in moonlight. The tender way she fed their pet birds, her eyes gentle on the tiny fluttering creatures with the rapid hearts. Her patience with him when he'd been young and angry and pushing her away.

Pushing her away because he was grateful for immortal life and had hated to admit it.

He pressed his eyes closed and whispered into the air. "You left *me* this time."

They had danced for years, closing in and pushing away, but since the moment they had shared blood, there had been very little time they'd been apart.

He felt her heart in his own chest. He was the only one who could make it move.

"Where are you?" He rose and paced the small light-safe room where Carwyn had stowed him.

Could he accept her? Could he accept that she was a killer? She'd asked him to, and he'd agreed. He'd said yes. He'd made a promise.

Whatever he was going into, Tenzin was his mate. And if she was the cause of all this, he had eternity to work beside her to make things right.

But first he had to find her.

Ben closed his eyes, tore his shirt from his body, and opened his arms wide in the darkness. He drew air into his lungs, suffusing his body with as much of his element as he could.

He reached out with his amnis, searching for the pull of her power. A thread. A flicker of elemental dust in the wind. Anything that could connect them.

They were wind and air and the void. The void was in everything. Even the matter of things in bodies was visible to Ben if he looked long enough. He saw the space between.

He turned slowly, his arms stretched out, searching for her.

He turned south and immediately knew she wasn't there.

He turned again, spinning slowly as the air around him swirled, caressing his bare skin and traveling from his blood, through tiny cracks in the vents, the seams of the shutters and the windows, through the rafters and into the open air.

Bathed in darkness, his amnis touched the sun and flew away, north and west and over the water. She existed in darkness, and that's where his element met hers.

I see you.

He whispered her name. "Tenzin."

Tenzin, holder of wisdom.

Guardian of secrets.

The ancient girl. The newly mated. Blood of his blood. His mate and his destiny.

She was the darkness and he called to her.

———

CARWYN COULD FEEL the young vampire's restless energy in the light sleep where he drifted. He was over a thousand years old, and the only time he slept deeply anymore was after a full meal and a thorough fuck.

The agitated vampire was keeping him awake, and it was annoying. The moment night fell, he opened the door to his room to find Ben already in the middle of the living room.

"They're in Alaska. Somewhere near the ocean."

"Brilliant." Carwyn's voice was dry. "So exactly where Katya suspects Zasha is causing trouble? Truly a deduction for the ages." The young one looked deflated, so Carwyn took pity on him. "Katya told me yesterday evening that she thinks Oleg has been trying to expand his territory and push her out. Boats have gone missing, both pleasure yachts and fishing boats the same. There have been violent confrontations and attacks on compounds. She asked me to look into it."

Ben frowned. "I thought you were looking for Brigid."

"I am." The young man truly didn't know how these things worked. He went bounding through life like a giant, lethal puppy. "But Brigid is working with Oleg. Do you think she'd be working with Oleg if he was behind a bunch of violent attacks on the Alaskan coast?"

Ben's eyes went wide. "It's not Oleg—it's Zasha."

"Of course it's Zasha, but try telling Katya that. Oleg is her nemesis at the moment, but if we're going hunting for bad fire vampires and we want Katya's help, then we agree to look for Oleg. We can't just roam around in another vampire's territory; we need some kind of permission to be here." He muttered, "Especially you."

"And if Katya tells me to get out?"

"I'll tell her to fuck off and create an international incident." Carwyn forced a toothy grin. "But since she knows that would be a bad idea, she won't say no."

"So we're looking for Oleg, but we're really looking for Zasha?" Ben lifted one shoulder. "No offense, but I came looking for Tenzin so I could help her kill this vampire. I want to find Tenzin first."

"Before she goes on a vampire-killing spree and pulls my wife into her madness? That's an excellent idea." He pulled a flannel over his shirt before he reached for his heavy jacket. "But there's an order to these things, Benjamin. An order to our world that your mate often ignores because it annoys her, but protocol *matters*. Territories matter." He shrugged into his jacket. "I hate being cold. Why couldn't they go hunting for a vampire who was causing mayhem in Rio?"

"I don't even notice the cold anymore."

Of course he didn't. The boy was a wind vampire.

"Also? You travel with me, you're not flying," Carwyn grabbed his keys from the dish on the counter. "I'm not following along after you like the tail on a dog."

"That's fine. How do we get north? How do we get to that part of Alaska without flying? Driving could take days."

Carwyn waited for Ben to pull on a black jacket he'd dried the night before. He'd need to get the boy—

Man.

The vampire was in his thirties at this point. Wouldn't do to call his best friend's child a boy anymore. Not when he'd gone and gotten himself turned into a vampire and then mated with a small and unpredictable monster.

"We're going to meet Katya, and then we're going shopping." Carwyn eyed him up and down. "You're never going to blend in, Tall, Dark, and Pale, but you could stand out a little less."

Ben stared at Carwyn. "You're wearing a Hawaiian shirt and a Red Hot Chili Peppers T-shirt."

"But I have a flannel over all that." Carwyn plucked at the well-worn plaid. "You look like a vampire from New York City."

Ben narrowed his eyes. "Can't imagine why."

"City boy." He walked toward the door. "Come on. You think Tenzin is on the Alaskan coast, and that matches where Katya thinks Zasha is. Let's go introduce you and get you permission to be in her territory. Then we'll get you some proper clothes."

———

"BENJAMIN VECCHIO." Katya was curled up in front of a roaring fire, but she didn't look cozy and she wasn't pleased to see him. "So now I have to assume your mate is also in my territory."

"To help Brigid find Zasha." Ben sat across from the vampire, who looked barely older than his little sister, and tried to take her seriously. "That's all."

"Not as an agent of Penglai Island?" Katya raised an eyebrow. "Not as a representative of your sire? Not in cooperation with Oleg, who has expressed interest in the past in taking Alaska with the help of the Eight Immortals of Penglai so they can expand their shipping channels and access the Arctic when the planet warms up?"

Ben opened his mouth, then closed it again. Carwyn was right. There was a lot of this stuff he didn't understand.

"Hold on," Carwyn said. "You didn't mention that last bit when we spoke last night."

"Because I thought I was dealing with you and Brigid alone." She jerked her head at Ben. "Not these two. I don't trust either of them."

"Well, I do." Carwyn's voice was blunt. "And I vouch for them. Are you questioning me?"

Ben raised both his hands. "I'm following my mate, who is following Brigid Connor, who is tracking Zasha Sokholov. I promise you, Tenzin is not an agent of Penglai."

"Are *you*?"

Fuck. "No."

"You're Zhang Guo's first child in thousands of years," Katya said. "He must have had a reason for turning you. Maybe it is for your extensive connections in Europe and North America. I understand you're also a close associate of Gavin Wallace. Is Gavin looking for new investors in his software business? Maybe you're here to negotiate with Oleg."

Carwyn burst out laughing and leaned forward, slightly breaking the laser focus Katya's eyes had on Ben. "Katya, you know why he's here. Why are you interrogating him?"

Katya narrowed her eyes and smiled a little bit. "I was having fun breaking his brain. You spoil everything."

"He's stressed about his mate. You don't want to piss this one off."

Carwyn flicked a hand at Ben, and Ben felt his fangs fall at the airy dismissal. His temper was building again.

"Boats." Katya kept her eyes on Ben. "I'll get you up to Alaska, but you'll be on a boat."

"You don't have a plane?"

"Not one for you. Zasha has taken my boats. I want you and Carwyn to find them. I'm sending you to one of my oldest lieutenants. She can help you look for your mates."

"After we find your boats?" Carwyn asked.

"You wanted to go to Alaska, I'm sending you there."

"Winter seems like a bad time for piracy," Ben said.

"It is. That's why they took the boats in the fall, but we haven't seen a trace of them since then, and we haven't seen a trace of their crews either." Her eyes flashed to Carwyn. "Three of my vampires and two dozen of my people in the crews. I don't have anything to tell their families. Find me some answers if you can't find the boats."

"Where?"

"It won't mean anything to you now, but they were off the Queen Charlotte Sound. International waters. The humans have no jurisdiction there."

"Any vampire ships in the area?" Ben asked.

"My boats. Oleg's people. And Penglai."

That's why all the questions about Penglai. The islands off the coast of China—as well being the seat of East Asian immortal government—were also the center of the vast business interests of the Eight Immortals.

"All the big and dangerous players then," Ben said. "I'm a

wind vampire, and I'm willing to help Carwyn look into the thefts."

Katya looked him up and down. "Can you grow a beard?"

Vampire hair grew very slowly. "Not in the next day or two."

Katya sighed. "You're going to stick out like a sore thumb, but fine. You have my official permission to be in my territory, which stretches from San Francisco to Point Barrow. I offer no protection for you, and any aggression not officially sanctioned in this meeting is subject to my judgment and punishment should any of my people, mortal or immortal, bring me a complaint."

"What aggression are you officially sanctioning in this meeting?"

Katya narrowed her eyes. "Get Zasha Sokholov out of my territory. Kill them. Maim them. I don't care. Arrest them and take them back to Russia—I wouldn't really suggest that one because others have tried—but get rid of them and get my people back. I'm sick of this shit." She huffed loudly. "This is supposed to be the quiet time of year, Carwyn. I gave people vacation time."

"I know." The big vampire tried to soothe the tiny, irritated vampire. "You know we'll deal honestly with you. And we'll get results."

"And when you run into him—because I know he's involved in this shit too—tell Oleg his taxes just went up for not taking care of his damn sibling."

Ben had a feeling Oleg was going to care about the increased tax bill much more than any threat to Zasha. From what he'd heard, there was no love lost between the Russian and most of his extended family.

"Done." Ben rose. "Thank you, Katya Grigorieva. We'll find our mates and get rid of the fire vampire."

"Not Brigid," Carwyn muttered.

"The other fire vampire."

"Or Oleg," Carwyn muttered.

Katya curled her lip at Carwyn. "I thought those bastards were supposed to be rare. I do not have a single fire vampire in my organization right now, nor do I want one, but it seems like I have fire vampires coming out of my ears all of a sudden."

"We'll take care of it." Ben nodded at the woman, who looked like a grumpy teenager. "Thank you."

CHAPTER SEVEN

Saint Petersburg, Russia 1765

Tenzin watched Giovanni from across the room, making every attempt to blend into the wall in the dark public house. She had trained him in the delicate art of poisoning, but this was his first attempt in public.

And they were very public.

The human they were killing was a detestable individual, but his manners toward his female servants weren't the reason they were killing him. He was a political rival in the court of Catherine the Great, and the duke who wanted him dead happened to have a Turkish blade and a property in the Crimea that Tenzin desired.

She'd promised the property to Giovanni if he succeeded; she only wanted the blade.

A vampire walked into the public house, drawing both her and Giovanni's attention.

Don't react. She willed the thought into his mind. *Trust me.*

It was her job to deal with complications. It was his job to kill the count.

Luckily, he kept his position at the table next to the one where the count was regaling a group of other men and a few barmaids with his story about boar hunting.

Humans were so boring.

The vampire who'd entered the pub lingered in the doorway, keeping to the shadows. Tenzin kept her eyes on the tall figure, searching the shadows for any other compatriots. Something made her amnis twitch, but her attention was divided between the young fire vampire she was training and the immortal at the door.

The figure strode forward, revealing an elegant man dressed in rich clothing with long black hair and aquiline features. His cheekbones were high, and his eyes were dark brown. Tenzin stared at the vampire from the shadows, searching for any hint of recognition.

Nothing.

If they'd met before, she didn't remember it. Then again, she met many faces she didn't bother remembering. The vampire's gaze caught on her own, but he swiftly looked away and turned his eyes to the woman behind the bar. The vampire kept their amnis close, and Tenzin couldn't discern his element, but since the immortal kept to himself, so did she.

Tenzin kept one ear on the new arrival but turned her attention back to Giovanni. The count had just refilled his vodka; it was the perfect time to dose his drink. All he'd need to do was get up from the table, ease around the man in the velvet jacket, and casually tip his hand over the count's drink.

The vampire approached her, but she kept her eyes on Giovanni.

"I didn't realize they allowed Mongols in this establishment." The vampire spoke in French, so Tenzin responded in kind.

"I am but a manservant of my lord." Tenzin kept her face turned to Giovanni, but her gaze turned to the vampire at her side.

Humans were within listening distance, but that didn't deter the vampire. "I am surprised to see you here," he continued in French. "Don't you remember me?"

"I meet many in the service of Signor di Spada." Tenzin's eyes remained on Giovanni. There was something familiar about the vampire, but she couldn't place it and she didn't care that much.

Underneath the restrictive masculine garments typical for servants of the day, she wore three blades, all of which she could access quickly and easily. Before this vampire drew a breath, she could have her dagger in his neck. If any of the humans saw anything, her amnis would wipe their memory, but it was more bother than she wanted.

"I would never have predicted seeing Elder Zhang's only daughter in the service of any man."

Her sire's name made Tenzin turn her face to the arrogant vampire beside her. "I think you have me confused with someone else." Who was he? A thread of smoke reached her nose before the vampire quickly pulled his amnis back.

It was enough. He was a fire vampire.

"Wouldn't it be lovely," the man whispered, "to tear their throats out, feast on their blood, and burn this wretched place to the ground?"

"A waste of time," she replied. "Why bother?"

Humans like this were a mix of cattle and prey to her. The rich and powerful were prey. The others were harmless cattle, humble people trying to survive in a world that didn't care about them. She had the same amount of concern for the cattle that she did for the winter fox or the deer hiding in the forest.

"We bother because we can," the tall vampire said. "The count?"

"*Our* prey, stranger. Not yours."

He nodded slightly.

Giovanni rose, joked with the man next to him in Russian, and appeared to drunkenly stumble past the count's table so he had to brace himself.

There!

The poison was in the vodka.

The count lifted the glass.

"Should I warn him?"

Tenzin's eyes flashed to the strange vampire, her fangs growing longer at the threat. "This is none of your concern."

"But it might be amusing." The corner of his mouth turned up.

Tenzin's hand moved to the dagger hidden just under her ribs as she watched the count from the corner of her eye. The dosed vodka disappeared down the human's gullet, and Giovanni moved toward her through the room, keeping up the appearance of a drunk human stumbling through the crowd and pulling on his overcoat.

Giovanni brushed against the strange vampire, eyeing the man from his carefully set hair to his polished boots. His chin lifted and his gaze turned haughty, the internal aristocrat coming to life before her eyes.

"Is there a problem?" he asked Tenzin.

"None." Tenzin glanced one more time at the stranger, then returned her attention to Giovanni. "Come, my boy. You've done well."

Giovanni and the other fire vampire locked eyes for a long moment; then Tenzin tugged Giovanni's arm and pulled him toward the door.

They walked out of the public house without another look back, crunching their way down the snowy streets of Saint Petersburg and dodging a carriage that rumbled past as it churned up icy slush.

"We'll wait for a few days to make sure he's dead," Tenzin said. "No one will be able to trace it back to the duke."

"I'd appreciate a bit of warmer weather," her protégé said. "An escape to the Black Sea is just what I was thinking."

"A nice relief," she said. "I'll be sure to fly ahead and check it out. It should only take you a month or so traveling by horse."

He laughed a little. "You're such a braggart, Tenzin." He looked over his shoulder. "Who was that back in the public house?"

"No one." Tenzin shrugged. "Probably someone I met before I knew you."

"You can't remember?"

"My boy, I have lived a long time."

———

"THE BOSS IS HERE."

Tenzin looked up to see Lev standing in the doorway that led to the stinky room. "Who is your boss?"

Brigid nudged her arm. "Oleg." She looked at Lev. "I didn't know he was in the area. You said he hated the cold."

"Oh yeah." Lev nodded. "That's probably why he's so grumpy, you know? And the dogs. He doesn't like the dogs."

Tenzin muttered, "What kind of human doesn't like dogs?"

"Maybe it's just the sled dogs," Brigid said. "I can't lie, they are really feckin' loud."

"Hmm." Tenzin stood up from the pictures she was examining. There was something about the photos that tickled her brain, but she couldn't place the irritation, so she just kept looking at them long after Brigid had lost interest.

"Is Oleg staying in the big house?"

Lev nodded. "Oh yeah, he doesn't stay here."

"Because it stinks like sweat?" Tenzin's nose twitched. "And pickled eggs?"

Brigid snapped her fingers, and a spark lit the air. "That's what it is. Pickled eggs." She wrinkled her nose.

"No, he stays at his house because..." Lev looked hurt. "He likes his privacy. Does it really smell like pickled eggs here?"

Tenzin and Brigid exchanged a look, and then they both nodded.

"Oh." Lev frowned. "Okay, so the boss said he wants to talk to you both in an hour. He doesn't want to come here. He says he'll have his housekeeper make tea."

"Okay, great." Brigid waved, and Lev returned to the front room. "Bollocks."

"What's wrong?" Tenzin returned to the map, trying to estimate how long it would take to fly to the burned villages.

"I don't have anything for tea."

"So?"

"Gift giving is a big thing for Oleg," Brigid said. "Anne said I should never show up to anything that Oleg is hostin' without some kind of gift."

"So he knows that about you," Tenzin said. "This is why he has invited us to his house instead of coming here and he specifically told Lev that he was preparing tea. He's challenging you."

Brigid's lip curled. "Yeah, but that doesn't help me at the moment." She lifted the pile of pictures. "What am I gonna give him? Snapshots of destruction?"

Tenzin shrugged. "I'll find something."

Brigid frowned. "Are you sure?"

"Yes." She pointed to the pictures. "Every type of attack. Every element represented. How likely is that? Usually our kind hunt in like groups. Wind with wind. Water with water."

Brigid crossed her arms and looked at the pictures. "You're spot on. Every single frame shows evidence of fire, earth, air, and water violence. It has to be intentional."

"This isn't chaotic," Tenzin said. "It's not random even though it's meant to look that way. Zasha is choosing vampires of each element and then letting them loose on these villages for fun."

Brigid sat down in a chair and stared at the fire. "Do ya know all the cruise ships that come up here to Alaska?"

"Cruise ships?"

"Humans all group together on large boats. I'm talking massive boats, Tenzin."

"Yachts?"

"Bigger than yachts." She spread her arms out. "Hundreds of bedrooms. Restaurants. Swimming pools. Nightclubs and pubs. Theaters sometimes."

"Like a floating city." *A vampire buffet.* She didn't say that part.

"Yes, like a floating city."

The idea of that had some appeal even without the human-buffet part. Tenzin traveled quite comfortably in boats even though Benjamin hated them. "If I could stay below the waterline, it wouldn't bother me. Ben stayed in a freighter once when we were—"

"Focus," Brigid said. "So on these human cruise ships, they travel to different spots, and then when they get to those locations, the humans will go off and do different things. Tour historic sites. Visit national parks or museums. Things like that."

"I like museums."

"You like stealin' from museums," Brigid said.

"Not always."

But often.

Tenzin didn't have a problem with stealing from museums. After all, most of the things in museums had belonged to someone else to begin with. She was hardly going to feel guilty about stealing things that were already stolen.

"What if, instead of running hunts like Ivan, Zasha is running vampire tours? 'Here, come to a place with long nights and cold weather where a lot of isolated vampires and humans are settled in for the winter, and then we can hunt them.'"

"For a price?"

"Of course for a price."

Brigid stared at the fire, and Tenzin watched the vampire and the fire react to each other.

Did the woman know the flames followed her? If she gestured, the fire moved in tandem. If she grew animated, the flames jumped. Sparks glowed when she stared at them, dying down when she looked away.

Fascinating.

Tenzin had never been particularly interested in fire. Giovanni's had been useful in certain situations, but they rarely burned vampires to death when a blade was so much quicker. She found herself curious about how Brigid and the fire worked together.

Giovanni wielded his fire like a warrior swung a sword.

But Brigid? Tenzin felt like the flames were almost reaching for her. As if the fire was an extension of her body.

Fascinating.

"...what you'll bring?"

She frowned. "What?"

Brigid said, "I was askin' if you had an idea what you'll bring? To Oleg's house." She glanced at the clock on the wall. "We should be there in about thirty minutes. I'm gonna go change into a clean shirt."

"Good idea. You are also starting to smell like pickled eggs."

"If I am, so are you." Brigid stood up. "We've gotta get some fresh air."

———

TENZIN WAITED at the front door of the luxurious wooden house in the middle of the forest. In the summer it would look out over a broad river teeming with fish. Bears probably rambled through to feed, and the sun from the long summer days would bake the wooden shingles on the steep, angled roof and warm the broad double porch.

The house's shutters were painted bright green with delicate flowers in red and yellow, a surprisingly feminine touch in an otherwise masculine abode. Elk and moose antlers decorated the face of the house, and two purebred white dogs lazed on a corner of the porch, looking for all the world like two miniature polar bears soaking in the snow.

"I guess he likes dogs after all," Tenzin said.

"I told you it's probably the barking." Brigid glanced at her. "What did you bring?"

"A gift." She shrugged. "He'll like it."

They had already clanged the heavy bell by the door, so Tenzin took advantage of the view. "It's beautiful here."

"It's Baltic cold."

"Yes, and beautiful." The broad river was frozen over on the edges but not in the center of the channel where the moon reflected in the black water. The snow refracted the lunar illumination, lighting up the world around them with an unearthly glow, and green lights danced in the night sky, waving like slow-moving banners across the velvet black.

The door opened behind them and Tenzin turned.

"Brigid." A tall man with medium brown hair and moderately handsome features greeted Brigid like a friend. "It's fucking cold out here. Get inside."

"Cheers, Mika."

Brigid walked in, and Tenzin approached the front door only to have the man step in front of her.

She stopped, looked up, and raised an eyebrow. "Mika Arakas."

"Tenzin of Penglai."

"It's been a long time."

"Who are you trying to kill at the moment? If it's Zasha, you can come in."

"I'm not going to kill Zasha."

Mika's blue eyes drilled into hers. "Then we will have a problem."

"I *can't* kill Zasha because I made a promise a very long time ago." She had no idea why she was telling this vampire anything save for the instinct that he was completely uninterested in her and would dismiss anything not pertinent to his master. "I am here to assist Brigid in killing Zasha," she said graciously. "So I suppose, as you guard Oleg, I guard Brigid."

Mika smirked. "You're playing bodyguard?"

"For the moment, and right now I'm outside and she's irritated. Can I come inside?"

"Fine." He opened the door and stepped aside to let her in. "Don't try anything."

She crooked her finger at Mika. "Come here," she whispered.

Mika indulged her and bent down since he was nearly a foot taller than Tenzin.

"If I wanted to kill you or Oleg," she murmured, "you'd never see it coming. You're welcome."

Mika stood up straight, and he looked perversely amused. "I heard you mellowed when you took a mate. I'm pleased to see the rumors are untrue."

"Oh no, this is me mellow." Tenzin rose a little in the air, patted his shoulder, then floated over to Oleg. "Hail, Varangian."

The corner of his mouth tipped up. "Welcome, Khazar."

Tenzin smiled and rested her feet on the ground before she nodded deeply. It was nice to meet a fellow immortal whose history the modern world had forgotten.

She dug into her pocket and brought out the bullet that had

struck her thigh. She held it out to Oleg and dropped it into his outstretched palm. Brigid gasped and Mika cleared his throat.

"Oleg of Kiev, here is the lead and steel your people gave me on my arrival in your territory. I return it to you. This is the *only* lead or steel that I will return while we remain friends."

Mika released his breath, and Oleg nodded carefully. "Understood." The corner of his mouth inched up. "An acceptable gift. Brigid usually brings cake."

"If you wanted us to bring food, we were limited to pickled eggs."

Oleg grimaced. "The bullet will suffice."

———

"YOU SAW the chaos that Zasha is playing with along the coast." Oleg sat back in a massive chair near the fire, his hand stirring the flames every time they died down. "I have been more than patient with the blood of our sire. They are working with the Grigorieva now and must be eliminated."

"Katya?" Brigid asked. "You think Zasha is workin' with Katya?"

"I heard the large one surmise it," Tenzin said. "I thought he was being foolish." She turned to Oleg. "Now you are being foolish."

Mika shrugged. "Katya wants us out. And all we want to do is use the property we have enjoyed peacefully for so many years."

"Yes," Oleg said. "The fishing in the summer is superb. Worth the short nights."

Lies. Brigid didn't seem to suspect anything, but Tenzin met Oleg's eyes and saw the calculation behind the facade. He was planning to take this territory back, and he was annoyed that Zasha might muck up his plans.

"Why not eliminate Zasha yourself?" Tenzin asked. "Why is this Brigid's problem?"

"Zasha is blood of my blood," Oleg said. "I have had to kill more than one of my sire's more... feral children, and my brothers in Moscow enjoy Zasha's antics. If I eliminate them..." He curled his lip.

"Awkward holiday dinners?" Tenzin asked.

Oleg muttered, "They will be unbearable."

"But if the results of Zasha's own antagonism caught up with them?" Mika spoke to Brigid. "That would be Zasha's own fault."

"Your brothers won't question why you didn't defend them?" Brigid asked. "Or why you won't avenge their death?"

"No," Oleg said. "They all know Zasha is a problem, but they all feel guilty."

"Why?" Brigid asked.

Oleg turned to Tenzin and met her silent gaze.

Zasha was different. The vampire was not like their brothers.

When Tenzin had first met Zasha, they were living as a woman. She could easily imagine what life had been like for Zasha in a warrior's compound because Tenzin had known that horror herself.

"Oleg's brothers are guilty because they are the ones who turned Zasha into what they are," Tenzin said.

"It was not a gentle house," Oleg muttered. "That's why I killed my father. That's why my brothers hate me even though they all know it was the right thing."

"And Zasha?"

"The only thing I could do for Zasha was kill our sire. I did that, and Zasha fled." He shrugged. "I let anyone who wanted to leave go. I am not my sire."

Mika muttered something in Russian that Tenzin couldn't hear, and Oleg snapped at him.

"Mika says I should have killed Zasha." He spoke to Brigid.

"Perhaps he is correct, but we cannot see the future. I wanted to give them a chance."

"It's not your fault," Brigid said.

No, it's mine. Tenzin stayed quiet, watching the civilized vampires speak about plans and strategy, listening to them talk of traps and lures as if Zasha Sokholov was a particularly clever wolf they could trap.

Not a wolf. Not a wolf.

Zasha was a wolverine.

Ferocious, stubborn, opportunistic, and able to take out prey far larger than one would expect. After all, Zasha was only one vampire.

One vampire to cause this much mayhem.

"Tell us where to find Zasha," Tenzin said quietly. "We will hunt them and we will kill them. You don't have to be involved."

Mika and Oleg looked at each other again.

"We don't know precisely where they are," Mika said. "We never do."

"But we have ideas," Oleg said. "And you have wings."

CHAPTER EIGHT

B rigid stared into the fire, ruminating over everything she'd heard at Oleg's house.

And everything she hadn't heard.

I'm not going to kill Zasha.

   I can't kill Zasha because I made a promise a very long time ago.

   I am here to assist Brigid killing Zasha. As you guard Oleg, I guard Brigid.

Brigid hated the idea of Tenzin being her guard dog, but she could accept it in a way that she couldn't accept Carwyn's protection. Carwyn wasn't an innocent, but he'd done nothing to create this situation, and he would be collateral damage in a battle that wasn't his.

Tenzin, on the other hand, had done something. Brigid didn't know what, but there was definitely something.

Brigid heard the whisper of movement in the air that meant Tenzin was in the room. She caught a flicker of movement from the corner of her eye and reached her amnis out. The wind vampire was floating in the rafters of the giant hall, her energy humming in a low, steady way. The humans were all sleeping; Lev and Oleg's other men were busy in the barn where they kept the snow equipment. Their laughing voices and shouts carried in the frigid night air.

That left Brigid with Tenzin.

God, she missed her mate.

If Carwyn was with her, he'd be telling her a story or a joke, making her laugh and then dreaming up a trip or a scheme or something to make her look forward to the endless stretch of eternity she faced.

"How do ya do it?" Brigid blurted.

Tenzin's voice came from a distance. "I need more information to answer that question."

Another question jumped into her mind. "Why don't ya have an accent?"

Tenzin had a slight accent, but nothing like Brigid's Irish.

"I got very good at not having one," Tenzin said. "I've had time to practice."

"Do you know how old y'are?"

"Not really." Tenzin floated closer to the fireplace, then sank to the floor. "Too hot up there. The air is stifling."

Brigid looked at her, a woman perpetually frozen in her late teens. Early twenties maybe. "You've no idea how long you've lived on the earth. I can't imagine being that old."

"Of course you can't." Tenzin shrugged. "It doesn't matter anyway."

"No?" She took a deep breath, inhaling the comforting smell of smoke and ash. "How do you live forever, Tenzin?"

"You don't live forever—you live now."

Brigid frowned. "What does that mean?"

Tenzin picked up a magazine sitting on the coffee table and opened to a page with nothing important on it, then carefully tore it out. "It means I rarely look forward and I avoid looking back." She started folding the paper in front of her. "Nothing is guaranteed, you know. We're not immortal. Immortal means we will live forever, but that's very unlikely. All things die, and in our world, we usually die violently. Or stupidly. I know of a vampire who had his head removed in an automobile accident. Isn't that a stupid way to die?"

"Yes." And how utterly common. If Brigid died by losing her head in a freak accident, she'd be pissed off.

Tenzin shrugged. "It happens. War. Accidents. Fire." She glanced at Brigid. "If you're looking for some grand purpose, you won't find it."

"That's just depressin'."

"It doesn't have to be." Tenzin held up a small paper crane and set it on the coffee table. "Be useful. Allow yourself to be bored. Take pleasure in small things, Brigid Connor."

"I was shite at being bored."

"Is that why you took drugs?"

Brigid's eyes went wide. "No."

Tenzin looked up. "Then why did you take them?"

"Because drugs made me feel amazin' instead of shite."

Tenzin nodded. "That's very logical."

"It is, isn't it? If heroin was free, I would have been high all the time. People hate hearing that, but it's the truth. I loved it." Her mouth started to water. "I was so fuckin' happy when I was high."

Tenzin tore off another piece of paper. "Heroin is like opium?"

"Yeah."

Tenzin nodded again. "I've seen humans on opium. They look like idiots to me, but they seem very happy."

"You don't care what ya look like. If you feel that good, you don't care if people think ya look like an idiot. You don't care about anythin'." The bitter tang sat in the back of her throat.

"That's why I stopped. Not because it was gonna kill me—well, it did kill me—or because I felt horrible on it. I didn't. I felt great. I quit because it made me a shite person."

"Because you didn't care about anything?"

"Yep. Not my family. Not other people. Nuthin'."

Tenzin pouted as she stared at the paper in her hands. "That's true. You should care about things." She methodically folded another paper crane. "Perhaps you care too much about everything now because at one point you were very selfish and cared only about dulling your pain."

She'd never thought about that. "Yeah, maybe."

"You cannot carry the weight of the world or it will break you." Tenzin finished another crane, then tore out another paper. "You asked me how I live forever."

"Yes."

"I live forever because I do not focus on the past or the future. I focus on the now. I have a very close circle of people I care about, and I care deeply about them. Also, I do not live alone."

"Ever?"

"No, I have lived alone in the past, and I know it is not good for me. Even in the half a century that I was silent in our world— before Stephen and Benjamin—I had Nima with me." Tenzin looked up. "Stephen was my first mate. He woke me from silence. Then I met Benjamin."

"And you weren't alone."

"I can be alone, but as I said, it's not good for me." Tenzin looked around the room. "You shouldn't have left your mate. You're like me. Being alone isn't good for you."

"I'm not like you." Brigid's voice was rough.

"In some ways you are."

"You left Ben."

Tenzin shrugged. "Only because I know he'll find me."

Brigid didn't want Ben to come. She didn't want him in Zasha's cross fire. That was the whole reason she'd left Carwyn.

"Do you think your giant earth vampire won't find you?" Tenzin smiled a little. "You are young. And you underestimate him."

"He was the legend and savior of my life," Brigid said. "I never underestimate him." Her voice grew rough. "He will shift mountains to find me."

Tenzin's eyes flashed. "So why?"

"Because I need time to find Zasha first."

"No."

"No?"

Tenzin crossed her legs under her body and focused on the crane. "No, that's not why you left him."

"Ya think so, really?" This should be good. "So tell me, wise sage of Penglai, why did I leave the love of my eternal life?"

"Because you think that you're not good enough. That you're not strong enough. You think you're going to die." Tenzin looked up. "And if Zasha is going to kill you, you don't want Carwyn to see it."

The lump in Brigid's throat kept her silent.

"You might be right." Tenzin set down a third crane. "You might not be good enough, but you could be."

"Because you're going to help me?"

"No." She cocked her head. "Yes. But not the way you think."

———

SHE WATCHED from a distance as Tenzin faced off against the giant fire vampire under a snowy cedar tree.

"You're going to do it."

"Why?"

Standing in the pure white snow, framed by dark cedars,

Brigid was reminded again of how utterly attractive Oleg was on a purely aesthetic level. His hair was a rich russet brown, his eyes were storm grey, and his beard with thick and luxurious. His amnis was old and there was something utterly wild about his energy, more like a fierce bird of prey than a dangerous fire vampire.

Brigid could clearly see why Oleg was rumored to have a stable of human mistresses.

"You're going to help her because she's cleaning up your mess," Tenzin said. "She's young and she has good control, but she's not a warrior."

Brigid cleared her throat. "Pardon me—"

"No." Tenzin turned and raised a finger. "This is not a debate. You are a fighter, but only in the human sense. This one" —she pointed at Oleg— "has razed villages. This one had scars that took centuries to heal." She looked at Oleg. "You think I wouldn't remember? I do. I choose to forget a lot, but not everything."

Oleg crossed his arms over his chest and said nothing.

"He's silent because he knows I'm right." Tenzin walked over to Brigid. "You fight with guns and daggers, but anytime I've heard of you using your fire, it's to explode and cause a distraction of some kind. You need to use your fire like I use a blade."

Brigid glanced at Oleg, keeping her voice low. "That's not how fire works, Tenzin."

"It can." Oleg's voice sounded like a low rumble of thunder on the other side of a mountain. "It can be like a blade." He walked toward her slowly. "Who trained you first?"

"Katherine Mackenzie."

Oleg curled his lip. "American. No wonder you explode so much."

"Hey, I very rarely—"

"Eh..." Oleg waved a hand. "Brute force is not a horrible thing. Sometimes it is necessary." He stepped closer. "But have you ever seen the slow suck of air when a fire is licking along a seam? Have you seen how it can flow like water?"

The scent of burnt cedar tickled her nose. Brigid looked up and saw a thin layer of fire coating the cedar branch over Oleg's head.

She hadn't even seen him start the flame.

The vampire raised a hand and called the burning flame to his open palm. The fire slid away from the branches, swirling into a glowing ball that floated over Oleg's palm.

"Our element isn't like the others," Oleg said. "The air, the earth, the water... they *exist*. They are matter, even the air. But fire?" His lips grew darker as he looked at the flames in his palm. "It is energy. Fire is a process. Like a woman's pleasure, fire must be fed to survive."

The ball of fire became a small rivulet of flame he slid between his fingers, the blue-and-yellow lick of heat floating just over his skin and singeing the fine hairs on the back of his hand, which turned to ash and floated away. "Don't think of your fire like rough matter, Brigid Connor. Don't think of it as something you must manage or tame. Think of it like a lover you must seduce."

Tenzin's lips were flushed when she spoke. "I would have sex with you if I were not mated and monogamous."

Brigid blinked and cleared her throat.

Oleg looked amused. "We could have tried, but there would probably have been casualties."

"Yes." Tenzin's eyes narrowed as she watched him. "But it might have been worth it."

The corner of Oleg's mouth turned up, and he turned his stormy grey eyes to Brigid. "I'll give you some advice. What you do with it is up to you."

Brigid cleared her throat, trying to ignore the flush on the surface of her skin. She could feel the heat pouring off her body.

"Okay, great." She nodded. "I'm always game to learn new things. Thanks."

———

"AGAIN."

It wasn't like any fire training she'd ever had before. She was in the barn and she was spilling fire slowly along the straw-strewn ground, channeling it from one pile of tinder to another. More often than not, her element collapsed on itself before she could feed it her amnis, leaving trails of ash along the concrete floor.

She let out a slow breath and took another, clamping down on the explosive temper that was starting to swirl in her chest.

"You're angry." Oleg wore a short-sleeved shirt and a pair of heavy khaki pants that looked military. He paced behind her in the barn. "Don't let it overtake you. That's what causes the explosion. You need control, not ignition."

"I'm not getting better."

"Don't be stupid," he growled. "You've only been doing this for six hours."

"Six fuckin' hours?" She glanced at the clock on the wall. "What the hell? Where is Tenzin? Is she—?"

"She flew out to survey the raid sites that Zasha left. Now focus." He stepped closer, inches from her back.

Brigid's instinctive reaction made her fangs drop, her shoulders turn, and she reached for a dagger that wasn't there. Her skin heated and her amnis jumped to attention.

She snarled at Oleg, who froze and narrowed his eyes.

"Touchy."

"I don't like people at my back."

Oleg angled his head, nodded slowly. "Understood." He stepped to the side, a few feet away. "Better?"

Brigid nodded. She was surprised how violent her reaction

had been, but she'd been away from her mate for weeks, she was low on energy, and she needed to feed. She was jumpier than she had been in years.

Oleg was still staring at her. "Someone hurt you in an unacceptable way."

They were alone in the barn. It was well past midnight, and the humans were asleep. Lev had probably followed Tenzin, and the rest of the vampires had left Oleg and Brigid alone while they practiced working with fire.

This was not a spectator sport.

"It was a long time ago."

"They hurt Zasha too. For many years." His voice was quiet. "If there is an excuse for their actions—"

"There isn't. Abuse isn't rare, Oleg. Lots of people get hurt every day, especially women and children. They get angry, but they don't all turn into sociopathic monsters."

Brigid snapped her fingers, brought the fire to her hands, and carefully fed it to the next trail of straw.

"You're already improving." Oleg stood at attention, watching her with his hands clasped behind his back. "Perhaps, though the world would be a slightly better place if more women and children expressed their anger."

It was the thought of a man who had probably never been vulnerable to anything. "That would be nice. It would be cathartic to rage and yell and scream, wouldn't it?" She carefully nudged her fire from the first pile of tinder to the next, coaxing it with amnis. "But we can't do that, Oleg. The world punishes our rage."

Oleg lifted his chin. "Perhaps that is your problem."

"What?" Fuck. The fire went out again before it reached the next tinder. Brigid tried hard not to be angry. It seemed like the fire in her responded to explosive energy or nothing.

Apparently her aunts had all been correct: subtlety was not in her DNA.

Oleg walked carefully over to the pile of ash that marked her last failed attempt. "Your rage has never had a voice, so your fire must always protect you. Your fire cannot serve you if it is always protecting you."

Brigid blinked. "That actually makes sense."

Oleg leaned back on one booted foot and smiled a little. "I cannot help you with that, Brigid Connor. Only you know how you must give your rage a voice. But I think that only after you do that will your fire be able to work for you."

CHAPTER NINE

The heavy churn of the water pressed against the cold hull, rocking Carwyn back and forth in a fishing boat heading north. He closed his eyes and tried to roll with the waves of the North Pacific, keeping his mind on his mate and on the problem at hand.

Find Brigid.

Find Zasha.

Kill Zasha.

Scream at Brigid for leaving him.

Don't puke.

"I hate you," Ben muttered from across the cabin he and Carwyn had been assigned.

"I told you I wasn't going to follow along after you like a puppy." Carwyn tried to focus on the metal of the boat, which was part of his element and provided some comfort.

Ben spat out, "I fucking hate boats."

"Huh. I do too."

"Useless pieces of crap with no air. No light."

"Light's not good for you these days." Carwyn kept his eyes

closed, wondering when Ben was going to figure out the very obvious solution to his predicament.

"Horrible food," Ben continued. "I was stuck on a freighter from Shanghai once when I was human and—"

"Benjamin." Carwyn had heard enough. "Just fucking float."

"We are floating. That's the problem."

Carwyn picked up a thick copy of *Birds of the Puget Sound* and chucked it at Ben's head.

"What was that for?"

"Fucking! Float!" Carwyn pointed at the ceiling. "In the air, you idiot. You're a wind vampire. Float in the fucking air so you don't feel the boat rocking. It's a very simple solution."

Ben was silent, but he immediately floated up to the top of the cabin and floated a foot or two from the top of the room. "That's better."

You think?

Carwyn closed his eyes again and tried to focus on the feeling of the metal against his palms. Steady, cool, beautifully solid metal holding the terrors of the vast Pacific Ocean at bay. It was fine. Even if the seams cracked and the water rushed in, he couldn't drown.

But he would be fucking cold and wet.

"Why do vampires get motion sickness anyway?"

Benjamin Vecchio was incapable of being silent.

"It's not actually sickness; it's an imbalance of the inner ear," Carwyn said. "If anything, we're more sensitive to it than humans are. It would be worse if there weren't water vampires on board."

Katya's ships were all captained by water vampires who both kept the worst of the chop away from the boats and also knew the water better than the fish. It was one of the reasons her fleet was one of the most successful in the area.

"Is commercial fishing a big part of her business?" Ben asked. "How many boats does she have?"

"Dozens, I imagine. All around this size." The *Pacific Lady* was a 120-foot vessel that fished for all kinds of seafood and shell-fish off the coast of the US and Canada. It was registered to one of Katya's many companies and held seven human crew members along with the vampire captain. The men were crowded into two cabins at the moment since they were carrying vampire cargo, but as two of the crew members had missing relatives on the boats that vanished, no one was complaining.

"The food will be better on this ship if you get hungry." Carwyn was starting to get thirsty. He would need to hunt when they reached the first site. "In my experience, most fishing boats don't put up with bad food."

"I do like fish."

"You're in the right place then." He could feel the boat turn, and he waited for it.

Wait for it.

Just a second longer...

"Fuck!"

Carwyn smiled and opened his eyes. Ben hadn't felt the boat turn, and the sudden rocking had smacked his head on the corner of the hull.

"You all right?" Carwyn poked his head out from under his bunk.

"Yeah," Ben muttered. "I'm fine."

Carwyn looked at the black circle of the porthole. There was a light-safe shield that covered it during the day, but it was night. He could barely make out a few sparkling stars in the cold night and the sliver of the edge of the moon.

"You could go up to the deck if you wanted."

"That sounds like a recipe for me flying my ass away from here and leaving you behind," Ben said.

"Not if you want my help."

Ben muttered something in Mandarin that Carwyn pretended

not to understand.

"Is this how you crossed the ocean back in the day?" Ben asked.

"Yes, and trust me when I say this is very much an improvement."

"Why don't you buy a plane like Gio and B?"

Carwyn had money. He had plenty of money. What he didn't have was the patience to pay bills. "Too permanent. Your uncle has a plane, which also means he has a pilot, a crew, a hangar to keep it in, and rent for that. He has bookkeepers and money managers and—"

"Butlers. Don't forget the butlers."

Carwyn smiled. "Exactly. Which is why I love to visit your uncle, but I do not want to be him."

Ben rolled over to look at Carwyn. "Are you telling me you don't have a bookkeeper? That you don't pay taxes?"

"I don't think so."

"Carwyn, you tax dodger."

"I keep my money in gold, Ben. I don't have a job. I just cash in some gold every now and then when I need to buy things." He pursed his lips. "I need a Winnebago."

"Why? And won't you eventually run out of gold?"

"I really have a lot of gold," Carwyn muttered. "And I need a Winnebago so I have more room to stretch. I love a sturdy recreational vehicle."

"Okay, this is ridiculous." Ben floated down to the ground. "Is the crew working?"

"If you mean are they fishing, no. This is a passenger transfer up to Ketchikan, and then we're meeting another one of Katya's people up there."

"Where is Baojia?"

"On vacation in Indonesia apparently." Carwyn had a feeling that his old friend was going to be more than a little angry that his boss hadn't called him back when Carwyn showed up.

"I'm going to talk to the crew." Ben walked to the door, stumbling a little as the boat shifted to port. "Want to come?"

"No." Carwyn sat up and swung his legs over the side. "But I'll come anyway."

———

THE CREW of the *Pacific Lady* were a cool and serious group of professional fishermen consisting of six men and one woman. They ranged in age from the fresh-faced greenhorn to the woman, who looked like she had to be close to her seventies judging by the lines on her face.

Five of them sat in the mess hall, chugging coffee and playing cards while the cook that night—a middle-aged man everyone called Guff—cooked in the galley.

"What's for dinner?" Carwyn asked when he sat down.

The old woman stubbed out a cigarette and grinned. "Not us if you know what's good for you."

The men laughed, and Carwyn was immediately put at ease. "No worries, friend. If I took your blood, I'd definitely wipe your memory."

"See? Manners, Frannie." A red-faced man with yellow-blond hair and a Northern English accent grinned. "I told you they were gents."

"Brick, your idea of gents and my idea are gonna be very different things." She winked at Carwyn anyway.

The easy jokes led to more laughter and a few stories being passed around about different vampire captains the crew had worked under.

Ben was surprisingly easy with the men. Once they'd gotten him out of his stark black wardrobe and into some worn jeans, flannel, and a beat-up parka, he fit into the tapestry of the crew just fine. He was paler than most, but that didn't even stand out much in the Pacific Northwest, where the sun was covered about sixty percent of the year.

"So these two ships that went missing," Ben started. "The ones Carwyn and I are going to look for. What can you tell us?"

There was a hush for a moment, and then Frannie spoke. "Nothing special really. One was a little smaller than this one. Five guys and a good captain. Her name was Maureen, and I worked with her before I transferred to Jeb." She jabbed a thumb over her shoulder toward the bridge. "Irish water vamp. Kept her head down and her hold full. Her boys made good money."

"You get paid based on how much fish you catch, right?" Ben asked.

All of them nodded.

"We get a stipend, right?" Brick added. "When things are lean. Not much, but it keeps the bills paid. But the bonuses go to us when the catch is good. The big boss is good to work with."

"And the catch is almost always good," Frannie said. "The only times we don't come back with a decent catch is when the rest of 'em get suspicious, right? You can't be that boat that never comes back empty."

"Got it," Ben said. "So the two boats—"

"Three." The young man at the end of the table spoke quietly. "There was the *Ranger* and the *Amaranth*, but the yacht that went missing—that one had Grigorieva crew too. My girlfriend was the cook on the *Dolphin*. The *Flying Dolphin*, that was the yacht that went missing. We haven't heard from her in months."

He opened his phone and held up a picture of a brightly smiling blond woman in a blue-and-white striped shirt with a red scarf at her neck.

"That's her on the *Dolphin*," he said. "She started working for

Katya, but the money Paulson offered was so good she switched over. We were saving up to get married."

"Paulson?" Carwyn asked. The name sounded vaguely familiar, but it wasn't immediately unique. The majority of Scandinavians were a -son or -dottar of something. Paulson was far from a rare name even in vampire circles.

"Henri Paulson," Frannie said. "He's the rich vampire that went missing along with his crew." She reached over and patted the young man's hand. "Christy's a smart girl. Don't you worry."

Christy was likely dead, and the young man knew it from the look in his eyes. He was already using the past tense when he mentioned her.

"She's not a vampire though." He glanced at Ben. "Is she?"

"We don't know if we're going to find any survivors," Ben said. "I don't want to give you any kind of false hope here. The chances that any of these crews are still alive after this many months is slim. I know Katya had people out looking, but..."

"It's a big-ass ocean," a voice rumbled from the galley.

"Yeah." Ben glanced toward the galley. "It's a big-ass ocean."

Everyone went silent for a long moment.

Frannie finally said, "Hell, accidents happen. Anyone who works on the water knows that. People get lost. A lot of us *want* to get lost when we come up here—that's why we don't take an office job in Spokane. But having three vessels go missing that close together is no accident."

"No," Carwyn said. "It's not. Have any of you seen the redheaded vampire named Zasha? Not as good-looking as me, sadly. Fire vampire. Tall, very noticeable. They don't try to keep a low profile."

All of them shook their heads.

"Rumors and whispers," Frannie said. "Humans up here try not to pay attention to most of that stuff. It's a quiet place. The whole coast is laid-back. Nobody goes there to cause trouble."

"Katya can lay the hammer down when she needs to," Brick said. "No one wants that to happen. The Russians, the Chinese. Everyone stays cool."

"Zasha didn't though," the greenhorn said. "I know who you're talking about. Christy said he..." The young man cocked his head. "They?"

"They," Carwyn and Ben said together.

"Yeah, well, I never met them, but Christy said this vampire visited the *Dolphin* one night at the end of the summer. Made her real nervous. She said his—their vibe was real jumpy. Gave her the creeps and made Paulson—her boss—she said he seemed kinda serious. I mean, he's from Sweden or something, so he's not mister jokey or anything, but he's usually real relaxed."

Paulson.

Henri Paulson. Something was tickling the back of Carwyn's brain. It was a familiar name, but he couldn't picture a face. But there were many Scandinavian water vampires who lived on boats. It was one of the more common places to find them.

"How close was this visit to when the *Dolphin* went missing?" Ben asked.

The greenhorn shook his head. "Maybe three, four weeks?"

Ben and Carwyn exchanged a look. Was Zasha visiting marks before they attacked, or was there another explanation for the visit to Paulson? Could the Scandinavian vampire be one of Zasha's allies?

"What kind of boat was the *Dolphin*?" Carwyn asked.

"Beautiful, mate." Brick pulled out his phone. "I have a picture of it. The boss wanted a word with Paulson last summer, and Jeb and us took her to where he was anchored, up around Admiralty Island." He pointed the phone at Ben, then at Carwyn.

The yacht on the screen was a beautifully equipped ship painted gleaming white and navy blue. It had modern electronic equipment and stunning woodwork on the deck.

"Got there in the middle of the day, so we got to hang out with the crew all day and enjoy the boat until sundown." Brick smiled a little. "That was a fun day. Hate to think of anything happening to that lot."

"Was Paulson one of Katya's people?"

"Don't know," Frannie said. "But he was a regular in the area. I've heard his name for a lot of years. Mostly he hired from her people."

"So that's the *Dolphin* missing first? Then the two fishing boats?"

Frannie looked at Brick, and he nodded.

"Yeah," the man said. "That sounds right."

Carwyn's mind kept circling back to his original question: Was Paulson a victim of Zasha or an ally? He needed to speak to someone who knew Paulson, but that probably wouldn't happen until they reached Ketchikan.

"Thanks," Carwyn said, glancing at the greenhorn at the end of the table. "What was your name, son?"

The young man sat up straight. "Jack. John, but everyone calls me Jack."

"My friend and I" —he nodded at Ben— "we're going to do everything to get you some answers. If we can't find Christy, we'll at least find out what happened to her. And if anyone hurt your girlfriend, you know our type doesn't wait for a judge and a jury."

Carwyn left it at that; Jack could fill in the blanks.

"Yeah," the young man said. "Thanks." He shrugged one shoulder. "Her family would appreciate it."

CHAPTER TEN

There was no snow falling when they made port in Ketchikan, but it was pouring rain. Ben stepped onto the dock and felt the space under his feet. The crisp night air, redolent with water and chilled from the northern wind, swirled around him, kissing his skin and filling him with a fresh burst of energy.

"Vecchio?" A middle-aged man in a heavy green parka nodded at him. "You the priest?"

The human had a beard and mustache, his brown hair threaded heavily with steel grey. His skin was weathered and tan; Ben guessed he'd spent his life on the water.

"The priest would be my friend." Ben turned to see Carwyn clambering off the boat.

Despite the vampire's age, he never seemed to have developed sea legs, so there was visible relief when the earth vampire set foot on the dock. "But he's not a priest anymore. Name's Carwyn."

The man said nothing but gave Ben a nod that told him he understood.

He didn't reach out to shake Ben's hand, which told him the human was accustomed to vampires. He waited until Carwyn had bid effusive goodbyes to the crew and exchanged phone numbers with Jack, the young man with the missing girlfriend.

By the time the big man made his way to meet them, the cold had crept down Ben's neck and wrapped icy fingers around his throat. He didn't mind winter in most places, but he was quickly learning that winter in Alaska was a whole new level of cold. It reminded him more of his training time in the northern mountains of Mongolia. But wetter.

"You Katya's man?" Carwyn asked, stomping his feet a little as he walked toward them.

"Bradley Buckland," the man said. "Just call me Buck. You Carwyn?"

"Yes, and you've met Ben." Carwyn looked up at the pouring rain, his red hair quickly getting soaked. "Can we get on real land and indoors?"

"Sure thing." Buck led them toward a walkway to dry ground. "We've got about six hours of night left. Where do you want to start?"

"We came up here to look for Katya's ships," Carwyn said. "I was told we were meeting one of Katya's lieutenants. That you?"

"That'd be my wife, Jennie. She's in charge, but she's tied up with some local stuff right now." He lowered his voice. "You heard about the raids?"

Carwyn nodded, and Ben kept his mouth shut.

"We've heard there were no survivors," Carwyn said. "She dealing with—"

"The families. Most of the dead were Tlingit like her. Big extended family."

"We're deeply sorry about your community's loss," Carwyn said.

"Goddamn Russians," Buck muttered. "Katya's folk excepted, of course."

Ben asked, "People around here think Oleg was involved?"

"Who else?" Buck shrugged. "They were happy to be rid of him a hundred years ago, and now he's back. Jennie thinks he's taking revenge on some of the folk who went to Katya when she took over."

"What do you think?" Carwyn asked.

"Ah hell, I wasn't even alive then, what do I know?" Buck said. "Come on, what're your elements? Where you gonna be comfortable? We got rooms for all kinds."

Carwyn nodded at Ben. "He can fly, but I prefer a ground floor. We've got time tonight, so catch us up with whatever information you have on the captains, the crews, and the last-known locations of the boats that are missing. Also, how am I getting around? You have any seaplanes that can take our kind?"

"Seaplanes can go in the winter with a good captain and the right conditions, but not at night. This time of year, boats are about the only way to get around the area."

"Damn."

Buck smiled a little. "My Jennie don't mind, but she's a water vampire." He pointed to a squat building in the distance, the only one with glowing gold lights in the windows. "I have all the information you were asking about laid out in the office along with what we know so far about the latest raid."

Ben froze, and Carwyn nearly slammed into him. "Wait, there was another raid?"

Buck turned to them with a frown. "I thought Katya's people had already contacted the captain of the *Lady*. There was a raid we found last night—that's what Jennie's dealing with. We think it happened three or four nights ago."

Ben and Carwyn exchanged a heavy look.

"They didn't tell us," Ben said. "Let's get inside. We need to know more."

"SKALA WASN'T REALLY A TOWN. More of a village," Buck said, pointing to a map spread out on the table. "Tucked back into an inlet not far from Annette Island, which is Metlakatla land."

"Metlakatla is a Native reservation?" Carwyn asked.

Buck nodded.

"Tlingit?" Ben asked.

"No, Tsimshian," Buck said. "Neighbors, but not related to the Tlingit."

He asked, "And are the Native people here associated with the Athabaskan Confederation at all?"

"Why do you want to know?" Buck frowned.

"Just being... friendly." Ben looked at Carwyn. "No offense meant."

Buck's expression shouted suspicion, but Ben tried to put him at ease. "Seriously. No offense intended. I apologize. You're probably wary of outsiders right now, and I'm sure it seems like I'm prying."

Buck took a deep breath. "You're friends of Katya's, so I should probably get over it. All this is real disturbing. Things are quiet around here. These raids aren't like anything anyone living has seen before."

Carwyn got Buck back on track. "Tell us about the latest raid."

"Skala was run by an old wind vampire. He took a Tsimshian wife way back when, and he's been living there for a couple hundred years with her people."

"What happened?"

"Mike—Mikael, but he goes by Mike—ordered some supplies last week. Nothing special. Canned stuff mostly, but he didn't want to fly into town and haul back that much stuff for his people, so he asked for a delivery. Pretty routine, but when my guys showed up yesterday, the village was..." Buck pursed his lips. "They said they never seen anything like that."

"Any survivors?"

"We have to assume anyone there is dead, but there were no bodies that my guys saw. Some blood in the houses, but mostly just ruins. Buildings torn up. They said it looked like the foundations had been ripped up." Buck glanced at Carwyn. "Only thing I know that can create that kind of damage is an earth vampire."

Ben leaned on the table. "Do you have pictures?"

Buck shook his head. "It was nearing sunset by the time they got out there, and my guys were spooked. They rushed through the houses nearest the dock, looking to see if anyone needed help, but they knew it wasn't a human attack. They wanted to get out of there quick before dusk. They didn't even grab the supplies they'd already unloaded on the dock, just jumped back in the boat and took off."

Carwyn sat down in the chair next to the table. "How long to get out there by boat?"

"Three hours at least," Buck said.

"And by air?"

He nodded at Ben. "Faster."

"I could make it," Ben said. "I could take a look around."

"Problem is," Buck said, "I don't know that you're gonna find the place in the dark on your own. Mike hid his people well."

"Which makes me wonder how he was found?" Carwyn spoke softly. "Zasha?"

Ben cocked his head. "We have to assume they were involved with all these attacks. The timing lines up." He looked at Buck. "Anyone else been causing problems around here? Anyone with a grudge against Mike?"

"That vampire has been living in that village for over a century. He doesn't bother anyone. He takes care of his wife's family. Last I heard, he was bitching about the tuition bills from UDub because one of the kids just got accepted and he was paying for it."

"Sounds like a family man," Carwyn said.

"I mean, he was a stoic old bastard, but he took care of his people. He must have been loyal because I don't think he even drinks human blood. I remember him making some remark once about how delicious moose blood could be."

"It's less gamey than you'd think," Carwyn said.

Buck and Ben both stared at him.

"What?" Carwyn shrugged. "Let's find out what happened to Mike. He seems like a good man."

Ben nodded. "So tomorrow at nightfall." He looked at Buck. "You take a boat out there with Carwyn and I'll follow. See if I can see anything from the air your men might have missed. You feel comfortable going out there with the two of us? We have no idea how many vampires Zasha might be working with, but it sounds like there was definitely a group, and there's no way of knowing if they're still hanging around."

Honestly, Ben was hoping they were still hanging around. He wanted to break some necks after hearing about Mike and his family home.

"We won't force you to go," Carwyn said. "If you give us coordinates, we should be able to find it on our own."

"Jennie would kick my ass if I sent you out there on your own, and honestly, coordinates won't help you find Skala." Buck shrugged. "I'll go. If the vampires who did all that are still out there? Well, we all have to die sometime."

———

THE FOLLOWING NIGHT, Buck took them out in a fishing boat roughly a third of the size of the one they'd taken to Ketchikan. This time they weren't chugging over the open ocean but speeding along the narrow passages and inlets of the Pacific coast.

Ben stayed with Carwyn and Buck for the first half of the trip, then took to the air to survey the dark coast, keeping the lights of Buck's boat in sight so he didn't get lost.

The expanse was nearly oppressive. There were few lights along the coast, and the dense forest reached right to the edge of the water.

The darkness wasn't dark for Ben, and the waning moon was over half full; its light cast shadows in the clouds and along the surface of the water as he flew.

He dipped low, spotting the occasional surfacing of marine life and the churn of large schools of fish as they coasted through the current below.

Occasionally, the bellow of what he thought might be moose sounded in the darkness, and he found himself reaching for any sign of life in the vast expanse of wilderness.

South from Ketchikan and then east and north into an interior dense with evergreen forest, void of human habitation and the bustle of civilization. Ben felt as if he was seeing the world as it rose from the ocean thousands of years before, damp, muddy, and ripe with life.

There was nothing but darkness before him, but he followed the tiny light from Buck's fishing boat north into a fist-shaped inlet with a lone island in the center of the water.

The wind was steady, but the water didn't churn as it did on the open sea. The forest and the slopes protected this inlet from the worst of the weather, but the sea was still choppy and a silver wake spread from behind the boat like a bird's tail.

Ben saw the boat approaching the end of the inlet and slowed. He flew closer and noticed the long dock that cut across the choppy water and led to a scattered group of buildings that spread in a fan around a large stone house.

He landed on the dock and immediately spotted the supplies Buck's men must have been sent to deliver. They sat on pallets at the end of the dock, and a forgotten dolly was tipped to the side. Beans, canned fish, and bags of rice made up the bulk of the delivery. Staples that would last through a cold, wet winter.

Buck nodded at the food supplies. "Guess I might need some help getting those back on the boat."

Carwyn's face was grim as he started walking toward the shore. "Let's look first." He motioned to Ben. "Want to fly over and scan the area? See if anyone escaped into the woods maybe?"

Ben nodded. "Good thinking."

He took to the air and flew over the village and the surrounding forest, but if there was a living human, he found no trace of them. He did see a small cove on the other side of a jut of land that looked like it might have held smaller boats, but there was nothing but a shed with a broken door visible from the air.

The big house was made of stone with a slate-tile roof and wooden beams that wrapped around it to create a massive porch on the second floor. It would have been protected from the sun and the rain, and Ben could see various signs of life on the wraparound porch. A barbecue, a child's play set. Porch swings and a few rusty space heaters stowed in a corner near the stairs.

This house had been alive, and it hadn't been empty for long.

But while it might have once been a bulwark of strength along this small stretch of coastline, it was leaning to the side, the ground around it ripped up like a child destroying a sandcastle at the beach.

The roof was partially caved in on one side, and sun umbrellas were tossed along the shoreline, their bright colors slowly being dragged into the sea.

Ben landed after his short circuit around the settlement to find Carwyn and Buck standing in front of the house, both men staring at the massive dwelling with their arms crossed over their chest.

Carwyn looked at him. "Anything?"

Ben shook his head and pointed to the right. "There's a little cove over past those trees with a beach, a shed. Maybe a landing spot for kayaks or something."

Buck nodded. "Yeah, not usable this time of year, but in the summer they'd take kayaks out in that spot."

"No kayaks that I could see," Ben said. "It's possible that some of them escaped, but..."

Carwyn shook his head. "Do you see this water damage?" He pointed to driftwood pushed up against the base of the house. "It almost looks like a tsunami. Or a hurricane." He kicked at a dead fish on the rocky ground. "Water vampire pushed water from the inlet up onto the shore. That's probably what started the attack."

"Did you check the houses?" Ben asked.

Carwyn nodded. "Nothing alive. I found..." His voice caught. "There was one body and a leg. A woman's leg, I think. Lots of blood in that house, but no bodies."

"No whole bodies anyway." Buck's face was a blank page. "I've never seen..." He shook his head. "I ain't ever seen anything like that."

"I have." Carwyn's voice was soft. "The bodies weren't taken then, but this looks like a raid. Not unlike the Viking raids in Wales. The looting, the destruction for destruction's sake. The... thoroughness." His jaw was tight. "That's what it reminds me of."

Ben asked, "How many people lived here?"

Buck glanced over his shoulder. "Mike ordered a pallet of supplies like that every couple of months. They hunted. Fished. This place was pretty off-the-grid. They were self-sufficient most of the year. Maybe a dozen people? Twenty at most."

"And a vampire," Carwyn said. "But one vampire and a dozen humans aren't going to be able to fight off at least four vampires when they have the element of surprise."

"Four?" Ben saw damage that had to be from an earth vampire, and the water vampire had wreaked havoc. Damage to the trees and the roof definitely looked like wind damage, but—

"Look." Carwyn pointed at the house.

The door had once been wood, probably as beautifully carved as the shutters and the trim, but now it was black, and the charred body of a human was curled into the fetal position, right at the threshold of the blackened door.

"Fire." Ben breathed out.

"Four vampires," Carwyn said. "At least four. Maybe more." He looked down and kicked at a rock, shoving it across the rocky beach. "Humans didn't do this. This was all vampire."

CHAPTER ELEVEN

Darkness. Fire. A twisting ache in her gut and a burning in her throat. Burning. Everything was burning.

"Brigid?"

She heard his voice calling from a distance. Was she dreaming? She'd thought she was in hell, but he wouldn't be there. No, he couldn't be there. He was good. Pure in a way that she'd never been.

The smell of smoke filled her nose, and the fire rippled along her skin, soothing and burning at the same time.

Pain.

It was the consuming thought in her mind. Burning. Tingling. Snapping tiny bites along her flesh. Stripping bare every nerve with its vicious claws. Pain. Consuming, breath-stealing pain. But she was no longer breathing, and suddenly she knew.

Fire.

"Brigid?"

She blinked awake to the darkness of a room in Alaska, frigid air seeping in from around heavy shutters that held back the light. The darkness was lighter along the edges of the windows, but it was still pitch-black.

"Brigid, are you awake?"

Tenzin.

"Yeah." She sat up and shook the dreams from her mind. Talking with Oleg the night before had been confusing, and she'd dreamed of fire all night. "Gimme me a few minutes."

It wouldn't take her long to get ready. She ran a hand over her head instinctively, but there was nothing but the smooth velvet of buzz-cut black hair. She ran a hand over it once, twice, remembering the feel of Carwyn's massive palm on her head. He would hold her head between his massive warm hands, brushing her temples with his thumbs.

"I don't like it when most people touch me, but I don't mind it when you do. Why do you think that is?"

"Why don't you let me take care of you for a bit? Will you let me, Brigid?"

"I'm a monster."

"No, you're not. Just hold on to me. I've got you. Don't let go."

She felt like her chest caved in at the memory of her mate's arms around her, holding back the world when she'd been a brittle, screaming mass of anger and fear.

Brigid wanted him so badly she felt like her skin would erupt with it, the fire would spread out along the whole of the Alaskan wilderness, searching for anything to consume the void that Carwyn's absence left in her chest.

"Brigid, I smell smoke."

She blinked and saw that the blanket clutched in her hands was burning. She smothered the flames, wiped the burning tears from her eyes, and sucked in a hard breath.

"I'm fine." She cleared her throat and rolled her neck to the right and the left. Then she pulled a jumper over the black tank she'd worn to sleep and thrust her feet into the boots next to her bed. "Give me five minutes and I'll be ready."

"They found another raid." Tenzin's voice was soft. "From weeks ago. Lev's supply boat just went out and found the damage. There was one survivor, but Mika doesn't think he'll last much longer."

———

THIS TIME they traveled by water, and Brigid's usual aversion to that mode of transport was the last thing on her mind. Tenzin, Brigid, and Lev caught a boat at Oleg's dock and sped across the waters of the Cook Inlet in a fast boat, heading toward open water and the tip of the Kenai Peninsula where the gusting wind and churning sea battered their vessel even with a water vampire standing at the bow.

Brigid glanced at Tenzin. "I'm surprised you're not flying."

Tenzin sat next to her in the enclosed cabin. "I don't mind boats."

"Ben hates them."

Tenzin shrugged. "That's probably my fault. I trapped him on a freighter for several weeks once."

Brigid blinked. "Why?"

"He needed to practice his Mandarin." She leaned forward and spoke to Lev. "Why didn't your men bring this human back to Oleg's camp if he's injured?"

Brigid answered. "Mika said he shouldn't be moved. He's elderly, and he managed to keep himself alive despite the blood loss, but survival is still in question."

"Sheer spite," Lev said. "That's what my men said. The human was alive purely from spite."

Brigid glanced at Tenzin. "You could prob'ly move him with the least damage."

"I'm willing to try," she said. "The men who found him obviously couldn't fly."

Lev said, "Oleg says he can't be moved to a human facility. There would be too many questions about his injuries."

"Fuck that," Brigid said. "I'm not lettin' anyone die because Oleg doesn't want inconvenient questions."

"It's not a problem," Lev was quick to add. "We have a clinic we use near Seward. If he survives being moved, they can help him."

"Human doctors are butchers," Tenzin muttered. "But I'll try to fly him there if he'll let me. If he fights me though, I'll drop him in the ocean."

Lev laughed as if he thought Tenzin was joking.

Brigid knew she probably wasn't.

She didn't like any of it. She didn't trust Tenzin's opinion of human doctors since she thought all of them were frauds, but since Brigid couldn't oversee this human's healing herself and she had no way to transport him, there was nothing she could do. She didn't even know if healing was an option.

"The only survivor," Brigid muttered. "How did he manage?"

"Apparently they thought he was too far gone, so they flew him out over the water to dump his body and he survived the fall, then swam to shore."

Brigid's eyes went wide. "In this water?"

Tenzin nodded, clearly impressed.

Lev shrugged. "I told you. Sheer spite and a lot of vodka."

Jesus, Mary, and Joseph, that was either severe spite or miraculous vodka.

"Ya know Katya didn't do this, right?" Brigid looked at Lev. "Katya would consider these people hers."

"Maybe she didn't mean to, but maybe if she works with Zasha she has to give them something?"

Lev was determined, Brigid had to give him that.

The boat slowed, and Tenzin and Brigid walked out on the

deck. Brigid stared at the low black rise of land in the distance, which grew slowly as they approached.

"What is this place?"

"An island." Lev followed them. "No one comes here."

"And the town?"

He shook his head. "No town. One vampire, her human, and the human's family. At most there were ten people."

"So why bother?" Brigid tried to think like Zasha. "Were they wealthy?"

"Not according to Walter." He looked down at Brigid. "That's the old man. The grandfather of the human mate."

Alaska was definitely living up its reputation of a place that humans and vampires could go to be left alone save for the current crisis. The other two raids had also been on vampire and human clans in isolated locations.

"They're using that to their advantage," Brigid muttered.

Lev frowned. "What?"

"Zasha is using the isolation to their advantage," Tenzin answered for Brigid. "This attack happened weeks ago. If there hadn't been a scheduled delivery of goods from Seward, it would likely have been months before they were found. And at that point, we would have no idea what had happened. If they want to stay under the radar and still have their fun, they're attacking at the right time."

"We wouldn't have any details now except for Walter," Brigid said. "And clearly they didn't plan for Walter to survive."

"What is the purpose of this?" Lev looked confused. "I understand raiding for resources. I understand raiding to eliminate an enemy. But these people had nothing valuable. They were fishermen and hunters."

"They were human prey," Brigid said. "With one vampire to keep things interestin'."

"Poor Rachel," Lev whispered. "She was happy with her husband."

Brigid blinked. It was the first time anyone had mentioned the name of the vampire who had been at the center of this small homestead, and hearing her name made the loss all the more real.

"There." Lev pointed. "I can see it now. You?"

The house was almost hidden by the trees, but Brigid could make out the grey stone and dark wood beams that leaned to the side as if they had been knocked off-balance by a tidal wave.

"It's the same as the others," she said. "We'll find damage from all the elements."

"I'm going to fly in," Tenzin said. "I'll survey from the air in case there's anything Oleg's men didn't spot from the ground."

They pulled into what was left of the dock, tying up to broken timbers that the ocean was already pulling into the deep.

Brigid walked off the boat and made her way across the remains of the dock to the shore where two humans were sitting under a propped-up tarp with a fire burning nearby.

"He didn't want to go in the house," one of the men said to Lev. "We tried to move him, but—"

"You move me and that leg'll start bleeding again," the old man said.

The old man was covered by a silver emergency blanket and two large furs. His face was bleached of color; his normal skin tone was probably dark brown, but his lips were cracked, his cheeks sunken, and his eyes had a slightly yellow tinge to them.

"Your leg?" Lev asked.

One of the men said, "It's mostly gone, Lev. Walter put a tourniquet around it to keep it from bleeding out."

"Tight." The old man's lips were nearly blue. "I know how to tie one proper. Needed to make sure someone was alive to give a report."

He smells of death.

Brigid had no idea if the human would survive, so she walked over and crouched down next to the man. "Your name is Walter?"

"Evans. Walter Evans. My grandson Jackson was Rachel's husband." He blinked, and darkness flickered behind his eyes. "They killed him right in front of her. I never seen..." His lip quivered for a moment before he firmed it up with a harsh, sucked-in breath. "We thought we'd be safe up here. The location is isolated but easily defensible. We had weapons. We kept a low profile."

Brigid saw Tenzin from the corner of her eye as she landed on the beach and approached them silently.

"My name is Brigid Connor," she told Walter. "I'm a fire vampire, and I work in private security. No affiliation with Oleg, just old friends." It was close enough to the truth for the human. "You sound like you might have some military or police experience. Am I right?"

"Enlisted in the Marines when I was nineteen and stayed until retirement," Walter said. "Lost Mary, my daughter's mama, when I was in my thirties. Raised my girl. She married a good man." Walter's voice caught. "Our whole family was here. I told them it would be safe."

"I'm so sorry." Brigid's heart ached. "I'm so very sorry."

Lev asked, "Did they kill Rachel too?"

Walter glanced up. "I think so. I was trying to protect my daughter. They killed my son-in-law first. We were checking crab traps on the dock, just about to pull things in when they attacked." Walter's shaking hand went to his chest. "It was a spear. A goddamn harpoon right in his chest. Jesse went down."

Brigid pried for details. "Did you see how they approached?"

"Two from the air, three in a Zodiac." Walter glanced at Tenzin, then back at Brigid. "Small vessel. They were coming from a bigger boat."

Brigid nodded. "Was there a vampire with red hair with them?"

"Maybe. It was hard to tell in the dark."

"They killed your son-in-law first," Brigid said. "You ran?"

He nodded. "I got to the main house, but the boat had already landed. House was burning. Outbuildings were ripped up like..." He frowned. "Like something had torn up the foundation. Jesse and Sandra's house looked like a tornado hit it."

Wind and earth damage. Fire too. "Was it only vampires? Did you see any humans?"

"It's hard to tell sometimes, ain't it?" Walter's voice dropped. "I think it was all vampires. We didn't stand a chance."

"You said they killed Rachel and Jackson," Brigid said. "Did you see them? Is there any chance anyone else might have survived?"

Walter's face went blank again. "Jackson shoved his mom toward me and told me to run. There's a barn back in the woods. The snowmobiles are there. He told us to run."

Lev asked, "And Rachel?"

"Jackson ran back to her." Walter kept his eyes on Brigid. "She's a water vampire. Was trying to put out the fire they set in the house. They grabbed him and ...tw-twisted his neck." Tears pooled in Walter's eyes. "Dead. Just like that. Dropped hard like his daddy."

Brigid kept her voice soft. "And Rachel?"

"I heard her scream his name, and then I didn't hear anything. She would have done anything for Jackson. She loved..." He cleared his throat. "She loved him. But there were three of them on her. Sandra—my daughter—almost ran back to the house, but I grabbed her and took off."

"Trying to get to the barn."

He nodded slightly. "We were running into the woods and two of them just— They scooped us up like barn owls catching mice. Flew us up over the ocean, tossing us back and forth." His eyes were blank. "They were laughing. It was like a game to them."

Lev muttered something low and dark in Russian. Tenzin was an eerie blank void beside her. The two men holding Walter had clearly heard the story before, but their faces remained stoic.

Brigid wanted to rage, but she kept her focus on Walter's face and her expression open. Carwyn called it her "trust me" face, and clearly it was working. "They dropped you in the ocean."

"Lost their grip on us, maybe?" He shook his head a little. "I swam in circles, trying to find Sandra, but I couldn't..." His voice caught. "I couldn't find my girl. Felt the current pulling me, and my God..." His voice turned cold. "I wanted to go under so bad. My whole world was on this island, and they took it."

"But you swam back."

Walter's eyes narrowed. "I knew someone would come. Eventually someone would come. Swam back, tied off my leg, and I waited." He glanced at the man to his right. "Knew these boys would come soon enough."

Walter's strength humbled Brigid.

If someone killed your entire family—

Hush. No. She couldn't go there. Even a whisper of the idea took Brigid to such a dark place that she felt her blood start to churn and her skin heat up.

"You gonna find who did this?" Walter kept his eyes on Brigid. "You gonna kill them?"

"I swear." Brigid nodded. "With my own fire."

He kept his eyes steady on her. "I've seen a body burn before. Vampires burn the same as humans?"

Her gut twisted. "At the beginning? Yes."

Tenzin moved, crouching down next to Brigid and speaking directly to Walter. "You should imagine the vampires who killed your family turning black, curling into twisted shadows of their previous form, and scattering like ashes in the wind. Because

Brigid is going to kill all of them, and I am going to help her." Tenzin never broke her stare. "Do you believe me, Walter?"

He nodded slowly. "Yes, I do."

"Will you let me fly you to the human doctors so they can try to save your life? I can smell that you are bleeding internally and your chances of survival are small, but they do exist."

Brigid saw the man considering it. Saw the ache of longing to leave the world and the hard pull of survival battling in his yellow-tinged eyes.

"Do you have other kin?" Brigid asked.

One of the men holding the old man said, "Jackson has a sister in Louisville." He put his hand on Walter's shoulder. "Jackson said she just had a baby. That's your great-granddaughter, Walter."

"Survive for them," Brigid told Walter. "Your granddaughter has lost her brother and her parents. Don't make her lose everyone."

The old man gave a curt nod and then looked at Tenzin again. "Fly me to the docs then." He looked back at Brigid. "And I'll be seeing you again. When it's done."

"Yes." Brigid stood, keeping her eyes locked with his. "You will."

CHAPTER TWELVE

Tenzin was meditating when she heard Brigid return from her lessons with Oleg. The young fire vampire was disciplined and hardworking, but she was still disconnected from her element in a way that told Tenzin that even after a decade of being immortal, Brigid still thought more like a human than a vampire.

Tenzin had just returned from ferrying the wounded human Walter to the clinic Oleg ran, and she had very serious doubts the man would survive, but she wasn't dismissing anyone who'd managed to drag himself back to land through a freezing ocean with sharks and orcas, then last for nearly two weeks before someone found him, all while taking shelter in the ruins of a home that housed the ashes of his family.

"I need you to be honest with me."

She looked to the right and saw Brigid standing in the doorway of the room she'd been assigned in Oleg's compound. "Why?"

"Because you lie."

Tenzin nodded. "It's good you accept that. Your mate usually gets deeply offended."

"By lying? Can't imagine why."

"Neither can I. It's not as if we don't lie by our very natures." Tenzin leaned back, propping herself up on the low bed. "What do you want?"

Brigid was still wrapping her brain around something. "What do ya mean that we lie by our very natures? Vampires don't lie any more or less than humans do."

"You heard Walter earlier."

"Walter said a lot." Brigid leaned against the doorjamb.

"It's hard to tell us apart," Tenzin said. "Humans and vampires."

"Yeah."

She almost smiled. "Yet the wolf will never be mistaken for the deer. What other predator mimics its prey so completely?"

"Humans."

Tenzin nodded. "Fair point. The only thing that preys on humans more than vampires is other humans."

"I don't have a single iota of proof, but I'd guess more vampires are killed by other vampires than anything else." Brigid crossed her arms over her chest. "We're our own worst predators."

"And I suspect you're correct." Tenzin stared at the wall. "I'm bored. When are we hunting Zasha?"

"We need to find a boat," Brigid said.

"What boat?"

"Walter said they came in on a Zodiac, which means they're on a larger vessel between these raids."

Tenzin nodded. "That is a good insight. What do we need to do to find a boat?"

"It may require coordination with Katya's people. I'm tryin' to convince Oleg that she's not working with Zasha in all this. He's thinking deep thoughts and talking things over with Mika."

How boring.

Tenzin sighed.

"I'm sorry we can't satiate your bloodlust more quickly," Brigid said. "But it's a big ocean."

"I suppose it is." Tenzin had found a boat once, anchored in the middle of a storm in the Philippines, carrying the vampire who had ended Ben's human life. She was probably dead now, but Tenzin had no way of knowing.

"What do you want me to tell the truth about?" Tenzin asked.

She wouldn't get Brigid to leave until she'd vomited up the information the fire vampire was seeking, and Tenzin was considering the idea of calling Ben with her tablet, which she had turned off so Gavin couldn't track her.

She missed her mate. Life was much more boring without Ben.

"What did you do to Zasha?"

Ah, so that was the question.

"I took something valuable from them."

"You stole something?"

"In a manner of speaking." Tenzin closed her eyes again, picturing the slant of the snow falling in the moonlight. There was a vivid memory that lingered, even after millennia, a type of flowering tree that grew along the riverbanks when she was human. When the wind blew, the flowers fell and swirled in the air like snow.

That's what had popped into Tenzin's head the night she'd killed Zasha's mate. The last memory of her human life that had been happy, when her daughter laughed in a basket on the riverbank, waving chubby fingers at the flower petals as they fell around her.

"I had a daughter once." Tenzin stared at the blank wall across from the bed, the flat white paint dirtied with fingerprints and smears.

"I didn't know that." Brigid's voice was soft and sorrowful.

Ugh.

She didn't want the woman's pity.

Tenzin looked at her. "Human life is brief and harsh and painful. And beautiful for those reasons. Mine was taken from me very early, and the first centuries of my immortal life were terrifying and horrible and no one should know about them. I was the single immortal female in the middle of a male vampire horde. Do you understand why it was terrible?"

A mask fell over Brigid's face. "Yes."

"Exactly. That horde was led by a vampire my own sire created, and his name was Temur."

Temur, Temur, Temur, whom the girl in her had loved in a sad, sick way even as the vengeful hunter drove the knife into his back. He had broken her too many times.

They feared your madness, and I trusted you!

He shouldn't have trusted her. Not ever.

Tenzin looked at Brigid. "When I was strong enough, I killed Temur, and then I killed every one of Zhang's other children—they were all sons—and I hunted down any vampire they had sired and I killed those too."

Brigid sat on the narrow bed across from Tenzin. "Including Zasha's mate."

"Yes. It took me over a thousand years, but I killed them all. Except for that one. I didn't know he existed until I heard stories. I smelled him." She wrinkled her nose at the memory. "Zasha's mate was the last of Temur's blood, and he was living quietly in..." She frowned. "Siberia, I think. He had hidden himself very well because he knew what would happen if I found him."

Brigid kept her voice low. "If he was living quietly, why would you kill him? Had he been in Temur's horde?"

"No." She turned her eyes back to the wall. "I doubt he'd even been born when I killed Temur."

"Then why kill him?"

"Because I made a promise." Tenzin frowned and looked at the young one. "Who are you to question me? When I was born, your human ancestors were living in the mud."

Brigid lifted her chin. "I'm allowed to judge you."

"Why?"

She didn't have an answer, because of course she didn't.

Whatever small indignities the human Brigid had endured, they were nothing to what the girl Tenzin had survived. "I killed those who needed to be killed. My *mercy*, Brigid Connor, is the reason that Walter's family is dead."

Brigid blinked. "What?"

"Zasha's mate pleaded with me to spare her. Zasha was living as a woman then. Their mate begged me to leave Zasha alone. He begged me to spare them, and I was stupid enough to have mercy. 'I will only kill her if she tries to kill me.' That's what I promised him. I vowed it on my children's blood." Tenzin smiled a little bit. "And ever since then, Zasha has never tried to kill me."

Brigid frowned. "New Orleans. You and Zasha were attacking each other and—"

"Please." The girl didn't know what an attack really was. "That was Zasha playing. With you as well. I don't think they ever really wanted to hurt you. In an odd way, I suspect they want to be your friend."

"That's fuckin' disturbin'," Brigid muttered.

"Yes, Zasha is very disturbed," Tenzin whispered.

She saw a flicker in the corner of the room and a tiny wind vampire crouched in the corner, pointing and laughing at her, a hand clapped over her mouth to hide the fangs.

Nearly as disturbed as you are.

"So Zasha wants to kill me but knows that they can't do it directly," Tenzin asked. "If they do—"

"Then you can kill them and not break your vow." Brigid caught on immediately. "So why draw me in?"

"They probably heard about you from Oleg or some of Oleg's clan. There aren't really that many fire vampires in our world. In my life, I would estimate there are only ever about a hundred active fire vampires at any given time." Tenzin looked at Brigid. "You are one. Oleg is another. Giovanni. Two fire elders in Penglai."

"And Zasha."

"Yes. You've tripped along the edges of vampire life in Europe for a while now. You have friends in high places, and you know me. Zasha probably heard of you and was intrigued. And then..."

"Then?"

Tenzin raised her eyebrows. "You killed their child."

"Ivan."

Brigid and Carwyn had helped in the hunt for Zasha's last progeny when the earth vampire was running hunts in Northern California.

"Yes. Ivan. I don't know that Zasha has any parental instincts that we would recognize, but they did care for Ivan if for no other reason than as Zasha's offspring, Ivan carried a hint of their mate's blood. Temur's blood."

"Ivan was a horrible human being."

"Do you think Zasha cares about that? He was their son. Technically their grandson, but I doubt Zasha made note of the difference. Ivan was theirs."

Brigid looked as if her brain was about to break.

"Zasha's sire did that, you know." Tenzin looked at Brigid. "He ran hunts on humans for his own amusement."

"Ivan would have made his great-grandsire proud."

"Yes, Oleg and Zasha's sire was awful. He raped and murdered all along the river systems in Europe, traveling by boat and raiding human towns. Then the old ones stepped in and told him to stop. I believe he was rather irritated at the time."

"Why?"

"Because to him, humans were somewhat amusing food. He never believed they were equal to vampires, and he thought the natural order of the world was to have vampires lead it."

"No, why did the ancients tell him to stop?"

"Oh." Tenzin shrugged. "I think he was drawing too much attention. I wasn't in Europe then. I was in Tibet, but I heard the stories later when I was traveling with Giovanni. It was around the same time that my sire retired to Penglai. The age of vampire conquest was over. The humans were becoming too many. Some had even stopped believing in the gods." She smiled. "It was time for vampires to become a legend, not a reality."

"So Zasha's sire stopped."

"In a manner of speaking, but he never stopped believing he had the right to treat humans as his food."

"No matter what the ancients said?"

Tenzin sighed. "How much honesty do you really want, Brigid Connor?"

Brigid slid down to the floor and sat across from Tenzin. Her eyes were defiant. "Tell me."

Maybe it would help her start thinking like a vampire, which would be good for Tenzin and for Carwyn too. The girl was far too idealistic.

Tenzin started. "Why do you judge me for killing Temur's sons?"

"We're being honest?"

Tenzin nodded.

"Because that man didn't do anything to you. My stepfather abused me. He has family, but I wouldn't dream of murdering them because *he* was awful. They had nothin' to do with it."

"And you believe human life has innate value."

Brigid blinked. "Of course it does."

Tenzin shook her head. "No of course. Why? Why is it valuable?"

"Because it is?"

"Is ant life innately valuable?" She glanced out the window. "How about insects? The cow meat you ate last night? The pickled egg from the chicken or the eagle nesting in the tree outside?"

"All life is valuable, but human life—"

"Is brief, harsh, and painful." Tenzin lifted her chin. "And most of all, it is small. It is small in the way that a flower petal is small. Beautiful and fleeting and valuable for those very reasons. That is my philosophy, and you are allowed your own. Because human life is so short, it should be allowed to exist for the brief flash that it is. I do not crush beauty for no reason. That would be as stupid and crude as crushing a flower."

"But you're not going to lose sleep if you accidentally trip over it while you're walking," Brigid said. "Flower crushed. Sad, but not a tragedy."

Tenzin nodded once. The young one was beginning to understand. "Brief. Harsh. Painful."

Brigid whispered, "And beautiful because of it."

"No ancient I have ever known—save for Giovanni's grandsire Cato maybe—really believes humans are anything more than amusing food or pretty flowers. Remember that."

"So preserving human life is only a form of self-preservation," Brigid said, "that allows them to live the lives they want in peace."

"And Zasha's antics are disturbing that peace," Tenzin said. "Which is why no one powerful in the vampire world will be bothered when they are dead."

"Do you think Zasha knows that?"

Tenzin laughed a little. "I think they revel in it. Whatever lies they have told themself, they are asking to be caught."

The realization came a fraction of a second later.

Oh.

Tenzin's heart softened just a little.

The memory flashed in her mind. A vampire on her knees, pleading with Tenzin, not for life but for death.

Kill me. I don't want to live without him.

Zasha had a death wish. They had been nursing one for years. But like a phoenix flaming into ash, they would burn as many as possible in their desperate attempt to die.

"Leave," Tenzin whispered. "I want to call my mate."

"You can't tell him where we are." Brigid's voice was petulant.

Tenzin glared at her. "Out. I'll tell my mate whatever I want."

Brigid curled her lip, baring a single fang, and Tenzin had to admire her bravado. She could crush the young vampire against the wall and force her own fire down her throat, but she wouldn't.

New Year's resolutions.

She heard Ben's voice in her mind and wanted to see his face. "Out."

————

HE WAS angry and so beautiful Tenzin nearly wept.

She had turned off most of the lights in the room save for the one illuminating her face. There was a darkness in his eyes, and she longed to be with him. She would roll around in that darkness and wrap it around herself, holding his light safe in her hands.

"I miss you."

He laughed a little, but it wasn't from happiness. "You left me."

"You're already in Alaska or near it," she said. "I can feel you."

"You're full of shit. You cannot."

"Did you feel when they shot my leg?"

His nostrils flared and his eyes narrowed. "Who did it?"

That was a yes.

"It was a misunderstanding, and you know I'm already healed." She leaned closer to the electronic tablet, and it flickered. She forced herself to lean back. "I miss you."

"You said that already," Ben said. "You knew that was going to happen when you left."

"Yes."

"So why did you do it?"

Tenzin pursed her lips. "I thought I was doing the right thing, but I was..." She trailed off when she realized what she'd been about to say.

"What's that?" Light finally came to Ben's eyes. "Finish the sentence, Tiny."

"No."

"Because you were about to say that you were wrong?"

How could she love him and also want to hurt him at the same time? Emotions were far too complicated.

Something about seeing her stymied must have brightened his mood. "I'm getting closer."

Tenzin sneered. "If you weren't with that large earth vampire, you'd already be here."

"How do you know I'm with—?"

"Because men are predictable." Tenzin plucked at a string on her tunic. "You knew I was going to Brigid. You knew Brigid had left Carwyn. So you went to Carwyn. Did you fight him?" She smiled a little. "I wish I could have seen that. What did you do to him?"

"Not much. It was muddy, and he's a lot stronger than I thought."

"Yes, he does like being underestimated, but he has very

ancient blood. If he fed from humans, he'd be a terror." Tenzin cocked her head. "You're so beautiful."

"Stop." He angled the tablet so she couldn't see his face.

"Benjamin!" She sat up straight. "Turn it back."

"No, I'm not going to let you look at me until you tell me what you've found out so far."

He fought dirty. "Why? You're going to be here in a couple of nights at most. I know you're traveling north."

"And the air tells me you were moving around a lot tonight, so tell me why."

She was mentally plotting how she was going to get her revenge for Benjamin hiding his face when he reached over and snapped his fingers in front of the camera.

"Focus," he said. "What were you doing?"

"Turn the camera back so I can see you and I'll tell you."

CHAPTER THIRTEEN

He turned the camera back, and his heart relaxed when he saw her face.

I love you so much it hurts.

"Tell me," Ben said.

Tenzin rested her chin in the palm of her hand and stared at him. "I want to kiss you."

"You could do that if you didn't leave, so I refuse to feel sorry for you."

Her eyes were soft, and she mouthed something he couldn't hear, probably in a language he couldn't speak.

"Zasha is raiding along the coast," Tenzin said. "We found a survivor today. An old man. I flew him to the hospital, and he told me about his grandson who had married a vampire he met three years ago. He'd convinced the family to move with him up to Alaska, and they were all living together."

Ben's heart ached at the soft sadness in her voice. "The family?"

"All dead except for him. He has one granddaughter left somewhere in the south." She looked down. "If he lives long enough to see her. He probably won't live. I think his organs were bleeding."

"I'm sorry."

She shook her head. "He was human and already old."

"It's okay to feel sad about his family, Tenzin."

"I don't know them."

"But you know *him* now, and you know they were probably nice people who were just trying to live." Sometimes Tenzin's humanity was hard to find, but other times it was swimming just below the surface like a fish under ice. "So it's okay to feel sad. That's empathy."

She wrinkled her nose. "He is a great-grandfather now. I promised him that Brigid and I would kill the vampires who did it." She quickly added, "They're dangerous and they need to die or they will kill more humans."

"I know." Ben nodded. "That was a good promise, Tiny. There have been raids around here too. More humans and vampires killed farther south. No one is going to try to save these guys. The problem is finding them."

"Brigid thinks they are on a boat. Zasha is on a boat somewhere, and they are raiding from that boat."

That was as good a theory as any. "Brigid's smart."

Tenzin curled her lip. "She also said it is a big ocean."

Ben sighed and ran a hand through his hair. He needed a haircut, but he didn't want one. "She's not wrong. I was at a raid site last night. Carwyn said it reminded him of a Viking raid in Wales."

Something sparked in Tenzin's eyes. "Like Zasha's sire."

Ben frowned. "Was he a Viking?"

"Yes, or something that came before. Maybe he gave them the idea in the first place. He was an earth vampire, but he traveled the rivers by boat and he raided human villages at night."

"Name?"

"I don't even know it." Tenzin frowned. "I've never asked."

Ben would make it a point to ask Carwyn. "Okay, so Zasha was sired by some horrible Viking vampire and now they're re-creating that with other vampires. Why?"

"Oleg thinks Zasha is working with Katya."

"Katya thinks Zasha is working with Oleg."

Tenzin narrowed her eyes. "That's very... convenient."

"For who?"

"Whoever Zasha is actually working with."

"Maybe they're not working with anyone," Ben said. It was the sick fear in his belly. That Zasha was doing all this just because they could.

For fun and nothing else.

"We could ask why they're doing it," Tenzin said. "But maybe the better question is why wouldn't they? Where are you?"

She might be secretive, but Ben wasn't. "We're in Ketchikan right now."

"Ketchikan," Tenzin whispered. "I love the names in this place. They are fun to say."

"Is Oleg with you?"

"Yes, but only because I asked him to train Brigid. He's not really helping us, but he's giving Brigid whatever she asks for."

Ben tried not to smile. "You asked Oleg to train Brigid?" He was not going to share that with Carwyn. The man was already on edge, and the last thing he needed was the knowledge that a well-known lothario of the immortal world was working closely with his wife.

"He's a fire vampire." Tenzin spread her hands. "Zasha is a fire vampire. Most vampires go their entire life without siring one fire vampire, and Oleg's sire made *two*."

Knowing how closely fire and trauma were related, Ben was getting an even more hideous impression of Oleg and Zasha's sire. "God, he must have been so awful."

"Yes, but for Brigid, it is convenient. Oleg is strong, and his amnis is probably similar to Zasha's. His fire might have some of the same characteristics."

"Every fire vampire I've ever met has used fire in different ways," Ben said. "You think Oleg is going to be able to help Brigid understand Zasha better or something?"

"Maybe." Tenzin leaned back against something that looked like a bed. "I'm not sleeping. I think I only do it when I'm with you."

Ben narrowed his eyes. "You're lying."

"Not exactly," Tenzin murmured.

"Are you dreaming again?" Ben knew that Tenzin dreamed and it wasn't always pleasant.

"Something like that." She stared at something off-screen. "Was it wrong to come here?"

"No. You just shouldn't have left me."

"But if I hadn't left you, the large flowered one would be all alone." Tenzin closed her eyes. "You're going to bring him, aren't you? I hate his judgmental face."

"His mate is the one Zasha is after."

"I don't know how accurate that is."

Ben forced himself to ask the question that had been plaguing him for days. "Did you do something to Zasha, Tenzin?" *Did you cause all this suffering?*

He didn't expect her to answer. God knows she rarely answered anything about her past and when she did, it was usually cryptic.

But this time she was staring at something, her head cocked, her eyes softer than he expected. "I think...", she started. "I think I did the worst thing."

Ben drew in a breath and braced himself. "What?"

"I let Zasha live."

———

"THEY'RE AROUND SEWARD." Ben walked into the common room under Buck's house. "Somewhere on the Kenai Peninsula. That's the most she could tell me. I doubt she really knows where they are."

The basement had been converted into guest quarters for Katya's people, so there were locked, reinforced doors, and a large fridge stocked with stored blood and bottles of blood-wine along with plenty of frozen red meat.

Carwyn was cooking something on the stove. "Did you talk to her?"

"She finally turned her phone on. I tried to track it on the network and called Gavin right after I got off the video call, but he said the most he could narrow it down to was the area around Seward. He said towers are pretty sparse around there."

Buck was sitting at the counter and drinking something with steam. Not coffee; Ben would have smelled that. "The Kenai Peninsula isn't massive, but it's not small either."

"Yeah, I looked at the map." He sat next to Buck. "They found a survivor from one of Zasha's raids."

Carwyn froze. "When?"

"Earlier tonight. Well, he was found two nights ago, but they went out tonight. I think Brigid was still on the boat on the way back. Tenzin flew the guy to get medical care."

"Who was it?" Buck asked.

"An old man who was living in a vampire compound with his family. His grandson was married to a water vampire named Rachel."

Buck cursed. "Jennie knew Rachel. I met her. Quiet gal. Dammit, this is awful. That woman never hurt a soul. She was..." Buck swallowed hard. "And her whole family? Damn it to hell. I know roughly where she was—it's around Seward—but she was real private. I've never seen her place."

Carwyn frowned. "I'm surprised there was a survivor at all. Based on that site we found the other night, I wouldn't expect Zasha's people to leave anyone alive."

"A couple of wind vampires dropped the old man and his daughter in the ocean," Ben said. "I imagine they didn't think he'd survive the swim back to shore. His daughter didn't."

Buck set his mug down. "That's weird though. The raid out here being just a few days ago and then one at Rachel's place the next night?"

Ben shook his head. "Tenzin said the raid on Rachel's place actually happened a couple of weeks ago."

"Still," Buck said. "That's all over the place. Where are they coming from?"

"The middle," Carwyn muttered. "They have a base between the two places. A central location."

Buck shook his head. "Central between Kenai and the Alexander Archipelago is open ocean, my friend."

Carwyn was staring at something in the distance. "What did Brigid find out from the survivor? Was he speaking? If he was, she would have questioned him."

"The old man said they came in on a Zodiac."

"They're on a bigger boat." Carwyn and Buck spoke at the same time.

Ben nodded. "That's what Brigid thinks. So we just have to find the boat where Zasha is hiding."

"Find a boat," Buck said. "No problem." He muttered, "Too bad it's a big fucking ocean."

———

CARWYN KNOCKED at Ben's door when Ben was starting to feel sleepy. The night was still dark, but his body wanted rest. He could smell the earth vampire on the other side of the door, and he pulled it open.

"How was it?" Carwyn asked. "Seeing her?"

"I was pissed." He opened the door wider and motioned Carwyn inside. "But Tenzin taking off is not exactly a surprise. She hasn't done it since we've been back together, but when I was still human, she'd run off and I wouldn't see her for six months sometimes."

"Before you were mated." Carwyn sat in a chair near the old boxy television in the corner of the room.

"Yeah." Ben sat on the edge of the bed and combed his fingers through his hair. "It's harder to be away from her now."

Carwyn smiled a little bit. "You know, not long after we mated, Brigid took off to America. Hopped in your uncle's damn plane and flew over to Los Angeles. I had to follow her in a boat that time too. I'd pissed her off somehow. Don't even remember what it was at this point."

"Tenzin told me about that. She thinks it's hilarious when you fight."

"She would." Carwyn sighed. "This feels different though."

"It is different. Zasha is dangerous and has zero check on their power. Answers to no authority. Has no sire. And their clan is unwilling to police them."

"But I don't worry about Zasha hurting Brigid, especially with Tenzin with her," Carwyn said. "I worry about the collateral damage. Brigid left the lower States and came up here to decrease the collateral damage, but Zasha is only turning up the heat. It'll kill my darling girl."

"Well, she shouldn't have left you."

"No, she shouldn't have." Carwyn stared at the ground. "We're stronger together. I thought she knew that by now."

Ben felt a twist in his chest. "She knows it, but she's scared."

"And I feel every doubt and fear in my blood," he whispered.

Ben didn't know what to say. There was nothing to say. He felt as abandoned as Carwyn even though he knew Tenzin was expecting him to find her. It was impossible not to when the air that surrounded him linked his blood to hers.

"Did Brigid really think Zasha was going to meet her on an empty plain in the Arctic and they would duel or something?"

Carwyn shook his head. "Don't ask me how that woman thinks. I've only been alive a thousand years. You think I know the mind of my wife?"

Ben fingered the gold ring he wore on his left hand. "If I flew out of here at nightfall tomorrow, I could find Tenzin in a matter of hours. If I wanted to do that."

Carwyn frowned. "How long have you been mated?"

"Doesn't matter." He kept his eyes on his ring. Gold matter, ruby crystal.

The space between.

If he focused on it long enough, Ben would stop seeing the solidity of what he was holding and instead see the void that existed in all things, the space between its molecular structure. He was beginning to own that space in a way that even Tenzin struggled to understand.

It wasn't a normal wind vampire trait.

"The wind is different for me," he softly confessed to Carwyn, a vampire who had known him since he was a child. "I'm seeing things differently. Even from my sire."

"Does this have to do with the Bone Scroll?"

Ben shook his head. He had been given that object of enormous elemental power a few years ago, but whatever power it held was still locked in a dead language. Then again...

"I don't think so, but the whole reason I was given that was because my human blood was unique, so who knows?"

143

"So what are you saying?"

"I don't know," Ben said. "I'm not going to find her tomorrow night. I don't think it's time yet."

"Could you fly both of us?"

Ben looked up. "Do you think that would be a good idea?"

"I don't know." A muscle in Carwyn's jaw twitched. "I'm starting not to care if things are good ideas or not."

"Maybe we should stay here," Ben said, "no matter how much we want to find them. We need to find a boat in a big ocean, right? Hard to think of anyone who would be better at that than Katya and her people."

Carwyn curled his lip and bared a single long fang. "It's fucking annoying when you're sensible."

"I know, it really is. Blame my uncle."

CHAPTER FOURTEEN

B rigid was squinting at a map on a computer screen where tiny green, yellow, orange, and red arrows blipped on a white background. Lee was talking on the speakerphone.

"So every ship is supposed to be linked up to this system via satellite," he said. "Freighters to fishing boats. This is the live traffic on the North Atlantic right now."

Moments later, the screen flickered and the arrows moved slightly.

"This is the overhead view." Brigid glanced at Tenzin. "Look familiar?"

"No. This is... kind of useless," Tenzin said. "When you get out over the water at night, you can't see anything this clearly until you're really close. This map greatly underestimates the distance."

Brigid frowned. "But these are live trackers."

"And if this map was to scale, those arrows you see right in front of you would be grains of sand, not flashing colored arrows." Tenzin shook her head. "The only thing this helps with is seeing routes."

"Routes?" Brigid knew almost nothing about ship traffic even though she'd spent half her immortal life working for a shipping magnate in the North Atlantic.

Lee spoke again. "Yeah, I think she means that most of these boats, to get from port A to port B, would use roughly the same routes. The captains are going to know where the best channels are closer in to land. The currents are probably going to affect that."

"But it's also possible that a ship could be on this map and we would never see it," Tenzin said. "How likely do you think it's going to be that Zasha and their hunters are using a satellite?"

"Maybe it's not far-fetched," Lee said. "Remember that they're going to have to head closer toward land at some point. They'll need to get fuel. Need to resupply. If they don't have any kind of call number or signature, that might be more noticeable than having one."

"We don't even know what kind of boat they're on," Brigid said. "But Lee, let's eliminate anything that's a freighter. Big and expensive to fuel, right?"

"Oh yeah." There was a tapping sound, and then all the orange arrows disappeared. "We can do that. Narrows it down some."

"Cargo ships could be adapted to carry passengers," Tenzin said. "But maybe take out the biggest ones?"

"I can try."

More arrows disappeared, but there were still dozens dotting the board.

"Small fishing boats?" Brigid suggested. "Unless the small boats are the ones that have the satellites and the larger boat is flying under the radar."

It was something her old boss would do, mask a larger vessel with the signature and information of a small one.

"That's quite clever," Tenzin said.

"Taking notes?"

Tenzin shrugged. "I don't want any boats at the moment, but that could change."

"Lee, is there a way that you can isolate the smaller boats—ones that could go in shallower waters—and see if any of them might be way out in the middle of the ocean?"

"I can." More tapping. "You realize that all these signatures could be completely legitimate vessels, right?"

"I know, but it might narrow it down." Brigid braced her arm on the table and stared at the screen. It flickered and a bunch of arrows disappeared. "Okay." She nodded. "That's more manageable."

"More over by Ketchikan than out on the open ocean," Tenzin said. "Staying closer to the shore because of the time of year."

"Start there, Lee. Can you run profiles of all the names and whatever info we have about the boats around and near the Alexander Archipelago?"

"Absolutely, boss." Lee started tapping away. "I'll do that tonight and see if I can write some kind of program that will track the boats over a period of time too."

"Good thinking."

Tenzin was staring at the wall. Not the one that was illuminated, just a random wall. "Ignore anything that has a regular route. Zasha won't be on a schedule."

"Uh-huh. Got it."

Lee's voice was starting to sound distracted, and Brigid knew they were losing him to his computers.

"Okay, call us with your progress before you go to sleep," Brigid said. "Send us what you have, and we'll see if we can get any information from Oleg's and Katya's people."

"If Katya's people are answering phones tonight, they're not answering calls from me."

Brigid felt a prick of annoyance. "Have you tried calling Carwyn?"

"Yeah, he's not answering me either."

Fuck. He was really pissed off.

"Thanks, Lee. I'll see you soon."

"Hope so, Mini. Talk to you later."

Tenzin was frowning at her. "Mini."

"Short for Mini Firecracker," Brigid said. "Lee said I should consider it my traditional name. I think he was joking, but honestly I'm not sure."

"You do explode outward, so it's not inaccurate."

The corner of Brigid's mouth turned up. "Do you have a traditional name?"

"Tenzin."

Brigid nodded. Yeah, that fit.

"Patron goddess of the Sacred Mountain," Tenzin continued. "Scourge of the Naiman Khanlig. Commander of the Altan Wind."

"I get the idea."

"Protector of Penglai Island. Protector and scribe of New Spain." Tenzin narrowed her eyes. "There're more, but I'm not remembering—"

"No, really. I get the idea."

"But Mini is nice," Tenzin said. "Very affectionate."

"He's a good guy." Brigid heard her phone buzzing on the table and glanced at the number, which she didn't recognize, but that wasn't unusual. Lee often routed calls through numbers she didn't recognize. She picked it up. "Did you forget somethin'?"

"So many things."

Brigid sucked in a breath. It wasn't Lee. She pulled the phone away from her ear and touched the Speaker button, putting her finger to her lips when Tenzin frowned at her.

"Hello, Zasha."

"BRIGID CONNOR," the vampire continued. "Are you following me?" Zasha's voice was teasing. "I thought I was the one to follow you. Did you miss me?"

"I do miss you, Zasha. Tell me where you are right now and I'll visit." Brigid bit the edge of her lip. Would the vampire be just maniacal enough to do it? "You and me, Zasha. We can go look at the northern lights. I hear they're a sight."

"They're beautiful. Is Tenzin with you?"

Damn it, how did they know?

"I'm here." Tenzin kept her voice quiet. "Did you want to speak to Brigid alone? I can leave."

"You can lie."

"I can, but I also keep my promises."

Zasha was quiet for a few moments, and Brigid wondered if they'd lost them.

The vampire on the other end of the call came back. "Do you remember me now?"

"Yes," Tenzin said.

"Good. You should remember me." Zasha's voice had lost its amusement and stung with acid. "Brigid, I didn't tell you to invite intruders into our little game. You're not playing nice."

"I'm not playin' at all," Brigid said. "I'm finding destroyed homes and dead bodies, Zasha. You think that's a game?"

"I told them to clean up after themselves." Zasha tsked over the phone. "I promise they'll be neater in the future. Some of them are very excited."

"So it's hunts, is it?" Brigid sat on the edge of the bed and tried to picture the vampire in her mind.

Zasha was tall, well over six feet, and as elegant and deadly as a poisonous snake. They had a shock of red hair they did nothing to hide and eyes the color of volcanic soil. Unnerving from a few paces away, as it appeared that their eyes were black with no pupil at all.

"Back to Ivan's old games?" Brigid asked. "Back to your sire's hunts?"

"Who told you about my sire?" Zasha sounded genuinely curious. "Are you talking to my brother?"

"Which one?"

"There are so many," Zasha whispered. "Oleg left so many alive. Not like Tenzin, huh?"

Brigid looked at Tenzin, but her face was a blank.

"Tenzin killed all her sire's children. Not a single one left to carry on his blood. Except for her own mate, I suppose. I hear stories about him. Stories about power and secrets. Stories that Tenzin might not even understand. Is he with you too? Is Benjamin" —Zasha drew out his name— "with you? Is he, Tenzin?"

Brigid waited for Tenzin to answer, but the vampire's face was utterly blank.

"I would like to meet Benjamin Vecchio. Or is it Benjamin Rios? Or Benjamin—?"

"Shut up," Tenzin snapped. "He has nothing to do with this."

"Doesn't he?" Zasha purred. "Think, little hunter. Why would your blood mate interest me?" Zasha's voice turned cold. "I'm sure if you think hard in your frozen, adolescent mind, you might come up with an answer."

Brigid felt her blood still. Was that what all this was about? Was all this about luring Tenzin's mate north so Zasha could kill Ben? Had she just put one of her closest friends in the sights of a sociopathic immortal with no qualms about killing anything in their path?

"Shhhhh," Zasha said. "Don't worry, Tenzin. I don't have anything against your mate. This is an old argument, and I'm only disappointed that you've inserted yourself between Brigid's and my growing friendship. We've gotten so close since she killed my son."

Acid burned at the back of Brigid's throat.

"Your son was a monster," Tenzin said.

"I know. I was so proud."

Tenzin stared at the phone with narrowed eyes. "I think that in your own mind, Zasha, you think we are alike. That you and I are the same in some way. But we're not."

"I didn't say that, but the fact that you did proves that you've considered it. And I think you believe we are more alike than different. Brigid, are you still there?"

Brigid considered hanging up. Her finger hovered over the button, but Tenzin reached over and pulled it away. She shook her head vehemently and nodded her chin at the phone.

Speak.

Brigid forced herself to speak. "I'm here."

"Tenzin invited herself into this, didn't she? She's always sticking herself in places where no one wants her. But I know that you and your lovely mate have an affection for Ben Vecchio. I'm telling you, I have nothing against him. They speak very highly of him in New York, and let me tell you, I adore that roof garden. I saw the pictures. It was stunning."

Brigid saw Tenzin start, and then the wind vampire pulled back, stood, and fisted her hand at her side.

"Get to the point, Zasha." Brigid felt her heart start to beat. "Tell me what you want."

"Tenzin. Obviously."

Brigid looked up and saw Tenzin staring at her. The wind vampire nodded silently.

"I think you know our little bargain now, don't you? I can't kill Tenzin. She can't kill me." Zasha's voice was a soft whisper. "But send me her head and I'll walk into the sun the next morning. Would that be enough for you?"

Brigid froze. "What?"

"You kill Tenzin and I'll stop. All of it. The hunts. The death.

All of it will stop, Brigid Connor. Your innocents will be protected. Civilized vampires" —Zasha's voice dripped with condescension— "will be safe. Just send me Tenzin's head and it's over."

Tenzin sat on the edge of the bed, a smile teasing the corner of her mouth.

"Is that understood, Brigid?" Zasha's voice was playful again. "I know you won't do it, but I at least wanted to offer. I'm not *unreasonable*. Give me a word, Brigid Connor. Tell me you've received my proposal."

Brigid could barely form the word. "Noted."

"Good." There was a clicking sound and the line went dead.

SHE STARED AT THE WALL.

"You have to consider it." Tenzin held up her phone and spoke. "*Cara.*" She looked back at Brigid. "You have to at least consider it. I won't *let* you kill me, but you'd be a fool not to consider it."

"Don't be ridiculous."

"It's not ridiculous." Tenzin gripped her phone. "Cara!"

Cara was the virtual assistant built into the Nocht software that let vampires run their electronic devices with minimal touch.

"Cara doesn't work up here." Brigid couldn't take her eyes off a spot on the wall. "Do you think Zasha meant it?"

"You've interacted with them more than I have. Do they lie?"

"Constantly."

"Then they might have meant it or they could change their mind." Tenzin threw her phone on the bed. "Call Chloe for me."

Brigid frowned and looked up. "Who?"

Tenzin bent down and snarled in Brigid's face. "Call Chloe Reardon. *Now.*"

The corner of Brigid's mouth turned up and her fangs dropped, but she had Chloe's number. "Wake." Her phone came to life in her hand. "Call Chloe Reardon."

The phone rang and rang, but finally a voice picked up. "Who is this?"

"Chloe, are you safe?" Tenzin shouted at the phone.

"Oh my God, Tenzin." Chloe sounded as if she'd been crying. "Tenzin, I'm so sorry."

"What happened?" Tenzin stood, and her feet left the floor. "Is Gavin with you?"

"He's talking to the firefighters right now." Chloe sniffed. "Tenzin, it's— I don't know how it happened. Maybe an electrical fire or something. I know I didn't leave a candle burning, and I haven't cooked anything there since you guys left, so I don't know what—"

"Firefighters." Tenzin was frozen, her eyes blinking rapidly. "They burned the loft."

Brigid's heart sank.

Ben and Tenzin's loft in New York had been their sanctuary. A refuge from the world. Brigid knew that especially for Ben, his place in New York was his pride and joy, a home he'd built for himself and Tenzin. Maybe the first home that had ever been truly his own.

"The birds," Tenzin whispered. "Chloe, did you get the birds?"

"I don't think anyone could have... I mean, they said the glass shattered, so it's possible they flew away but—"

"It's winter in New York." Tenzin's face grew very calm and still. "The birds are dead." She curled her hand into a fist.

Brigid stood up. "Chloe, it's Brigid Connor. Tell Gavin and the O'Briens that whoever did this was connected to Zasha Sokholov."

"Gavin's furious because I stay at the loft sometimes when

he's out of town and I was there two nights ago. He said it was an attack on him. That I could have been killed and—"

"You could have been killed, but you woulda been collateral damage." Brigid glanced at Tenzin. "You weren't the target. Zasha was showing off."

Poking the bear.

If Zasha had wanted to make Tenzin angry, they'd done it. Brigid had never seen Tenzin as cold as she was in that moment.

She stood up and moved toward Tenzin, only to be met with a raised hand and a fist of wind that slammed her back against the wall of the room.

"Tenzin!"

"If you even think about killing me before I can kill Zasha, I will end you." Tenzin's voice was a soft monotone. "They burned his home."

Brigid gritted her teeth and managed to force out "I'm not gonna kill you."

Tenzin dropped her hand, the wind died to nothing, and Brigid fell to the ground. Her phone was still sitting on the bed, and Chloe was shouting.

"Brigid, what's happening? What is going on? Where's Ben?"

Tenzin knelt next to the bed and spoke carefully. "Chloe, do not leave Gavin's side until I tell you that you are safe. I am going to take care of this."

"Is Ben okay?"

"Benjamin will be safe." Tenzin gently touched the phone speaker. "You will be safe. Tell Arthur and Drew to stay at Gavin's for now. Gavin will know what to do."

"I'll look for the birds."

"Not without guards." Tenzin closed her eyes. "The birds aren't important now."

"Should I call Ben?"

"No, I'll call him. I'll tell him when it's time. Tell Gavin to dig up any trace of Zasha Sokholov in Alaska. I want to know any place Zasha or the Anker clan might have property—ships, ports, anything. Any financial tie." She cut her eyes to Brigid. "We're not waiting on the Russians anymore."

"Okay." Chloe sniffed. "Okay. Zasha Sokholov. The Ankers. Alaska."

"British Columbia too," Brigid added. "And the Yukon Territory. I don't think it'll be farther than that."

She took a deep breath and waited as Chloe and Tenzin said goodbye. Then Tenzin tossed Brigid's phone back at her. "You can't kill me."

"I wasn't plannin' on it, but you claim that you can't kill Zasha, so I don't know what your plan is."

Tenzin stared at Brigid to the point where Brigid felt her skin start to crawl. The small, silent vampire was as unearthly as her legend described in that moment.

"I'll kill them," Tenzin said. "Or you will. As long as I see them dead."

"You swore on the blood of your children," Brigid said.

"My children are dead." Tenzin walked toward the door. "I don't think their blood will care."

CHAPTER FIFTEEN

"How would a castle attack?" Carwyn murmured into the frosty air outside the house that looked over Annette Bay. The night was nearly over, Ben was sleeping, but Carwyn couldn't rest.

Unlike his younger companion, he couldn't sleep until dawn called him. During the long winters in North Wales, he'd often spent more time outside than in, reveling in the rich darkness of the mountains and enjoying the snow on the peaks that surrounded the tiny valley where he'd hidden from the world.

Now the world was laid out before him, the brutal reality of it, the slithering politics and the destruction. What Ben had told them about the attack that Brigid and Tenzin had found the night before disturbed him on a deeper level.

He knew there was evil in the world. He'd seen the cruelest acts of war and the desperation of the survivors. He'd seen good men turn to darkness when there was no place left in the light. He knew that keeping a code of morality was considered useless to many of his kind.

After all, what god could judge those who never died?

What he could never reconcile was evil for evil's sake. The

wanton destruction of a family, the death of an immortal who had found a modicum of peace. Useless, disgusting cruelty.

"Carwyn?"

He turned to see Buck standing in the doorway, offering a steaming cup of something. Carwyn walked toward him and realized it was herbal tea.

"You don't seem like the type to drink much," Buck said, "or I'd offer you a whiskey."

"I do love a whiskey." Carwyn took the mug. "But I appreciate the tea too." He sipped it, glad to taste honey instead of sugar. "Where are we with finding that boat?"

"I've called the main office in Seattle, so they're on it. Katya's tracking all of Oleg's fleet that we know of and trying to get information on all his unregistered vessels too."

"So she's still convinced that Zasha is working with Oleg?"

Buck shrugged. "You have to admit it makes sense. You want to disrupt the territory of your enemy before you try to take over. Makes the new boss look like a better bet than the old one, you know?"

Okay, the human had a point, but Carwyn knew that Zasha wasn't working with Oleg. Brigid would have figured that out by now.

"Henri Paulson's boat," Carwyn said. "The one that went missing. Could Zasha be working off that?"

"The *Flying Dolphin*? It's good-sized. Possible. That might be the reason they were meeting. Zasha wanted to buy his boat. Or they took it."

"No one's seen or heard from Paulson in months, right?"

"Not that I know of, but that's not unusual. He's real private."

"But his crew has gone missing too. Is that normal?"

"No."

Paulson. Why did that name sound so familiar? Henri Paulson. There was something there. A thread that begged to be tugged.

"Any idea how we're supposed to get around?" Carwyn asked. "I can't fly. I never wanted to, but I have to admit, it'd be convenient right now."

"Katya's sending the *Pacific Lady* back to Ketchikan for you."

"The boat that carried us here?"

Buck nodded. "I'll go with you, help out Jeb so Jennie can stay here. He's the water vampire who captains the *Lady*."

"So no choice but to get around by boat?"

"It's the best option here."

Carwyn sipped his tea and stared out over the water. "How would a castle attack?"

Buck looked confused. "How do you attack a castle?"

"No." He sighed. "It's a chess thing. I don't know much about chess, but a smart young man told me that I fought like a castle, which apparently used to mean a chariot."

Buck frowned. "Attacking like a chariot? That's a chess thing?"

"I'm told it is."

The older man pursed his lips. "So a direct frontal attack by *Roman* chariots wouldn't happen until the opposing army was in disarray. They'd be circling the ground troops at first, the archers riding in the chariots would be shooting arrows into the battle until things were all messed up, and then once that shield line was broken, they might do a unified frontal assault."

He blinked. "That's a surprising knowledge of Roman military history, Buck."

The old man shrugged. "It's an interest."

Carwyn frowned. "I feel like I should know that better than you."

"Were you a Roman?"

"No, hated the bastards, but I've spent a lot of time in Rome."

Carwyn finished the tea in one gulp. "I appreciate the insight. I'm not a wind vampire like Ben or a water vampire of any kind, so finding a boat is one hundred percent *not* my strength. But I am very good at breaking things."

Buck nodded slowly. "And... would that be helpful?"

No, but it might be satisfying. "Maybe. Let's see if we might be able to throw this army into disarray, shall we? Shoot some arrows from the perimeter. Is there anything that you know of, any particular base on land that Zasha is attached to?"

"Nothing jumps to mind, but I might be able to find something. Zasha was in town a bit last summer, and I can make some calls."

"Do that." Carwyn started to go inside. He wasn't tired, but he wanted to try to call Brigid if she'd pick up the phone. "I'll see you at nightfall, Buck."

"Sleep well, Carwyn." Buck raised his mug. "And I'll find something. Just give me a few hours. I know a lot of guys who know a lot of people."

"Good man."

HE STARED at the blank screen and contemplated what he'd say to Brigid if she picked up.

I love you.

I know why you did this.

Where the fuck are you?

No, not the last one. He was starting to understand why Ben was holding back from finding his mate. Currently there were two fronts to this battle; in theory, putting pressure on Zasha from two different directions.

Carwyn liked the idea of shooting arrows from the perimeter. It wasn't as satisfying as rolling through the middle of a battlefield like a tank, but he could shoot arrows. He was Welsh, wasn't he?

If Brigid and Tenzin could focus on finding that boat with Oleg's help, maybe he and Ben could find Zasha's base. Shoot arrows around the perimeter until they knew where to barrel in and demolish.

He really wanted to demolish something.

Carwyn hit the button on his tablet that called his wife and waited.

And waited.

He was nearly ready to throw the thing against the wall when she answered.

"Carwyn?"

Fuck me, who else would it be? He swallowed the anger and stared at the screen, trying to judge her mental state from a wavy digital image on the screen. "I'm here."

She released a long breath and closed her eyes. "I miss you."

"So tell me where you are."

"Moving soon," she said. "It wouldn't matter, and I still can't tell you because I promised."

"You're on the Kenai Peninsula at Oleg's compound, and Tenzin is with you."

Brigid pursed her lips. "She can't keep her mouth shut to save her life, can she?"

"Not from him."

"So Ben's with you."

"You know he is."

"That means you could find me."

"I *will* find you. All I'd need to do is set foot on the ground there and you know I'd find you."

"Carwyn—"

"But a young wind vampire convinced me that it was a good idea to let you and Tenzin work together. Is he wrong?"

She shook her head but said nothing.

"Is this some sort of strange bonding ritual between you and the psychopath?"

"Zasha or Tenzin?" Brigid ran a hand across her forehead and rubbed her temple. "Sorry, that's not fair. She took a test."

"Only passed by a slim margin from what I heard." If there were vampires he'd trust with his mate's life, Tenzin was not on the list. But she was as terrible as Zasha, so that was something. "Is Oleg helping you?" He hated the Russian on principle, but at least he had faith the fire vampire wouldn't want to piss off any of Brigid's many powerful friends.

"Oleg is helping me work with my fire," Brigid said. "We need to find a boat."

"Because Zasha is coordinating hunting parties on a boat somewhere, then sending vampires ashore to wreak havoc on isolated vampires and their humans."

She blinked. "How did you—?"

"Ben tells me everything."

Brigid leaned closer to the screen. "Is he with you?"

"No. But I heard about the raid." He reached out his hand, then pulled it back. "How are you?"

"It was bad." Her voice was rough. "That's not why I'm asking."

Carwyn sat up straight. "Did something happen to Tenzin?"

"No, but someone set fire to their loft in New York. No one was hurt, but it sounds like their home was pretty much destroyed. Don't tell him yet. Tenzin is..."

"Angry."

"I've never seen her like this," Brigid said. "We're lookin' for anything that's connected to the Sokholovs in Alaska. She's got Gavin looking."

"Good." He didn't want to talk business with her. He wanted

to scream at her, but he knew it wasn't productive. "Listen, Brigid—"

"I shouldn't have left. Mo chroí. My heart." Her voice was barely over a whisper. "I'm sorry I left. I wanted to protect you, but most of the time I feel like I'm stumbling around in the dark up here. It's a bog. There's nothing I can hold—" Her voice caught. "I want to do something, but I don't have a plan for this, Carwyn. There're too many variables. And this place is giant. Vast on a level I can hardly wrap my brain around. I don't know what I'm doin', and now Tenzin says that she's gonna kill Zasha and I'm really not sure how she plans to do that but—"

"Shhhh." He ached to reach her. He wanted to grab her, shake her a little, then hide her away from any harm. "The first thing you need to do is listen."

Brigid closed her mouth.

"Maith an cailín. Good girl." Carwyn took a deep breath. "We're coming around to the same ideas from different places. For now we work apart. We utilize Oleg's *and* Katya's resources. If Gavin finds anything on land, you tell me. If we find anything from our side, we'll tell you. Ben may be strong as hell, but he's not as experienced a hunter as Tenzin is. I may not like the woman, but she hunted a clan into extinction because they wronged her. She can find Zasha Sokholov."

"That seems to be the reason she needs to find them."

Carwyn leaned forward. "Zasha was part of her sire's clan?"

"Not exactly."

Carwyn thought back to their last time together in Las Vegas, before Brigid had left and he'd gone half-mad. "Mate. Zasha had a mate."

Brigid nodded.

"And that mate was part of the clan." It all fit together. "Tenzin killed Zasha's mate."

"What would you do to avenge your mate?" Brigid asked. "Even after centuries."

"I'd tear down the world for you," Carwyn whispered. "I'd break every rule. I'd demolish this world from the foundations if you were taken from me."

Brigid rested her head in her hands. "You're still really pissed at me, aren't ya?"

Carwyn didn't want to respond, so he just stayed quiet. "The next time I call, you answer your phone, Brigid."

"Is ea," she whispered. "Yes. I'll answer."

"And the moment you find a hint of Zasha's presence on land, you call me. You tell me immediately. I may not fly, but I have ways. Anywhere on land and that psychopath is mine."

She nodded.

"Good." He took a deep breath and let it out slowly. "You have Gavin looking?"

"Yeah, Tenzin called Chloe."

"Have him search for a vampire named Paulson. Water vampire and captain of the *Flying Dolphin* out of Vancouver. The ship went missing a while back, a few weeks after Zasha was seen meeting with the owner. That might be the boat we're looking for. Katya hasn't been able to find it and the crew is all missing, but Gavin might have better luck."

"Paulson," she said. "I'll pass it along."

———

THE FOLLOWING NIGHT, Buck and Carwyn took the boat out to a small island within spitting distance of Ketchikan where a luxurious house rose from the shores of a small cove thick with frosty pines.

"It was snowed in a month ago," Buck said. "But melted now. Zasha rented this place at the beginning of the summer. Not a bad report from the owner. The place was spotless when the party left."

"How many?"

"According to the human who owns it, there was the 'tall, redheaded fella' and three others. Two men and a woman. He thought they were Russian. Their secretary said something about a fishing trip. They didn't make any trouble." Buck pointed to a boathouse that sat on the water. "There's a twenty-five-foot fishing boat stored in there. According to the owner, they used it but they didn't buy fishing licenses or any gear from what he heard."

"So maybe they were exploring," Carwyn said, "not fishing."

"Possible." Buck looked over the dark water. "There are countless coves and inlets in the interior like this. Alaska has more shoreline than the entire rest of the United States combined, and the Alexander Archipelago has over a thousand islands. Only a few of them are populated. It's mostly national forest."

"*Dense* forests." Carwyn sniffed the air. "Isolated places. Lots of wildlife."

"They're only accessible by air or boat," Buck said. "The Inside Passage protects the area from heavy weather. If you wanted to hide out here, you could do it. Lots of people have."

"That's why Katya keeps a loose grip on the area," Carwyn said. "Because mostly it's impossible to police."

"Partly." Buck nodded. "And there aren't really enough people to create problems. Like I said before, most of the vampires who come up here want to live quiet."

"Which gives one vampire who wants to wreak havoc an easy place to hide." Carwyn nodded at the shoreline where he could see Ben waiting. "Let's go ashore. See if Zasha and their party left anything for us to find."

CHAPTER SIXTEEN

B en explored the area around Zasha's rental house while he waited for Carwyn and Buck to reach the shore. He'd already circled the island where the luxurious cabin was tucked between the forest and the sea. It was a sportsman's paradise with dense wooded property stretching back from an inlet bordered by a curved pebble beach.

There was a boathouse built over the water, and the two-story cantilevered chalet had massive windows overlooking the cove where a wooden dock stretched out from the shore.

A meadow filled the area behind the house. It would be lush with wildflowers when the sun peeked through the heavily clouded sky, but when Ben flew over it, it was nothing but a dense green patch bordered by mud.

He floated through the forest behind the house, following muddy paths that wound through the trees. Pine, cedar, and a few hardwoods created a dense patchwork, dripping with moisture from the air. They were in the cool, temperate rainforest of the Pacific Northwest, and moss covered every surface, ferns filled the underbrush, and bugs the size of his palm flew next to him.

There were scents in the forest, but none of them spoke of

humans or vampires. Deer, bear, and fox. The low hoot of owls calling as he passed silently through their realm.

It was completely dark; the moon and stars were covered by a dense cloud, and no light shone from the empty house save for a small security light at the end of the dock.

He heard the putter of the boat engine in the distance and flew to greet Carwyn and Buck, waiting on the rocky beach while they walked down the dock toward him.

The earth vampire had spoken to his mate, and Ben could see the slight ease in the set of Carwyn's shoulders.

Ben lifted a hand in greeting. "How was the water?"

"Wet," Carwyn muttered. He heaved a visible sigh of relief when his feet touched land, then froze. "Ben, what did you see from the air?"

He frowned. "Nothing. House looks good. No damage that I could see. Paths through the forest. Lots of mud and trees. Why?"

Carwyn's knees hit the soil, and he dug his hands into the mud.

The hairs on Ben's arms rose as the old vampire's amnis stretched out, touching everything connected to the earth.

Ben's instincts went on alert, and his feet lifted from the ground.

"Not you," Carwyn muttered. "It's not you. But he's some-where." Carwyn stood up, kicked off his shoes, and sank his feet into the earth. "There's a vampire here. *Deep* underground."

Buck frowned. "I don't know anyone who lives out here. None of Jennie or Katya's people—"

"He's none of Katya's. He's much older than Katya." Carwyn started walking barefoot across the rocks, then straight into the trees and back into the forest, moving at a pace that didn't match his size.

From Ben's perspective, the vampire appeared to float through the trees, moving with so much speed that he appeared to be flying. He moved over the ground like a boat skimming over water.

Ben flew after him, leaving Buck alone on the rocky shore, Ben dodged through the canopy as Carwyn ran through the forest. He was as silent as an owl in flight, his body slipping through the dense underbrush, and the only way Ben could keep him in sight was watching for the bright red shock of hair appearing like a spark in the forest.

Carwyn had stripped down to his shirtsleeves, and mud streaked over his arms and legs. He stopped every now and then to crouch down, altering his angle before he moved again.

Ben had no idea how long they'd run before they came to a mound that rose in the center of the trees, ferns blanketing the steep rise of earth. A hint of old logs poked out from the edges of the moss and the dirt.

He landed next to Carwyn. "What is it?"

"He was hurt. Surprised by them. This place is old, and he came here to heal."

"There's a vampire in there?" Ben reached for one of the blades worked into his jacket.

"You won't need that." Carwyn spread his arms, and Ben gawked as the earth hollowed out beneath him, the mud and the rocks peeling back as Carwyn stepped down into their depths. "Stay here. He may not trust you."

The earth was silent after it swallowed Carwyn, the ferns dripping water onto the churned soil and the moss gently creeping over the scarred ground as Ben watched the ground begin to heal itself.

Like most of the vampire world, Ben sometimes forgot how formidable earth vampires could be. They were the humble folk of the immortal world, living in isolated places and gathering communities around them, more enmeshed in the human world than most vampires and their retinues.

But as Ben watched the ground open up for the old vampire, he remembered how powerful the earth could be.

Minutes passed; silence reigned.

Finally the ground began to move again, the moss and ferns pulling back like a blanket tugged from a bed. The soil beneath Ben's feet heaved up, and as he backed away, he saw Carwyn emerge from the earth with a blackened figure in his arms.

"I don't speak his language." Carwyn's voice was a low growl. "Buck's wife is Tlingit. Does he speak the language?"

"I don't know. What happened to him?"

Ben could sense the vampire was alive but just barely.

"Burned," Carwyn said. "Maybe by Zasha. Maybe by someone else. I have no idea."

Ben held out his arms. "Give him to me. I can fly—"

"I have no idea what condition he's in or what he's capable of," Carwyn said. "Right now he's barely alive. He needs blood, and I don't know if you can control him if he loses it." Carwyn began to move through the trees the same way they'd come. "Buck has blood on the boat. Meet me there."

———

THE VAMPIRE WAS COVERED in mud, and his skin was blackened from fire, but his fangs were long and pure white when they sank into the bag of blood that Carwyn held for him on the deck of Buck's boat.

"I don't know him," Buck said. "But he doesn't speak Tlingit. Or at least he doesn't right now. If we get him back to my place, Jennie might be able to talk to him. He might just not recognize my accent; it's not great."

"He's Tlingit?" Ben asked.

Buck nodded. "I mean, I think so. He looks Tlingit, but then if he's as old as you think he is, he might be something else. Whoever came before them, you know?"

"He's old." Carwyn reached out a hand toward the blackened forehead of the vampire before he pulled back. "He's older than me. I want to comfort him, but touching him might be painful. The best thing we can do is leave the mud on him."

"He might have been living back in those woods for a thousand years without anyone bothering him." Buck kept his voice quiet. "Like I said, there aren't too many vampires who come out here. It's possible Zasha just happened on him, or this one came looking when he sensed other vamps in the area."

"There's no way of knowing," Ben said. "We just need to focus on getting him stronger. Something tells me that if he's been living out here all this time and no one even knew he was here, he was probably feeding on animal blood like Carwyn."

"This is human blood," Carwyn said. "Donated. He'll heal faster with human blood." Carwyn muttered something quietly in a language Ben didn't speak, something that sounded soothing and reassuring.

Hopefully the desiccated vampire would recognize the tone of the words even if he didn't understand their meaning.

Buck had already pointed the boat back toward Ketchikan.

"Do you think it's a good idea to move him?" Ben asked.

"It might take him centuries to heal from burns like this with no help," Carwyn said. "He'd be alive but barely. Getting blood into him is better."

Buck added, "If we get him back to our place and Jennie can't talk to him, I know someone else we can call. She's older than my wife and might know this guy. Either way, we'll make sure he gets better." Buck scowled at the vampire curled in the corner, hidden under emergency blankets. "I don't understand it. I don't understand any of it."

"Zasha was there with friends most likely." Carwyn pulled

another bag of blood from the refrigerator. "Brigid said there was at least one wind vampire with them in the desert. That's how they got away."

"A child?" Buck asked.

"No." Ben shook his head. "Zasha's sire was an earth vampire. Any child they sired would go to the earth. This has to be someone else."

"Someone who's following them around. A friend. An ally."

"Doesn't matter," Carwyn said. "We finish anyone involved in this." He looked at Ben. "Judge, jury, and executioners. This cannot continue."

"Agreed." Ben looked at Buck. "We have permission from Katya to get Zasha out of her territory by any means possible. This is the second survivor found from one of Zasha's attacks. The first one happened a couple of weeks ago. This one might have been in the ground for months. We need to find out where they're hiding."

"In this place?" Buck spread his arms out. "Sorry, gentlemen, but you're lookin' for a needle in a haystack."

THEY WERE GREETED BACK in Ketchikan by a round-faced woman with light brown skin, wavy black hair that fell to her waist, and fine lines of tattoos decorating her chin.

Buck stood at the wheel and waved. "That's my lady. That's my Jennie."

Katya's top lieutenant in Alaska wore a serious expression on her face and a blood-red parka dotted with rain. There were two humans waiting with her as she stood on the dock, a tall man and a woman who could have been her sister.

"I'm Jennie." She nodded at Carwyn, who was carrying the burned vampire in his arms. "Sorry I haven't been able to meet you before. What the hell, Buck?"

"I know, honey." He leaned over and kissed her cheek. "Just glad the earth vampire was with us or we never would have known."

"Sounds like you've had a lot thrown at you," Ben said, "from what Buck has said. Do you recognize him?"

Ben held out a hand to stop her when she reached out to the burned vampire in Carwyn's arms. "His skin."

"Right," she murmured. "I think I might know who it is. We didn't know if he was alive or not 'cause no one's seen him in so long." She bent her head to the curled-up vampire and whispered something in his ear that seemed to get a reaction.

"Yeah." Jennie nodded. "Come on then. We already made a bed for him. Let's get him out of the water and onto land."

Carwyn muttered, "He needs blood."

"That's why they're here." Jennie nodded at the two humans. "He gonna hurt 'em?"

"I don't think so. He took some donated blood on the boat and didn't lash out." Carwyn followed Jennie off the dock. "He didn't seem aggressive."

"Yeah." She nodded. "That sounds right if he's who I'm thinkin' of."

Buck and Ben hung back, tying up the fishing boat to the dock as a misty rain fell on them.

"Does it rain every day here?" Ben asked the man.

"Pretty much." The man smiled. "Water vampires love it."

"I bet." He glanced at the retreating figures. "Will he be okay?"

"Friend, you probably know better than me about that. I'm just married to one of you folk." He stood up straight when the ropes were secured and pulled out a mobile phone. Something dinged and he stared at the screen for a few moments, his mouth a grim line.

"Everything okay?" Ben asked.

If there was one thing he missed from mortal life, it was his damn phone. The lumpy miniature tablets they had to carry to use any technology did not match the sleek black phone that had been his constant companion before he turned.

"Everything's fine," Buck said. "Let's get in the house. Carwyn was asking about Henri Paulson the other day."

Ben nodded. "He was thinking that Zasha might be working off the *Flying Dolphin*."

"I put a word in with Katya's people in Seattle after Paulson's name kept coming up. Tried to find out what all I could tell you."

"Okay." That made sense to Ben. "You hear back?"

"Just now. Let's head in and I'll fill you in on what I know."

———

BEN CHANGED out of his damp clothes, listening to Buck as the man moved around in the living area upstairs. He could hear the human talking to someone on the phone and suspected Buck was filling Katya's office in on what they'd discovered at Zasha's rental house.

If Paulson was under Katya's aegis, that meant he was afforded some privacy from outsiders. Vampire aegis went more than one way. Katya would expect immortals in her territory to show her loyalty, but that meant they were under her protection as well, so sharing private information with an outsider would be frowned on unless there was a reason.

But Ben wasn't sure if Paulson was under aegis or just residing in Katya's territory independently. He was leaning toward the latter.

By the time Ben walked upstairs, whatever permission Buck needed must have been granted, because the human had his laptop out and was projecting his screen on a wall across the room.

"I've been looking through the file Katya's people just

emailed," Buck said. "Paulson is the current name of Henri Paulus." He pointed to a grainy black-and-white picture. "Water vampire from what's now Denmark. About three hundred years old or so—not sure on that one, to be honest—and apparently the quietest billionaire you've never heard of."

Ben blinked. "Billionaire?"

Millionaires weren't uncommon among the undead. After all, when you lived for centuries, it was almost impossible not to acquire wealth. But billionaire wealth was a level that few vampires reached because it required too much interaction in the human world. Of course, the richest vampires in the world— including his mate—really had no way of measuring wealth since they kept most of it in gold.

Ben frowned. "How did he make his money?"

"Technology if you can believe it. And pharmaceuticals. He quietly invested in a bunch of internet start-ups over the years and some very successful pharma companies. He pays Katya boatloads to keep his location a secret. No one is supposed to know where he is. He lives only on the water and has no citizenship of any kind."

"Like one of those marine colonies humans talk about?" Ben asked. "What do they call it? Sea-steading or something?" He leaned forward, watching as Buck flipped through pictures.

Buck nodded. "Somethin' like that."

There was Paulson on the deck of a yacht in the moonlight. All the pictures were at night save for some of large watercraft that were taken during the day with what looked like staff on deck.

"All these boats are his?"

"And more. I was told that Henri Paulus has a network of ships that he loans to immortals who are trying to keep a low profile."

Ben blinked. "You don't say."

"The ships are unregistered and move around constantly."

"And Katya allows that?" Ben murmured.

"Hey, I don't make the decisions." Buck shrugged. "I suppose it's not really a problem as long as they're not causing trouble."

"But Paulus has disappeared," Ben said, "along with his boat. So where did he go, and who is in charge of his fleet?"

"That would be the billion-dollar question, because if one of them is being loaned to Zasha Sokholov and used as a base to attack the mainland, Paulus has now become a major problem."

"Is it possible that Zasha took it and Paulson doesn't know?"

"Possible? Yes. Probable? No idea." Buck flipped the picture to an overhead shot of a giant marina. "This is Vancouver. Normally the *Dolphin* would be moored there this time of year. It's gone."

"And the last report about it was from crew who got in touch a couple of weeks after Zasha Sokholov came to visit?"

"Yeah." Buck clicked to another grainy image of Paulson on the deck of the *Dolphin*. "So how is Paulus involved in all this? Is he a victim or an accomplice?"

"And if he's an accomplice, where are he and Zasha right now?"

CHAPTER SEVENTEEN

Prague, 1822

T enzin stared at the crumpled body of the human, his innards splayed on the damp grey cobblestones of a narrow street in the old Bohemian city, blood pooling beneath his body and leaking in ever-spreading rivulets between the stones.

She pulled a wool cloak around her face, hiding her features. Her cover in Prague was as the foreign wife of a rich merchant, but in the human world, fear and suspicion often found their target in unfamiliar faces.

She wore a long wool dress in the modern fashion of a wealthy married woman, the heavy fabric shielding her from the worst of the damp cold and rain in the old city. Her boots were tight and unpleasantly stiff, but they were practical for the stone streets.

She glanced up at the stone balcony and the figure with pale blond hair peering over the ledge. It appeared the man had jumped from the balcony. Or he'd been pushed. Either one was possible.

"They just keep doing this."

Tenzin looked to her right to see a tall figure in a black cloak staring down at the body. The stranger was clearly a vampire, but Tenzin had a hard time pinpointing what type of element he wielded.

His collar was elegant and pure white—barely contrasting with his pale skin—and his neck was wrapped carefully to ward off the cold. A dark top hat made the vampire appear even taller than he already was. A hooded cape with red trim flowed from broad shoulders, the fur-trimmed collar turned up to cover most of his face.

The stranger nudged the body with the toe of his black leather boot. He was speaking German, not unusual in the old Bohemian capital. "What a shame."

She responded in the same language, hoping her accent wasn't too difficult to understand. "They do seem to like this type of execution."

"Execution is a softer word than murder."

What a curious thing to say. "Did you know him?"

His amnis was cloaked with a very heavy buffer that told Tenzin he was powerful but clumsy. Maybe young, maybe simply uneducated. It was as if a somewhat clever child had thrown a blanket over a wolf, but the animal was fighting to break free.

"I knew him." The stranger's voice was close to a sigh. "At least, I knew a part of him."

She nodded. "A social acquaintance then."

"Yes, I only knew his sexual organs." The cloak tipped back, and a faint smile lifted the corner of beautifully curved lips. "They were quite nice."

"Ah." Taking human lovers was common among her kind. They were amusing pastimes, and some vampires even became attached to them.

Not Tenzin.

"An unfortunate loss for you." Tenzin was debating her next move. "My condolences."

"Poor Josef." The vampire kept looking between her and the body; she caught a glimpse of dark eyes and pale skin, not unusual for immortals who couldn't survive sun. "Did *you* know him?"

"No."

"Then what are you doing here?" The corner of his mouth turned up. "Just passing by?"

Tenzin looked up at the balcony, but there was another person now. She'd been planning to use that balcony as an entry point for the theft, but now that was definitely out of the question for the night.

She wasn't going to follow her plan anymore, so there was no harm in telling the stranger. "I was supposed to be stealing a particularly beautiful clock from this human's house."

"I see." The vampire nodded. "The gold Boulle on the third floor?"

"Yes, exactly." Tenzin moved her foot as the human's blood seeped down the channel between the cobblestones. "I have a client in Paris who would like to retrieve it. It was given to this human without their permission."

"So irritating when that happens." The vampire's tone was casual. "The Boulle is a lovely piece."

She nodded. "I saw the drawings, but I haven't seen it in person."

Voices rose from down the street, and a few doors opened and slammed shut. Someone rang a bell in the distance, and the distant sound of carriage wheels made Tenzin go on alert.

She hated carriages.

"You wouldn't miss it," the other vampire said. "He kept in on the mantelpiece in the upstairs library."

Tenzin narrowed her eyes and looked at the balcony again, where three people were shouting. "I think the humans are coming. I should retrieve it another time."

"Not a bad idea. Perhaps tomorrow night?"

I'm not telling you when I'm coming back. She couldn't see the vampire fully, but she didn't trust him. His clumsily cloaked amnis put her on edge. "Perhaps."

"They call you Tenzin, don't they?"

She kept her face carefully blank as she looked at him from the corner of her eye. Her faithful bronze blade was secured in a pocket built into her skirts, she had a garrote in her waist pocket, and a thin blade was tucked in her hair, disguised as a hatpin.

She kept her voice low. "Some call me that."

"I mean no offense." He clicked his heels together and bowed a little bit. "Your reputation precedes you."

She had no idea if that was a compliment or a threat. She wanted to see more of the stranger's face, but the vampire kept it hidden, and he was too tall to make out his features clearly. "Are you native to this city?"

"No." The stranger bent down, swiped a finger through the blood pooling under the broken body of the human, and licked the viscous red liquid that was quickly turning black. "I enjoyed the sex. And the blood."

Tenzin watched the cloaked figure straighten to his full height. She took a step back, unnerved by the vampire who was so casually acting inhuman in public.

Physical strength wasn't as important to immortals as it was to humans, but it wasn't nothing. The vampire beside her dwarfed her tiny frame, and he was physical in a way that made Tenzin think he might be an earth vampire. He had broad shoulders, a long neck, and long arms. He would run faster than her; he could reach farther.

Tenzin survived by hiding, and this immortal's actions tempted discovery.

"Good night to you." She took another step back. "Perhaps I'll tell my client that this job must wait."

Tenzin turned and slipped into the shadows, taking to the sky as quickly as she could.

Once she reached the roof of a nearby building, she crouched behind a brick chimney and peered over the edge at the tall vampire, who had remained in the crowd gathered around the dead man.

There was something familiar about him. Something that tickled her vast memory.

A face gusted by, then disappeared like smoke into the night sky. There was too much. Too many eyes and scents and dark nights to account for in her mind.

She took to the air after making sure the vampire wasn't following her.

Charles and Emil could wait for their clock.

———

"WE'RE FLYING YOU TO JUNEAU." Oleg lounged in a large easy chair in front of the fire burning in the massive stone hearth at his fishing lodge. "Lev will go with you. And I'll send Olaf if you want. He can fly."

Someone grumbled in a deep voice from another room. It sounded like Olaf wasn't thrilled with his assignment. Tenzin didn't blame him. She didn't like carrying earthbound vampires around like cargo either.

"Juneau?" Brigid looked at Mika, who was watching them from the corner. "That's all the way on the other side of the state."

"Ketchikan," Tenzin whispered. Ketchikan was near Juneau. Maybe. She was still confused by Alaskan geography, and from the sky, too much of the state looked the same.

Trees.

Ocean.

Large rivers of ice.

More trees.

Oleg glanced at Tenzin, then back to Brigid. "That is where you need to be. Zasha is not here."

Brigid persisted. "Did you find them?"

"According to some information that has come to us, there is a house that Zasha used as a vacation rental near Sitka. That is closer to where we think they are hiding now."

"But you don't know." Brigid kept looking at Mika for some reason. "I kinda feel like you're tryin' to get rid of us, Oleg."

Tenzin had been thinking the same thing.

Oleg spread his arms and opened his palms to the sky. "I do not know what else you would have me do, Brigid Connor. It is highly unlikely that Zasha is in this area anymore. Perhaps they have gone back to Katya's home territory after trying to rile the vampire residents in Kenai and Seward against me."

"Oh, pull the other one, Oleg," Brigid countered. "You know she's not involved in this."

"No? Three raids in the course of a few months? All coming from the sea? And all against vampires who are loyal to me?"

Tenzin felt prompted to speak. "Katya has had attacks in her territory too."

"A ruse. Perhaps a smoke screen. Or perhaps she is eliminating those she might see as loyal to me when the time comes."

"The time?" Tenzin smiled. "The time for what?"

Oleg smiled back but said nothing.

The vampire was full of shit; he was speaking for an audience, and Brigid and Tenzin were not it. This was a performance for the men and women listening with big ears and waiting tongues.

Brigid was trying to reason with Oleg even though this was all bullshit.

"We're not under Katya's aegis, Oleg. We're not workin' for her or for you. We're just trying to take care of a problem that both you and Katya share."

"Good," he said. "Then you should be happy I am flying you to Juneau."

"There are whispers," Mika finally said. "Whispers that Katya's people are now finding raids in their own territory."

"Which means she can't be involved in any of this," Brigid said.

"Which means" —Oleg took command of the room again, his eyes landing right on Tenzin— "that unless *two* rogue vampires have suddenly decided to start attacking human and vampire compounds in Alaska, Zasha has moved on and you two have no reason to be here."

"So you're sending us to Juneau?" Brigid asked.

Mika shrugged. "Zasha seems to attack where there is isolation and secrecy."

"And they have a base somewhere central in Alaska to be attacking both you and Katya," Brigid said. "We need to explore the islands across Prince William Sound and—"

"They're on a boat," Mika muttered. "You know they're on a boat, Brigid. It's the only thing that makes sense."

Tenzin *didn't* know they were on a boat. Zasha's sire was an earth vampire and they were sired to fire, which meant that water was basically the opposite of everything that made them comfortable. If Zasha was basing themself on a boat, Tenzin would eat her sword.

"If you go south from Juneau," Oleg said, "you'll be in the heart of the Inside Passage. There are countless places to disappear there if one wants to. It is more protected from the weather. You've flown over it, Tenzin."

She looked at Brigid and nodded. "It's huge, cold, and damp. Take the airplane. I'll even go with you just to avoid the windchill."

Oleg knew something. Sending them to Juneau was too specific to be a coincidence, but once again, he was rationalizing and performing for an audience that was neither Brigid nor Tenzin.

Yes, Oleg knew something, but he wasn't going to share it, at least not in front of the others.

"Brigid, we should take the plane," Tenzin said quietly.

"Really?"

"Or I can fly you over Prince William Sound and drop you," Tenzin said. "Maybe."

Brigid huffed out a breath and crossed her arms over her chest, her eyes going back to Mika Arakas, who said not a word.

"According to my men," Oleg said, "a wind vampire can probably make the passage in four or five hours depending on the wind, but as I said, I will make my plane available to you." He spread his hands graciously. "As a gift."

"So we can go kill *your* insane sibling." Tenzin wasn't fooled by Oleg's magnanimity.

"What happens when you find Zasha is between you and Zasha," Mika said. "Oleg and the Sokholov family have no knowledge of your plans, nor do we want any."

Brigid looked toward Mika. "And Lev and Olaf?"

"Lev and Olaf are there to see you safely to Katya's territory. After that, they will return with the plane."

Translation: we'll get you to Juneau; then you're on your own.

Tenzin looked at Brigid. "You tried to avoid bystanders by tracking Zasha to an isolated location, but Zasha is now using isolation as an advantage. This is the right decision."

"At least it's a sparsely populated wilderness instead of downtown Las Vegas this time." Brigid stood and gave Oleg a nod. "I appreciate your... insight. And your plane."

"If I could have found Zasha and kept this away from others, I would have," the fire vampire said. "Don't forget what we talked about. Now leave before we start fighting."

Brigid couldn't stop the smile. "Excellent idea."

Tenzin cocked her head and watched them interact.

Air vampires didn't care who they shared space with. Water vampires and earth vampires glommed on to each other like sticky tape.

But it was highly unusual for two fire vampires to share space as peacefully as Oleg and Brigid had been. Collaboration was not their element's strong suit, and their instincts warned them away from others of their kind.

Fire vampires in the same vicinity?

Like two sparks competing for the same kindling. Inevitably, one of them was going to devour the other.

"Thanks for your help," Brigid continued. "I'll be sure to say hello to Anne and Murphy from you the next time I call Dublin."

Oleg rolled his eyes. "I appreciate the thought, but you only need to say hello to Anne."

She shook her head. "You and Carwyn. Exactly the same." Brigid stood and walked to the door.

Mika met her and the two put their heads together, speaking in low tones that Tenzin didn't care to interpret.

Tenzin remained in her chair, staring at Oleg.

The fire vampire turned his eyes to her. "Khazar."

"Varangian."

Oleg looked at the guard at the door, and within moments, every human and vampire in the place disappeared.

The corner of Oleg's mouth turned up. "What do you want?"

"You've been oddly cooperative. What is your angle?"

"Angle?" Oleg raised a cutting eyebrow. "I don't have one. One might say that I owed you a very old debt that's now been repaid."

"We were hired to kill him." Tenzin turned her eyes to the fire. "The fact that you assisted us has never been an issue."

"Fine then. I don't want Zasha killing harmless people. It's bad for business and my reputation."

"And you want Alaska back."

He lifted one thick shoulder. "There are opportunities I might pursue if Zasha was no longer a problem."

"The last time I saw you, you were glaring at the pretty new leader of the Poshani caravan."

"Your memory is... interesting. Do you think she's pretty?"

Tenzin said, "If I weren't a mated vampire, you'd be out of luck."

That made him smirk. "What do you want, Tenzin?"

She wasn't sure, but she felt like her business with the Russian was far from concluded.

"Tell me how to kill Zasha," she said. "You know them better than I do."

"No." Oleg shook his head. "No one ever knew Zasha. We weren't allowed."

"Why?"

"Because our sire kept Zasha like a pet. They were a curiosity, and they weren't allowed to have normal relationships with anyone. They never had a friend. Never had a lover. Nothing was allowed."

"And after you killed your sire?"

Oleg shifted in his seat, clearly uncomfortable with the turn of the conversation. "After Truvor was dead, I killed all those who tried to defend him, and then I killed everyone who challenged my claim on his territories. It was a very bloody few weeks in Irbosk."

"Zasha wasn't one of those challengers."

"Of course not." His reply came quickly. "At that time, Zasha was nothing. A shy dog kicked too often. They were happy to leave, so I let them." He shrugged. "I had no idea that Zasha would become a gadfly the way that they have."

"Why not kill them yourself?"

A flicker of guilt in Oleg's eyes was all that Tenzin needed to understand the vampire's thinking.

She rose and looked down at Oleg. "You are not responsible for the monster Zasha has become. I know what they suffered, but I also know that Zasha made choices. Those choices are what made them who they are now, *not* the violence they survived."

Oleg folded his hands and rested his chin on them. "Didn't you kill everyone in your clan in judgment for their actions?"

Tenzin didn't mind her reputation; it was well-earned. "I killed those who needed to be killed. See that you never become someone needing to be killed and we will remain friends."

The Russian looked amused. "We don't really have friends, do we? Immortals like us? We don't have friends."

Tenzin thought about Ben first. Then Giovanni. About Beatrice. About Chloe and even about Gavin. Arthur and Drew. It was an odd assortment of mortal and immortal connections she had collected in the past thousand years. Brigid might even join the list.

"I think I do have friends," Tenzin said. "And if you ever harm any of them, you will know who they are."

Oleg still looked amused. "You're not going to give me a clue?"

She wrinkled her nose. "No."

Oleg's cheeks turned a little red. He almost looked like he was going to laugh. "I have no desire to make you my enemy, Khazar."

"Nor I you, Varangian." She started walking to the door.

"But your reputation is expanding."

Tenzin turned. "To what?"

He plucked at a loose thread on his sleeve, pinching the string between his fingers until a small puff of smoke escaped. He flicked the ash from his fingertips and looked at her. "You used to be an assassin. Now some are calling you the executioner."

The difference was subtle but not without meaning. "They

can call me an executioner if they want. Someone in our world has to be."

"And you think it should be you?"

She shrugged. "Is there anyone else who wants the job?"

———

BRIGID WAS PACKING in her room when Tenzin found her. She glanced over her shoulder and noticed Tenzin standing there. "Lev wants to leave within the hour."

Tenzin shrugged. "I don't have anything to pack. Everything I own is in my bag." It was pretty much clean socks and underwear, a spare tunic, and her tablet so she could contact Ben.

And gold. She had gold sewn into the seams.

"Good. I'm almost ready too. I'll take the dogsled back into town. You'll fly of course. And then I think Oleg's plane will meet us there. It's only a few hours to Juneau after that. We'll have plenty of dark."

Tenzin watched her. So efficient. So precise. She ordered her life as if she'd served in an army. "You have the habits of a soldier."

"Do I?" Brigid didn't look up.

"Did Murphy teach you that?"

"No, that was recovery."

Tenzin frowned. "Recovery?"

"The drugs, remember?" Brigid zipped up her backpack and turned, slinging the bag over her shoulder. "I had a mentor in the first rehab I ever went to after I became an addict. He emphasized how keepin' your life organized could help your recovery from substance abuse. It didn't work for everyone, but it worked for me."

"Until you overdosed on heroin?"

"It's a process, not a destination," Brigid muttered. "And thanks for reminding me. I'd almost forgotten that my failure in drug recovery led to me becoming a vampire. Wouldn't wanna forget that."

Tenzin pointed at her. "Sarcasm. You and Ben both like it."

"It's our common language." She pointed toward the door. "Shall we?"

"I have a question."

Brigid put her other arm through her backpack. "What is it?"

Tenzin closed the door and lowered her voice. "Why didn't you tell Oleg that Zasha had offered to end this if you killed me and delivered my head?"

Brigid kept her voice barely over a murmur. "Because he might have believed Zasha and tried to kill you."

"He wouldn't have succeeded."

"Yes, but then we wouldn't be gettin' a quick plane ride to Juneau, would we?" Brigid shrugged. "Besides, Zasha wasn't serious. If they were, they would have told me where to deliver your head."

"I do like that you considered it." Tenzin nodded. "I respect you more because of it."

"Cheers."

"You're welcome."

———

OLEG'S PLANE wasn't nearly as luxurious as Giovanni's, but it did do the job. Tenzin flew herself to the airport outside Seward where she met a frosty and windchilled Brigid before they were loaded into the cargo compartment of the plane that would fly them to Juneau. After that, Brigid would be limited to boats since fire vampires and small planes didn't mix.

Tenzin, of course, could fly.

Benjamin, I am coming to you.

She could feel him in her blood as they moved southeast. He

would be sensing her too. The wind whispered that her mate was closer. His amnis was tied to her, woven through her blood as inextricably as a thread through a tapestry.

I am coming to you.

Tenzin endured the few hours in Oleg's airplane and tried to remember how cold and wet the wind was outside. When they landed, she shot out of the plane and into the air, flying over a deep ocean of forest green. On one side there were trees as far as her eyes could see, and on the other side was the intense deep green of the winter sea threading through the archipelago that covered the northwestern edge of North America.

She took deep breaths of the cold air, filling her lungs and surveying the land below her. There were a few sparks of light, but most of the landscape was a combination of velvet green and endless water chopped with whitecaps from the cold northern wind.

Somewhere in the vast landscape of the Inside Passage, Zasha Sokholov was waiting for her, waiting to take their revenge. Waiting for Tenzin to break her vow.

In the back of her mind, she felt the memory of a delicate bird's wing brush across her cheek. The warm press of humidity in a garden springing to life within a concrete forest.

She heard the whisper of a song overtaken by the bursting crash of glass shattering in flames.

Something delicate and beautiful destroyed for no reason.

Another flower crushed in the grip of careless power.

Zasha, I am coming for you.

CHAPTER EIGHTEEN

B rigid stepped off the plane in Juneau and saw Tenzin shoot out of the plane behind her, disappearing into the blackness as Brigid followed Lev onto the small private runway cloaked in darkness.

"I don't like leaving you here," Lev said. "But I'm not technically supposed to be in Alaska at all."

Brigid narrowed her eyes. "And how long have you been here?"

The big man shrugged. "About fifty or sixty years."

"Yeah, you don't wanna push that." She stuck out her hand. "Nice to work with you, Lev. Cheers to you."

"Oh, I have a name for you." He pulled a wadded paper from his pocket. "The name is Pam. She's a vampire and she knows people."

Brigid took the paper. "Knows people?"

"If you have to move around. Take a boat maybe." He gave her a broad wink. "Call Pam if you need a boat."

"And she works with Oleg?"

"Absolutely not, but sometimes we share a cabin in the

summer." Lev lifted both eyebrows suggestively. "The days get very long here."

"I can see that." She held up the wadded paper. "I'll tell her you're a pal o' mine."

"Oh no." He shook his head. "She might get jealous."

"For real?" She frowned. "I'll be sure to mention that I'm a mated vampire."

"That might help. But really, all Pam cares about is money. Just pay her and she will send a boat for you."

"Got it."

Mika had given Brigid the address to a safe house where they could rest during the day, but she doubted they'd be there more than a night.

"Lev?"

The big man turned back from walking to the cargo plane. "Yes?"

"Where do you think Zasha is?"

He frowned and crossed his giant arms over his chest. "You know, Zasha likes people. I think they will be somewhere where people will pay attention to them."

That was an interesting take. "So no isolated cabin in the woods?"

"Maybe if it's close to a city or a town." He shrugged. "Or maybe not. I'm not the smartest vampire." Lev's voice went quiet. "But I feel sorry for Zasha. Even now. Life was very cruel to them."

"They don't deserve your pity." She hiked her backpack over her shoulder. "I'll see ya around."

"Unless Zasha kills you." Lev sighed. "So in case that happens..." He walked over and threw his massive arms around Brigid's stiff shoulders, hugging her with a hearty embrace and kissing first one cheek, then the other. "It was good to know you,

Brigid Connor. I would like to meet your mate someday. If he comes to avenge your untimely death, I will help him."

"Right." She patted his back. "That's sweet, Lev. Thank you."

"You're welcome. Say goodbye to the small violent wind vampire for me."

"Sure, I will." Brigid turned to walk toward the dim outline of a hangar in the distance, leaving the Russian earth vampires behind her.

She and Tenzin were on their own.

———

WHEN SHE REACHED the safe house, Tenzin was still nowhere to be found, but she pulled out her phone and put a call through to Gavin Wallace, the immortal tech tycoon Lee used to work for.

"Brigid?" He answered her video call after one ring. "Are you with Tenzin?"

"Not at this exact moment because she's flying over Juneau right now." Brigid looked up at the ceiling. "I'm staying at a safe house that Oleg—"

"I'm sending you another address. Are you on a Wi-Fi network?" Gavin snapped his fingers, and someone handed him a pen and paper. "Get off Wi-Fi."

Brigid disconnected from the house Wi-Fi that had connected to her tablet and walked outside, using an insulated hotspot that Lee had engineered for her and Carwyn. "I'm on Lee's network now."

"Always use Lee's network." Gavin scribbled something on the notepad and held it up. "Write it down."

"You think this place is compromised?" She didn't hesitate to set her tablet on the backyard picnic table and write the address

Gavin gave her on the back of a receipt. "Oleg hasn't betrayed us in the past."

"And he might not intend to" —the note disappeared— "but he also might not know who in his organization is vulnerable. Don't use any connections he gave you from now on. I have people in that area."

"You're really pissed off about Tenzin and Ben's apartment, aren't you?"

The Scotsman glowered at the screen. "My wife could have been injured. No matter her associations, Chloe should be off-limits."

Gavin wasn't only a technology entrepreneur—his main business was a network of very exclusive clubs around the world that operated like neutral territory for various immortal factions. Going after Gavin Wallace or any of his people meant that you forfeited the shelter of his businesses and had no safe ground to meet with a rival.

In a world of ancient predators and skilled assassins, having that neutral territory could mean the difference between a peaceful resolution to conflict and outright war. Only a fool or a lunatic would cross Gavin Wallace.

Zasha had crossed him.

"I'll head to your address as soon as we get off the phone."

"Chloe has already sent the address to Tenzin," he said. "She might be there by the time you arrive. Are you hiring cars?"

"Taxis," Brigid said. "Reliable when I can find them."

"As long as they're not electric," Gavin muttered. "Come to think of it, that could be an opportunity."

"Can we talk about your next business another time? Tell me what's happenin' in New York."

"Cleanup," Gavin said. "Chloe is dealing with the insurance. Ben left his uncle on the paperwork for the house, so Giovanni's flying out to deal with it. I told him not to say anything to Ben until Tenzin does. He agreed it was a good idea."

"He loved that place."

Gavin pursed his lips. "Sometimes a house is more than just a house."

"Tenzin is furious."

"She should be. Any leads on Zasha?"

"Henri Paulson," she asked. "Do you know the name?"

Gavin narrowed his eyes. "I do. He's working with Zasha?"

"We're not sure," Brigid said. "Carwyn's convinced there's a connection. He told you to dig. He's maybe under Katya's aegis, maybe not. But she can't find a connection with Zasha. He may just be another victim."

"If there's a connection, I'll find it." Gavin lifted his chin. "I know Paulson a little." He frowned. "He approached me a few years ago—this was some time after the Ankers took Chloe. He had heard I was looking for investors."

"For the computer things?"

Gavin covered his face. "Thank God you have Lee working for you. Yes, the 'computer things.' That's how Paulson's made most of his money in the past hundred years. Telegraph. Radio. Then computers. He's brilliant and ferociously private, but he saw an opportunity. He wanted to invest, but I didn't need the money and I didn't want the tie."

"Why not?" It sounded like Gavin had opinions on this vampire.

"Paulson has always been a bit of a fringe thinker. I'm not surprised he ended up in Alaska."

"Describe fringe when it comes to vampires." Brigid tapped her fingers on the table. "It's not as if we're a mainstream crowd."

"Yes, but most of us don't believe in the destruction of modern human civilization and a return of vampire empires." Gavin raised an eyebrow. "That's Paulson."

It took a lot to surprise her these days, but that was a surprise. "What the feck?"

"Paulson isn't old, but he is old-school. He's one of those vampires who gets very nostalgic for the era when humans were peasants scraping for survival under kings, warlords, and emperors."

"Because it was easier to hunt them?" Dear God, and she thought Zasha was a problem.

"I suspect Henri Paulson hunts as much as he wants, but he's quiet about it. Doesn't make waves, so to speak. But he doesn't care about humans, he cares about wealth, and it was far easier for his kind to accumulate wealth when you only had to curry favor with a few powerful men—and it was almost always men. He hates women. He considers humans like cattle. And he's a snob. He sires no children because he doesn't want to share his wealth, and I doubt he'd ever find a human up to his standards."

"What a charmer." She stared up at the dense, cloud-covered night sky. "He and Zasha sound like a match made in heaven."

"I don't know. Zasha isn't Paulson's usual style—he's usually very quiet—but if Zasha had something on him?" Gavin shrugged. "Maybe."

"What could Zasha have on Paulson?"

"I have no idea, it was just a thought," Gavin said. "He might have made some concessions, exchanged favors if it was convenient or profitable. Paulson doesn't have a conscience that would get in the way."

"Understood." She leaned her arm on the table. "Can ya find him?"

"Paulson? Doubtful. He only lives on boats." Gavin smirked. "I might be able to find some of his money. It would give the children something to do."

"The children" were Gavin's small army of brilliant computer programmers and hackers.

"See if they can help." Brigid glanced at the dark forest behind the house. "I want to leave now. I'll send a message when I'm at your place. I'm startin' to see assassins behind every tree lately."

"I don't blame you," he said. "I'll see what I can find on Paulson's assets and let you know. Send Chloe a message when you and Tenzin are safe."

———

BY THE TIME Brigid reached the nondescript wood-sided house in a small residential tract near Mendenhall Lake, it was still dark, but it was well past six in the morning and she was getting tired. She noticed the open door off the upstairs deck before she entered the house with the code Chloe had texted her.

Her gun was out before she walked in. "Tenzin?"

"I'm upstairs. Put that thing away."

Brigid kept her 9mm out just to be contrary. Also, she liked the weight of it in her palm. She closed the door, fastened the dead bolt, and took off her jacket, hanging it by the door before she tossed her backpack in an overstuffed chair.

"The bedrooms are in the basement," Brigid said as she climbed the stairs.

"I know." Tenzin's voice sounded hollow. "I want Benjamin."

Brigid stood in the doorway where Tenzin had set her tablet on a desk. The door to the deck was open, and the bedroom was frigid. The picture on the tablet was a picture of two brightly colored birds.

"I didn't know ye had pets." Brigid walked over and closed the door as rain started to fall.

"They were at the house in New York."

Damn. "I'm sorry, Tenzin."

"They were old, but they should have lived at least a few more years." Tenzin stared at the picture.

"It's shite." Brigid sat on the edge of the bed.

"It's my fault they're dead."

Part of Brigid wanted to console her, but Tenzin was correct. The birds were sad collateral damage in a fight that Tenzin had willingly entered.

"You made their lives beautiful while they lived," Brigid said. "That's all we can do for delicate things."

Tenzin glanced at her. "Thank you."

"For what?"

"For not trying to tell me it wasn't my fault. Ben would have tried to make me feel it less."

"He woulda tried to make the feelings *softer*, not less," Brigid said. "Cos no one did that for him when he was young."

Tenzin swiped the picture of the birds to the side, and a picture of Ben appeared. It must have been taken when Ben was human because he was lying in the sun, smiling at whoever was behind the camera. His beard was half grown in, and hair was falling in his eyes. He looked like he was about twenty-one or twenty-two.

Older than Tenzin looked. As old as she was, Ben physically looked older and had for years.

Tenzin stared at the photograph. "Sometimes I think I do not know him at all. And other times I think I have always known him."

Brigid stared at Tenzin. She'd known Ben before he mated Tenzin, but she'd never known a Ben without Tenzin in his life. She had a hard time separating the two of them in her mind. As opposite as they were, they were two sides of the same coin.

"If you want to call him, you should," Brigid said. "I don't think we can do this without him and Carwyn."

"I don't want to call him." Tenzin stared at the sun-washed picture. "I want to send him far away so I can dispose of this weight hanging around my neck. Then I want to build him a beautiful house and fill a garden with birds and flowers so he can remember the sunlight."

Brigid's heart ached at the longing in her words. "That's a beautiful thought."

"But he won't let me do it." She turned, and she was frowning. "He would be angry if I did that."

"Because he loves you, and he wants to protect you."

"I am nothing compared to him." Tenzin shook her head. "I have never understood why he doesn't see that."

Brigid stood. "Maybe ya need to realize that the way you see Ben might just be the way he sees you."

The corner of Tenzin's mouth ticked up. "He is beautiful, and I am a blade in the night."

"Yes. But Ben doesn't see the blood on that blade." Brigid walked to the door. "He only sees the polished edge flashing." She smiled a little bit. "And he thinks it's beautiful."

Tenzin stared at Brigid with an unrelenting focus. "You deserve better than the hulking earth vampire."

Brigid lifted her Hellcat and tucked it into the discreet holster at her waist. "Insult him again, Tenzin, and I'll shoot you someplace more painful than your leg."

CHAPTER NINETEEN

"Here." Buck pointed at a map spread on the scarred coffee table. "One of Jennie's people spotted one of Paulson's unregistered vessels here." He placed a yellow pin in the middle of a cluster of islands near the mouth of a river north of Ketchikan.

Spread on the table before Carwyn was a large map of the Inside Passage, the patchwork of islands, sea, peninsulas, and river deltas that made up the stretch of coast that started at the Puget Sound and stretched north into the lower reach of Alaska.

Carwyn leaned closer and peered at the area where Buck was pointing. "Do we know why one of his ships is in this location?"

"No more than we know why any of his ships are anywhere. It's probably one of those... need-to-know kind of things."

Ben asked, "Do you know who's on it?"

"Nah. It's a bigger ship." Buck shook his head. "Converted cargo barge, probably used to move timber. It'll be looking to avoid the weather in that area." He put two more pins in other locations. "And these are the last known of two of his other vessels, a fishing boat and a yacht. Trying to track down exact locations right now with Jeb's help. He's docked in Sitka at the moment, but he's been on the radio all night, asking around."

The straits and islands that made up the Inside Passage were a common route for sea vessels of all kinds. Because the channels were deep, they allowed shipping vessels and cruise ships to avoid winter storms, but even in a heavily traveled region, it was still... a very big ocean.

Ben had his arms crossed over his chest, and he was staring at the map next to Carwyn. "Any other vessels we can confirm belong to Paulson?"

"Katya's sending a list," Buck said, "but it won't be complete. I know of at least two vessels he staffed with Russians and Asians. They're ghost ships. Don't dock anywhere. They stay at sea pretty much constantly. Use other ships to refuel, don't ever come into port."

Ben looked at Carwyn. "Those would be the caravan ships?"

"Possibly." Carwyn nodded. "But it's important to remember we don't know that Zasha is working with Paulson or if Paulson is a victim. Remember, the crew on board his ships that we know of haven't been seen by their loved ones in months. If Paulson was cooperating willingly, I suspect he wouldn't want to raise suspicions like that."

"Very true," Buck said. "Katya pointed that out too. As of right now, we're treating Paulson like a victim."

"Victim or ally, we need to find him," Ben said. "If for no other reason than we know he talked to Zasha."

Carwyn sat back and tried to put the puzzle together in his mind.

One vampire antagonist with no conscience, an ultra-private immortal billionaire, and a fleet of ghost ships in a vast, cold ocean. Couple that with seemingly random attacks on vampire compounds in isolated locations, two territorial leaders with deep suspicion toward each other, and Carwyn could see a larger situation with the potential to explode.

"Are we not thinking big enough?" Carwyn looked at the

two men with him, both of whom were far younger than he was. "Fleets of ships that aren't used for business are historically used for two things—conquest or exploration preceding conquest."

Ben frowned. "But Katya said that Paulson uses them for safe houses, like the sea-steading thing."

"Sea-steading is limited. Maybe it's not enough for him anymore." Carwyn unfolded the map on the table and spread it out to include the entirety of the Alaskan Peninsula and the Arctic Sea beyond it. "The planet is getting warmer—every vampire who's lived over a century can feel the difference."

"Hell," Buck said. "I'm in my fifties and I can see a difference in the ice."

"Paulson likes money." Carwyn tapped the sea ice around the North Pole. "So maybe he's looking for his next investment."

"In... ice?" Buck frowned. "Melting ice for that matter?"

Carwyn stared at the map. "Melting ice is exactly the point."

Buck leaned one arm on the table and narrowed his eyes. "You're talking about the Northwest Passage, aren't you?"

"The Northwest Passage?" Ben asked.

Carwyn ignored the young one and looked at the older man. "I'm talking about a very lightly controlled area of the vampire world" —he spread his hand over the map, concentrating on the blue water— "that could become a major shipping region over the next century. Paulson didn't make a fortune without thinking ahead. He might be betting that this area will be a gold mine in the very near future."

"I don't know about that." Buck shrugged. "But I know Katya is watching the Russian for that exact reason."

"Oleg?" Ben asked.

Carwyn closed his eyes. "Oleg and Zasha are not working together."

"Same sire," Buck said.

"Oleg's not a sociopath. This was his territory for centuries; it's not exactly unexpected that he would—"

"You on his side or something?" Buck asked.

"I don't take sides in—"

"Can someone explain this to me?" Ben interrupted them. "What's the Northwest Passage?"

"A shipping lane." Carwyn dragged his finger across the edge of the Arctic Sea north of Asia. "And potentially a gold mine. Europe to Asia through the warming Arctic Ocean instead of going through the Panama or the Suez Canals. It would cut the shipping time of goods and the fuel used by a huge margin."

"People have been speculating about it for years," Buck said. "Hell, explorers died tryin' to find it back in the day. Katya knows that Oleg has his eye on it."

"I'm sure he does, but that doesn't mean he's working with Zasha," Carwyn said.

Buck leaned on the table. "There'll be a conflict eventually, or some kind of settled agreement. I imagine Katya's gonna depend on the Athabaskan Confederation preferring stability over Oleg."

"Why?" Carwyn asked. "They're interior. We're talking about water."

Buck looked stumped. "I don't know. I guess I always assumed—"

"You're thinking like a human." Carwyn stared at the map. "Because you are one, so of course you are. But we're vampires. What happens on the water and what happens on land are very different things. The Athabaskans won't be consulted if water vampires go to war."

"That's what Zasha wants then?" Ben frowned. "War? I don't see them as a general for anyone to command."

"And we don't know that Paulson is involved in any of this." Buck pointed back at the yellow pins. "For all we know, he's another victim like these vampire compounds along the coast."

"One way to find out." Ben looked at the map. "I think it's a good idea to pay this barge a visit."

"You're right." Carwyn glanced at Ben. "I don't think it's smart for you to go without backup."

"Five hours by boat," Buck said. "And that's making good time if the weather holds steady."

Ben crossed his arms and looked at Buck. "Can you get Carwyn in a boat during the day? That'll put him up there right about nightfall, right?"

"Not a bad idea." Buck nodded. "Carwyn?"

"More boats," he muttered. "I'll do it." He glared at Ben. "Only time in my life I've wished I could fly."

———

CARWYN CLIMBED out from the ship's hold and into the small enclosed bridge just in time to see faint lights in the distance through the rain-dotted windows beyond the control panel of the fishing boat. An old man in a dark blue sweater and a ragged base-ball cap sat in a bouncing chair behind a cracked helm in the center of the sealed compartment.

"Evening." The old man pointed over his shoulder. "There's some blood in that fridge if you're hungry. I am not on the menu."

Carwyn smiled. "I hunted before we left this morning, but thank you." He looked around the compartment. "Are we close?"

"Almost there. Name's Clovis, and I don't need to know yours."

"Understood."

"Your friend meeting us?"

Carwyn peered out into the dark, overcast night. "He's flying. Said it would only take an hour or so after dusk."

The captain nodded. "I'll put the lights on then. Give him a place to land if he's coming from above." The wiry human captain glanced over his shoulder. "Ain't really a place for earth types. Kinda surprised to see one of you this far out."

"I'm not with the Athabaskans." Carwyn reached out to balance himself as the boat hit a rough spot. "I'm from Wales."

"Eh yup." The man nodded. "You'll see them out here too."

Carwyn blinked. "Athabaskan vampires?"

"Nah, whales."

Right. Carwyn nodded and gave the man a smile. "Well, I thank you for the lift. Buck said you know these waters much better than he does."

"I been around a while, but Jennie calls the shots in my world. She tells me to take one of you boys where you need to go, I don't ask questions."

Carwyn looked at the darkness all around him. He could barely make out the dim outline of islands rising up out of the water, covered in dense trees, but there was no moon and no stars reflected on the water. The sun had only been down for half an hour, but it was already pitch-black.

"We're not sure what we're looking for," he warned the old man. "It might be a while."

"No worries. I got a book with me. Take all the time you need. You got about sixteen hours before the sun comes up, so plenty of time to go exploring." He nodded at the glowing panels in front of him. "I pick up anything on the radar, I'll let you know."

"Hopefully once my friend gets here, he can give you directions."

"I gotta say, I don't envy the blood-drinking thing, but that vampire night vision would sure come in handy."

"You're not wrong, Clovis." Carwyn settled into a bench seat to wait for Ben.

No more than half an hour later, he heard a thump on the back of the boat. When he looked out the back window, he saw

Ben's tall figure dressed in black, crouched on the deck and clearly trying to find his balance.

Clovis smiled. "Wind vampires hate small boats."

"Lucky they don't have to take them often." Carwyn threw a yellow slicker over his shoulders and walked out of the enclosed compartment. "You're here."

The young vampire straightened. "I saw the barge coming in. If he takes the boat toward the shore and around this island here" —Ben pointed to the right— "it's in a cove."

"I'll tell him."

Carwyn poked his head into the bridge and said, "Around the island and to the right. There's a cove?"

Clovis nodded. "Eh-yup. I know the place." The old man walked out on the deck and flashed a lantern toward the shore. "Just callin' Gus."

"Gus?"

The human frowned at Carwyn. "You didn't think I was gonna take this big thing close into that barge, did you? You want eyes on that boat, you need a water vampire. Jennie said to call Gus."

Carwyn had to assume that Gus was one of Katya's people too if Jennie said to call him.

A few moments later, a flash from the shore came back, and Clovis headed back to the bridge. "He'll bring 'er around."

"Good." Carwyn didn't know what was happening, but he was going to follow the old human's lead.

They rounded the cove as the rain poured down, and Clovis shut off the lights as he approached the turn where the land met the water.

"I'll fly over," Ben said. "Go lower and scope things out."

"Good."

Clovis nodded. "And we'll wait for Gus."

Carwyn walked out to the bow of the ship and waited in the

darkness as Ben took off into the night. He saw the vampire circle the barge, which was lit with dim blue lights along the deck. There were three lights glowing from portholes, and the faint sound of music drifted across the surface of the water.

He squinted through the rain and watched Ben fly lower. "What are you seeing, boy?"

———

BEN WAS FREEZING COLD, but he didn't let it distract him from surveying the converted barge. The deck was flat and broad and had to be at least a hundred and fifty feet long. It had been altered from its original job as an industrial vessel to a pleasure craft with attractively lit walkways, raised container gardens bursting with evergreen plants, line-fishing stations, and freshly painted storage containers that must have been the cabins.

Near the bow, a cedar-sided sauna pumped steam through a round chimney; in the center, what looked like an outdoor kitchen sat cold and lifeless under a large cover. On the other end, opposite the sauna, five steel containers sat on the deck, not a window visible from the outside but each bearing outdoor stairs that led to a wood deck atop the industrial-chic cabins.

Ben didn't want to get too close in case someone was watching, so he flew at a distance, waiting to see any sign of life. But though there were lights on and Ben could hear music, there was no movement atop the barge.

He flew to the shelter of a nearby cedar that hugged the edge of the cove and sat to wait in silence. The faint sounds that emerged from the vessel gave no indication of anything other than general habitation. He could smell food cooking, but that could mean either human or vampire inhabitants.

Henri Paulson had bought this barge from a salvage ten years ago, renamed it the Sea King Alpha, and then it had disappeared from all commercial enterprise, at least officially. Unofficially, Katya suspected that this boat was one of Paulson's shadow fleet of sea havens for vampires who wanted to disappear from modern life.

Disappear in luxury, of course.

Ben heard movement in the forest behind him, but when he turned, all he could see was the head of a bright red fox popping out from behind a fallen, moss-covered log.

The fox ducked down, spooked by something to Ben's left.

When he followed the animal's gaze, he saw her.

Perched in a pine tree and cloaked in black with her hair covered in what looked like a balaclava, her storm-grey eyes watched him across the lush green expanse.

Tenzin.

Ben blinked, and in the space of a heartbeat, she disappeared.

Without a word, he pushed off from the cedar, ignoring the crack of the branch beneath his feet, and took to the air in pursuit.

CHAPTER TWENTY

It was her own fault for tracking him. The lure of his amnis had been too much to bear at nightfall. She knew he was close, and she allowed herself to take flight, her blood drawing her to him like the proverbial moth to a flame.

And just like a flame, his anger was burning.

She could feel it as he pursued her. In proximity, she could feel the desperation, longing, and pure rage in his blood.

He chased her, and the dark, competitive part of Tenzin reveled in it.

She darted through the treetops, leading her mate on a wild chase in the dark shadows laden with the heavy scent of rain and animal musk.

A crashing sound followed her, and she knew he was breaking tree branches in his pursuit. He was bigger than her, his shoulders wider, and his amnis a broadsword instead of a rapier.

She turned in midair, twisting around a moss-laden outcropping of rock to swiftly change direction, leading Ben away from the water and into the dense forest that blanketed the Alaskan coast. She flew over rushing creeks, dipping low over the water to hide her scent, knowing that it was ultimately useless. At this proximity, her mate's pursuit would only be stopped by daylight or violence.

You want him.

She did want him.

Fly!

Instinct was her enemy, driving her away from him and deeper into the forest.

In the distance, she heard a faint roar that could have been an animal or Ben's frustration.

She twisted up a threaded river that led to the sea, flying low over the gravel riverbed as the scent of salt gave way to moss and granite and churning, mineral-laden air.

There was a bear waking in the forest nearby, and the heavy musk of its scent hit her nose as she passed.

Tenzin was just passing a tumble of granite rocks when she felt it.

A creeping sense of ribbons around her ankle, airy threads of Ben's amnis that slid up her leg, twisting and wrapping around her left leg, then her right.

One day you will be infinite.

Her fangs fell at the challenge.

His amnis was powerful—it would be more powerful than hers with time. He'd been born of an ancient whose amnis had not thinned in thousands of years. He was swimming in Zhang's ancient power, mated to her blood, and had been raised by a vampire assassin.

Heat churned through her veins as she felt him grow closer. He was using their connection to draw her in, gaining ground as she flew up the riverbed.

She didn't want to lose him; she wanted to fight.

Tenzin flipped in midair, spiraling upward and into the night, breaking through low-lying clouds, and she felt his grip on her ankles falter.

He followed her, bursting through the clouds with rage-fueled speed.

"Tenzin!" He roared her name.

She spun around, baring her fangs with a satisfied smile as she spread her arms and let the wind take her higher.

The air lifted her outstretched arms and whipped her hair around her face as she thrust her hands forward, bashing her mate with a wall of elemental energy.

Ben wasn't expecting the sudden turn. He flipped end over end, tumbling back toward the earth.

Tenzin's chest was pounding. It was the most her blood had moved in centuries, and the thrill of it lit her from within even as Ben righted himself and arrowed toward her. He reached out an arm, grabbed for the wind around her, and yanked.

She felt his amnis wrap around her and shove her downward as Ben flew upward.

He was on her in seconds, wrapping a fist around her hair and pulling her mouth to his.

His fangs cut her lips when they came crashing down, and she drank in their mingled blood, sucking hard on his tongue as Ben's hand continued to grip her hair as the other ripped away the cloth that had covered her face to shield it from the tearing wind.

They were a tangle of arms, legs, fangs, and amnis as they plummeted to the earth.

Tenzin let herself fall.

At the last minute, Ben's power wrapped around them both and lifted them back into the clouds, past the rain, and into the light of the nearly full moon.

"Damn you," he hissed as he sank his fangs into her neck.

She threw her head back and held his head to her neck, her own fangs aching to pierce his skin. She ripped at the heavy clothes covering his body and keeping his skin from her own. She could feel him, already hard and ready against her thigh, his arousal piqued by his pursuit.

"Why did you run?" He growled. "Why do you always run?"

"Because you chase," she whispered into his ear as he bit her again, bruising her skin and leaving marks she didn't want him to heal. "And in the whole of my life, you're the only one I ever wanted to catch me."

He froze in her arms, but the wind around them spun like a tornado.

"Damn you." He pressed his cheek to hers. "Why do you do this to me?"

Because you love it. She didn't say it. She didn't need to. She turned in his arms, yanked his neck to the side, and sank her teeth into his flesh.

Tenzin felt him grow harder against her thigh. His erection was straining against his clothes, and her body was ready for him. He scented her arousal and ripped at her leggings, tearing them down her body and letting the wind take them away.

Ben rolled over, lying on his back in a cushion of air as he freed his erection and pulled her onto his body. She braced herself on his shoulders and sank to the hilt, her eyes rolling back at the pleasure of their joining.

His heavy canvas pants rasped against the sensitive skin of her inner thighs, but the wind obeyed him, pressing around them like a cocoon that felt as solid as the earth.

His blood coursed in her body, his erection invaded her. Tenzin was full of him, and in the safety of his arms and their element, she allowed her mind to go blank. Her body was full of the pleasure of their joining and their amnis finally together after weeks of aching need.

Ben pulled her down to his chest and took her mouth in a bruising kiss, his hand still gripping her hair. She felt a sharp tug of pain at her nape, but it only fueled her desire.

She reached down, dug her fingers into his buttocks, and pulled him into her body, driving her nails into his flesh.

He hissed and arched his hips upward.

Their bodies joined and held by the wind, she rode him over the clouds, her gasps snatched away by the frigid winter air that curled around them.

His amnis kept her warm, and moments later she felt the roaring climax barreling toward her, shaking her body and shattering her from the inside out.

He felt her break apart and followed, one hand still gripping her hair and the other gentle at her hip, coaxing her through a release with skillful, teasing fingers that knew her body better than hers.

When he came, the air around them exploded outward, and they dropped for five long seconds before she bundled the wind with tender whispers and it held them aloft again.

They came to rest on a rocky outcropping that overlooked the threaded river, and when Ben's eyes opened again, they were still furious. Sated but furious.

"You left." He sat up, holding her to his body and keeping her captive with his embrace.

———

HER STORM-GREY EYES were nothing but curious. "Are you still erect?"

"You *left*." Ben was enraged, turned on again, and relaxed, all at the same time.

Being a mated vampire could be really confusing.

His amnis didn't know he was angry, it only knew that his mate was in his arms and they'd exchanged blood. She was on him, her body wrapped around his erection like a glove, and that glove fit so well his body never wanted to leave. In fact, it was ready to go again, weeks of frustration forgotten in the heat and pleasure of sex.

"You found me," she said, as if it was the most obvious thing in the world. "I knew you would. You could have found me weeks ago."

"That's not the point, Tenzin."

She leaned forward, her hands braced on his shoulders, and her kiss was a soft, drugging seduction. "What is the point?"

"You…" He kissed her back; it was impossible to resist. His blood was pumping, and his body was primed. "Fuck me now." He wrapped an arm around her waist, flipped them over, and started moving in her again. "Talk later."

———

HE LAY ON THE GROUND, the sharp rocks digging into his back, and he didn't care. He didn't care about any of it. They were sheltered in a depression, warded from the wind and rain by the stones and his amnis.

Tenzin was curled into his side like a cat, and he'd come twice more before his body had been ready to take a break and he could think clearly again.

His voice was a low growl when he could finally speak. "It's not that you left, it's that you left without telling me."

"I've done that many times."

That was true. Except…

"Not since we've mated," Ben said, trying to appeal to her logic. "Our amnis is joined now, and doubly so because we're of the same element. When you're not there, Tenzin…"

It hurts.

He didn't want to say it, but it was the truth. Behind the anger and the rage and the frustration, he was hurt. It hurt to be away from her.

She propped her head up on his chest and looked at him. "We're not as effective apart as we are together."

"Exactly." Let her think it was a battle strategy if it kept her close. "And honestly, we're coming at the same problem from two different places, and we might be more effective if we joined our efforts and—"

"Or we might be less effective if Zasha only has one target instead of two."

He put his hand on her head and forced her eyes to his. "What did you do to Zasha? Why do they hate you so much? I want to hear it from you."

She narrowed her eyes. "Sometimes I don't like how smart you are."

"Too bad."

She stared at the rock over his shoulder. "I don't want to tell you what I did because I think you'll judge me."

"So?"

She blinked and looked at him. "So you *will* judge me?"

"Of course I will. And you should trust my judgment more than anyone else's because I love you more than life or eternity, and I will judge you and still love you at the same time."

Tenzin stared at him for a long time, not saying a word.

"Blood of my blood." He kept his voice soft. "You are my mate and my destiny. Tell me what you did to make Zasha so angry."

"I let her live after I killed her mate." Tenzin frowned. "They were living as a woman then, so the picture in my mind is feminine."

"Vampires go back and forth," Ben said. "That's not the important part."

"Zasha's mate said she had no one but him," Tenzin said. "And I killed him."

"Because he was part of Zhang's bloodline. The blood of Temur."

Tenzin's eyes flew to his. "I told you I didn't want you—"

"You have a reputation in our world, Tiny. I didn't have to guess much." Ben had learned a lot, but he needed to let Tenzin know that her secrets were not as secret as she thought. "The Scourge of the Naiman Khanlig. Did you think I wouldn't hear the stories just because you didn't tell them?" He played with a strand of her hair. "You didn't recognize them in Louisiana?"

Tenzin sat back. "I didn't remember Zasha for a long time. I didn't connect the woman I left in a cabin in Siberia hundreds of years ago with the sociopath who was tormenting Brigid and wreaking havoc for no reason."

"But Zasha remembered you."

"Yes." She looked over the rainy landscape that spread before them. "Their mate was the last of Temur's line."

Ben whispered, "The blood of Temur remembers who you were."

"He'd been living quietly, but I found them in a house in Siberia. He had been taking humans from the village to feed her, so stories started to circulate. I tracked them down eventually and killed him. When I did that, I promised him I would let Zasha live."

"So this vampire was hunting humans to feed his mate instead of teaching Zasha to feed quietly," Ben said. "You killed him and let Zasha live. Where is the guilt coming from? Neither of these two were innocent, Tenzin."

"I don't feel guilt."

"Don't you?"

"It's not guilt." She frowned. "I... recognized her. I could tell the woman I saw had not had an easy life. I didn't want to kill her for surviving the only way she knew how."

"Okay, but that's bullshit," Ben said. "You said this guy— Temur's descendant—had been living quietly for centuries. So if

Zasha hadn't come along, you probably never would have found him."

Tenzin blinked. "What are you trying to say?"

"I'm saying that whether you realize it or not, you have been feeling guilt about killing Zasha's mate. But he wasn't an innocent, Tenzin. They were killing humans long before you found them. They were probably taking the most vulnerable people they could find and then feeding on them and throwing them away."

She looked at him but didn't speak.

Ben started to feel her stare like she was drilling into his brain. "What?"

"Should I have let Zasha live after I killed their mate?"

Ben drew his head back. "I'm not your conscience, Tenzin."

"You should be. You're better at it than I am."

Ben took a deep breath. "You want to evolve, right? New Year's resolutions? You can grow a conscience again. You already have a moral code."

It was shaky and prone to flexibility, but she did have a code.

"Yes." Tenzin nodded. "But I also think my conscience was broken long ago while yours was not. You are a better judge of these things."

"I don't think that's a good idea. I think—"

"It's an excellent idea." She leaned forward and repeated her question. "Should I have let Zasha live after I killed their mate?"

Ben cocked his head to the side. "Were they stealing people, feeding on them, and killing them?"

"Yes."

As a human, Ben had never believed in capital punishment. He thought it was useless and outdated. But vampires couldn't be kept in prisons for the rest of their life.

Vampires needed to *fear* doing evil. They were predators who fed on the innocent because they were easy. Vampire killers had to be stopped, and usually the only way to do that was by executing them.

"Yes." His voice was firm. "You should have killed both of them, Tenzin. If you feel guilty about anything, it should be letting Zasha roam free for centuries."

She nodded. "See? You're much better at this than I am."

"Are you going to kill Zasha now?"

"It would be better if Brigid killed them," Tenzin muttered. "But if the chance comes, I won't pass it up."

CHAPTER TWENTY-ONE

C arwyn heard something rustle and break in the forest, as if a tree had fallen, but before he could ask Clovis if the old man had heard the same thing, he heard a soft whistle from the port side of the boat.

He looked over the edge to see what looked like a young man with the unmistakable energy of a water vampire, standing in a long canoe that curved up at the bow. It was smooth and silent in the choppy water, as if the vampire in the boat was holding the water still with his presence.

He stood at medium height, his legs spread wide in the belly of the canoe, a slick leather cape hanging over his shoulders. His hair was buzz-cut, and his cheekbones were high, his face showing the planes typical of Native humans in the area.

"Hey, Clovis."

The old man nodded. "Ey-ah, Gus. This is the one Jennie was talkin' about."

Gus shifted his eyes to Carwyn. "You the digger who found our elder?"

"If you're talking about the old one who was injured, I am."

"Cool." Gus nodded. "Happy to help you out. You good on boats? Most of your kind ain't."

"It's not my favorite form of travel." He glanced at the rocking canoe no wider than a Volkswagen Beetle. "But I'll manage."

"I'll keep the boat easy," Gus said. "Head over to the stern and Clovis has a ladder."

Without a sound, Gus crouched down, stuck his hand in the water, and the canoe began to move to the back of the boat.

He might have looked young, but the vampire's amnis was strong.

"Good luck." Clovis slapped Carwyn's shoulder. "You want a life vest before you get in there?"

"I can't drown."

"Nah, but it's plenty cold if you sink to the bottom." Clovis's grin showed two missing teeth. "Anyway, Gus'll take care of yeh."

Carwyn climbed down to the canoe, surprised by how steady it was under his feet. Gus was waiting in the middle of the vessel and quickly directed him to a broad bench a little forward of center.

"You're heavy," Gus said. "That's good. Nothin' worse than light cargo in winter water."

"Glad to help." He turned to look at the distant blue lights of the converted barge. "Have you seen this boat before?"

"Here and there." Gus stuck his hand in the water again, and the boat started moving as if propelled by unseen oars. "I keep to myself though. Don't want anything to do with the Russians."

"This boat is owned by a Danish vampire."

"Russian," Gus muttered. "Dane. American. Whatever." He shrugged. "Not our people."

Carwyn was curious. "Do you mind? Katya's the regional power here, and she's Russian."

The corner of his mouth turned up. "Katya deals with the Americans and the Russians. She's good at paperwork."

"And she leaves you and Jennie and the rest of the vampires up here alone."

He nodded. "Exactly."

"What about Oleg?"

"Eh, most Russians aren't too bad," Gus said. "Don't like hearing about that elder though."

"There might be rumors that Oleg's people are responsible for that, but I don't think that's right." Carwyn leaned to the right to look around the bow. "For what it's worth."

"You're old," Gus said. "I can tell. You probably know some stuff."

The canoe approached the barge, and as Gus and Carwyn stopped talking, the heavy weight of silence fell over them. The wind hushed through the trees and the slow creak of the forest occasionally broke through the night, but the only sounds of humanity came from the long barge with the three glowing portholes.

Carwyn glanced back at Gus, but the vampire said nothing, piloting the vessel close and silent around the flat ship tucked back in the cove.

Where was Ben?

Carwyn listened for voices, but they were speaking rapidly in accents that weren't familiar. Occasionally a snippet would break through.

"...thinks we don't know."

"...the plan? Because from what I've heard..."

"...the point. Nothing is clear and that's where—"

"Do you hear something?"

Carwyn held his breath, and Gus pulled his hand from the water, letting the canoe drift.

"...nothing. Probably crew."

"You're right... human..."

He let out his breath.

"...desperate for some new blood."

"Unless you want to go on a shore excursion with—"

"Absolutely not. Those Neanderthals..." More words lost to a gust of wind. "...don't need that kind of..."

"I feel the same way. ...just want to live my eternity in peace and not have to hide."

"The hiding is *exhausting*."

The last answer was spoken in a voice that told Carwyn the speaker had never been truly exhausted in her life. He thought it was two women, but he couldn't be sure.

"Hey," Gus whispered to Carwyn. "Gonna take us up the side unless you want to stay here."

"No, let's go around." Carwyn was curious to find out who else was on the boat. There were two female vampires from what he could glean from the previous conversation. Were there other vampires too? And where the hell was Ben?

Gus gave Carwyn a low grunt as they approached another set of lit portholes. This time there was more sound of equipment and business than voices. Someone was washing dishes, and another voice was shouting orders at what sounded like servers.

"—grab that tray. Number three is going to want that blood fresh or she'll..."

"Yes, Chef."

Chef, huh? Of course Henri Paulson's vampire safe havens had professional chefs on board. What would hiding from humans be without human servants?

It was one of the chief ironies of immortal life that most vampires considered themselves superior to human beings, but they could not survive without them. It grated on every vampire Carwyn knew, either because they hated having to hunt humans for blood—like his wife—or they hated being dependent on something they considered inferior, which was most of the rest of the immortal world.

Humans provided their chief sustenance, took care of their daily needs, staffed their homes during the day, ran errands and did tasks that vampires couldn't do because they happened during daylight.

Humans didn't *need* vampires. A good case could be made that vampires offered them nothing of value and their lives would be better if the last bloodsucker died out.

But vampires? Vampires were nothing without humans.

"Sounds like the staff quarters," Gus muttered. "I hear at least half a dozen."

Carwyn wondered if any of that staff were from the *Flying Dolphin*, the missing yacht that had belonged to Henri Paulson.

"On a boat this large, how many crew members would you need?" Carwyn asked.

Gus looked up and down the barge. "Depends on how many passengers. To just pilot the thing? Not that many. You could get by with two or three. But this is a passenger ship now. And passengers need crew."

"Take it around," Carwyn said. "I want to see if I can get on deck."

Gus's eyebrows went up. "You sure about that?"

"Those two vampires we heard didn't know what 'the plan' was," Carwyn said. "I want to see if I have better luck figuring it out."

———

THEY FOUND a ladder on the far side of the barge, metal rungs welded to the body of the ship. Carwyn put his finger to his lips and turned to Gus, who nodded and waited for Carwyn to climb the first rung before he drifted the canoe away from the barge.

The water in the cove was calm, but the wind tugged at his

clothes, making climbing a challenge. Luckily the ship and the rungs were metal, which had always liked Carwyn.

His elemental energy had always gotten along well with metal. Raw metal in the earth loved him, and even forged and manufactured metal appreciated his touch.

He clung to the side of the ship, crawling up the rungs until he was just under the deck. He paused, waiting for any voices to pass by, but he heard nothing.

Carwyn's size belied his swiftness. He swung his legs up and heaved his body onto the deck of the barge, immediately crouching down to lower his profile. If any guards were watching, he didn't want to raise alarms.

Fortunately, the only guard he could see was on the far side of the deck near what looked like an outdoor kitchen covered by a metal shade.

He scanned the deck of the barge, his eyes sweeping from the tip of the ship where it looked like someone was fishing to a wood-clad building in the middle of the deck with steam pouring from the top.

A sauna? Interesting.

To the right, he saw five containers that all looked like they were wearing a fresh coat of paint. There were lit walkways that led from one to the next, raised containers spilling over with plants in the winter, which meant they had to be heated. The air was full of the scent of pine, not from the forest around them but from strategically placed stations along the walkways that pumped fragrance into the environment.

It was as luxurious as a five-star hotel, but it was floating.

Carwyn walked quickly and silently toward the containers, curious if they were what he thought. He put his ear to one and heard movement, so he quickly moved to the next.

Two vampires in the stern of the ship, one in a container. That was three at least.

He glanced at the door and saw that each of the containers was numbered.

Number three is going to want that blood fresh...

The memory of the chef's barking voice matched the number on the container where someone was stirring.

Carwyn moved to container five, the last of the containers that was sitting at the back of the deck. He put his ear to the side, listening for movement.

Nothing.

Trying the door, he discovered it was locked, but he twisted his wrist to the side with a sharp crack and the knob came loose, dangling on the freshly painted door. He pushed his fingers inside the lock mechanism and pulled the pieces out, crushing them in his hand before he tossed them overboard.

Carwyn pushed the door in and blinked, waiting for his eyes to adjust to the pitch-darkness There was a lamp near the door, and he reached for it, closing the door before he switched it on.

A low light filled the container, and Carwyn could see exactly why the chef had been barking orders.

While they were industrial on the outside, these containers had been converted into luxuriously appointed small apartments, complete with a living area, a kitchenette and bar, and a door at the back that likely led to another reinforced sleeping compartment for daytime.

Carwyn walked to a marble-topped desk in the corner to pick up a gold-leaf piece of stationery with an engraved elephant at the top of the page, painted in sky blue. The name Henri Paulson was written at the top, and under that name was a single line.

Welcome to Blå Havn, the beginning of a new world.

"A new world, eh?" He flipped over the page, but there was nothing else. There was, however, a leather portfolio sitting to the right, and when he opened it, he saw a menu of services not unlike a room service guide at a luxury resort.

There was a guide to the ship, including a map that showed where the sauna, the spa, the library, and the entertainment rooms were. After that, there was a Menu tab he flipped open.

"Caviar," he murmured. "Oysters. Lobster and salmon, of course."

Under a light menu of human food were more offerings to tempt the vampire palate. A list of blood-wines and fresh and preserved blood. Exotic blood like caribou and moose had a note that advance order was necessary.

He flipped to the next page and saw a menu of humans on staff, including pictures and a note that sexual favors were included with all meals upon request.

And then two lines under that: *Complete live meals arranged by ship's porter.*

Complete. Live. Meals.

What the fuck did a complete meal mean? Carwyn could guess, and it was enough to make his blood boil.

He flipped through the staff pictures, looking for the face of a cheerful blond woman he'd seen on a cell phone screen wearing a blue striped shirt and a red scarf, but she wasn't in the directory. Either Christy the chef had been taken to another boat that Paulson owned or she was dead.

Unfortunately, with things like complete live meals on the menu, the chances of Christy being alive after so many weeks were slim.

He quickly searched the rest of the container, but the back room had a combination lock, and he didn't have the time. He grabbed the leather portfolio along with a clump of papers in a folder that was shoved in a desk drawer and headed back toward the door.

Carwyn opened it and came face-to-face with a mustached guard whose eyes went wide.

The vampire opened his mouth, but before he could shout,

Carwyn rammed his fist into the man's face, knocking him across the walkway and into the container opposite the one he'd just searched.

The guard thunked against the steel wall before he slid to the ground and rolled to the side. In seconds he was back on his feet, and Carwyn had to make the quick decision whether he was going to put the guard out of commission or run.

The cautious part of him said run, but then he thought about Gus waiting silently in his boat. The last thing he wanted to do was put one of Jennie's people in danger.

The guard came charging again, still not shouting for help, and Carwyn wondered whether keeping appearances up was so built into the crew of this ship that they'd lost all common sense.

He reached out, trying to wrestle Carwyn to the ground, but the big earth vampire ducked to the right, punched into the man's kidney, and the guard fell to his knees.

The guard reached back, throwing a punch over his shoulder and into Carwyn's face. It hurt and split his lip open, but there was little force behind the awkward attack.

Carwyn locked his elbow around the guard's neck and wrested it to the side, twisting the man to the deck in a headlock that made an audible crack as he fell.

The man shuddered for a second, then went still, his neck broken. He was still alive, but he wouldn't be moving for twelve hours or so. Carwyn stood, bracing himself as he looked around to see if anyone had heard the fight, but the whipping wind must have carried the sound of their violence away.

Carwyn remembered Clovis's words before he'd left the fishing boat with Gus.

"You want a life vest before you get in there?"

"I can't drown."

"Nah, but it's plenty cold if you sink to the bottom."

Despite what he'd seen in the portfolio, he didn't want to kill the guard that night until he got more information. He could, however, throw him overboard and let the ocean decide his fate.

"I'd say I'm sorry" —Carwyn kept his voice low, glad that the wind was coming off the stern and heading up the bow where he was planning to dump the motionless guard— "but I'm not. If you're working with Zasha Sokholov, I hope the fishes eat your liver by dawn."

With a giant heave, Carwyn tossed the vampire overboard, then grabbed the portfolio and gathered the papers that had scattered in the wind before he ran for the ladder and the waiting boat.

If the sound of the guard's splash made it to the deck of the freighter, he didn't want to know.

CHAPTER TWENTY-TWO

Brigid heard Tenzin land on the roof of the house in Juneau and started when she heard a second set of feet.

Thunk.

Thunk.

She pulled her Hellcat and unlocked the trigger, taking position across the room within sight of the door that led to the stairwell.

"Brigid," Tenzin called, "I brought Ben. Don't shoot us with your gun."

She relaxed a tiny bit, somewhat certain that Tenzin wasn't being coerced but still cautious.

"It's me, Brig."

She recognized Ben's voice and released the breath she'd been holding.

Tenzin walked through the door, quickly followed by Ben.

Brigid lowered her weapon. "Took ya long enough to find us."

Her old friend rolled his eyes. "As if we didn't know exactly where you were for weeks now."

"Sure ya did."

Tenzin looked at him. "You said that you didn't know until I called you."

"I mean, it wasn't exact but..." Ben looked at Brigid.

"Don't expect me to cover your arse for ya."

He lifted an eyebrow. "Like the hair, baldy."

She flipped him off. "It's practical."

"And cold."

"Because I had such a mane before." She walked over and held still as Ben enveloped her in a hug. He was such a touchy-feely person, and she tried not to mind.

She didn't find it easy to touch people save for her mate. "Where is he?"

"Last I saw, he was climbing back on an old fishing boat and heading to Ketchikan."

"Which is where we're going," Tenzin said. "You should come too."

"Did you find Zasha?" Brigid asked. "Is that where they are? Ketchikan?"

"Not exactly, but—"

"Then it's premature." Brigid was quick to correct them. "I can't fly. Juneau is centrally located. Until we know where Zasha is, I don't need to be wastin' time moving round."

Ben frowned. "But Carwyn is headed back to Ketchikan."

And the pull for him was a tangle in her gut. "Until we know where Zasha is, I'm stayin' put. The last thing we need is for all of us to relocate south and then be stuck there when Zasha attacks farther north."

Ben leaned against the wall. "Katya thinks Oleg is working with Zasha."

"Go foirfe." Brigid threw up her hands. "Because Oleg thinks *Katya* is working with Zasha. This is perfect." She knew someone had to be pulling strings behind the scenes, but this was getting ridiculous.

Ben walked over to the refrigerator. "Do you have any blood here?"

"Scourge of the refrigerator," Tenzin muttered. "So fitting."

"I'm hungry." Ben flashed his mate a grin. "Someone wore me out."

Brigid held up a hand. "And I don't need to hear about it, so hold yer whist!"

She wasn't jealous but...

Who was she kidding? She was jealous as hell.

Ben grabbed for a bottle of blood-wine in the refrigerator door. "Right now Katya's people have identified four different raids on compounds in her territory. Only one survivor so far."

"There were three in Oleg's... *not*-territory," Brigid said. "Maybe more we don't know about because it's all shadows and rumors in that part of the state."

"And there are boats missing," Ben added. "And billionaire vampires."

Brigid frowned. "Are you talkin' about Paulson? What's his role in all this? Victim or ally?"

"We don't know for certain," Ben said, "but he's looking suspicious. Did you ask Oleg about him?"

"No, but I asked Gavin. He said that Paulson was a fringe thinker who wants to make vampires into emperors again or some such shite. No conscience, according to Gavin, but he didn't sound like he liked the fella, so he might be unreliable."

"Gavin can be very judgmental." Tenzin sat down at the table. "We need to put all of our information together. Right now there are too many threads, and they're all frayed. Brigid, we have three hours before light. That's enough time to take you to Ketchikan with us."

Brigid blinked. "As in... carry me? While you're flyin'?"

"That has to be how Zasha is moving around so quickly,"

Tenzin said. "Didn't you say they were picked up in the desert by a wind vampire? They clearly have allies."

"We're not going to drop you," Ben said. "And even if we did, you'd survive. It would hurt like hell, but you'd survive."

Tenzin lifted a finger. "René du Pont once survived a fall from seventy stories in New York. I saw it."

Brigid snorted. "You prob'ly caused it."

Ben said, "*Seventeen*, Tenzin. I don't think it was seventy."

"Either way." Brigid was cringing inside. "I don't think that's a good idea."

"The last I saw your mate, he was climbing onto a fishing boat in rough water." Ben sat next to Tenzin and stared at Brigid. "You're going to make Carwyn travel by boat, and you're too afraid to travel by air?"

"We can carry you." Tenzin shrugged. "If it comes to it, I can carry you and Ben can carry that block you're married to."

Brigid pulled her gun faster than a vampire could blink and pressed it right to Tenzin's knee. "I told you, insult him again—"

"It's not an insult." Tenzin glared at her. "He's built like a concrete block and is just as hard to get through."

"Ladies." Ben sounded nervous. "Can we not threaten bodily injury while we're catching up on news? Just a suggestion."

Tenzin kept her eyes locked with Brigid. "I followed you up here because I know that Zasha wants me dead. I know that I'm the cause of this, and I'm sorry that you and Carwyn got pulled into a mess that I created—even though I thought I was doing the right thing."

Brigid tried to wrap her mind around the idea of Tenzin apologizing. Had she ever done it before? Brigid couldn't remember.

"I can't lose him," Brigid said. "I could lose my own head, but if I lost him, I'd turn into a monster."

"No, you wouldn't." Tenzin brushed the barrel of the gun away. "You need to leave this thinking in the past. I've seen monsters. I've been a monster. You're the opposite of one, Brigid Connor."

"Who told you that, Brigid?" Ben's voice was soft. "You're one of the most honorable people I know, mortal or immortal."

Brigid blinked back heat in her eyes.

"You love it. Fire, temptation, bloodlust. They're the only things that make you feel alive."

"I'm no monster. I am nothing like you!"

"I never said you were. But you said it. Because deep down, you believe it. In your heart, you know what you are."

"Whoever told you that is playing with your mind," Tenzin said bluntly. "And it's working. I've used that tactic myself. Was it Zasha?"

Brigid said nothing.

"They are perceptive," Tenzin said. "If they know you fear being a monster, they'll use it against you. Don't let them win."

"Come with us," Ben said. "Go to Carwyn. Right now he's working on his own, angry at you for leaving him behind."

"We can chase this ghost together and win, or we can split up and probably lose." Tenzin leaned forward. "But there's no way to keep them safe. Not Ben and not Carwyn. Not from this. He won't let you, and you're only making him hurt because of your stubbornness."

Brigid pulled her hands from the table; the edge was singed and black, but it wasn't burnt.

Tenzin glanced at the burn marks on the wood. "Your control is improving. Even a few days working with Oleg helped."

Brigid felt the fire in her belly, felt the burning snap of it reaching from inside, aching to get out. Aching for her mate. The fire wanted Carwyn, and the longer she let it smolder, the worse it was going to be.

"Fine," she whispered. "I'll go with ye."

———

FLYING across the Inside Passage on the back of a wind vampire was as completely terrifying and freezing as Brigid could have imagined. She tried to close her eyes, but her relentless curiosity had her peeking over Ben's shoulder more than once.

"It's amazing, right?" Ben was obviously in his element. "People dream about flying all the time, and now I can actually do it. Do you know I called you from the top of a cathedral in Russia once?"

"I did not know that."

Jesus, she was turning into her Aunt Sinead with the number of times she'd held her breath only to let it out in a minor explosion.

"...but once I figured out how to keep the bugs away, it got a lot better."

"Completely missed the first part of that one." She gasped and ducked down as a bird nearly sideswiped them. "Dear God in heaven."

"My uncle and aunt refuse to fly with me, but my sister loves it."

"That's mildly terrifying." Ben's sister was something like thirteen. Perhaps she had a death wish.

"Nearly there." He pointed off to the left. "I recognize that old lumber mill."

"Great!"

Let her die. She'd had a good life—she could just die now. Surely it was possible for vampires to have heart attacks. Was that possible? What about a stroke? If he dropped another time to avoid a seagull, something in her head was bound to explode.

"You're not getting tired, are you?" Ben yelled over his shoulder. "Tenzin and I exchange blood, so the short days have been great. But I don't need as much sleep as most new vampires."

"Yeah, it's fine."

It wasn't fine. None of this was fine. She wanted her feet on the ground. Even a boat would be better than this terror.

"Banking to the right, then going down."

"Okay."

For the love of all things holy, let that mean they were almost there.

Brigid saw lights in the distance, a cluster of them sitting between a peninsula and an island, straddling a narrow strait dotted with smaller lights that were probably boats.

Beyond that strait was a vast stretch of dark water as they looked over the cold Pacific Ocean. As they'd crossed the maze of land and sea dotted with tiny moving lights, she'd had one thought repeating in her head over and over.

Well, one thought other than contemplating death.

How the hell were they supposed to find Zasha Sokholov in this huge stretch of wilderness? She'd thought the Alaskan interior was vast.

This maze of islands was so much worse.

———

WHEN BRIGID'S feet finally hit land, she understood the humans who kissed the ground. Despite the pouring rain and the mud that squelched between her boots, she was tempted.

In the distance, she saw a house clinging to the edge of land, a dock sticking out into relatively calm waters while two wooden decks wrapped around a wood-clad house.

Behind the house was a raised cedar-plank longhouse with smoke pumping from a stone chimney, and next to it rose a mound with a door cut into the earth.

"I see Clovis's boat," Ben muttered, "so they must have gotten back already. I wonder where—"

"He's here." The moment she touched the ground, a pull in her blood had started. "He's comin'."

The door to the mound house swung open, and silhouetted in the gold glow, she saw Carwyn's outline.

Her blood leaped, and she felt the whisper of Ben and Tenzin as they took to the sky, leaving her alone in the drizzling rain.

While Brigid's blood was a riot, he walked slowly. Deliberately.

It took a lot to make her mate angry, but when he was, he went stone-cold and silent.

Brigid walked to him, halting a dozen feet from him, lifting her chin and pushing back the hood that protected her head.

Carwyn stopped and stared, his face a mask.

Brigid lifted her hand. "Hello." She wanted to cry. She wanted to leap into his arms. She wanted to hide in the safety of him, and he was cold as ice. "Carwyn—"

"Do you need to feed before daylight?"

That was the first thing he asked her?

"No." She swallowed hard. "I've been feeding regularly. I haven't been skipping. I've been—"

"Good." He looked her up and down. "You flew."

"I did." *Please don't do this. Please don't shut me out.*

"I wondered where Ben disappeared to." He glanced up. "I should have known it was her."

"Carwyn—"

"It's almost dawn." He started walking toward the house. "There are rooms on the ground floor that—"

"I'm sorry!" Brigid choked on the sob that erupted from her throat. "I'm sorry. I love you so much, and I'm sorry, mo chroí. My heart, tá brón orm. So very sorry."

He spun on her. "You left me!"

The ground beneath Brigid shook with his anger. "I know."

"I begged you not to leave me behind. I called you and I _begged_ you to let us do this together and you left me, Brigid." The corner of his lip curled up and his fangs fell. "You are my _mate_."

"I don't deserve you."

"Oh fuck off!" The ground shook again. "I'm not a saint. I'm not a savior. I'm as selfish as the next bastard, and you left me." He stomped toward her, the ground firming under his feet, lifting up to meet him as he stalked her. "Why?"

She whispered, "I wanted to protect you."

"But you can go to Oleg?" He threw out an arm. "You can call on Tenzin? You can call in favors from any number of the worst criminals in our world but—"

"Yes!" She lifted her chin, not caring if he saw her cry. "I will call in any favor and rake the absolute muck of our world if that means keepin' you alive and away from Zasha Sokholov."

"I'm not weak, Brigid." He stood up straight and lifted his chin. "But apparently you think I am."

CHAPTER TWENTY-THREE

The look on her face made Carwyn feel as if he'd slapped her.

"No." Brigid shook her head. "Carwyn, that's the last thing I could ever think. I know you're not—"

"Then why the fuck would you leave me when you're hunting one of the most psychotic immortals we've ever come across?"

Anger was still burning in his gut even though she'd apologized. It wasn't a pretty thing, and he knew it. It wasn't one of his finer qualities, but pushed to the edge, he had a very hard time letting go of resentment.

And this time his mate had pushed him.

He could see the sky changing color. The dawn would come soon, and he saw that she was exhausted. He couldn't bear to be parted from her for another day, but he wanted to shout at her and shake her until she realized how reckless she'd been.

"Carwyn," she stammered. "I... I know what I did was hurtful, but I was trying to—"

"Shut up." He spread his arms, and the ground beneath them opened up, pulling them both in. He caught her in his arms as the earth took them under, then tunneled toward drier ground.

The earth around him was fragrant with moss and organic matter, lush with scent and life. He held Brigid curled into his chest and carried her to the burrow he'd carved out two nights before when sleeping for another night by the crashing water had raked on his nerves.

He tunneled past the shelter he'd created for the elder, sensing the man's amnis as it worked to keep the old one alive and heal him from his burns.

The ground opened before him, emptying into a round chamber he'd lined with rocks and some of the furs he'd taken from the house.

As the earth settled around them and rested, Carwyn tossed Brigid on the pile of furs and blankets he'd made up to use as a bed, then went to light a small lamp in the corner. "You can sleep here."

She lifted her head, and her eyes went wide. "Are you gonna leave me buried in the ground?"

"Of course not, you idiot," he snarled at her. "I mean, yes, but I'll be here with you."

He felt her energy rise, the faint smell of steam as her skin heated up.

"Don't!" He bent down and got in her face. "You are safe here. Stop doubting me and trust your mate."

"I know I'm safe with you." Her voice was small.

"Your fire doesn't." He reached for a wet rag he kept on the table and wiped his face. Then he tossed another one to her. "You can clean up if you want. I don't have any spare clothes for you."

"I have my backpack."

"Good."

She stripped out of her muddy clothes and cleaned her face in silence, running the wet cloth over her head, her hands, and her shoulders. She said not a single word, then folded the washcloth into a square and set it on top of her black backpack.

She looked smaller somehow, more frail than she'd been the last time he saw her. Her hair was trimmed into a short buzz cut that did nothing but enhance the beauty of her stunning eyes and high cheekbones.

Carwyn felt his anger ebb as the fire inside her calmed and the room smelled of moss and green life again. "Are you armed?" he asked. "I don't want a gun under your pillow tonight."

"It's in my backpack." She looked around the dimly lit cavern. "You'll feel something before me down here."

"Yes." He took off his shirt and took a second towel from a pile sitting on a stone. He dunked it in rainwater and wiped the mud from his face and hands. "I know you don't like sleeping underground, but I'm sick of the damn ocean."

"I know the feelin'." She took a deep breath and let it out slowly.

A little more of Carwyn's anger ebbed as she released her breath. His amnis didn't care about righteous anger. Everything in him ached to reach out for her, join her, embrace her.

The combination of having her within reach and the tumultuous events of the night combined, slamming into him with the force of a freight train, and he leaned against the stone wall of the cave.

His shoulders slumped with exhaustion. "I'm tired, Brigid."

"Then come here." Her voice was soft.

Carwyn turned and saw her with her arms out, her beautiful eyes soft for him and her damp skin shining in the low lamplight. She was wearing nothing but a cropped tank top and a pair of practical black boxer shorts. Her pale skin was milk white on the dark furs he'd brought to the cave.

"My fine man," she whispered. "Come here."

Her softness broke him.

Carwyn stripped off his shirt and crawled into bed beside her, wrapping his arms around her and laying his head on her belly.

His amnis settled against hers, and he felt Brigid heat her skin to warm the chill in his.

"Why'd you do it?" He kept his voice low. "Don't you know it would *break* me if anyone laid a hand on you?"

"And I'd burn the world to keep you safe," Brigid whispered. "I'd burn... *everything*. Everyone. I was trying to do the least harm, and I hurt you instead."

He lifted his head and looked into her eyes. "Charred whiskey barrels."

She frowned. "What?"

"Your eyes. The first time I saw them after you turned, I thought about charred whiskey barrels. That beautiful brown with grey along the edges." He turned his head and laid his cheek on her belly.

He could hear a smile in her voice. "Did you?"

"And then I thought... I'll protect her from anything." He felt her hands hot on his shoulders. "She's my world now, and I'll protect her. I'd have abandoned all of them for you, Brigid. Every tie, every responsibility. Every obligation was nothing compared to that need to protect you."

She brushed a lock of hair from his forehead. "I learned to protect myself years before I turned vampire."

"And don't you know that it makes me crazy that you had to do that?" He gripped her on either side of her torso, his large hands spanning the delicate rib cage that protected her heart. "I hate that you had to learn that. It makes me want to break things."

"Carwyn—"

"No." He lifted his head. "I have spent my eternity seeking peace, but no one *fucks* with you, darling girl. This vampire, they aren't only killing and burning and destroying, but they're trying to get in your head. Turn you into someone you are not. Trying to ruin what we are."

She shook her head. "No one can do that. I won't let them."

He opened his mouth and let his fangs grow long. Then, keeping his eyes on Brigid, he slowly sank his fangs into the flesh of her belly, licking up the blood that released and easing the boxers down her hips.

She sucked in a breath and arched into his mouth. "Carwyn."

"I'm going to bite all over your body," he whispered. "I'm going to sink my teeth into your breasts and suck the blood from between your thighs. And you will scream with the pleasure of it."

"That a promise?"

"Yes." He lapped up the blood on her torso, sealing the wounds he'd made before he made more. He licked down her body and between her thighs, holding her in place as her body became engorged with pleasure.

He nicked the tender flesh with the tip of his fangs, sucking the wound into his mouth and hurling Brigid into her first climax.

Carwyn turned his head while she was still coming and sank his teeth into the flesh next to her sex, sliding his hands under her buttocks and lifting her body into his mouth. He feasted on her rich blood, sucking in the amnis that purred for him.

Brigid reached for his hand, grasping for anything as she convulsed in pleasure. Carwyn reached his hand toward her neck and growled when she grabbed it and sank her fangs into the vein at his wrist.

He felt her enter him, the true joining of their kind. Her amnis curled around his like smoke around cedar, and the scent of their joined blood filled the cave.

Carwyn carefully sealed the wounds in her thighs before he moved up her body, kissing and licking along her torso, raking his fangs along her flesh and raising welts.

He tore down the center of her shirt and parted it, revealing the gentle rise of her breasts.

"I'll bite these too." He put his mouth on the right breast. "Mark you, Brigid. Give you a reminder not to leave me again."

"Talk is— Fuck me!" She gasped as his teeth sank into her flesh on either side of her nipple. He bit down and sucked the tip into his mouth, teasing the sensitive flesh with his tongue before he sucked hard, leaving her bloody and engorged before he moved to the left breast and did the same thing.

Her skin was gritty and he didn't care. They were streaked with mud and blood, and the scent of smoke filled the room.

She was gripping a blanket so hard it had started to burn.

Carwyn reached over and smothered the flame with the palm of his left hand before he licked at her wounds, sucking and then sealing them as he slowly worked his way up her body.

She scrambled to shove his pants down his hips. "Please."

"Not yet." He still had a little bit of anger to work out before he trusted himself.

"Carwyn—"

"Kiss me." He braced himself over her, caging her with massive arms, this tiny, lethal predator he'd managed to capture and make his own. "Kiss me, Brigid."

She lifted her hands, and the water that dripped from his hair sizzled when she touched his cheeks.

Brigid framed his cheeks with hands so hot they nearly burned his skin. She lifted tentative lips and pressed a kiss to his mouth.

He softened a little bit, but his fangs were still down.

She licked up the length of one, then the other. She ran her tongue along the edge of his lower lip, sucking it into his mouth.

Carwyn closed his eyes at the pleasure of her kiss.

She nibbled softly along his jaw, and he grew harder, his erection straining against the heavy canvas pants he'd worn on the boat.

She lifted one leg, wrapping it around his waist and drawing him down to her body.

"I want your weight," she whispered. "Please."

He jerked his head from her ministering lips and gazed at her, blood marking the border of his kiss. He looked down at her red-smeared breasts, which were still swollen with pleasure, and her body, bare and wet. He could smell her arousal as heavy as her blood.

"Never leave me again."

She shook her head. "Wherever we go, we go together."

"Never use yourself as a shield for me."

She blinked. "Carwyn—"

"Promise me." He bared his fangs. "Promise. Me."

She lifted her chin. "I'll shield you, and you'll shield me. Try to make me promise otherwise and you'll be disappointed."

"Fucking stubborn woman." He pushed away from her, stood, and shoved his pants down his legs, stepping out of them as he fell on her. "You infuriating, stubborn woman."

"Infuriating." She wrapped an arm around his neck. "Stubborn." Threw a leg around his waist. "Man." She arched up, and Carwyn drove into her body, sinking to the hilt as she wrapped her other leg around his hips and pulled him in.

The earth around them shuddered as he made furious love to her. She kept her arm around his neck and sank her fangs into his shoulder. Carwyn erupted in pleasure, and she wrung him dry, holding him to her body as his chest heaved and he paused, waiting to grow hard again.

"I love you." She kissed his neck and whispered, "I missed you every day. I wanted to cry every time I went to sleep without you."

"Damn you, woman." His body grew hard at her tender words. He closed his eyes, rolled them over, and pulled her on top of him. "Ride me."

Putting his hands on her hips, he slowly lifted her up and down his body, stroking her clitoris as she arched back in pleasure.

"I'm going to make you come again," he said, "then I'm turning you over and biting your sweet arse, Brigid Connor."

"Is this how you teach me a lesson?" She closed her eyes and let out a soft moan. "Because if it is, you can teach me every night."

He spread his hand and smacked her backside as she rode him. "Every night and every day."

"Yes please."

For the first time in weeks, he felt like laughing. "What you do to me, Brigid."

"Likewise." She bent down and placed a gentle kiss on his swollen lips, tapping his fangs with her own. "I love you, you infuriating giant."

"I love you too... you unholy imp."

CHAPTER TWENTY-FOUR

B en felt the ground rock with several minor earthquakes that were probably going to confuse human geologists for a while.

"It's good," Tenzin said from her position curled into his side. "It lets off tension."

"Yeah, they both looked pretty worked up."

"I mean from fault lines. Alaska is very geologically active."

He smiled. "Right."

Tenzin looked up at Ben. "This was the longest we've been apart since we mated."

"Trust me, I know."

"I missed you."

His eyebrow went up. "Were you surprised?"

"A little bit." She stared into the darkness of the light-secure room. "I do understand why Zasha hates me."

"I do too. That doesn't mean you were wrong to kill their mate." His arm tightened around her. "Did you kill humans for food when you were young?"

"Rarely. I wasn't allowed to hunt when I was newly turned. Sometimes they gave me humans to feed on. Or animals. Mostly they didn't let me have fresh blood. They wanted to keep me weak."

His arm tightened. "Tenzin."

"I'm not going to tell you things if you're going to react emotionally."

He let out a frustrated huff. "How can I not react emotionally? I love you and I hate that you were hurt."

She turned her face to his. "I survived. That's the part you should remember."

"I know." He bent down and kissed her forehead. He set his questions and reactions about Tenzin's past to the side. "We have hours before nightfall. Tell me what you discovered at Oleg's."

"Well." She took a long breath. "He's more attractive than I realized. And he has a very dry sense of humor. His personal chef is excellent, but his men almost all smell like pickled eggs. Is that a Russian delicacy? If it is—"

"I'm talking about Zasha." Ben closed his eyes. "I don't— You think Oleg is attractive?"

"Aesthetically yes, but we would probably kill each other if we spent much time together, so he would make a terrible lover." She patted his shoulder. "And of course I am loyal to you, and you desire monogamy."

"I appreciate your consideration," Ben muttered. "About Zasha?"

"Ah." She nodded. "It has the appearance of chaos, but I think it is just the opposite. This was all carefully planned."

"What was carefully planned? The raids?"

"Yes. And the missing ships you mentioned." She squeezed his hand. "I do not think it is a coincidence that Zasha's violence in Alaska coincides with Oleg's aggression."

"*Oleg's* aggression?" Ben frowned. "Are you saying that you think Katya's right? That Oleg and Zasha are working together?"

"No, but maybe Zasha wants Katya to *believe* that they're working with Oleg and—"

"Then Oleg might think that Zasha is working with Katya." Ben nodded. "Why take on your enemies when you could simply turn them on each other?"

"But why?" Tenzin shrugged. "You think Zasha wants this territory? They have never given an indication that they want an empire."

"No," Ben muttered, "but maybe Zasha heard about global warming."

She narrowed her eyes. "Global warming?"

"It's this thing that's happening because modern humans burn a ton of—"

"I know what global warming is," she snapped. "Why would Zasha care about it? They have plenty of money. Global warming is going to affect poor humans, not wealthy vampires."

"If enough sea ice melts, there'll be new shipping channels through the Arctic Ocean."

Tenzin said, "Oleg controls half the Arctic shipping lanes from his territory in Russia."

"And Zasha could control the rest if they take Alaska. They *are* stealing ships."

Tenzin cocked her head to the side. "Zasha wouldn't take on Oleg directly."

"No, they wouldn't. But remember, Katya thinks Zasha and Oleg are working together."

Tenzin muttered, "And she's overextended. She's not really in control of this place. She's losing control of it just like Oleg did."

"Maybe that's inevitable," Ben said. "It's so massive."

"But if this was your *only* territory..." Tenzin turned to him. "Maybe Zasha finally wants to settle down."

"Settle down?

"Yes." She remembered a snowy valley between two mountain ranges and the scent of cold ocean in her nose. "Maybe they want to settle down in a place that feels familiar."

Ben sat up. "But Zasha knows there are two powerful vampires who want to control those shipping lanes."

"They see an opportunity." She sat up and crossed her legs. "Zasha starts attacking the coastal villages. They go back and forth between the territories."

"Katya blames Oleg." Ben nodded. "Oleg blames Katya."

"Put the bear at the throat of the wolf and see which one kills the other first. Whoever survives will be weak, and the other will be finished.

"It fits what's happened, so why doesn't it feel right?" Ben raked a hand through his hair. "These endless nights are throwing my head in a blender. At this point I'd murder Zasha Sokholov just so I could get back to New York."

Tenzin opened her mouth, then shut it quickly.

Ben could tell she had something to say. "Tenzin?"

"I have to tell you something and you're going to be upset, but I want you to remember that no humans were hurt and I am telling you this now because if you lose your temper—"

"Tenzin." His entire body went stiff.

"—we are contained in this room and no one will see you out of control."

Ben felt dread curl in his belly. "What happened?"

She turned to Ben and met his gaze. "Someone burned our home in New York."

He felt a fist squeeze his heart. "Our place?"

"Yes."

"How much damage—?"

"It's basically gone," she said quickly. "Chloe sent pictures, and whoever did it used an accelerant of some kind, and we're on the top floor so the firefighters..." She took a breath and held it.

"It's gone?"

She nodded. "It's gone."

It was a house. It was just a house, and she'd already told him that no one was hurt.

No *humans* were hurt.

He choked out the question. "The birds?"

"Probably they are dead."

They were birds. They were *birds*.

Their life was always going to be short.

Except those brightly colored creatures had brought Tenzin joy and peace, and some nights seeing that was the only thing that kept Ben from cursing eternal night.

"Tenzin—"

"They could have flown away. We probably won't ever know."

He whispered, "Tenzin."

"Gavin is investigating because he's very angry that Chloe might have been hurt, though I suspect that whoever burned our house timed it so that she was not hurt because hurting her wouldn't have distracted us—which is doubtless the intention—it would have simply provoked even greater enemies."

His heart ached, and it wasn't only for himself.

It was just a house, and it shouldn't matter so much. In the centuries of life stretching before him, he would gain and lose property. There would be homes that were lost because of natural disasters or simply because they became too exposed.

But their town house in New York was where he'd fallen in love with Tenzin. It was the nest he'd created to tempt her to New York with him. It was the place where she'd held him when life fell apart.

"It's just a house," he whispered.

"It was your home." She reached over and stroked the back of his neck. "I know that it was important to you."

"We're going to kill Zasha," Ben said woodenly. "And every person who is working with them. Not because of our house but because it's the right thing to do to keep them from harming anyone else."

But also maybe a little bit because of Tenzin's birds.

———

Hungary, Ninth Century CE

TENZIN WALKED through the rubble along the edges of the Duna River, stepping over corpses that humans had left to rot.

Waste. So much waste.

The blood was already spoiling in their veins, which made her lip curl. It was dark along the riverbank, and she could hear other vampires in the distance, scavenging among the victims of this raid to find humans with enough life that they could use them for food.

Her kind were predators by nature, but they were scavengers when the opportunity presented itself.

She came across a barely living victim a few moments later. The girl was no more than thirteen or fourteen and had propped herself on an overturned boat. She was holding her intestines in her lap, watching the water flow by as she blinked slowly and faded away.

A vampire approached from the forest, but Tenzin flung out an arm and grabbed them by the neck. "What are you doing?"

The young man was ravenous, probably a newborn. "She's alive; her blood is still pumping."

"There are others. Leave her."

He shrieked, and it sounded like a ferret screaming. "I want her!"

"Are you willing to die?" Tenzin bared her fangs and hissed.

His eyes went wide, and Tenzin saw the water behind him stir, so she threw the young one in the air and punched him with a column of wind that sent the creature soaring into the forest on the opposite side of the river.

Tenzin turned back to the girl and bent down. Her skin was milk white, and her lips were turning blue. "You're dying."

She had hair the color of polished copper and clear brown eyes that looked up at Tenzin, but there was no sense of comprehension. The girl murmured in a language Tenzin didn't speak. Magyar, perhaps.

Tenzin watched the girl as her eyes drifted back to the river. She sat down in the mud next to the girl, wondering if she was in pain or if shock had settled in.

"It's not a bad place to die," Tenzin murmured. "The air hasn't turned rancid yet. There's no scent of rot. Most of the blood washed away when it rained today."

The girl let out a soft breath and reached out, bloody fingers reaching for Tenzin's hand.

"I can't give you any healing." Tenzin glanced at her wound. "I'm surprised you're still alive."

She said something else, and her fingers curled around Tenzin's.

"You want me to hold your hand?" Tenzin frowned. "I can do that."

She held the girl's hand in her own, squeezing her fingers and snarling at the dog that lurked on the edge of the river.

The Duna flowed south and east, the water gathering all the blood and dirt from the violent land it crossed, flowing down to a sea that entered another sea and another and another until it returned to the sky to spread over the earth again.

"Your blood will be part of that," Tenzin said. "You're not dying really. Your body will feed flowers and grass. Your tears will return to the sea. One day the blood that is leaving you right now will fall as rain on the grass that your people walk on, and your spirit will exist in them and in another form." She turned to the girl, who was staring at the river again. "Nothing is wasted in the end. Everything has a purpose."

She spotted a vampire from the corner of her eye, not a newborn like the first but a vibrant warrior with long braids the color of chestnut lying over his shoulders and leather armor with silver trim covering his chest. He was probably one of the many who'd raided this river town the previous night at dusk.

She spoke in a Slavic tongue she thought he might recognize. "Hail, Varangian."

The vampire lifted a single hand, then put it on the hilt of the blade at his hip. "Hail, Khazar."

Tenzin looked at the dying girl. "I will sit with her until her spirit leaves."

The vampire looked at the human, then at the rubble around him. "I was sent to finish any survivors."

"That is a kindness."

"Is it?" The man blinked grey eyes that were not unlike Tenzin's own.

"Killing those who have survived this raid will end their suffering," she said. "So yes, it is a kindness. But this girl no longer feels her pain, so you will leave her alone."

The hand went back on the hilt of his blade. "I was sent—"

"You were not sent." Tenzin knew who had done this. "Truvor has no regard for humans, and you're one of his sons, aren't you?"

The warrior frowned. "Aren't *you*?"

Tenzin smirked. "Does Truvor hire or sire female Khazars? I didn't know." She wasn't a Khazar—she was something much older, but that name was one the raider would know.

The vampire looked closer. "I didn't realize you were a woman."

Tenzin wasn't surprised. She'd been dressing like a man since she started her journey at the Black Sea. It was an easy way to avoid attention.

"You should leave," the vampire said.

"What is your element, Truvor's man?"

"A dangerous one."

Tenzin looked up when she smelled the hint of smoke.

Interesting.

"So Truvor has a fire vampire with him. No wonder other immortals have left him alone. You're attracting attention from human regents though. Tell your sire he needs to stop."

"I'm not the reason they leave him alone."

"You're one of them, and you know it. It's why you have crept from the camp and are going to ease the suffering of the humans who are dying slowly. You know he values you, and you feel guilt."

The girl's breath turned ragged, and there was a rattling sound in her chest. She tried to sit up but fell back on the rock she'd crawled to.

She muttered something; then her breathing grew worse.

Tenzin shifted and put her arm around the girl's back, lifting her so she could watch the river as her breath grew more and more labored.

The warrior stepped closer, his hand reaching out before he clenched it into a fist. "She's suffering."

"Very unlikely." Tenzin had sent a wave of amnis over the woman as soon as she touched her hand, clouding her mind and easing her into the darkness.

"Why don't you kill her?" the man asked.

"Because you already did."

"I didn't." His voice was bitter. "What do these people have? Nothing we need. I didn't want—"

"Whether you wanted it or not, you did." Tenzin stroked a hand over the girl's copper hair. "Isn't she pretty? Such unusual hair." Tenzin hadn't seen hair so bright in a long time. Was that what sunlight looked like? It reminded her of rubies in firelight.

Beautiful.

The vampire stared at the dying girl. "She's... human."

"Is that all you can say?" Tenzin looked up, then reached over and plucked a purple violet from the base of a rock. "A flower. I should crush it because I can." She squeezed the violet in her hand and dropped it on the grass. "See how stupid that sounds?"

"Who are you?"

"Someone you don't want to meet if you make a habit of crushing flowers." Tenzin lowered the girl's head to her shoulder and stroked her hair. "My name is Tenzin."

He sucked in a sharp breath.

He'd heard of her. Good.

"Go, Varangian." Tenzin glanced at the young fire vampire before he melted back into the darkness. "If you survive, I suspect I will see you again."

CHAPTER TWENTY-FIVE

"Someone is attackin' Katya Grigorieva's territory and people." Brigid tapped her tablet with a stylus, and blurry images popped on-screen. "And I believe we are in agreement that Zasha Sokholov is most likely the perpetrator of all these attacks."

Brigid, Tenzin, Ben, Carwyn, Buck, and Jennie were in a makeshift conference room in the community hall set back in the woods behind Jennie and Buck's house in Ketchikan. The building was long and narrow, roofed with wood beams with a stone fireplace on one end. Running down the center of the great room was a carved wooden table with benches along either side.

A large TV hung from the ceiling opposite the fireplace, and Buck had done something with Lee on the phone to make Brigid's case files jump onto the screen.

"Yeah," Buck said. "I mean, that's what all you folks seem to think. And what we're hearing around."

"To clarify, Zasha is the one *leading* the attacks," Carwyn said. "All the raid sites so far show evidence of violence from fire vampires, water vampires, earth, and wind."

Brigid put up more pictures. "And these are copies of the pictures we took in Kenai and a few other spots farther north."

More burned houses. More blood. More destruction. "These attacks were also orchestrated by Zasha Sokholov. In two cases, there were eyewitnesses that spotted them."

"Zasha and their friends are running wild," Ben said. "And they're doing it in Katya's and Oleg's territory."

"Correction," Jennie said. "Katya's territory. The Russian does not have territory in this state."

Brigid barely kept from rolling her eyes.

Buck said, "So this Zasha character wants to run Alaska? Take it from Katya?"

"That's one possibility." Brigid continued with the briefing that Jennie had requested at dusk. "It would be out of character for them—they only expressed interest in takin' over Las Vegas because they'd been hired by the Ankers; Zasha didn't want it for themself."

Carwyn handed her a thick manila envelope, and she opened it.

"But I want all of us to consider that there's another likelihood based on what Carwyn found on Henri Paulson's barge last night."

"One could call it a barge." Carwyn was sitting at the conference table and looking at a heavily insulated tablet in his hands. "Or one could call it what it is."

Brigid switched to another slide that brought up a picture of the welcome letter Carwyn had found on the boat.

Welcome to Blå Havn, the beginning of a new world.

"Blå Havn." Brigid flipped through more of the papers in the welcome packet. "Blue Haven. A new world according to Paulson."

Jennie and Buck were both leaning forward, reading the letter projected on the television.

Brigid continued. "Henri Paulson might be a tech billionaire and a very successful businessman, but he's also a conspiracy theorist with aspirations of empire."

She flipped through more of the welcome information that explained to Paulson's "guests" that they were part of a new world of vampire domination.

"He outlines his plans," Carwyn said. "Not in detail, but we can read between the lines. Fostering human dictatorships that will give immortals free rein. Dominating shipping and currency trading. Taking control back from the..." Carwyn read off the screen: "'Irresponsible human element' that could endanger the most desirable class of vampires."

"The desirable ones are the rich ones?" Ben asked. "I'm assuming."

Brigid checked for Jennie's reaction, but her expression was a blank.

"Blå Havn is only one of the boats we think Paulson has." She continued with the briefing she'd hastily put together. "And there are about a dozen vampires on it from what Carwyn could tell. All ridiculously wealthy guests with lots of money, lots of connections, and a hunger for..." She brought up the menu page of the welcome packet and let her audience scan it.

She'd been shocked, horrified, and unsurprised by what she'd seen in the files Carwyn had taken from Paulson's barge. It matched perfectly with what Gavin had told her about the vampire, and in Brigid's mind, there was no question what role Henri Paulson was playing in the sudden rash of violence that had marred the peace of Alaska.

"Complete live meals," Ben murmured. "Paulson's running hunts?"

"Isolated locations. Human and vampire victims." Brigid flipped to a blurry picture of Zasha. The only definite feature outstanding in the frame was a shock of red hair sticking up from a dark coat. "Remind ya of anyone?"

"Wait," Buck said. "You think the vampires on that barge, the ones hiding out on Paulson's ships, are the ones that are killing people with Zasha? Why would they do that if they're hiding out? That's dumb as shit."

"They're not hiding." Tenzin stared at Jennie. "Or at least, they aren't hiding anymore."

———

CARWYN WATCHED her present the mass of information to Buck and Jennie, marveling at a mind that could pull all these disparate threads together and weave a picture of conspiracy that was as grand and twisted as any he'd seen.

Brigid set one of her tablets to the side and pulled up another picture of Henri Paulson on the screen. "Let's look at Paulson again. For sure, it was his ship, the Blå Havn, that Carwyn boarded. His guests who have menus of people presented to them on a silver platter," Brigid said. "How long has he been in this area?"

Jennie was silent for a moment while she thought. "He showed up about twenty years ago. He was already rich; he was in computers even back then."

Brigid nodded and typed out a note on her tablet.

- 1990s—Paulson in Alaska

Ben sat back and crossed his arms. "Paulson's a billionaire. According to Gavin, he invested in technology at the end of the 1990s. Now he has fingers in so many pies he's had to get new fingers."

Tenzin blinked. "He has extra fingers?"

"It's a figure of speech," Ben muttered.

"And he's been missing for months now," Jennie added.

"Whatever you all may suspect Paulson of, we don't know he's not one of Zasha's victims."

"Fair enough," Brigid said. "You're completely correct."

Carwyn made a mental note. Jennie was protective of her people, even those who might be on the grey edge of vampire society. It wasn't a bad thing as long as she could think with a clear head when she saw all the facts.

And as long as she wasn't a conspiracy theorist herself.

"But there *were* reports that Paulson was hosting strange vampires about a month before he went missing." Buck piped up, shooting a look at his wife. "Not strange as in unusual—Paulson was hosting vampires from out of the area and no one had reported them to Jennie."

Tenzin stared at Jennie. "Are you the VIC here?"

Jennie frowned. "My name's Jennie, not—"

"Vampire in charge," Ben jumped in to answer. "That's all she means. Are you the vampire in charge?" Ben leaned toward Tenzin. "Jennie is Katya's lieutenant." He looked back at Jennie. "Was Paulson having strange vampires on one of his boats unusual?"

Jennie took a while to consider the question before she answered. "We keep out of each other's business. Paulson had dealings with people from out of the area. That's none of my business, and I don't think it concerns Katya either. As long as strangers don't hang around much or create problems, we're not going to make it a big deal."

Tenzin said, "But these strangers have 'complete live meals' on the menu. On Paulson's menu. Does Katya know about that?"

Jennie leaned forward and rested her hands lightly on the table. "What are you trying to say?"

"Tiny." Ben put a hand on Tenzin's arm. "We're not casting blame here; we're trying to figure out what is happening."

"So Paulson shows up twenty years ago." Brigid raised her

voice and tried to get the meeting back on track. "And by all accounts—as Jennie said—he lives a quiet life."

Jennie nodded. "Yeah. He's even hired some of Katya's people over the years. Who are *fine*. From what we know, the guy's a good boss."

"Except for the crew of the *Dolphin*," Ben added quickly, "who disappeared the same time that Paulson did."

"Exactly." Jennie's tone was more than a little terse.

"One thing to add." Carwyn glanced at Brigid, and she nodded. "Paulson does have ties to the Ankers." He looked at Ben and Buck. "The name sounded familiar, but I couldn't place it until the other night. One of my sons—his mate has distant ties to the Anker clan, and I remember she mentioned Paulson to me after the Ankers took Chloe."

Tenzin narrowed her eyes. "One of your children's mates is an Anker?"

Carwyn glared at Tenzin. "No, I said she has distant ties. Just like you used to have ties to some... less than upstanding vampires. We don't control who sires us." He turned back to Brigid. "She mentioned Paulson as a possible ally of the Dutch Anker clan, but only in passing. I would be surprised if Paulson would risk anything of his own for them."

"So maybe don't classify them as allies," Ben said. "They're more like stray dogs who frequent the same streets. They help each other if it works, but mostly they trade information. Feed from the same gutter."

Brigid cleared her throat. "Jaysus, thanks for that vivid mental picture, Ben."

He shrugged. "If the shoe fits."

Tenzin was staring at him. "I feel like you just insulted stray dogs."

Brigid jumped in. "Getting back to the briefin'."

His poor wife. Herding cats. It was absolutely herding cats to keep Ben and Tenzin on track.

"We know Paulson has been here for some time." Brigid flipped to another frame and another picture of Henri Paulson, this time a shadowy figure in the background of a picture that looked like it had been taken in the summer based on the lush flowers on the deck of the boat. "We know he has a connection to the Ankers."

"Maybe after the Ankers were defeated in Las Vegas," Tenzin said, "Paulson noticed that Zasha needed a new project."

"That's *very* possible." Brigid made another note on her tablet.

- Last summer—Zasha and Ankers lose in Vegas

"Vegas was an expensive loss," Carwyn said. "And the Ankers will not hire Zasha for any new projects when the last two went south."

"So Zasha comes to Alaska to lie low after things got kyboshed in Las Vegas." She made another note and put it on the screen.

- ???—Zasha goes to Alaska

"They must have a house... somewhere," Brigid said. "A hideout. Probably away from both Oleg's and Katya's eyes."

"Wait." Buck raised a hand. "They rented that house around Sitka last summer, right? Did they do that and then go kidnap that kid in Vegas?"

Ben stood and walked to the screen, looking up. "They must have."

Carwyn frowned. "So if Paulson and Zasha started working together, it wasn't because Zasha was bored. Whatever happened must have started before Las Vegas. This was planned out well in advance."

Brigid added another note and amended the previous ones.

- ???—Zasha back to Alaska

"And sometime later in the fall," Carwyn said, "Henri Paulson and Zasha meet again."

Ben said, "That's when the crewman on the *Pacific Lady* said his girlfriend saw a very scary redheaded vampire who seemed to spook Paulson."

"Which probably means that Paulson is a victim in this," Jennie said. "Why would Paulson be spooked if Zasha and he were working together?"

Brigid remained silent, but she updated the timeline.

- 1990s—Paulson in Alaska
- Last summer—Zasha rents house outside Sitka (meets with Paulson?)
- Last summer—Zasha and Ankers lose in Vegas
- ???—Zasha back to Alaska
- Last fall—Zasha and Paulson meet on the *Dolphin*
- A few weeks later—The *Dolphin* goes missing along with the crew

Brigid looked around the room. "Zasha Sokholov is an opportunist. There's no way of tellin' if they approached Paulson or Paulson approached Zasha. But at some point last year, I think they decided they could benefit each other."

She used her stylus to bring up pictures of boats on the TV and looked at Carwyn.

"These are all vessels of various size and utility that Gavin Wallace sent to us last night," he said.

Brigid flicked through a dozen pictures, one after another. A barge. A fishing trawler. A yacht. Something that looked like a ferry. More barges.

Carwyn continued. "All these vessels were bought by anonymous buyers or shell companies inside of shell companies. And none of them are currently registered in any legal way."

Buck stared at the screen, shaking his head. "I don't recognize any of these ships."

Brigid leaned on the table. "They've all been tracked to the Pacific Northwest over the past twelve months, and then they disappeared."

Carwyn said, "And every single one belongs to Henri Paulson."

Dead silence filled the room.

Jennie narrowed her eyes. "How do you know?"

Ben raised a hand. "I actually know this part. Gavin is really pissed off, and he has a team of hackers. He followed the money. Paulson suddenly started shifting a lot of gold from known accounts in the Netherlands to vampire gold exchanges in Vancouver. Regular amounts sent monthly."

"To pay crew," Buck said. "I mean, you gotta have crew to run that kind of fleet, and you gotta pay 'em. And if it's off the books, they're gonna want cash."

"It may be a big ocean," Tenzin said, "but money is harder to hide."

Brigid continued, flipping the screen to more boats. "Paulson has mixed this growing shadow fleet with his legitimate fleet to expand his operations. These are not all in the Pacific Northwest —a good few of 'em are in Northern Europe." She looked at Jennie. "Have his tariffs for doing business in Katya's territory increased? Reportin' to human authorities is one thing, but he should have reported them to Katya."

Jennie glanced at Buck. "I don't deal with financial stuff. Not my area. Like I said, Paulson doesn't cause trouble."

Carwyn spoke quietly. "Are you sure about that? Why does he have all these ships? Why is he expanding so quickly?"

"He's a smuggler," Ben said. "That's obvious. And you know he's hiding vampires who want to disappear."

"That's not a crime in our world." Jennie leaned forward. "And Paulson's not the only one who's disappeared in the past, is he?"

Ben smirked. "I didn't disappear so I could avoid paying taxes or quietly foster a vampire regime change."

Tenzin opened her mouth, took a breath, then shut it, pursing her lips and letting out a soft "Hmmm."

Ben glanced at his mate. "I'm not answering for her."

Brigid raised her voice. "Smuggler or not—and all of us have known a few smugglers, hardly uncommon in our world."

Carwyn nearly laughed. Brigid would know. She'd worked for one.

"Paulson seems to be somethin' different," Brigid continued. "And thanks to Carwyn, we now know he's a conspiracy theorist who is attracting other immortals to his vision for a new world. A *blue haven* on the ocean so they don't have to be accountable to any vampire or human government."

Carwyn said, "Paulson has quietly amassed a shadow fleet of ships captained by humans and immortals who are only loyal to him, and he's hiding them along the Alaskan coast."

Jennie still wasn't convinced. "Katya's still in charge of this territory."

"But does Paulson recognize that?" Ben asked quietly. "You know where these facts are pointing." He looked at Jennie's husband. "Buck?"

Buck took a deep breath and watched his wife, but he kept his mouth shut.

Carwyn was watching Jennie herself. She was Katya's lieutenant. She was the one responsible for the vampires in this area.

And Paulson had floated under her radar.

"But it's not only the vampire boats." Carwyn kept his eyes steady on Katya's woman. "The Northwest Passage is no longer a rumor. It's *going* to be a reality in the next fifty years, and Paulson has money, power, and a fleet of ships in Katya's territory primed to take advantage of a new shipping lane."

"But he's a greedy fucker," Brigid said. "Oleg on one side of the Bering Strait, Katya on the other. He might not want to pay the tariffs they'd both charge to keep his fleet movin'."

Buck finally spoke. "Okay, so you're saying that Zasha is the one attacking these villages, but Paulson is the one pulling the strings?"

"It's exactly the kind of job Zasha would revel in. Maximum chaos. Very little risk for themself. Zasha doesn't want to be an emperor, but Paulson's been dreamin' about it for centuries I'd bet. I guarantee Paulson thinks he's too brilliant to answer to any authority other than himself."

"So Zasha is Paulson's attack dog." Tenzin's eyes lit. "He's trying to start a war between Katya and Oleg. Then, when they are weakened from fighting each other, Paulson will be well-positioned to make Alaska his vampire kingdom with all the rich vampires he has persuaded to join him."

Carwyn sighed. "Please don't sound impressed."

Ben put a hand on Tenzin's. "We are definitely *not* impressed, because Paulson's plan would be horrible and not desirable at all. But it would be clever."

"That's all I was saying," Tenzin muttered.

"It's also a real big stretch." Jennie leaned on the table. "*Oleg* is a Sokholov. If there's a vampire pulling Zasha's strings, doesn't it make more sense that it's someone from their own clan? I'm telling you, Oleg is behind these attacks, Katya's missing ships. All of it."

Brigid shook her head. "Oleg hasn't had anythin' to do with Zasha in years. And Tenzin and I saw the attacks in the north first-hand. Oleg's people didn't cause them. They think Katya is responsible."

Jennie rose to her feet and slammed a hand on the table so hard it cracked. "That's bullshit. Why would Katya attack her own people? Oleg may think he's got a foothold in Kenai, but those humans and vampires were under our aegis, not his! She would never attack humans or vampires she was responsible for."

"We agree," Carwyn said. "But the two of you have been blaming each other for months now, and Brigid and I needed both of you to hear each other before we could move forward and cooperate against a common enemy."

Jennie blinked. "What are you talking about?"

Carwyn looked at his wife, who nodded.

He flipped his tablet around to reveal Katya Grigorieva's face on the screen.

Then Brigid flipped her tablet around to reveal Oleg Sokolov's face on the other screen.

Jennie looked between the two vampire rulers. "Katya, give me the word. We have a perimeter."

CHAPTER TWENTY-SIX

B en had felt the gathering of vampires—air and water mostly
—the moment they stepped inside the meetinghouse, so he
knew that Carwyn, Brigid, and Tenzin felt them too.

His amnis stilled, joining his mate's, as the room fell silent.

He smelled a faint whiff of smoke that had to be Brigid, and
the ground vibrated slightly beneath his feet.

Carwyn's voice was a warning. "Careful, everyone."

Despite the smell of smoke, Brigid took a deep breath and
spoke in a calm voice. "Oleg, I told *you* that Katya wasn't behind
this, and you've heard everythin' we said here."

"And Katya" —Carwyn's voice remained a low growl— "you
know us. We have lived peacefully in your territory and recognized your authority for years. You've listened to Brigid. You've
seen the files Gavin sent you, I'm assuming?"

That day, while the vampires were resting, Gavin's people had
sent through a treasure trove of information, and Ben had
forwarded everything about the ships, the gold transfers, and a list
of known associates who were working on Paulson's new fleet to
Katya's and Oleg's email addresses as Brigid and Carwyn had
requested.

"I read the files," Oleg said in a low voice. "Ekaterina Grigorieva, I swear on my honor that I had nothing to do with these attacks. When I attack you, I will not use humans as my shields or sneak behind your back like a fox."

Ben looked at Katya's face, visible on Carwyn's tablet.

Brigid prompted her. "Katya?"

The small woman was sitting in the dark, and a faint red glow illuminated her pale skin. Her chin was propped on two delicate fingers, and her lips were slightly pursed. "What do you want from us, Brigid Connor?"

"We need to cooperate," Brigid said. "We need *both* your resources and both of your permissions to share information. Zasha is workin' with Paulson, and if you've seen Gavin's files, you probably both have come to the same conclusions."

Oleg grunted. "Brigid Connor, you have my permission to share the information I gave you with whomever you deem necessary to rid this territory of this menace."

Brigid looked at Katya.

The small vampire didn't look pleased, but she didn't look angry either.

"Jennie, you can work with them," Katya said. "Give them what they need. Paulson isn't our friend and he never has been. Whatever he's been paying me isn't enough to make up for unleashing this on our people and whatever fucked-up plans he has to take over." She looked from Jennie to Brigid. "And make no mistake—the people lost in Kenai *are my people*." With that statement, the screen went blank.

"What a pleasant evening." Oleg sounded amused. "If you need reinforcements—"

"We don't need anything from you." Jennie cut him off. "And Brigid, I want to see what you have on Paulson. I'm sick and tired of being in the dark."

Tenzin laughed, and everyone looked at her.

"It's amusing because the nights here are long," she said. "We're all in the dark."

————

BUCK AND CARWYN spread a large map of Alaska on the center of the table and another one beside it that was a larger detail of the Inside Passage.

Tenzin floated over the table, trying to picture the geography in her mind. "Tell me the dates."

"Paulson's boat wasn't the first," Buck said. "A fishing boat went missing two weeks before Zasha met with Paulson."

Tenzin saw Buck put a pin on the map. It was just north of Vancouver.

She made a mental picture of Zasha's movements. They'd moved from Las Vegas up through Katya's territory, possibly skirting into the sparse interior of Western Canada to avoid the prying eyes of the Athabaskan Confederation.

"The first attack was outside Vancouver." She closed her eyes and pictured the two vampires she was tracking. "Where did Zasha meet with Paulson?"

"Not far." Buck placed another yellow flag. "Within the Hecate Strait."

"The Hecate Strait is north of Vancouver." Tenzin blinked her eyes open. "They met about their plan. The crew gossiped that Paulson didn't look pleased to see Zasha. Perhaps they were more than Paulson bargained for. Perhaps Paulson didn't like Zasha drawing attention to themself in Las Vegas."

"Either way," Carwyn said, "at that point, Paulson was committed. A few weeks later, he and the entire crew of the *Dolphin* drop off the map just outside Sitka."

Buck placed another two flags. "And after that, another fishing boat goes missing."

Brigid stood, looking down at the maps, her arms crossed over her chest. "Now Zasha's movin'. There's a gap between the incidents. Nearly a month that nothin' happens after Katya's second fishing boat disappears."

"But then the attacks start up north." Tenzin's eyes moved to the western edge of the Alaskan Peninsula. "The first compound that Oleg reported was south of Katmai Bay."

"Lev called it a village." Brigid went over and pointed to a spot on the map, and Jennie placed a red dot. "At least twenty victims that we know of. They estimated somewhere in the beginning of September, but they didn't find it until weeks later."

"Then another one on Kodiak Island." Tenzin drew a mental line on the map. "Moving across the water. Maybe a week or two later."

Jennie lifted a small yellow flag. "That would be the beginning of October?"

Brigid nodded.

Buck said, "We had another ship go missing in that time, but it was in Prince William Sound."

Tenzin blinked. "Zasha isn't a wind vampire. They can't move the way Ben and I can."

Carwyn's booming voice interrupted Tenzin's train of thought. "Zasha has wind vampires working with them, and it's clear from what we know of the attacks that they have hunting parties with every element. Isn't it possible that Zasha sent someone to grab another boat in Katya's territory to sow confusion?"

The priest was right, but Tenzin wasn't going to say it.

Ben added, "It's logical that there would be multiple raiding parties at work, especially if the goal was to get Katya and Oleg fighting each other. Steal a boat in Katya's territory, attack a village in Oleg's."

"It's not Oleg's territory." Jennie's voice was sharp. "And I resent the implication that—"

"Officially it might not be." Tenzin stared at the map from her position overhead. "But this part of Alaska looks east to Oleg for protection" —she waved a hand over the territory west of Anchorage— "and this part of the state looks south to Katya. Let's not get caught up in politics when we're hunting."

"So they attack a village in the west," Brigid said, "then jump over and steal a boat in the east. But still movin' steadily along the coast."

"Zasha and Paulson don't want to go inland, and they don't want to draw the Athabaskans into this," Ben said. "If they do that, they're way outnumbered."

"Moving along." Carwyn stood and started pacing around the room. "The attacks continue along the coast, roughly one every couple of weeks."

"And then back toward the tip of Seward," Brigid said. "We know that one was only a few weeks back because there was a survivor."

"More confusion," Buck said. "Keep moving south but send a few people to attack Oleg's people so there's not a clear pattern."

"There were ten victims in the Seward attack," Brigid said as she placed another red dot. "Last I heard, Walter was hangin' in there."

"Spite," Tenzin whispered. She had to admire the old man she'd flown to the hospital. He's survived a vampire attack *and* human doctors.

Go, Walter.

"Zasha's overall trend is east and south though, pushing toward the Inside Passage," Tenzin said. "Why?"

Ben looked at the flags and the dots on the map. "I think we have to assume that Paulson is on a ship here somewhere." He waved a hand over the map of the watery maze that curved south from the Gulf of Alaska.

Buck said, "Most of this area has deepwater channels and pretty decent traffic, so you could move ships in and out of the area without anyone noticing. And there are" —he shook his head — "thousands of places to hide."

Tenzin surveyed the area. It was still huge. "Somewhere among all these islands, Paulson and Zasha have some kind of base."

"A base?" Carwyn frowned. "That doesn't sound like Paulson. From what we've heard, he's always mobile."

"He has a base." Jennie's voice was soft.

Every eye in the room turned toward her.

Tenzin stared at the quiet woman. "What do you know?"

"The elder that Carwyn found." She nodded at the big vampire. "He was talking in his sleep a little bit. Said something about a floating city." She shook her head. "I thought he was talking nonsense, maybe remembering old stories, but what if he was talking about a larger vessel, like one of these sea-steading things people talk about?"

"A floating city?" Tenzin pictured Penglai Island floating in the sky. It was a beautiful image. And terrible. That many dangerous vampires shouldn't be comfortable *and* mobile at the same time.

Ben shook his head. "As far as I know, none of the sea-steading environments that have been proposed are anything more than theories. And I definitely don't see anything of that type surviving an Alaskan winter."

Carwyn laughed a little. "It's obvious what he saw."

"A floating city is obvious?" Jennie asked.

Carwyn smiled. "What's a common sight around here? Something one of the old ones might see as a floating city."

Jennie shook her head. "I don't—"

"Large enough to survive the winter," Carwyn said. "Might be a little unusual this time of year, but not unheard of. And in the summer you wouldn't think twice."

"A cruise ship," Brigid answered. "Paulson must have a cruise ship."

Tenzin remembered Brigid talking about them before.

"Cruise ships?"

"Humans all grouped together on large boats. I'm talking massive boats."

"Yachts?"

"Bigger than yachts. Hundreds of bedrooms. Restaurants. Swimming pools. Nightclubs and pubs. Theaters sometimes."

Tenzin repeated her thought at the time. "It is a floating city."

Carwyn nodded. "And one that would blend into the background in a place like Alaska."

"It wouldn't in the winter," Ben said. "Don't the cruise ships float south in the winter?"

"Yes, but that elder was attacked in the summer months," Jennie said. "Maybe he saw something he shouldn't. Maybe that's why Zasha tried to kill him."

Tenzin looked at the many islands and peninsulas dotting the map. "Could you hide something that big?"

Everyone in the room spoke at once. "It's a big ocean."

She narrowed her eyes. Yes, the ocean was big, but vampires still had to drink human blood, and humans had to eat and sleep. If Paulson had created a floating city, there would be trails leading back to it.

If Paulson, Zasha, and all these vampires were hiding out on a giant boat somewhere, Tenzin would be able to find it.

———

SHE WAS WRAPPING herself in every warm layer she could find when Ben walked into their room.

"What are you doing?"

Tenzin looked at him. "It's cold."

"In our bedroom?" He frowned. "Why do you have a wool blanket tied around your torso, Tiny?"

She looked out the window of the house where they were sleeping. "There are at least five hours of darkness left. I love the winter here, but it's cold. Why are all the really dark places so cold?"

Ben leaned against the doorframe. "Sometimes I really question if you listen to yourself speak."

Fine. Whatever. She wasn't looking for a scientific answer. "A boat that could be mistaken for a floating city would be massive," she told him. "And it wouldn't be easy to hide even in a place like this."

"Are you sure?"

"It's a big ocean, but they'll need fuel, they'll need to hunt. They'll need food if they're keeping humans. Anything that big will have lights. I can find lights."

"Not necessarily," he said. "That barge I was watching had very few lights visible."

Tenzin considered that. "Then what do you suggest?"

"I suggest planning." He pushed away from the door, closed it, locked the dead bolt, and began to unwrap the layers around her body. "Zasha hasn't attacked anyone in nearly a week. They're going to start getting restless, so right now Jennie is putting out an alert to every vampire compound in the area, trying to warn everyone that they could be at risk."

"That sounds wise, but what are we supposed to do?" She spread her arms. "I'm not going to wait around for another attack."

"You and I?" He smiled. "Well, after I get finished taking all these blankets off—Buck has modern rain gear, you know—I'm going to strip you naked, lick between your thighs, and make you come very hard."

Tenzin's fangs were always down, but they got longer when her blood moved. "Is that the plan?"

"Then, after a couple of hours of that, if we still have some night left, you and I are going to go through Gavin's list and start tracking all the day people we can find who have worked for Henri Paulson. I want to find out who's picking up that cash in Vancouver and where they're taking it."

"A couple of hours?" Her lips heated at the thought. Ben was very good at the thing he was describing.

"Mm-hmm." He unwound the last scarf from around her neck and trailed his fingers around her collarbone. "I'm still mad that you left me." His light touch skimmed over the top of her clothes, circling her nipples, which rose at the sensation of his fingers over her skin. "I might need to torment you a little bit."

"This is not tormenting behavior, Benjamin."

Ben reached down and cupped her sex with one hand as he put the other around her throat, holding her still as his fangs scraped along her exposed neck.

"Not yet." His tongue flicked against the sudden pulse that rose in her veins. "But don't worry; we'll get there."

CHAPTER TWENTY-SEVEN

Carwyn didn't waste time after they ended the calls with Oleg and Katya. Those two vampire regents would have to figure out their territorial disputes eventually, but before that, they had a usurper and a sociopath to deal with.

"I wonder," Brigid muttered.

He looked over at his wife, who was finally beside him, working next to him like she should have been for months.

His heart took a quick double beat when he looked at her.

She noticed and glanced over. "What's up?"

"I'd break the world for you," he said quietly. "You know that, don't you?"

Brigid's focus broke and her eyes softened. "I don't want you to break it. Not for me or anyone."

"That's why I'd do it without a second thought." He took a slow, measured breath. "It was a risk doing that. Jennie had twenty vampires gathered around."

"We calculated the risk of danger against the danger of continuin' to work on parallel tracks."

"I know, and you were right." He frowned. "You understand Oleg better than I do."

"Yeah." She nodded. "I asked some mutual friends for their opinions before I went to him for help last autumn. Talked to Anne and her sister Mary. Reached out to Terry in London to get his read. He's had some dealin's with Mika in the past."

"Look at you, my brilliant woman." The corner of his mouth turned up. "How did you get so smart?"

"Genetics and a lot of fuckups." She leaned over and pressed a long kiss to his mouth. "And I've learned a few things about human nature from the wisest man I know."

He caught her around the waist. "How dare you call me wise."

"Don't worry," she whispered. "I won't let your secret get out."

Carwyn pulled her down to the bench and settled her between his spread legs. "It was still a risk. Katya could have gone either way."

"I know, and we're in her territory." She looked up. "But I also know that my husband is a force of nature who'd break the world for me."

He rested his chin on her shoulder. "And my wife is a warrior who commands fire."

She snapped her fingers and brought a glowing yellow flame to her palm, holding it just over her skin. "You might break the world for me, Carwyn ap Bryn, but if anyone tried to hurt you, I'd turn this forest into ash, and I don't think I'd care who I hurt."

"No, you're wrong." He reached out, warming his fingers over the yellow-gold flame in her hand. "Your heart is bigger than the ocean out there, Brigid. You do what needs to be done, my girl, but you're never thoughtless about it."

"I wondered." She turned her face to his. "After Zasha seemed to become so... infatuated with me. I wondered why. I wondered if there was somethin' about me that they recognized. Somethin' I wasn't seein' in myself. Some weakness or cruelty."

"There's nothing about you that's the same as Zasha."

"No." She put a hand on his cheek. "That's not true. I think

Zasha's life was quite horrible as a human. I'm certain of it. They've been powerless. They know what that feels like."

"Lots of people—human and immortal—suffer in life, Brigid. And the vast majority never hurt other people. At least not intentionally."

"I know." She nodded. "Mika Arakas told me once that Zasha is fascinated with me because they see my fear but I live with it and haven't allowed hate to consume me."

Carwyn never expected to find wisdom in the words of an Estonian assassin, but there you go. Life still held surprises. "Mika isn't wrong. You know fear, but you don't allow it to control you."

"I was workin' with Oleg when I realized somethin' else."

He narrowed his eyes. "What do you mean, working with Oleg?"

She turned the fire in the palm of her hand. "On my fire. On controllin' it. I only ever trained with Kathy, and that was right after I turned."

"I'm surprised he helped you."

She rolled her eyes. "He's not that bad."

"He'd like to restore the empire his sire allowed to fracture, and he'll do it in such an underhanded fashion people won't even realize he's consolidating power."

Brigid opened her mouth, then closed it.

Carwyn raised his eyebrows. "You know I'm right."

"But is that necessarily a bad thing? Not for humans, but for our kind?"

She had a point, but Carwyn hated to admit it.

"He'll run into problems in Central Asia if he keeps going." Carwyn pulled her back. "What did you realize when you were working with Oleg on your fire?"

"I didn't realize it really. It was him."

That damn Russian. If he wasn't dead certain that his wife would incinerate Oleg if she spent too much time with the

Russian, he might actually be jealous. "Fine, what did Oleg say?"

"He said: your fire cannot serve you if it is always protecting you." She looked at Carwyn. "Do ya think he's right?"

Carwyn let out a soft breath. "I know he's right."

Elemental energy was a curious thing. Carwyn's element was earth, but his relationship to that element was entirely different to Brigid's connection to fire.

The earth was a nurturing mother. It grew life and held all of nature and human civilization on its sturdy back. While Carwyn commanded the earth, he did so as a supplicant.

Any request he made of his element was a gesture of humility because he would never be more powerful than the whole of earthly matter. But the whole of earthly matter was also designed to nurture life.

Fire wasn't a mother or a foundation. It was a feral lion that had to be mastered. It could be protective. It could be territorial, and it was ferocious in battle.

But it was still a lion.

Carwyn said, "Old fire vampires are dominant personalities for a reason."

Brigid lifted her chin. "Like me."

"I know." Carwyn knew she had to be. Any immortal not strong enough to hold that leash would be consumed by it. Carwyn whispered, "But you're also at the average age."

Brigid blinked. "What's that?"

"You're at the average age of a fire vampire," he repeated softly. "You've been a vampire for roughly fourteen years."

"And?"

"That's about average," he said. "It's not like there've been studies, my love. But after a thousand years, you notice things. And one of them is that if a fire vampire makes it past fifteen, chances are" —he nodded— "they'll survive."

Her expression was bleak. "Because most of us die young."

Carwyn nodded. "Your element isn't a kind mother, Brigid. It's a lion."

"It'll serve me, but only if it doesn't have to protect me," she murmured. "So how do I let my lion know that I don't need to be protected?"

He shook his head. "I don't know."

"Maybe a better question is: Does that man at the circus ever really tame the lion?" The corner of her mouth turned up. "Or is it all an elaborate trick?"

———

SUMMER MACKENZIE TAPPED the tablet to end her call with her sire before she turned to the vampire sitting on her right. "Well, that's interesting."

"What is it?" Her best friend, Raven, was flipping through files across the room, fingering the short twists she'd just had braided into her normally short-cropped hair.

"Leave your hair alone. It's cute."

Raven huffed out a breath. "It feels weird. What did the boss want?"

"Do you recognize the name Henri Paulson?"

Katya's office in Vancouver was a concrete apartment building in the Beach District. Perched on the seawall and overlooking the harbor, the building housed most of the vampire's support staff in the city. It sat right on the water, which made water vampires like Summer happy, but it also had wraparound balconies, which made air vampires like Raven content.

Raven shrugged. "Paulson's a tech billionaire of the fanged persuasion. Water type. He's in and out of the port in the summer, but he doesn't cause trouble."

"Does he have day people around here that you know of?"

Raven narrowed dark brown eyes and looked at the glowing lights of Vancouver out the window. "I can think of two or three people who would probably work with him, but I don't know that they're exclusive."

Summer had discovered that around any vampire community, there were contract employees who were hired to do daylight jobs but not permanently attached to any particular vampire. They were kind of like immortal gig workers, and Summer had even used a few in her time for... personal errands.

"Katya wants us to go to the gold exchange tomorrow night."

Raven's eyebrows went up. "Why?"

"Sounds like Paulson's up to something," Summer said. "Someone told the boss that he's moving a ton of gold into Vancouver, getting a lot of Canadian dollars. Enough to be noticeable."

"Okay," Raven said. "He might be buying a new boat or something. I think that guy is obsessed with boats. Mostly lives on one." She cocked her head. "Would you do that?"

"Live on a boat?" Summer considered it. "I might, but I like fresh water more than salt. I'd live in a houseboat in a hot minute though. Or one of those canal boats in Europe."

"Yeah, those are cool." Raven shook her head. "But I would not be your roommate."

"Fair enough." Summer looked at the notes she'd taken while she was on the phone with her sire. "Katya wants to find out what Paulson's doing with all the cash he's pulling out."

Raven put down her files. "Wait, he's taking all this gold out of the exchange in *cash*?"

"Yeah. Twenty million worth of green Canadian dollars, my friend."

Raven's mouth dropped open. "That's... a lot of cash. And Canadian currency isn't green."

Summer pushed away from her desk and spun in her chair. "Why aren't we tech billionaires?"

"We should be."

"Right? No more filing." Summer lifted up a manila folder. "We could hire people to do filing."

Raven stared into the distance. "And fill out incident reports."

"We could hire people to be us, and then we could be cool, badass vampires."

"Speak for yourself." Raven sniffed. "I'm already a badass vampire."

"Keep telling yourself that the next time you're arguing with Baojia about the new incident-report form and why it's not as good as the old one."

Raven flipped her off. "To be fair, we weren't even born when Henri Paulson started investing in Silicon Valley, so he has a head start."

"Details." Summer rolled back to her desk and pulled out the compact 9mm handgun Baojia had given her for her birthday the year before. "Dusk tomorrow, Katya said. She wants me to go inside and you watch from above. We'll need to get Lang to monitor their comms. She wants to know who they contact when I go in and start asking questions."

"They won't answer any of them," Raven said. "You know the exchanges run on privacy. They're independent of aegis."

"I know, but depending on who they call or what messengers they send after I go in, that might tell Katya what she needs to know."

"Gotcha." Raven stood. "I'll let Lang know. Tomorrow night?"

"Yeah." Summer leaned back and kicked her feet up on the desk. "We get to shake that apple tree and see where the rats run out."

Raven just shook her head. "You are the hickest hick that ever did hick, Summer Mackenzie."

"Don't be jealous of my colorful Carolina vernacular just because you come from the frigid north, Jessup."

"My people are from Chicago, okay? Not the Yukon." Raven shook her head and walked out to the balcony. "See you at home."

———

RAJ WAS on a plane to Vancouver before the captain even connected the call from his boss. "Why am I flying to Canada?"

"Because I may need you there." Gavin's voice was clipped. "Did I inconvenience you?"

"I know who I work for." Though Raj had been doing some very amusing surveillance on a group of teenagers from a charter school in Long Beach who had been trying to hack into the Paladin servers.

The group of four boys and two girls had found rumors about Paladin on the dark web and decided that it must be full of spies, crypto-millionaires, and drug dealers instead of centuries-old vampires who were constantly forgetting their passwords or filing reports on YouTube videos that got historical events wrong.

"If you open your email," Gavin said, "you're going to find a file on Henri Paulson."

Raj recognized the name immediately. "I know him."

"Mild-mannered tech billionaire by day—"

"Nothing about Paulson is mild-mannered," Raj muttered. "Mila almost worshipped him. Thought he had all the right ideas. Vampires are the superior species. Humans are basically cattle, and immortals need to thin the herd so we don't suffer from their bad choices. Human governments shouldn't have any control over us or our resources."

"The whole buffet of vampire conspiracy, I see."

"Oh yeah." Raj tried not to think about his toxic former lover, especially since she was dead, but at times the security work he did for Gavin Wallace made it impossible.

"Tell me what you know," Gavin said. "Beyond the conspiracy buffet. The man has more money than nearly anyone in our world, so he's not an idiot."

"He's not an idiot, but..." Raj took a deep breath. "Paulson thinks he's a genius, but he's not. He has a nearly cultlike following among water vampires in South Asia. Lots of them into the floating-city thing."

"What about you?"

Raj shook his head. "I may be a water vampire, but even I know it's not a feasible plan. We need humans to live, and humans need land. Not that Paulson cares much about humans."

"Brigid called him an imperialist."

"That's not wrong as long as he gets to be emperor. Paulson's young, but he's got grand aspirations, and he does have a knack for spotting opportunities before they become obvious. He'll find an actual genius, pump up their ego, and then steal their ideas or cheat them out of their intellectual property. Remember, he thinks humans are a natural resource like timber or wheat. He has no respect for their autonomy or their lives."

"Hmm. So he steals ideas and profits from them. Any idea who might be thinking of a Northwest shipping passage and gaining control of Alaska?"

"No, but with the environment going the direction it is, it's not a bad plan."

Who would benefit? Katya Grigorieva was the obvious answer, but Oleg was just on the other side of the Bering Strait. Then there were all the interests in Northern Europe who would love a faster shipping channel to Asia.

"Shipping isn't really your area, is it?" Raj wrinkled his nose, but he had to offer the best suggestion he could think of. "Have you talked to Brigid Connor? She used to work for Patrick Murphy, and she's on the West Coast now."

"She's already there," Gavin said. "You may be working with her and her mate. You don't have to be friendly, but you do have to be polite."

The last time he'd encountered the small fire vampire and her massive mate, they'd been accusing him of betraying Gavin and conspiring with the Ankers.

"Gavin, does this have to do with the Zasha Sokholov mess?"

"Yes. Zasha is in Alaska, and we think they're working with Henri Paulson."

A knot of dread curled in Raj's belly. "Paulson isn't as smart as I thought he was."

"I can't disagree." Gavin's Scottish brogue got a little heavier. "I think Paulson met a vampire who saw through him faster than he could anticipate."

"So is Paulson leading Zasha or is Zasha leading Paulson?"

"Either way, these people threatened my wife and I want you there."

"Understood." Raj took a deep breath and glanced out the window as the lights of Los Angeles retreated in the distance. "I'm on my way."

CHAPTER TWENTY-EIGHT

She flew over the dark ocean, scanning the surface of the pitch-black water, looking for anything that stood out.

"It's no good," she told Ben. "I hate to say they were right, but the ocean is too big."

"That's why Gavin and Katya sent people to Vancouver. Once we narrow down where the cash is going—"

"How long will that take?" It had already been nearly two weeks since Zasha's last attack. They wouldn't wait much longer. "Zasha offered to give up if Brigid killed me. They said they would walk into the sun if Brigid delivered my head."

Ben halted midair, froze as if the wind wasn't even battering him. Tenzin turned and looked back at her mate, and what she saw reminded her that Ben was far more powerful than he even realized.

Water dripped down his face, flowing from the black hair that fell onto his forehead. His beautiful mouth was a thin line, and his silver eyes stared with flat fury.

But though a storm pressed into the coast of Alaska, bringing ice, rain, and ferocious wind, the air around Ben was calm, absolutely still, as if waiting for his command.

"She wouldn't," Tenzin said. "Obviously I wouldn't let her."

"Zasha is evil."

"They're..." Evil was a moral judgment, and Tenzin didn't know what belief system Zasha was raised to adhere to in their human life. What was permissible in one moral code could be reprehensible in another. "Zasha is practical. They have an aim—to kill me and destroy my life—and pitting those who consider me a friend against each other would be an effective tactic to achieve that goal."

"I would kill her," he said. "If Brigid killed you, I would—"

"Yes." Tenzin flew to him and put a hand on his cheek. "Which is exactly what Zasha would want. And then Carwyn would try to kill you, pitting him against your uncle, his oldest friend, and it would all spiral into a very horrible storm that Zasha could sit back and watch."

The corner of his lip twitched and Tenzin saw his fangs, fully extended and red with blood where he'd cut his lip. "Benjamin."

He reached out, put his hand at the small of her back, and pulled her to his body.

She felt his amnis riot, then calm as it recognized her own. "I did not tell you this to anger you."

"You know how to survive." His voice was soft. "You need to survive."

"I don't." Tenzin was far from sentimental about her own immortality. "Not really. I have had so much time. But you do, and you seem happier when you have me, so I will be less careless about my safety."

His gaze finally unfroze, and his eyes moved to meet hers. "Less careless? Like not flying off into the Alaskan wilderness and leaving me in order to meet a vampire who might have killed you?"

Tenzin kept her hand on his cheek. "She wouldn't have killed me. Her moral code wouldn't permit it."

"You're right." He blinked. "You're right." Ben took a deliberate breath. "My reaction is exactly what Zasha wants. They want to divide us."

"Like I said, Brigid's moral code would not permit it, and mine would not sacrifice myself because it would be detrimental to you."

Ben's eyes turned from rage-filled to calculating. "I wonder what Henri Paulson would have said if Brigid did kill you and then Zasha killed themself."

"I suspect he would not like it. He probably thinks Zasha is required to follow his directions."

"Zasha never follows directions," Ben muttered. "That's what killed the Ankers' plans."

Tenzin frowned. "Why did Paulson recruit Zasha? Is his ego really that big that he thinks Zasha Sokholov would do his bidding?"

"I'm guessing that Paulson thinks like other rich vampires. Well, rich vampires other than you."

She slid her hand from his cheek to his palm, knit their fingers together, and nudged him to fly next to her as they made their way south to Vancouver. "What do you mean?"

"Rich people love money. They're motivated by it."

Tenzin nodded. "I do like money."

"Why?"

Tenzin considered the question. "Because I can do whatever I want if I have money, and I can acquire the things I want."

"Yes. And if you had enough money to do all that, would you still want more?"

She closed her eyes and let her mind drift to the wind caressing her skin and threading through her scalp.

"Tenzin?"

"Why would I want more if I have enough to get what I want? Money isn't interesting anymore. Now it's only numbers that Cara reads off when I ask her." She curled her lip. "Boring."

Ben smiled. "You're adorable."

"Unless it's gold." She smiled. "I like gold."

"Gold is a shiny thing for you," Ben said. "But it's not really money these days."

She was glad he understood that, because she sometimes became concerned he didn't realize how fleeting modern human civilization was. "Because money is a human construct that means nothing."

"I know."

"And gold is gold."

"Exactly."

She quickly added, "And paintings are inherently worthless."

"Can we focus?"

The thread of irritation in his voice made her smile. "I know what you're saying. Paulson isn't like me. He *likes* the numbers on the screen."

"He likes the chase and acquisition of anything and everything. It's his form of hunting," Ben said. "How would you try to bribe someone, Tenzin?"

She turned toward the distant lights of Vancouver and sighed. "I would probably just threaten them. Bribery could be expensive."

"Okay, never mind." Ben tugged her hand and pulled her to float over him, cocooning her in the bubble of quiet he created as he flew. "Paulson likes money. He wants money, so he assumes everyone else does too. He offered Zasha money and thinks the lure of that money will control them."

"That's very stupid," Tenzin said. "Zasha is a living reaction, not a calculation. I doubt they've even considered what they would do with the money if Paulson actually paid them."

"Which he might."

"Which he won't" —Tenzin corrected her mate— "because we're going to kill Zasha."

Ben arched his neck up and kissed her. "Exactly."

———

THEY ARRIVED IN VANCOUVER, following the directions Katya had given them until they spotted the building she'd described, a four-story office building in a sea of office buildings on the edge of the commercial district in Vancouver.

"I haven't spent much time here," Ben said. "You?"

"No." Tenzin pointed her chin at the building opposite the one where they were perched. "But this is the gold exchange."

A wind vampire named Raven was already waiting, watching the building with steady eyes. Katya had described the vampire to Ben, and Tenzin had a hard time imagining there were two tall, ridiculously beautiful, Black wind vampires in Vancouver with golden-blond braids.

Ben looked at Tenzin gaping at Raven, and he snickered a little bit. "So if I got blond extensions, that would go over well, huh?"

She shook her head. "You couldn't pull it off."

"And now I'm a little bit hurt." He sent a gust of wind over to Raven, laden with their amnis and their scent.

The wind vampire turned her head, caught sight of them in the distance, and watched them with steady eyes before she pulled out a small device and spoke into it. A moment later, she waved them over.

"Ben Vecchio." Her eyes moved to Tenzin. "And Tenzin?"

"Mm-hmm."

"I've heard of you." Raven's fangs fell a little bit. "I'm a little intimidated to work with you guys if I'm gonna be completely honest."

"You won't be working with us," Tenzin said. "We're here for information."

The young vampire's expression fell. "Oh. Right."

"But obviously, it's really important information," Ben was quick to add. "And we were told you know the city really well, so you were the person to talk to."

"Thanks." Her expression brightened a little bit. "Uh, yeah, so we've been watching for a couple of hours now. Our tech guy, Lang, he's got a hook into their system, I guess. Less than an hour after Summer went in there—"

"Summer?" Tenzin didn't know a Summer.

"Katya's youngest daughter," Ben said. "Brigid and Carwyn know her."

"Yeah." Raven nodded. "So she went in there, asked some questions. No answers obviously because it's a gold exchange."

"Obviously." Tenzin didn't trust the exchanges to hold her gold as some vampires did, but they were a useful service if you wanted to move money in immortal circles.

"But messages started flying," Raven said. "Lang said there were some back to Amsterdam, which is where Paulson has his gold reserves according to what Katya could find out."

"Matches with what Gavin's people said," Ben muttered. "Anywhere else?"

"Lang said no phone calls other than Amsterdam, but there were messages sent—apparently their messaging security is something like tin cans connected by a string—to a server in Iceland, then it bounced around a couple of times before it landed back here in Vancouver."

Ben frowned. "So the gold exchange sent a message to... itself?"

"No, it didn't go back to the same server, but it did come back to Vancouver before Lang lost it." Raven shrugged. "And that's all we know so far."

"Did you find his day people?"

"That's Summer's job," Raven said. "She's better at interviewing people than I am. Apparently I'm seen as intimidating."

"Clearly that would be an asset," Tenzin said.

"Right?" The girl huffed out a breath. "But no, Katya wanted soft hands for this one. Said she didn't want to scare anyone off."

"We need to track the physical cash," Ben said. "Paulson is paying his people, and it's likely going to be in cash considering where they are."

"Where is Summer?" Tenzin asked. "She was the one you were calling when you saw us?"

"Yeah." She lifted a large phone. "She's got two day people she thinks might have taken gigs for Paulson." Raven looked Ben and Tenzin up and down. "You guys bring anyone who's slightly less..."

"Scary?" Tenzin asked. "Lethal?"

"Vampire-y." Raven looked embarrassed. "If Grim Reapers exist in our world, they would look like the two of you."

Ben muttered, "Fucking flannel shirts."

"You want someone who looks human and nonintimidating?" Tenzin asked. "He's already on a plane."

CHAPTER TWENTY-NINE

I f there was one thing that Carwyn loved, it was an American-style diner. They could be glossy, retro reproductions or gritty, dive-like holes-in-the-wall.

He loved the smell of burnt coffee, bacon grease, and hairspray. The scent of cigarette smoke that clung to the older staff. He even liked the cracked vinyl booths, though he could rarely fit into them.

"Oh fuck me, you're in heaven, aren't ya?" Brigid's smile was amused.

"This is *brilliant*." It was a retro diner, but one that hadn't been reproduced. The red vinyl booths were well-kept but cracked with age, and the chrome detailing along the edges was original and shined to a bright mirror finish.

The menu was on a board posted over the counter, and a young woman with blue hair stood waiting to greet them, wearing a white apron over her jeans and vintage bowling shirt.

"Hey, welcome to Janie's. Two?" She grabbed laminated menus. "You eating here or—"

"Meeting friends," Brigid said quickly, pointing to the redhead at the end of the diner who was already sitting down.

"Oh, for sure!" The girl quickly ushered them down the aisle to the large round booth that anchored the diner. "Hey, Summer. Didn't realize you were expecting more."

The young vampire looked up, her blue eyes meeting Carwyn's. She smiled, and his heart eased a little bit.

"Yeah, I wasn't sure if they were gonna make it in time." She looked at the waitress. "Thanks, Rose."

"No problem." She turned to Carwyn and Brigid. "What can I get you to drink?"

"Coffee," they both said at once.

Carwyn and Brigid had learned that tea was best left on the other side of the ocean unless they were making it themselves.

Brigid sat next to Summer, and Carwyn slid in behind her, angling into the booth the best he could. He looked at the two young men who were sitting across from Summer and staring at both of them with wide eyes.

"Hiya," Carwyn said. "How is it, lads?" He slumped his shoulders and turned on his best "friendly father" voice. "Thanks for coming to speak with us."

The dark-haired young man who looked South Asian turned to his friend. "Oh, I didn't think we had a choice about it. Can we just—?"

"Nah, he's just being nice." Summer cut him off. "Katya wants you to talk to them and answer their questions."

Carwyn smiled and said nothing, but the two young men seemed a little more at ease when they turned back to him.

The other young man looked like a surfer from California, and his ball cap was turned backward on his head with a fluffy sprout of curls poking over his forehead like blond broccoli. "So Ravi and I, we take turns with the gigs, right? But we follow the letter. We're looking for a permanent position. We've never skimmed cash or anything like that. We're *honest*."

"We wouldn't think of it," Ravi said. "Callum and I are very clear with our clients. We're a team, and that means if one of us if off duty, the other is on. We cover all kinds of clients—we don't discriminate against elements—and we are completely discreet."

"And honest," Callum said again.

Brigid piped up. "We're not worried about you skimmin', lads. We just need to know where you took the cash you picked up last week from the exchange."

Ravi and Callum exchanged a look.

"Listen," Callum said, "I just said we're discreet. This was a new client, but we protect all clients' privacy like we're regular employees. That's how we stay in business."

"We don't need to know who," Carwyn said. "You won't know their real name anyway. But Katya needs to know *where* it was taken."

Summer added, "Guys, this is a territorial security thing, okay? I promise Katya is not trying to jam you up or hurt your reputation, but she needs to know." Summer wiggled her fingers. "You know I can get you to answer if you don't cooperate."

Ravi sat back. "Summer, that is not cool."

"I thought we were friends," Callum said. "Why would you—?"

"Territorial." Summer spoke slowly. "Security. These are not people you want to work for, guys. We need a location."

Both Ravi and Callum were silent for a long moment, and then Callum muttered, "Dock on the west side of Granville Island."

"Dude." Ravi hit his arm. "Callum—"

"Thank you," Brigid said quietly. "The people you took the job from are dangerous sociopaths who've attacked humans and vampires along the Alaskan coast. They're extremely violent, and they're not under Katya's aegis. If they contact you again…" She slid a card across the table. "Call us immediately. Hide. Don't meet them. You won't be safe."

As soon as Brigid slid across the card, the boys' faces drained of color.

"Thanks, lads." Carwyn leaned across and held out his hand to shake. "None of us think less of you. You know Katya wouldn't ask you to violate that trust unless it was a true risk, right?"

Ravi shook Carwyn's hand and shrugged. "Yeah, she's cool."

"I appreciate it, y'all," Summer added. "You need to take off?"

They nodded, clearly ready to leave.

"I'll get your tab," Summer added. "It's the least I can do."

The young men stood, and the blond one hesitated before he walked away.

"If anyone asks...," Callum started. "I mean—"

"I was asking you to acquire a large-screen television for my boat," Carwyn said. "Obviously. I'm going to email you the details now that I know I can trust you."

"Awesome." Callum smiled and looked at Summer. "See you, Summer."

Ravi grabbed his friend's sleeve and hurried them out of the diner, leaving Summer, Brigid, and Carwyn alone.

"Look at you." Carwyn smiled at the girl they'd been hired to find years ago. Summer had survived, but she'd decided to give her mortality to Katya in exchange for revenge on the vampires who took her and her boyfriend. "You're looking happy."

"Yeah, my family's finally used to it, I think." She smiled awkwardly. "Mom and Dad came out last summer. Even said how nice the city was, which shocked me to hell."

"Eh, the Mackenzies aren't city people," Brigid said. "As a rule."

Summer belonged to an immortal clan in the Carolinas consisting of human and vampire family members, some of whom were related to Carwyn by marriage. She was a young cousin, in his way of thinking, and he'd been keeping track of her.

"Katya says you're thriving here," he said. "Do you know the area the boys were talking about?"

"I do." Her Southern accent was just a hint after years in the Pacific Northwest. "I know the area anyway. We have the time and the location now. We'll be able to find out where they went and who they talked to as long as there are security cameras."

"Is that likely?" Brigid asked.

Summer nodded. "In that area? Definitely. There are a lot of businesses around there. Lang should be able to hack his way in. As long as they still have footage from last week, he'll find it."

———

BRIGID STOOD over the shoulder of a young man with curly dark hair that fell into his eyes and tattoos all over his neck. He was sitting in a dark office with no windows even though he was human. The strange cave looked like it belonged to a wizard in a fantasy novel, and the walls were lined with shelves filled with books, small figures of dragons and soldiers, and several reproduction swords.

Over the long counter that served as the young man's desk were three large posters, one of a popular sci-fi movie character, another with the slogan Can't Stop the Signal, and the last emblazoned with the words: I Smoke and I Know Things.

The young man's name was Lang, and Brigid guessed he was Katya's version of their Lee.

"So there's a bunch of fishing charters going in and out of those docks all year round." He typed as he talked. "All I had to do was hack into their security systems, so" —he rolled his eyes— "opposite of hard." He did something on the computer, and color footage jumped onto the screen. "No cap, Ravi and Cal are good guys. They wouldn't mess with a chaos vamp, so whoever this was must have seemed legit."

She was mostly keeping up. "You think Ravi and Callum didn't know who they were meeting?"

"Bet," Lang said. "I don't recognize this guy, but the boat?" He whistled. "Whatever vamp is bankrolling all this has money, and lots of it."

It was Ravi on the screen, and he was carrying a duffel bag and looked like any average Vancouverite coming from the gym and heading home. He walked over to a large yacht with a back deck, spoke to a man in a raincoat, and the man showed him something on his phone.

Ravi scanned the screen with his own phone, nodded, and handed over the bag.

"Most of the gig day workers use security codes to verify," Lang said. "Keeps everyone safe from influence, you know?"

"Brilliant," Brigid muttered. "A human under vampire influence would still have to verify a code, like a digital receipt. And if they couldn't, you'd know somethin' had gone wrong even if you couldn't remember."

"Exactly," Lang said. "Code doesn't verify, you know someone got scammed. You may still be up shit creek and out of money, but it helps keep people honest."

Summer said, "Now this is during the day, but Lang already sent the boat's registration number." She pointed at the screen. "See there? We've already looked it up, and it's registered to a shell corporation in the Cayman Islands."

"What's the next step?" Brigid asked. "How do ya track a boat?"

"For sure, for sure, my lady vampire." Lang started typing again. "Every boat—even ones owned by shell companies—should be hooked into the automatic identification system run by the International Maritime Organization, especially if they're docking all legit-like in the city."

"An automatic ID system?" Carwyn asked.

"Kind of like flight control for maritime vessels, my dude." Lang clicked on a few more buttons. "So I don't know exactly who owns this ship, but I can tell you where it was last week." He brought up a map with tiny arrows all over it. His cursor hovered over a purple arrow. "And I can tell you it left Vancouver and two days later it was docked in Petersburg, Alaska."

"Where?" Brigid leaned in to see a narrow strait of water north of Ketchikan and south of Juneau with glaciers on one side and a narrow network of sea and islands on the other. "Has it been there before? Can ya tell?"

"I can get historical data with the IMO number." He tapped more keys quickly. "It docked in Wrangell one time and Port Protection another time, but it looks like Petersburg was the place he kept going back to." Lang tapped the map. "So I'd say whatever deliveries he was making, it's in this area."

Brigid murmured, "There're so many places a large ship could hide. Even with wind vampires lookin', it could take weeks."

"Maybe not as many as you'd think." Summer leaned on her back leg and hooked her hands in her pockets. "Check with a local to be sure, but this area is known as the Wrangell Narrows, and it's not very deep. You're looking for a larger vessel, right? Sounded like a small cruise ship or a large yacht?" She nodded at the surveillance video. "Something a lot bigger than this fishing boat, I'm thinking."

Carwyn nodded. "That's our guess."

"Petersburg isn't a deepwater port. Nothing in the Wrangell Narrows is going to be deep enough for a ship like you're thinking." She moved her finger up the map. "Now above that, Frederick Sound is a better bet. I think you'd have more luck looking in that area."

"Either way." Carwyn nodded at Lang. "We've got someplace to start, and that's an improvement over before. Thank you, lad."

"Straight facts, my lord and my lady." Lang reached over and held up his fist.

He was odd but friendly. Brigid bumped her knuckles with the young man. "We owe ya one. Good work."

"You owe *me*?" Lang smiled a little. "Dope."

CHAPTER THIRTY

B en flew low over the waters of the Frederick Sound, scanning the cloudy night for any hint of light.

Stars, ships, flickers of civilization. Anything.

He glanced over his shoulder at his mate. "You're loving this, aren't you?"

Her moon-pale face in the color-leached night was glowing. "There's nothing. No people. I smell air and water and animals."

"And no boats."

"Not true." Tenzin pointed at distant green lights. "There are many boats, including cargo ships, because I can smell the fuel, but not anything like what we're looking for."

What they were looking for was a floating city, a vessel that looked out of place but not too out of place. One with lights and activity despite the winter cold.

He scanned the mountains on either side of the long bay they were flying over. Hills rising on either side of frosty water, the eastern slopes a prelude to glacier-covered peaks and valleys while the western reaches of land were blanketed by velvet evergreen forests.

There were ancient stretches of spruce, hemlock, and cedar;

streams pouring down to the ocean from near-constant precipitation; fresh water flowing from the sky and into the vast and winding ocean channels of the Tongass National Forest.

Occasionally the dense evergreens or cold ocean would be dotted with evidence of humanity—a light on a watchtower, a buoy bobbling near a dock. The coastline was jagged and sweeping, over eleven thousand miles of shore in just this section of the Inside Passage.

Tenzin headed toward a cluster of lights, dipping down to survey a village consisting of a dozen shops running along a street that led down to a dock lined by fishing boats.

"Another human town," Ben said.

"Did Katya and Jennie get ahold of all the vampire compounds in the area?"

"Most of them." He glanced at the forest beyond the town, feeling eyes that probably weren't there. "Do you believe in Bigfoot?"

"Yes." Tenzin shrugged. "Why not?"

"What do you mean, why not?"

"I've been alive for five thousand years, and I am still surprised by this planet and its secrets. Why wouldn't a large human-type creature exist in the forest?"

He shook his head. "I will never be able to predict what you're going to say."

"Good."

Ben felt a gust of wind rising off the water and he pushed it away, keeping a bubble of air around him and Tenzin like a cushion. They curved around the end of the bay in a large arc and headed up to rise over the cold hills and back to the main channel where they were looking for a boat.

A large boat.

An *occupied* boat, most likely a small cruise ship or a very large yacht. Less likely a tanker with containers.

"Do you think we're looking in the right place?" Ben asked.

Tenzin was silent for a long while. "I believe Brigid calculated that this was the most likely region for Paulson to be hiding."

"That wasn't an answer."

"I trust Brigid. Somewhat."

Ben narrowed his eyes. "I have a thought and I want to know if you're having the same thought, so can you just tell me what you really think?"

Tenzin glanced at him from the corner of her eye. "Brigid thinks if she finds Paulson, she'll find Zasha. I don't know if she is correct."

It was the same idea Ben had been chewing in his mind. "You think they're somewhere else."

"I'm thinking that Zasha probably likes boats about as well as another earth vampire we know."

———

"IF I NEVER SET FOOT IN a boat again," Carwyn muttered, "I'll be happy. I'll celebrate that. Not a single thing could make me regret that."

"My, my." Brigid sidled up to him as he stood on the bow of their fishing vessel, which was trolling through the waters of the Frederick Sound. "I see someone isn't enjoying the fresh air."

"Fresh air? You mean freezing air."

"It can be both." She couldn't help but be amused. For a thousand-year-old European, her husband did love warm weather. "Let's go to Mexico when this is all over."

Carwyn's eyes lit up. "Warm mountain towns? Historic cities? Lucha Libre tournaments that go on for hours?"

"All of that." Brigid smiled.

"That's a brilliant idea." He put his arm around her shoulders.

"And let's spend all the time on land. Nothing special about oceans anyway."

In the distance, just to prove her mate wrong, a massive orca breached the water, its rounded dorsal fin cutting through the night air as two other whales in the pod skimmed the surface before all three plunged into the black water.

"Nothin' special about oceans at all," Brigid said. "I'm sure we'll see somethin' like that in the mountains around San Miguel."

Carwyn blinked at the magnificent display. "Fine, boats aren't the worst mode of travel in the world—that remains the bicycle—but they are very close. In the bottom five unless there are whales."

"Not just boat slander but bicycles too? Jaysus." She tsked under her breath as her eyes narrowed in on a figure flying toward them. "No wonder the Danish vampire hates us."

Carwyn spotted the figure approaching from the sky. "Is that Tenzin?"

"No, it's Raven," Brigid said. "Her hair's tied back."

The wind vampire landed on the back deck of the ship with an uneven thunk, and Brigid and Carwyn walked around to greet her.

She perked up as soon as she met them. "Cool. I got the right boat. I ran into Tenzin flying north into the Stephens Passage. They spotted something in a bay that they think looked promising. I mean... suspicious." She shook her head. "You know what I mean."

"So we head north." Brigid nodded. "I'll tell the captain. Anythin' else you spotted?"

"Eh..." Raven shrugged. "I'm not an expert here."

Carwyn said, "You have good instincts. Did you notice something?"

"The lack of something," Raven said. "I mean, I know it's winter, but life goes on, right? We're not that far from Juneau, and

I think boat traffic is down from what it normally is this time of year. Which again, it's winter, so I might be wrong, but it seems low."

Brigid looked up at Carwyn. "Maybe Paulson put out the word that other boats weren't welcome."

"Or maybe something is happening to boats that normally travel in that area," he said. "There are residents who live along there, in areas that are probably mainly accessible by boat this time of year."

"You think there are more attacks we haven't found yet?" Raven asked. "More than the ones Katya blamed on Oleg?"

"You mean the ones Oleg blamed on Katya?" Brigid nodded. "We might never know who all Zasha and their people killed. But if there's less boat traffic than usual for this time of year, we have to at least consider that Paulson and Zasha are behind it."

———

TENZIN LOOKED around the narrow fjord they were flying over. "Maybe we should sell the house in Shanghai and buy a place here."

"It's freezing cold in winter."

"And it's burning hot in Shanghai all summer."

"The only time the weather is nice here are the summer months when there's something like twenty hours of sunlight."

Her excitement did not wane. Ben was thinking like a human. "I'm just saying we should consider it."

"Or," Ben offered, "maybe Paulson has the right idea and we should all be living on boats."

She glanced at him. "Let's not be ridiculous."

"Think about it, Tiny. A ship with a huge deck. Privacy on the water. We could get a converted barge with a huge, light-safe hold."

She smiled. "*You're* suggesting this? *You?*"

"I'm just saying we're going to need a new base after..." He blinked. "I mean, we lost New York. Maybe it's a sign that we need to go somewhere new. I'm not saying I want to live on a freighter, but a nice luxurious river barge in Paris or Copenhagen? That's hardly like living on a boat at all. And you keep saying that things in Paris need to be shaken up. Maybe what they really need is a vampire coup, and we both know that's practically a guarantee when you come to—"

"This is an intriguing train of thought." Her voice was soft. "But why don't we talk about it after we lose the vampire who's been following us for the past few minutes?"

Ben didn't turn to look. "Raven?"

"No. A male. He's been following us since we first started flying up this inlet."

She started to turn to face the enemy, but Ben snapped at her.

"Head forward!"

"Why? I'll simply kill him now. His amnis is much weaker than ours, and we don't want him reporting our presence to Paulson."

"How do you know he belongs to Paulson?"

"Because he's not one of Katya's people or he wouldn't be following at this distance."

"Fair enough, but don't kill him."

"Yet?"

Ben sighed a little bit. "Let him tail us and see how he reacts. If he keeps on our tail, that means we're probably on the right track."

Tenzin considered it and decided it wasn't the worst idea in the world. "I think we're exploring the right inlet. The water looks very deep, and there are no settlements on the coastline."

"Exactly," Ben said. "Plus this isn't a strait, according to

Raven, but a bay. That means there won't be any random passing ships and the mouth of the inlet is easily watched."

A sharp, unexpected gust cut through Ben's amnis and sent a shot of ice-cold, damp air down Tenzin's back. "Plus this fjord is sheltered from the weather."

"Yes."

She rose over him, scanning the distant coastline, which was shadowed by the clouds blocking the moon. They passed over the first of a series of small islands in the center of the bay, and as they crested the rising hill at the center of the island, a cluster of lights appeared in the distance.

"There," Ben said. "Do you see it?"

"Yes."

As they approached, the cluster of lights took on a shape more akin to a pyramid, and as they got even closer, Tenzin saw that the triangular shape she'd been watching stretched back and back, revealing that it wasn't at triangle at all but a light-dotted vessel painted white on the top with a dark blue or black hull jutting proudly from the water.

Two rows of portholes lined the lower deck of the ship, and the faint sound of music could be heard coming from the ocean liner.

"And what do we do about our friend?" Ben asked.

"Are we sure this is Paulson's boat?"

"Who else is keeping a cruise ship in Alaska in the middle of winter?"

"Let's get closer and take a look," Tenzin said. "I don't want any extra humans or vampires in the middle of this. It will irritate Katya if we kill innocent humans."

"So what does that mean for our flying friend back there?"

She smiled a little bit. "It's time for him to get a new hobby."

Tenzin reached for the hilt of the Mongolian saber at her waist and flipped her feet over her head, walking herself backward and upside down, flying in the face of the man who'd been pursing them at a "safe distance."

The vampire gave a short gasp and immediately drew a blade of his own, a curved katana popular in Asia for those with little experience in air combat and even less imagination.

Not as worthy an opponent as she'd hoped. "Pity."

"Tenzin!" Ben's hissed warning alerted her a moment later to the second vampire following them.

It was a woman, her pale white hair cropped in a pixie cut, who pulled another sword from her hip, this one a much more imaginative hook sword.

Tenzin's heart raced at the challenge. "Much better."

A channel of wind gusted from her mate's amnis, curving in a river of air around Tenzin's body to re-form in front of her, blasting the first vampire off course.

The man tumbled backward and down toward the ocean, Ben following him to the water while Tenzin held up her hand and blasted a column of air toward the woman with the hook sword.

The wind vampire was clever, darting to the side and sending a wall of ice-laden air back toward Tenzin.

She twisted to the side, breaking the wall with her shoulder and flipping right side up to meet the thrusting hook sword aimed for her neck.

The vampire was fast even if her amnis wasn't as strong as Tenzin's. She twisted in the air, flipping over Tenzin's head and trying to pull the saber from her grip.

The clash of steel made Tenzin's fangs ache for blood.

The white-haired vampire bared her teeth, her hook sword locked on the tip of Tenzin's saber until Tenzin pulled back, pushing the air away from her body and hurtling her opponent through the air.

The vampire flipped head over heels until she righted herself and speared through the icy air back to Tenzin, her sword tucked against her thigh.

Tenzin had to admire her ferocity. The woman hadn't said a word; she was wholly focused on killing her.

She rounded on Tenzin, flipping in the air and spinning around to whip the hook sword with its twin, extending the reach of the lethal blades.

Tenzin felt the cut on her cheek before she could pull her face back.

She laughed at the woman's gall, only to flip her own blade upside down and force the tip of her saber into the sharpened crescent guard that had sliced her cheek. She felt the tension through her arm when the blades locked, and Tenzin tugged hard, at the same time pushing back with her element.

The vampire gave a hard grunt at the punch of air to her gut and faltered, her grip loosening enough that the hook swords spun away from her, flipping through the air and spinning into the water below.

The vampire watched her weapons fall with wide eyes, then looked up and tried to retreat.

Too late. A whorl of air formed in midair, wrapping around the woman and pulling ice from the heavy clouds overhead, crystals that sliced her pale skin, spraying bloody mist into the wind. The small tornado wrapped around the blond vampire, who struggled against the press of her element turned against her.

"Henri Paulson," Tenzin said to the captive vampire.

The woman's eyes flew open; she looked at Tenzin, then at the cruise ship floating low at the back of the fjord. Her pale eyes turned back to Tenzin, and she bared her fangs.

Tenzin smiled. "That's all the answer I needed." She swung out, cutting through the torrent of air and slicing the vampire's head from her body.

The snow-white head dropped into the evergreen forest

below, disappearing into the darkness, and a moment later, Tenzin released the body from its tornado cage, the limbs splaying out in the wind as the vampire's remains dropped to the forest floor where they landed with a soft thud.

Ben reached her only moments later.

"She cut you." He bared his fangs, growling low in his throat as he reached his hand out to grip her neck. He pulled her cheek to his mouth and licked up the small wound, healing it with his own blood.

She smelled a hint of blood somewhere on his body, but he was not visibly damaged. "Where's our other friend?"

"In two pieces at the bottom of the ocean," Ben said. "What happens when you cut a vampire in half?"

Tenzin frowned. "Not at his neck?"

"No." Ben floated a short distance away and pointed to his belly. "Kind of right at the waist."

"You have far more force in your blade strike than I do."

"He irritated me, and he was definitely trying to kill me."

Tenzin shrugged. "I don't actually know if you killed him. If he can find the other half of his body in the bottom of the Pacific Ocean, he might manage to put himself back together. But I imagine he's probably orca food."

"Sorry." Ben frowned. "I just realized we probably should have kept one of them alive to question."

"No worries," Tenzin said. "I know exactly where Henri Paulson is."

CHAPTER THIRTY-ONE

The air in the far pocket of the long bay was eerily still, and the whipping wind that scraped across the summits of the surrounding islands seemed to die down to a cool, licking breeze within the outstretched arms of the natural cove where the cruise ship sat moored.

Ben floated in the darkness over the surface of the water, peering into the portholes, most of which were covered.

He wasn't the only wind vampire in the area, so it was hardly surprising that the immortals in residence of Paulson's prize vessel valued their privacy and blocked out curious eyes.

Ben was surprised that he'd been able to get as close as he did without detection. Tenzin was watching from the clouds, making certain that no one noticed his surveillance, but even the vampires she'd alerted him to had ignored his amnis. If they felt him at all, they weren't bothered.

Maybe Ben was getting better at cloaking his power, or maybe Paulson's residents had simply become too comfortable in their hidden cove to fear discovery.

He saw a sliver of light from a porthole near the front of the ship and flew closer, peering into the uncovered window to the cabin lit with golden lamplight. Ben glanced inside and quickly looked away. The passenger was a female vampire in the throes of sex, blood dripping from two cuts over each breast while two men —who appeared to be human—licked the blood from her sides, smearing it across her pale skin.

Okay, so Paulson's guests were not preparing to invade or attack anything *that* night. It looked like it was leisure time for the immortals on this floating vampire city.

But that one glance did confirm that there were definitely humans on board Paulson's ship, which Ben and Tenzin had already guessed. How many was a mystery, but Ben knew that an oceangoing vessel like this would need a good-sized crew to run it, especially when vampires were only active during night hours.

He flew along the edge of the cabins, but there were no other portholes uncovered.

Maybe the first vampire was an exhibitionist.

Overhead, balconies rose over the icy water, and Ben could hear slips of conversation drift by before the breeze snatched them away. He floated up, moving just under the line of sight so he could listen in.

"...send him a message when the markets open in Tokyo."

It sounded like a vampire speaking on a phone but with some kind of headset Ben couldn't hear.

"No, I probably won't be back to Taiwan until the spring. I'm in the middle of a project at the moment." He laughed a little. "Yes, the one Paulson mentioned. I can't tell you."

Another silent exchange on the other side of the call.

"Soon enough. It's not even worth talking about until the Nikkei is over forty thousand. If that happens in the next month, get in touch."

The conversation settled into mundane business, and Ben moved on, looking for more clues.

Each cabin seemed to hold a vampire even richer than the one before, and there was more than one voice that tickled his memory. There was one immortal with a distinctly Corsican accent that Tenzin might feel conflicted about, more speaking Latin, and others speaking Russian. There was a whole section of the boat occupied by a clan from Singapore. Another area held a group of rich French aristocrats.

Ben wondered if they'd been on the run since the 1790s.

He was passing by another cabin and paused when he heard a familiar name.

"...seen Sokholov in days."

The name was spoken in an aristocratic British accent, and Ben flew closer, curious if he could identify the man.

"I don't care if Zasha is here or not," a woman with a similar accent responded. "I'm dying for some variety."

"I'm not sure when dinner hour is over, but we can go take a look at the buffet."

"Darling, can't we order room service?"

Ben flew closer to the second-level balcony, intrigued by this seemingly ordinary exchange that sounded like it could have been any wealthy, middle-aged couple on holiday.

The voices grew louder, and a man said, "We're limited to crew if we order room service, and you know what Henri said about the crew. And after the last incident—"

"That wasn't my fault." The woman's voice took on a distinct whine. "The girl was struggling to escape, and you know how that triggers my prey drive."

Okay, so not an ordinary couple on vacation.

The man was trying to placate her. "I'm just saying that if you want to be able to finish a kill, the ballroom is where we must go. We don't want to annoy our host."

"Ballroom hunting is *boring*. What a dreadfully banal way to spend an evening. Frightful, Reggie. Absolutely gauche."

Ballroom hunting? What the actual hell was Henri Paulson doing on this boat?

"Henri promised another shore excursion soon, Poppy."

"*Henri* promises a lot." There was a definite pout in her voice. "Why are we even listening to him? We're not under aegis here. That's the whole point, isn't it? We can fly out of here right now." Footsteps approached the balcony, and Ben slid to the side, keeping to the shadows.

"Patience, pet." The man soothed the petulant vampire. "Henri promised that once the fighting starts, we'll all have as much hunting as we like without anyone the wiser."

"Oh, I suppose—"

"Didn't we have fun at the last shore excursion?" He cajoled her in dulcet tones. "Didn't we, pet? Remember that funny old man who was hobbling with his cane?"

Ben heard the woman laugh.

"That was funny. But he tasted medicated. I like younger blood."

He struggled to keep from flying up and showing them what violence really looked like.

"And you shall have it." The man coaxed her back into the room. "Just be patient a little bit longer."

Ben silently shook his head.

Even if he and Tenzin had to raze this boat to the ground themselves, these spoiled and entitled immortals weren't taking another human victim.

———

"SO WE AGREE?" Brigid looked at Katya, then at Oleg on the screen. "You've both dealt with Ben and Tenzin before. We can agree they're giving an accurate report?"

"Agreed," Oleg said. "I am willing to deal with the blowback from any regents who complain. Whoever might be on Paulson's ship, their lives are forfeit for attacking humans and vampires in foreign territory."

"I can agree with that," Katya said. "Oleg and I may have our own disputes, but neither of us condones this. Paulson and everyone on that ship are fair game."

When Brigid had heard the report from Ben and Tenzin, she immediately knew that a group of powerful and wealthy immortals were going to have powerful and wealthy friends. The last thing she wanted to do was start an international incident, but they had ironclad proof that Paulson was hunting humans and that Zasha Sokholov was involved.

Whatever "soon" meant to those waiting vampires, she didn't want to find out what they had planned.

"We're all in agreement then." Brigid nodded. "So let's talk strategy."

CHAPTER THIRTY-TWO

Carwyn crouched low in the bow of the speedboat, hurtling through the night toward the long cove where Henri Paulson had parked the *Nautilus*, his "floating city" for vampire elites.

Using Ben and Tenzin's description, they'd identified the ship as a three-hundred-thirty-foot vessel bought by a shell company in the Bahamas several years ago. It had cruised up to Vancouver two years before; then by all official accounts, it had disappeared.

Katya had no idea how Paulson had managed to keep an entire cruise ship in her territory without her knowledge, but she was more than a little angry. Though, as Brigid had pointed out, if it was part of Paulson's shadow fleet, there was no telling where it had been and how long it had remained in Katya's stretch of the ocean.

Beside Carwyn, Gavin's chief of security on the West Coast sat on the deck, his eyes closed and his amnis positively swollen with power from the salt-and-water-laden air.

"Raj?"

The young vampire's eyes flickered open. "I'm so ready to be done with this."

"Sokholov?"

"Sokholov, Paulson. The Ankers. All of it." Raj took a deep breath and let it out slowly, the water in the air around them drawn to his skin, so it appeared almost as if the dark-skinned water vampire was sweating in the freezing-cold wind.

"I know we didn't make the best impression on you in New Orleans, and I'm sorry for that. You're entitled to your privacy. All of us have parts of our past we don't like to talk about."

"When you work for Gavin Wallace, you don't have secrets." Raj stared straight ahead. "At least not from your boss." He glanced at Carwyn from the side. "Remember that if you go in doubting any of our people again."

"I'll remember." He settled down next to the man, who was wearing a black wet suit. "You don't seem to mind the cold."

"I hate it, but this much water is always going to rev me up."

"I hate the cold *and* the water." Carwyn grinned. "I might not be a help at all."

Raj didn't even show a hint of a smile. "You know who else doesn't like water?"

"Zasha Sokholov?"

Raj nodded. "That vampire won't be on the boat. I guarantee it."

"Ben and Tenzin are already looking for someplace close by. Tenzin agrees with you." Carwyn looked at the dark water and the black outlines of land rising around them. "You know Zasha?"

"Mila had this weird fascination with them." He looked at Carwyn. "Mila Anker."

Carwyn knew from Gavin that Raj and Mila had a history before Gavin killed her. "Why fascination?"

"Zasha could be... very mercurial. One moment it was like they wanted to be your friend. They could be really fascinating when they wanted to be. Very... attractive."

"The same way a deadly animal can be attractive?"

Raj nodded. "Zasha always reminded me of a tiger. I never got too close—Mila kept me away from them—but they were beautiful and fascinating and very... relaxed. But with all this silent energy you could just sense anytime you got close."

"What happens when a tiger gets hungry?"

"Or bored?" Raj's voice got softer. "I think Zasha grows bored quickly. Mila tried to impress them, but Zasha ended up leaving her after a month or two."

That surprised Carwyn, and he didn't know why. "Mila and Zasha were lovers?"

"For a time. Mila tried to brush it off. I could tell she was angry though. She said Zasha would never stay with any lover for long. They were still in love with their dead mate."

"We only learned about their mate last year."

Raj looked at Carwyn. "Can you imagine loving a tiger?"

Carwyn looked at the deck and the sky reflected in the dark water that had pooled at their feet. "Maybe Zasha wasn't always a tiger."

"Maybe." Raj shrugged. "But I don't think you just suddenly turn into a sociopath like that. Even when life hurts you, there has to be something beyond that."

Carwyn took a deep breath and let it out slowly. Despite his firm belief that something Tenzin had done had precipitated the vampire's ire, he knew that Zasha wasn't the average vampire out to get revenge.

"I agree with you," Carwyn said. "I've seen many hurt people in my life. Human and vampire. Very few of them become monsters."

Raj sat up. "And I misjudged you. I thought you and your mate were bullies."

Carwyn laughed a little bit. "There's nothing my wife hates more than a bully, but she can be a little abrasive at times."

"I don't mind abrasive." Raj shrugged. "Abrasive gets results."

He nodded. "Yes, she does do that."

———

BRIGID STOOD ON THE BRIDGE, a paper map spread in front of her, as pelting rain bashed the glass enclosure. "We're passin' through the narrows. If Paulson has any security at all, he'll be able to see us soon."

Jennie was the captain at the helm. She glanced at Brigid over her shoulder. "I think there's already someone following us. Don't ask me how I know—it's a gut feeling."

Brigid nodded. "Not a shocker." The real question was: If someone was following them, how fast could they get back to Paulson with a warning?

Unless someone intercepted them before they could do that.

She poked her head out of the cabin. "Raj!"

Gavin's man stood and turned, giving her a terse nod.

"You ready to channel some of that aggression on an unwelcome guest? Make sure they don't make it to Paulson's ship before us?"

Raj nodded. "Someone following us?"

"Captain thinks so."

He looked at the churning water behind them. "Are any of Oleg's people in the area?"

Brigid shook her head.

Raj raised an eyebrow. "You're sure?"

Carwyn stood up and wiped water from his eyes. "Too much tension between his and Katya's people. They agreed that Oleg would focus on hunting down Paulson's shadow fleet for now while Katya's people planned this attack on the cruise ship."

"Good," Raj shouted as he walked toward her. "Too many unknown vampires in a fray just equals friendly fire."

"You have military experience," Brigid said.

Raj nodded but said nothing else.

"Then get to it, soldier." She nodded toward the rear of the ship. "You have your sticks?"

They'd given all of Katya's people bright pink glow sticks that had been left over from Jennie's granddaughter's birthday party to signal if any of them needed a pickup. Designated wind vampires were circling overhead, watching for the color in the water, while others joined the assault.

Brigid ducked back inside the boat as Raj leaped overboard into the freezing waves.

"This is goin' to get messy." She wiped the water from her eyes.

"It's already messy," Jennie said. "Paulson made it messy when he decided to get ambitious."

"I don't think it's ambition that Katya and Oleg object to," Brigid said. "Pretty sure it's the murder."

Brigid felt the boat shift to the right, and a looming black point of land rose in front of them before Jennie turned the wheel to the left and pointed the cruiser toward a channel that appeared between what looked like two pointed islands.

"There's another island running lengthwise down the center of this bay as I recall," Jennie said. "Though I haven't been here in years. The water's cold but the fishing's always been bad in this area."

"Any particular reason?"

She shrugged. "Personal opinion? There may be a water elder somewhere in the area, and the fish keep away from a powerful predator instinctively. But sailing boats love this area in the summer because the water stays calm."

"And in the winters?"

Jennie shook her head. "You're not going to catch any sailboats in this area past September. Paulson could have parked that ship for months and no one but locals would even notice it."

"And what if— Jaysus." Brigid held on to the back of the counter as a massive wave rocked the boat.

"Or you could have a water vampire" —Jennie's fangs fell— "guarding the entrance to the bay." She struggled to keep the wheel steady. "And making sure that no vessels come your direction. Sam! Take this and let me get out there. Keep it steady."

"Yes, Auntie Jen." A young human who couldn't have been more than twenty-five quickly took the wheel, and Jennie bolted off the bridge and ran to the bow of the ship.

Brigid tried to see through the increased onslaught of rain pelting the glass covering the bridge.

"You're not gonna be able to see anything not on the radar from inside," Sam said.

Brigid pushed her way through the wind and the water sloshing around the narrow side deck of the cruiser and peered around the corner to see Jennie locked in an epic battle with a massive wave bearing down on the ship.

"God in heaven." Brigid lost her breath as Jennie swept an arm out and seemed to grab her own wave coming from the side, gathering the water in a massive column of icy slush she picked up from both sides of the boat and bashed into the supernatural wave that rose to block the channel that led into the bay.

Paulson had some powerful allies.

Another boat appeared from the darkness to their left, and Brigid saw a dark-haired man standing in the bow, his arms out and his hair streaming behind him. He leaned forward, seeming to embrace the water beating against their vessels, as two more twin waves on either side of his boat rose like orcas frozen in midbreach before arrowing toward the wall of water and joining Jennie's assault.

The four waves speared through the barrier that guarded the bay and shattered the wall into a deluge that rained around them, and the two speeding cruisers shot straight into the heart of Paulson's hidden empire.

"Woo-hoo!"

Brigid turned to see Carwyn standing next to Jennie, his arms spread out and his voice rising over the din of the engine.

"That was *bloody brilliant!*"

Trust her husband to get a thrill from narrowly escaping a giant, boat-destroying wave. Brigid walked back inside and grabbed a towel that was hanging on the wall behind the ship's wheel.

Sam looked as pale as a vampire, but he was holding steady. "I knew Auntie Jen would get rid of that wave."

"Did ya now?"

"Uh-huh." He nodded quickly "She's the best."

A few moments later, Jennie was back on the bridge of the cruiser, soaked to the skin as she took the wheel from Sam. "Two of Kelso's crew are in the water, dealing with whatever vampire Paulson has stationed at the mouth of the bay." Her voice was grim. "Do we have any clue how many vampires are on that ship?"

"None," Brigid said. "The *Nautilus* has fifty-four cabins, but that could mean—"

"A hundred vampires? More?" Jennie growled. "Against thirty-four of us."

"Yep," Brigid confirmed. "Against thirty-four of us, and Ben and Tenzin."

Jennie shook her head. "That may mean something in the air, but it means nothing on the water."

———

BEN SWOOPED down and hooked Raj's arm, lifting him from the water and carrying him back toward the red-lit boat where Brigid and Carwyn were speeding toward the *Nautilus*.

"Raj," Ben shouted over the wind. "Good to see you."

"Been a while." Raj had a cut across his belly that was already closing. He also had a harpoon gun. "Take me to that ship. I'm armed now."

"Aww, did you find a new toy?"

"Oh yeah. I love it when toys nearly impale me," Raj shouted. "Luckily, my new diving knife works."

"I've been stabbed underwater myself," Ben offered. "Not an experience I'd like to repeat."

"Then fair warning." Raj looked up at Ben as they crested the island in the center of the bay. "Do not fall in this water." He pointed at a pool of black water and shook Ben's arm. "There."

"Still got your glow sticks?"

Raj nodded, then shook his arm free of Ben's grip and dropped into the icy deep.

CHAPTER THIRTY-THREE

Tenzin circled the ship, the thread tying her to her mate as strong as ever. She felt him dip down to the water when they saw the glowing pink color in the water, and she kept her eyes on him, blowing back the vampire who launched from the balcony with a massive wall of wind until Ben was back at her side.

"Don't keep them in the ship," Ben said. "We need them drawn away so Carwyn and Brigid's people can board. If we pick them off the air vampires, that will leave the rest unguarded. Mostly water vampires, I'd guess. Jennie's people will be outnumbered, but this is their territory."

"I can't imagine many earth vampires are part of Paulson's plan." Tenzin looked toward the cruise ship. "Do you think Zasha is on the *Nautilus*?"

"Doubtful." He glanced at her. "Zasha was sired to fire, but their blood comes from earth."

"I know." Tenzin was already peering into the forest that surrounded the bay. "They're probably not on the boat, but they may be nearby."

She turned when she felt the presence of four wind vampires approaching them on the left. "Four at three o'clock."

He frowned. "Wait, my three or your—?"

"Three o'clock!" She threw out her right arm and pointed. "Ben, they have harpoons!"

"Got it!" He drew the short Mainz gladius he preferred and dove toward the four silent wind vampires who were trying to be sneaky.

Tenzin felt a puff of wind near her face and batted the harpoon away before she thought twice, flicked her fingers, and brought the metal-pointed spear back to her hand.

She hadn't thrown a spear in too long. This could be fun.

———

BEN FELT the approaching projectile like a whisper at his back. He darted to the side, letting the harpoon pierce the belly of the vampire he was dueling, but while he was distracted, he lost control of the current of wind holding back the other three vampires.

"Hey!" he shouted at Tenzin. "That almost grazed me." He ducked to the side and threw up an arm, knocking the second vampire off-balance while Tenzin dove for the one carrying the harpoon.

"I knew you'd feel it." Tenzin flew over the harpoon shooter's head, twisting her body in a circle before the man realized where she was going, only to slice his neck from behind, sending his severed head spinning in an arc over Ben and his opponent, spraying them both with blood.

Tenzin swooped down and yanked the barbed harpoon from the belly of the wind vampire who was barely keeping a grip on her blade. "You're not an idiot."

"Gee, thanks." Ben held the last vampire in a whirlwind as he raised his arm and finished off the harpooned woman with a slash across her neck.

The vampire's amnis scattered in the wind, and her body and head fell to the dark water with a splash.

That left one vampire twisting in the wind, and Ben could see that he was trying to escape, knowing that fighting both of them was futile.

No.

This wasn't a battle that anyone could escape. Paulson's guests had raided and murdered too many innocents to let any escape.

No matter who they belonged to or what their connections might have been, every vampire who'd been a guest on the *Nautilus* was going to die.

CHAPTER THIRTY-FOUR

Carwyn leaped from the deck of the cruiser to the hull of the *Nautilus*, punching his fist through the porthole and gripping the twisted metal as he heard the deck above him erupt in chaos.

"Pirates!"

"Vampires!"

"—being boarded."

"This wasn't supposed to happen! Henri said this wasn't—"

"Shut up and find a weapon."

"—our kind. *It's our kind.*"

Beneath him, Carwyn heard the whoosh of grappling hooks whizzing by his head. One hooked on to the edge of the deck, and the rope was within reach. He grabbed for it, yanking down to make sure it was anchored before he swung his weight onto the rope and hauled himself up, the cuts on his arm healing as he moved.

He swung his leg onto the deck and immediately crouched in the darkness, but Jennie's people were already on board, dropped by air vampires who'd been patrolling overhead or climbing over railings from vessels that had come alongside the *Nautilus*.

Brigid crawled up the grappling line behind him. "Really?" She picked up his arm and glared at the healing cuts. "You're being careless."

He wasn't being careless—he was angry and pumped with amnis. It didn't matter that he was away from his element. His mate's blood was churning in his veins, and his body was primed for violence. What he didn't have in elemental strength, he'd make up in brute force.

The Almighty hadn't made him a giant for nothing.

"Let's go," he growled.

They moved quickly along the deck, Brigid with her gun drawn and Carwyn with the long bowie knife he preferred to use when he was hunting vampires.

The first immortal they encountered was armed even though he was wearing a tuxedo. Carwyn could smell human blood on his clothes, and his fangs were bared. He looked Norse, with brown hair and pale blue eyes set in a square face. He was as tall as Carwyn but not nearly as wide.

The vampire rushed Carwyn as soon as he saw him, his blade lifted, aiming for his neck.

They met like two stags colliding in the forest, Carwyn's righteous anger roaring as he drove the other vampire back, ignoring the icy, pelting rain the water vampire directed at his shoulders. It sliced through his clothes and cut his skin, but Carwyn was blind to the pain.

He knocked the water vampire to the deck, punching the blunt end of his hunting knife into the vampire's face. Bone cracked under his fist, but Carwyn didn't have time to relish in the man's injury. There could be over one hundred enemies on board this ship, and he needed to move fast.

The vampire under him wasn't rattled. He hacked at Carwyn's thigh with a short sword, flipping it to plunge the tip into his knee, but Brigid was backing her mate, and she fired at the man's hand, blasting the sword from it and making him scream.

Carwyn gripped the vampire's hair in his fist, yanked up, and sliced the back of his attacker's neck in one quick movement.

The vampire stilled, his amnis going dead, and his body thunked to the deck.

"Let's go!" Brigid yelled.

Carwyn could already hear more footsteps approaching.

Vampires were silent predators, but on the deck of the *Nautilus* with no humans to hide from, Carwyn was cast into a melee.

Pink glowing bracelets marked Jennie's people, so Carwyn aimed his fury at the dark figures without glow sticks, most of whom were wearing formalwear.

Apparently they'd interrupted an event.

A female vampire wearing a thick pearl necklace drew a sharp jian and braced for Carwyn's blade, but Brigid didn't waste time with an elegant fight. She raised her 9mm and fired directly into the vampire's neck, quickly shooting her two more times in each shoulder and driving her to the slippery wooden boards, which were starting to run with blood.

"Go!" Brigid waved him toward another vampire as she walked to the fallen woman in the pearls. His mate picked up the woman's head, sliced her neck with a silver knife, and let her body drop.

Just then he heard a rage-filled scream, and a column of water wrapped around Brigid's ankle, yanking her from the vampire in pearls and hurtling her toward the edge of the boat.

"No!" Carwyn ran to grab her hand, but whatever water vampire had Brigid in its watery grip was too fast.

Her eyes met Carwyn's and went wide a second before she went over the deck.

BODIES AND PARTS of bodies were strewn across the bloody deck—most of them wearing formal clothes—when Ben landed. He looked for anyone familiar and immediately saw Carwyn twisting the neck of a vampire in a black dinner jacket. The body fell with a thud to the deck of the *Nautilus* as Carwyn spotted him.

"Benjamin!" Carwyn pointed to the port side of the vessel. "Brigid is in the water, and I'm no use to her there!"

"Fuck." He lifted from the deck and flew down to the surface, careful not to get too close to the waterline where waves were churning with elemental energy and he was a prime target for a water vampire.

"Brigid!" he shouted into the darkness and the wind.

If a water vampire had her in its grip, she could be trapped below the surface and completely defenseless.

Many of Paulson's vampires were already overboard, battling with Jennie's people, who were fighting from boats or swimming in the darkness. He could see faint pink glow sticks beneath the surface as water vampires did battle undersea.

He saw an arm waving on the surface and recognized Brigid's pale face before the water pulled her under again.

Vampires couldn't drown, but putting a fire vampire underwater was a good way to neutralize her.

Ben saw Brigid bob to the surface again and speared down, grabbing her arm and yanking her from the deep even as the water tried to pull her back.

He forced a column of wind toward the surface, fighting back the waves as he scooped Brigid up and pulled her into his arms.

"Hey." He grinned. "So how are you?"

"Busy." She glanced over her shoulder. "Did ya see Carwyn?"

"On deck and cutting a swath through Paulson's vampires."

"We surprised them. Has Tenzin found Zasha?"

How did he know she was going to ask? "Maybe. There's a wooden house on the island in the middle of the bay. There was something about the roof that Tenzin recognized. She said it has to be Zasha's."

"Take me there." She glanced over his shoulder. "Then go back to help Carwyn. They haven't even made it inside that thing."

"If you think I'm going to let you and Tenzin take on Zasha by yourself—"

"Ben!" Her voice was desperate. "I need you to back up Carwyn. Leave Zasha to me and Tenzin. There are humans on board that boat."

He wanted to snarl, but he knew she'd argue with him for eternity. He flew Brigid toward the island. "I'll check on Carwyn, but he's going to tell you the same thing I am. The vampires on that boat are pampered socialites who hunt humans because it makes them feel tough."

"Yes, and those humans need to be saved."

"Zasha isn't pampered! You're going to need our help."

"We can do this." Brigid squeezed his arm. "I'm not bein' proud, Benjamin. Fire against fire. Let me and Tenzin work."

He dropped her off on the shore of the island near the jut of land where Tenzin had spotted the old Russian-style house. "I'll get Carwyn and come back."

"Ben!"

He flew away before she could argue with him.

Ben had no illusions about the vampires of the *Nautilus,* and neither did Katya's people. He had every reason to think Jennie and her crew could handle them and no reason at all to underestimate Zasha Sokholov.

He'd help Carwyn on the *Nautilus*. Then both of them would be back.

TENZIN SPOTTED Brigid walking through the forest and chirped a high, trilling note that caught the fire vampire's attention. She looked up toward the birdcall and saw Tenzin in the trees.

Brigid nodded and walked toward Tenzin, weaving through the needle-strewn forest.

Ferns brushed along Brigid's legs as she walked, and her footsteps sounded like a crashing animal to Tenzin's keen ears.

The house was sitting on a hill, built of rough-hewn cedar timbers and perched to look over the water. A sheer rock wall rose behind it, and a wooden deck ran along the second story. Narrow, wood-shuttered windows were cut into the face of the house, and a steep-pitched roof was clear of snow, but moss grew on the wooden shingles.

The moment Tenzin saw it, she knew it was Zasha's refuge. The house was a mirror image of the one in Siberia where Zasha and her mate had been sheltered so many years before, even down the faint stench of decaying bodies that drifted in the air. That same stench should be enough to cover their approach.

Tenzin had finally found the fire vampire's home.

It was the perfect location for them. Rainforest to keep their element under control. The lush greenery around the house showed evidence of blackened scarring, but the forest was too wet for any fire to find purchase, especially in the winter.

Brigid stood at the base of the cedar tree and looked up. "What are we doing?" she whispered.

Ugh. How inconvenient to be tethered to the ground. Tenzin tried to remember what it felt like to be bound with gravity, but she couldn't quite fathom it anymore.

Not the little fire vampire's fault. She swooped down, picked up Brigid under the arms, and plopped her on a branch in the cedar tree.

"That's Zasha's house." She nodded at the old izba peeking through the trees.

"Fuck fuck fuck fuck fuck." Brigid was hugging the trunk of the cedar. "Are you sure?"

Tenzin frowned. "What are you doing?"

The woman glanced down and clutched the tree trunk harder. "Tenzin, why—?"

"Even if you fell, you'd survive." Tenzin bounced on the branch a little. "And this tree is sturdy."

"Right." She gritted her teeth, and her fangs pierced her lip. "I know that. Really I do. But it would hurt. A lot. And you said you found Zasha's house."

"If you open your eyes, you'll see it." Tenzin peered through the branches to keep an eye on the windows. "I don't see any movement, so I don't know if Zasha is there. I find it hard to imagine they don't know the *Nautilus* is being attacked."

"Right." Brigid nodded, but she didn't let go of the tree. "Uh... they prob'ly don't care. Zasha doesn't have any loyalty to Paulson or those vampires. They were just useful idiots to them."

"Yes." The little fire vampire really was quite bright. "But on the chance that anyone *is* watching, they're going to see the top of this tree shaking, and it's obviously not from the wind, so could you calm down please?"

"Okay." Brigid took a calming breath. "Okay. Right. Right."

Tenzin rolled her eyes. "Oleg was right; you do still think like a human."

"You know, I consider that a feature, not a bug."

"I don't know what that means. Why would you compare yourself to a bug?" Tenzin wrinkled her nose. "Why Zasha became fascinated with you is a mystery to me."

"Me too." Brigid cautiously sat up straight, still keeping a hand on the trunk of the cedar. "Why don't we go knock on the door and ask?"

Tenzin pursed her lips. "That's an idea."

"I was jokin'."

"Maybe, but it's a quick way to get an answer." Tenzin floated away from the cedar tree and held her hand out. "And I think we've waited long enough. Don't you?"

Brigid's eyes went wide. "You're serious."

Tenzin nodded. "They won't kill me. They know they can't try to kill me without me killing them. So I'm going to go knock on the door and say hello."

"But you said that you didn't care about your promise anymore. That your children wouldn't care if you broke your word."

"I did." Tenzin nodded. "But Zasha doesn't know that."

CARWYN GROWLED at Ben when the wind vampire finally pulled him away from the fighting. "They did what?"

"Tenzin found Zasha's house," Ben said. "It's on the island we passed in the middle of the bay. I dropped Brigid on the beach."

"Why would you bloody do that?" Carwyn roared.

"Because she told me to!" Ben snarled and roared back. "Do you want me to take you to her or not?"

"Fuck!" Carwyn spun and slammed his fist into the face of an elegantly coiffed vampire who was barreling toward them with a harpoon spear in her hand.

The female vampire crashed to the deck, then popped up like she was made of rubber, only to be lassoed around the neck by Jennie, who pulled the vampire across the deck kicking and screaming before Jennie bent down, pulled the harpoon spear from the sequined vampire's hand, and plunged it into her neck, stilling her kicking feet.

"Have you seen Paulson?" Jennie wiped away the spray of blood across her cheek before the persistent flow of rain washed it away. "My people have the decks nearly cleared, but there's no sign of that bastard."

"Have you found any living humans?" Ben shouted the question in the roaring wind. He held up a hand and the wind stilled.

Carwyn was focused on finding Brigid. "Ben, you need to take me to that island."

Jennie shook her head. "We haven't found the humans. We're clearing the decks; then we'll go below."

"They could be killing them right now!" Ben shouted. "We need to get—"

He was cut off by an explosion off the port side.

"Fuck!" Jennie ran to the railing, and her eyes went wide when she saw one of Katya's boats go up in flames. "What the hell happened?"

Ben searched through the darkness and the smoke and saw a flash of bright red hair. "Zasha?"

Carwyn grabbed the front of Ben's shirt and lifted him in the air. "You fly me to that boat. Right the hell now."

CHAPTER THIRTY-FIVE

T enzin walked up to the house, her feet stepping lightly on the damp cushion of needles that blanketed the perimeter of the clearing.

> *"You have no quarrel with her. Your fight is with me, Saraal."*
> *"Sida, I do not know that name."*

She stood at a distance, watching the windows for movement. For light. For any sign of life. She heard a bolt turn, and the heavy front door of the wooden house creaked open a few inches.

Nothing else moved.

> *"Her name is Zasha. She has nothing to do with us."*
> *"You know why I am here."*
> *"I am not my sire."*

"Your god is a jealous god," Tenzin whispered, "visiting the sins of the fathers upon the children to the third and fourth generation."

She pushed the door open and walked inside.

Tenzin cast her amnis into the darkness of a room that was lit only by a small fire in a stone hearth. She could sense another vampire in the room, but there was no sound. No movement. Only the fire crackling and the motes of dust floating in the red-gold light.

Red-gold like the memory of long hair splayed across a floor, mixing with dirt and bloody tears.

"I'm here." She stood still and waited.

"Why?" The voice came from the darkness, a flat, dull intonation from a figure hidden in the periphery of her vision. "You found Paulson's guests," the voice said. "Is Brigid on the *Nautilus*, wagging her finger at the naughty, naughty vampires?"

"I don't know." The lie came easily to her lips. "I don't really care about them."

A spark in the low, wooden voice. "Now you're just *trying* to make me feel special."

Tenzin almost smiled. "I came to apologize, Zasha."

"For killing Purev?"

"I found you because there were rumors of an Eastern wind vampire who was stealing children from the trade routes."

"Orphans. Beggars. Children who had already been thrown away. No one would miss them."

"I miss them."

"No," Tenzin said. "I will not apologize for killing your mate. Benjamin was right; I was correct to kill him. He may have been kind to you, but Purev was a monster."

Zasha stepped out of the shadows. Their hair was long and flowing over their shoulders, and their beautiful face was lit by the flickering gold of the fire.

They wore a black shirt and a long black skirt wrapped around their waist. The shirt was open halfway down their chest, revealing a sharply defined musculature and countless scars that appeared to have been made by knives.

Tenzin couldn't look away. She let out a soft sigh. "You're beautiful. Was it ever anything but a curse to you?"

"No." Zasha held out their hand, and a small whirling fireball danced into their palm. "Truvor found me while I was hiding among the dead. He spotted my hair in the darkness. That's why he took me. He *loved* my hair."

"He was a monster too."

Zasha rolled their eyes. "We're all monsters. You should know that by now."

"Some of us are more monstrous than others." Tenzin didn't take her eyes off them. That had been her mistake for centuries. She had moved on, tried to forget.

But Zasha had never forgotten.

"I killed your mate," Tenzin said. "But I won't apologize for that."

The fire leaped in the grate.

"So why are you here, you useless little *thing*?" Zasha spat out.

"I wanted to apologize for not killing *you*."

Zasha's black eyes went wide, and a crooked smile spread over their face. "That is your apology, daughter of Zhang? That you did not kill me when you killed Purev?"

"Yes." She didn't blink.

Zasha took a deep breath, and a strangled laugh escaped them. "This hasn't gone at all like I had hoped."

Tenzin decided to play along. "What did you hope?"

"I wanted to get to know Brigid better, but she's so..." Zasha sighed.

"Abrasive? Self-righteous? Rigid?"

"Protective." Zasha rolled their eyes. "I wanted her and her soft mate to come up here, and then I would force them to lure *you* here as well. Then I'd strike a deal with the priest to trade you for Paulson."

"Ah." Tenzin nodded. "And that would have gotten rid of Paulson and also driven a wedge between the priest and Brigid."

"Paulson is a self-important ass," Zasha muttered. "I'd trade him for you in a heartbeat."

Tenzin leaned against a post that held up the landing on the overhead loft. "But you can't kill me. So why would you care if the priest handed me over?"

"Oh no, I was going to make the priest kill you." Zasha offered a rueful smile.

"Not a bad idea." Tenzin nodded slowly. "But that would have been difficult."

"He would find some moral justification for it—saving innocent lives or something like that—but you know he's wanted to do it for centuries."

Tenzin barely kept from laughing. Carwyn had little love for her, but the priest was nothing if not hopeful. He'd try to convert her before he killed her.

But Tenzin didn't want to disabuse Zasha from the notion, especially when Tenzin could feel Brigid lurking along the perimeter. "It might have worked if Brigid hadn't come to me first. The priest doesn't like me much, but I might have killed him if he tried to kill me."

Zasha's eyes were dancing. "Either way, Brigid's life would have been ruined."

"Why ruin her?" Tenzin shrugged. "Why bother, Zasha?"

Zasha shrugged. "She killed Ivan."

Tenzin didn't know if that was even true, but it was evident that Zasha believed it was. "Why did you destroy our house in New York?"

"That was actually a favor from an old associate, one that I enjoyed cashing in." Zasha stepped closer, rolling the ball of fire from one hand to another. "They may have gone a little too far, but it gave you a push, didn't it?" Zasha winked.

"You got our attention." *And I am going to kill you. Or watch happily as Brigid kills you. Either way is fine.*

"I would have liked to go to New York," Zasha said, "but I was busy with Paulson's little shore excursions up here. He actually thought he could draw Katya and Oleg into a war. Can you believe that?"

"It almost worked."

Zasha shook their head. "No, I knew as soon as Brigid came up she would see through it. She's really very keen. She understands how we think."

"We?"

"Monsters," Zasha whispered. "You're the worst, you know."

"Am I?" Tenzin felt Brigid's power building, and she noticed the fire in the hearth moving in ways it shouldn't. Had Brigid's power grown that much?

Interesting.

"You are." Zasha was staring at her. "You pretend to be on the side of the angels, but you're a monster who hunts down vampires for the sins of their sire." Zasha's friendly veneer cracked. "Hypocrite. Is your own sire blameless? Shouldn't you be hunted too?"

"Probably. And my sire isn't blameless." Tenzin stepped farther into the room, sensing the shift in the air. She could feel what Brigid was doing, and she wanted to stay well out of the way. "But he is useful. And he has" —she racked her brain for the word Ben had used once— "*evolved.* Have you?"

Zasha lifted their chin. "Why would I want to evolve? I am as I am." They spread their arms, both hands holding growing balls of swirling fire. "I am as I have always been. I revel in it, *Saraal.*" Zasha spat out her old name with ire.

Ah, Saraal. That poor girl buried in a tent beneath Temur's war chest.

"Saraal is dead," Tenzin whispered. "And I... have never pretended to be on the side of the angels."

In the space of a human heartbeat, the fire in the hearth leaped up and shot across the room, spearing from the fireplace to the window, blowing Zasha backward as it raked across their face, exploding through the room as the fire vampire screamed.

The flames blasted Tenzin across the neck, and she raised her arm to blow it back as she turned her face to shield herself.

Too late.

Tenzin pushed the air away from herself, but not before she felt Brigid's lashing flames eat into her skin.

———

CARWYN DROPPED from Ben's grip to the deck of the speedboat where two vampires were propping shoulder-held rocket launchers on the backs of dead-eyed human men.

"Fire!" One launched toward the front deck of the *Nautilus*, streaming though the black night and hitting the railing as it exploded and the deck where Jennie had been fighting erupted into flames.

Carwyn barreled toward the vampires firing the rockets and spread his arms wide, knocking both of them to the deck before they realized they were being attacked.

Thud.

He bent down and twisted one neck.

Scramble.

He pivoted on one leg, sweeping it out to knock the second human holding a rocket launcher to the ground.

"Conrad!" The vampire's shout was cut off when Carwyn gripped him by the throat and lifted him in the air, the blade of the hunting knife at the vampire's nape.

"Where's Paulson?" Carwyn growled.

"*Nautilus*," the man choked out. "Bridge."

He turned his head, spotted the *Nautilus* and the vampires already steaming upward toward the glass-covered deck that must have been the bridge.

"Good."

"Let me—" The vampire's words were choked off when Carwyn sliced the bowie knife across his spine.

There were three zombielike humans stumbling around the deck of the speedboat and slipping in the rain, but Carwyn could feel no other vampires, and the ones who had fired the rocket launchers were dead or neutralized.

The boat was bobbing in the stormy sea and drifting toward the immense black hull of the cruise ship. He ran to the controls, took the wheel, and gave the engine a short burst of power to point it in the correct direction.

Then Carwyn aimed the bow toward the beach where Ben had taken his mate and hit the throttle.

The speedboat jerked forward in the water, hitting the chop with rough slams until it reached a steady speed and rose to skim over the waves.

He had no idea how to properly drive it, but that didn't matter. He was planning to run it aground on the island where Brigid and Tenzin had gone to fight Zasha.

Carwyn aimed for the widest part of the beach he could see in the darkness, then braced himself and cut the throttle as he felt the first scrape of gravel on the hull.

The boat crashed up the beach, roaring over the rocky shore with a heinous grating *scraaaaaape* as it headed toward the tree line.

He crouched down as the dense cedar, pine, and hemlock grabbed the bow of the speedboat and forced it to stop. The boat rocked to the side, and the humans groaned as they rolled across the deck, shielding their heads and curling into balls.

Carwyn used the velocity of the boat to launch himself into the forest, crashing through the branches and digging his feet into the welcoming, rocky soil.

Ahhhh, that was better.

The moment he touched the ground, he could feel her.

Mate.

He started to run, weaving through the trees, his amnis reaching through the soil and the rock and the roots. Smoke drifted in the air, and he could smell the faint scent of charred flesh.

Brigid!

Carwyn's mind screamed her name, but he said nothing, barreling toward the fight with the single-minded focus of a man on fire.

———

"HSSSSSS!" Ben's shoulders retracted and the hair on his neck rose when he felt the burning sensation in his arm and across his neck.

Tenzin.

He felt her pain in his own body, but he also felt her rage, and his fangs ached as her amnis rose in defiance.

His mate's pain distracted him only for a moment before he swung the hammer from the toolbox he'd found on the deck, brought it down, and shattered the window covering the bridge, letting him and two other wind vampires inside.

For the first time, he saw Paulson in the flesh.

He was dressed in a tuxedo, and his arrogant expression didn't waver as he pointed his chin at Ben and barked a command at the dozen guards who flanked him. Some of the guards raised automatic rifles and pointed them at the vampires crawling onto the bridge.

"Kill him," the vampire billionaire said calmly. "Kill them all."

Ben smiled through bloody lips. "I don't think so."

Paulson dropped his radio and pushed the guards at his side forward.

Three of the guards dove toward the wind vampire on his left and three others toward the one on his right, driving both of Jennie's people off the bridge as Paulson's guards tackled them to the deck outside, leaving six armed vampires standing in front of Henri Paulson with their eyes on Ben.

Alone on the bridge, Ben speared through the air, ignoring the bullets that hit his body, shoved the guards blocking Paulson with a battering wind as he reached his hands out to grip Henri Paulson around the throat.

Ben's hands closed around the vampire's neck for only a moment before the guards pulled him away, one swinging a knife down toward his neck.

Ben swung his sword arm up, and the gladius sliced off the arm of the vampire, making the guard scream and the knife clatter to the floor.

He felt another blade hit his ankle, but he ignored the bite of pain.

More bullets hit his side, but none of them even came close to his spine.

Ben felt a deep slice along the small of his back, caught the scent of his own blood spraying the air, and time suddenly seemed to slow.

The black wind came to Ben in the scent of his own blood. It was a whisper in the darkness, wrapping around him like a shield as his vision went dark.

Ben closed his eyes and saw the room around him, the dead matter of the machinery mixed with the living elements of air and flesh and blood. The gold mist of matter woven through with silver mist of the water in the air, the flesh, the red threads of energy that hummed through the human-made machinery that surrounded them, all glowing against the wash of rain against glass.

And through it all, the darkness, the darkness in everything.

The precious space between.

Ben reached for the darkness that belonged to him and gathered it in, pulling it into himself, swallowing the emptiness like heated wine, gripping it in his fist and pulling hard until the gold compressed into a solid mass that fell like lead to the floor.

He expanded, his element stretching the borders of his physical form until he felt as if all the space in the metal-wrapped compartment was his to command. The air answered him, whispering that it had been waiting. That it was glad to be seen.

That it would serve him.

Ben opened his eyes and saw Henri Paulson frozen in front of him, his eyes darting from the crumpled lumps of flesh and blood that were barely recognizable as the guards who had made up his personal retinue.

Mangled steel, flesh, and fluid coated the ground, and Paulson had to steady himself on the control panel as he started to slip.

"What are you?" The vampire didn't sound afraid.

He sounded fascinated.

"I'm Ben Vecchio. And you're Henri Paulson."

The vampire's eyes lit up. "You're remarkable. I will make you rich beyond your dreams."

Ben frowned. Did this vampire think everyone was for sale?

"No, thanks." Ben inhaled, and the air was thick with a blood mist that entered his lungs and fed his amnis. "I'm good."

He drew his sword back and swung, slicing the billionaire's head from his body in one clean cut.

Henri Paulson's disembodied head thunked against what remained of the glass windows and fell to the ground, rolling into a messy mass of flesh that had once been a water vampire. Guns, swords, and daggers sloshed in the bloodstained water that flooded the bridge, turning it into nothing less than a scene of elemental carnage.

Ben flew back, desperate to hide the evidence of his violence before Jennie's people saw what he had done.

He was not ready for questions about his power.

He surveyed the battle on deck, but it was clear that Jennie and her pink-glow-stick army had taken control of the *Nautilus*, so he gathered his bursting energy and brought a violent whirlwind to tear into the elevated bridge, sweeping away the machinery, the bodies, the weapons, and what was left of Henri Paulson into the ocean.

Jennie looked up and shouted at Ben, but he couldn't hear her.

All he could feel was a burning pain on his skin.

CHAPTER THIRTY-SIX

Brigid saw Tenzin curled into a ball in the corner of the room, but she couldn't focus on her. She knew the vampire would survive. That was what Tenzin did; it was what Brigid did.

She survived.

Brigid had survived abuse, violence, addiction, and fire for this moment. It rang in her head with the clarity of a single struck bell as she pulled the flames from Zasha's hearth into her hands, coaxing it—not like the lover that Oleg had described but as a friend.

I see you, she said to the flames. *I see you protecting me.*

The flames danced around her, swaying with a kind of glee as Brigid commanded them to burn around Zasha Sokholov, spinning and swirling around the fire vampire who had created them.

You are mine now.

She drew the flames out of the house, charring the walls until the timbers fell away and Zasha strode toward her, their black clothes on fire, the flames licking at their feet. With each step, the damp ground hissed.

"Bri-gid!" Zasha screamed. "What have you done?"

"You're finished, Zasha."

The fire rose around them, the needles on the ground quickly drying and bursting into flames wherever either of them walked.

Brigid's feet sank through the smoldering detritus in the clearing until her feet hit the ground and the earth touched her skin, soothing her like her mate's embrace.

"You're done." She paced in front of the house, drawing Zasha away from Tenzin. "It's you and me. Just us. It's always been comin' to this."

Zasha screamed and bared their fangs, blood dripping down their chin and along their chest. The fire snatched their tunic away like singed black feathers, and a scarred white torso emerged from the black cloth.

Brigid's clothes were also burning slowly, but the flames licked over her body, teasing and energizing her as she finally, finally held them lightly in her grasp.

That was what the fire had always wanted, Brigid realized as tears rolled from her eyes, turning to steam on her heated cheeks. It wanted to dance with her, to sing with her, and sometimes, yes, to destroy.

> "I want to rage. I want to destroy everything, and I don't know where that comes from."
>
> "It comes from you and it comes from the fire. Don't try to run from it when it's what gives you your strength."
>
> "I can't become the destroyer."
>
> "Fire is no simple thing. It consumes and creates. Destroys and revives."

Brigid paced in the darkness, the fire licking away the black cotton T-shirt she'd donned. Minutes before, she'd been soaked to the skin. Now the damp cloth was as dry and brittle as paper.

Zasha gripped a short sword in their hand, and the blade turned black from smoke.

She and Zasha circled each other, walking along the flaming perimeter of the clearing as the lush green forest and the misty night held the fire on the edge of control.

"You should have stayed away," Zasha said. "This is between me and the vampire who killed my mate." They pointed their sword back at the house. "This is between me and Tenzin."

"No." Brigid shook her head. "I'm not here for you or for her. I'm here for Walter."

No hint of recognition on Zasha's exaggerated face. *"Who?"*

"For Jackson and Rachel. The people that you helped kill." She pictured the old man surviving icy water and winter wind, surviving to tell the story of the family he'd lost. "I'm here for Jesse and Sandra. For a baby who won't know her grandparents because of you."

"They were human." Zasha waved a hand. "They were nothing."

They were everything.

"I'm here for Summer," she continued. "And for Lee. For Nic and Bex and Lucas. Even for Chance. For everyone you used. For every relationship you destroyed. For every evil suspicion you planted. And for every human and vampire you killed." She lifted her hand and felt the fire wrapping around her legs, her torso, and her arms. The last of her clothes had burned away along with her hair. She had no weapon other than herself and her element.

In that moment, Brigid realized she *was* the fire.

The saint and the goddess.

The destroyer and the creator.

She blasted a column of flames toward Zasha, who held up a hand and diverted Brigid's flames toward the forest.

A hemlock tree, shaking from the heat and the dry air, burst into flames on the edge of the clearing.

"I'll burn it all." Zasha's smile was madness. "I'll burn it all, Brigid. You know I will."

"This time there's no one but us on this island." Brigid spread her arms, and the fire leaped to her side. "Have at it. Do your worst."

Zasha's expression faltered when they realized they had no leverage. There were no victims to threaten. No innocents for Brigid to protect.

Brigid smiled when she realized that she'd done it. She'd finally isolated her enemy. Tenzin could fly away even if she was injured. There were no humans on the island, and they were surrounded by water.

"Burn it, Zasha. Burn it all! You're only killin' yourself." Brigid threw out her arms and sent two more columns of fire at the vampire, who batted them away, but this time, instead of hitting the forest around them, the rivers of fire flowed around Zasha and arrowed straight toward the tall wooden house.

Zasha spun and looked at the fire as it leaped to the wood shingles on the roof. "No!"

The wooden house quickly caught, the hungry fire eating away at the roof, the wooden shutters, and the railings before it began to consume the walls.

Brigid lost her breath for a moment. "Tenzin."

A burst of wind from the side of the house as a small figure shot like a bullet from the burning building and flew into the darkness above them, whatever flames that had been trailing her quickly quenched by the misty night air.

But the gently falling mist was no match for the fire that burned Zasha Sokholov's haven in the woods. Brigid fed it, directing her fire to the woodpile in the corner where she could smell human remains decomposing.

Rest, the fire whispered. *We will spread their ashes to the earth. Nothing is lost in the end.*

Brigid saw it in the curling golden flames.

Nothing would be lost.

"Our element isn't like the others." She heard Oleg's voice in her mind. *"The air, the earth, the water... But fire?"* Brigid watched the flames take the trees that had been used to build Zasha's hideout and turn them into ashes.

Fire is a process.

Zasha was raging and stomping around the clearing, batting back every column of flame Brigid threw at them, hurling it at the forest and the cliff behind the house.

But fire was a process, and Brigid wasn't going anywhere.

"Everythin' comes to an end," Brigid told them. "Even us, Zasha. Even me. If that's what it takes to keep you from hurtin' anyone else..." She choked on her words when she thought about Carwyn. This would hurt him. She could already feel his anger in her blood. His amnis was in her. Dying meant part of him would die with her.

But part of her would always live in him. It was the only comfort she could take.

"You're not leavin' this island." Brigid threw another column of fire toward Zasha, and they diverted it to the other side of the clearing, setting even more trees on fire.

They were fully engulfed, and even though the fire was dancing for Brigid now, at some point she knew that she could be consumed. Maybe it wouldn't come from her own fire, but Zasha was hurling their flames at Brigid; both were evenly matched.

The two fire vampires were surrounded by an inferno. The house was fully ignited, and the forest around them was burning. Not even the dense rainforest and the mist could combat the churning, fiery battle.

"What do ya want, Zasha?" Brigid shouted. "Because I can't let ya live."

"Then you'll die with me." Zasha gripped the sword in their hand and charged at Brigid.

She had no weapon. If Zasha wanted to kill her, they would

probably succeed even if Brigid's fire consumed the vampire in the process.

But halfway across the burning clearing, Zasha seemed to trip.

"No!" They looked around, their eyes careening around the clearing. "That's not fair!"

Brigid frowned and looked down as the vampire in front of her seemed to shrink before her eyes.

No, not shrink.

The ground was eating Zasha from below.

"No!" they screamed again. *"Noooo!"*

Brigid saw her opportunity and ran, blasting a stream of fire at Zasha's hand.

They screamed and dropped the sword, which Brigid picked up, her flesh sizzling against the heated steel as she lifted the sword from the ground, drew her arm back, and swung.

Zasha's eyes went wide the moment the blade bit their neck.

Then the metal sliced through their spine and it was over.

The world around Brigid erupted in flames, and the ground beneath her opened up, swallowing her whole.

———

HE MOVED EFFORTLESSLY through the silent earth, using his amnis to protect her from the fire, pushing away the rocks and roots until he could sense her. He felt the hum of her amnis glowing like a banked fire in the darkness.

Carwyn pushed through the soil until he was next to her, stretching his body out with the earth between them. Then he moved his hand, clearing a pocket around her face but leaving the rest of her smothered in the cool soil. Her warm, loving eyes flickered open.

He couldn't stop staring. Her face was flecked with faint scars from Zasha's flames, but her eyes were the same, the warm brown charred with grey along the edges, her gaze holding his as firmly as she held his heart.

He said nothing. What was there to say?

"You came," she whispered.

"I'll always come for you."

"I didn't feel you near."

He smiled a little bit. "You had it, darling girl. I just gave you a little assist at the end. This was your battle to win."

"With you." She took a deep breath and laid her head on his shoulder. "I'm always better with you."

"Glad you finally realized it."

She smiled, but it died away quickly. "The humans on the boat?"

"Ben was fighting with Jennie when I left. They had the upper hand, Brigid. They'll get everyone out that they can."

"Tenzin was hurt."

"She'll survive. That little vampire will always survive. It's her blessing and her curse."

"Yes." Brigid blinked, and he could feel her mind already pulling away from that moment, already reaching for the innocents who might still be in danger. "I'm naked."

"I noticed that, yes."

"Might need to borrow your shirt if we need to get back to the *Nautilus*," she whispered.

"Or you could rest for a bit." Carwyn's heart ached. "Let others fight the battle for a while."

"Carwyn—"

"Will you rest, Brigid? Just for this night. There will be another battle to fight tomorrow." He leaned forward and kissed her forehead. "I promise. There will be others you can help. But just for tonight, trust our friends to do the rest. You've done enough for now."

She whispered, "It's not enough. It'll never be enough."

Her heart was a burning fire, and he loved her for it. A thousand years wouldn't quench it. A thousand innocents rescued wouldn't quell her need to help the next.

For his Brigid, eternity was only worth it if she could mend the hurt, find the lost, and give them the justice they deserved.

"For tonight, Brigid" —he brushed a gentle hand over the curve of her forehead— "it is enough. You've done enough."

CHAPTER THIRTY-SEVEN

B en sat on the deck of the *Nautilus* as the humans they'd rescued from belowdecks waited in the falling rain for more ships to come and pick them up. Jennie said human-captained boats were leaving from Juneau with doctors and other day people on board, but they wouldn't reach the bay until dawn.

"We'll need to find shelter before then," Jennie said. "I hate the idea of leaving them here, but—"

"There are a dozen wind vampires who can wait for a while longer. There are humans on board some of the boats." He was scanning the sky, looking for Tenzin, but though he could feel her near, she wasn't showing her face. "Let your water vampires go back with you, leave the human personnel on board, and go find shelter."

"The bodies have all been thrown overboard." Jennie kept her voice low. "I don't think any will float up, but try to keep them away from the railings if you can."

"I'll see what I can do." Ben wasn't sure that these survivors wouldn't benefit from seeing their tormentors' bodies, but he was no expert.

The fifty-some humans on board were a mix of staff for the

cleaning and the cooking—including the missing chef from the *Dolphin*—a few favorite "pets" that belonged to Paulson's vampires, and random human captives taken from pirated vessels and raids along the coast.

The staff had been better treated than the captives, but all the humans were traumatized except for a few who appeared to have been in thrall to vampire guests on the ship. Those Jennie had already secured in the hold of her cruiser since Katya would need to question anyone who might have collaborated with Paulson.

"I've already contacted Katya. She and Oleg are coordinating to round up every ship in Paulson's shadow fleet using that list that Gavin sent." Jennie narrowed her eyes and drilled her gaze into Ben. "You're sure he's dead?"

"Head. Off." Ben sliced a finger across his neck. "Did it myself."

"I'm still not sure what happened on that bridge, but I'm glad he's gone."

"So am I." Ben needed to see Tenzin. He needed to feed her blood. He needed to have his mate in his arms, and he needed Jennie gone and her people taking charge of the human survivors so he could find her. "I'm going to find Tenzin and check on Carwyn and Brigid as soon as I can."

"I've never seen a fire in this part of Alaska before." Jennie looked out toward the island. "Hope everyone is okay."

"I'll report back to your people as soon as I know."

She finally left on her ocean cruiser, and Ben immediately flew to the island where the fire was burning.

He reached out with his amnis and felt his mate answer. Her need was as ferocious as the burning pain in her side.

Ben flew low over the forest, catching her scent in the branches of a pine tree where she was huddled in what was left of an old eagle's aerie.

"Tenzin?"

She looked up, and Ben's rage roared in his chest.

"*Where is Zasha?*"

"Dead." Tenzin's lips moved slowly and painfully. "Zasha is dead. I saw Brigid kill them."

"Fuck." Ben cradled her unburned cheek in his hand. "Oh my God, Tenzin. What happened? What happened to you?"

Whatever fire had burned Tenzin had slashed from her right elbow up her shoulder and crawled up her neck to the lower part of her right cheek. Her tunic was burned away from most of her body, and angry red scars marred her pale skin in an angle from her wrist to the edge of her right cheek.

Ben stared at her, his hands hovering and unsure. "What do I do?"

She shook her head. "Nothing. I'll heal. It'll take a long time, but it's surface damage only." She bent her arm, breaking open an oozing wound in the curve of her elbow. "No tendons or ligaments seriously damaged. I can still fight."

"Tenzin, stop moving." He didn't know where he could touch that wouldn't hurt. "I have to be able to do something."

"Nothing." She shook her head. "I just need time."

He remembered something his uncle had said once: Vampire blood could heal human wounds, at least on the surface. That was how they healed fang marks. Maybe it would help Tenzin too.

"Is Paulson dead?" Tenzin was leaning against the tree, but she didn't move more than her mouth.

"You're in pain. Yes, Paulson is dead."

"Life is pain. I'll survive." She blinked, and he saw tears rolling down her cheeks.

Ben wanted to crush something, but there was nothing to crush. Their enemies were dead, but it wasn't without cost.

"I'm going to give you blood."

"And I'll take it," she said softly. "But we need to find shelter first."

"You're going to drink from me as soon as we find shelter." He gently pulled the bloody cloth from the burn. "But first..." He bit deeply into his wrist and watched the blood well up.

"What are you doing?" Her voice snapped at him. "Benjamin, you were just in battle, and I know you haven't fed. We haven't had time to hunt, and—"

"Tiny, shut up." He pulled his wound open, and the blood flowed over her shoulder. "I know it's going hurt, baby, but I need you to stretch your head so I can put my blood on your neck."

"Do not call me baby," she said through gritted teeth.

Tenzin stretched her neck up with aching slowness, exposing the burned curve of her shoulder, her throat, and her cheek to his gaze. "I've learned to live with Tiny, but I am not a child."

"Fine." Pissing her off was the quickest way to get her mind off the pain. "Keep your chin up."

"Don't order me around."

"Baby, I haven't even begun to order you around yet."

She hissed at him, and the corner of his mouth went up. He much preferred angry Tenzin to quiet and hurt Tenzin.

The blood started to work, flowing over the open, angry wounds and smoothing them out until they weren't weeping fluid. The skin would still be rippled and would probably take years to regrow since vampires healed slowly, but it wasn't breaking open every time she moved.

"I didn't lose an arm or anything bad," Tenzin said. "I lost my right hand a long time ago. That took nearly a hundred years to grow back."

A hundred years? "Fuck me."

"Maybe tomorrow night." She let out a slow breath. "After I hunt."

"That wasn't an order, but feeding from me will be," Ben muttered.

He coated the surface of her wound again, smearing his blood from her neck down her shoulder and to the curve of her elbow, covering every inch of the wound. By the time he was finished, her skin had knitted together in angry red swirls that looked almost like an intricate flame tattoo over a quarter of her body.

Ben let out a sigh of relief. "Okay, that should help— Whoa."

Tenzin lunged at his neck, sinking her fangs into his vein and settling in his lap as she wrapped her unhurt arm around his neck and stroked the hair at his nape.

Ben blanked out the pain of her bite and stroked a hand down her back as she fed. "Good." He traced his fingers lightly across her back. "Take everything you need."

She was safe. She would heal.

Paulson was dead. Zasha was dead.

His mate was wounded, but she would heal.

As soon as they found shelter, he could rest.

———

Two years before

TENZIN WATCHED the small bird hopping down her arm. Harun the green lovebird tossed her an indignant whistle before he flew across the glass house and perched next to his mate in the branch of a ficus tree, glancing at Tenzin before he started grooming the feathers along Layah's peachy-orange neck.

They had been in Penglai for the winter holidays, and even though her sire had tried to persuade them to stay for the Lunar New Year, Tenzin had been anxious to return home.

Now she was stripped down to a thin tank top, staring at the remarkable plants she and Chloe had managed to keep alive through the chilly winter on a rooftop in New York City. The heater was running, as was the humidifier, creating a mild sauna effect in the glass house that kept the plants and the birds warm.

She stared at the lush greenery but could only picture a frozen night in Siberia and the wailing cries of a vampire whose mate was dead.

The same cries she'd echoed on a riverbank in the Wuyi Mountains in the not-very-distant past. Tenzin leaned forward and stared at the weeping, arched branches of a potted maiden-hair fern.

She whispered, "The blood of Temur remembers who you were."

Stephen's body lay in a bed of wild ferns on the edge of a beautiful river that tumbled over rocks, and Tenzin knelt beside him, stroking his cold cheek.

In his brief years of immortality, this water vampire had never learned to regulate his body temperature to appear more human. He'd never enjoyed the taste of blood. Her mate, in the end, had not been particularly good at being a vampire.

But he had been kind. He had loved. He had made her remember gentleness and laughter. Stephen had woken Tenzin's frozen heart, which had been so angry after Nima refused immortality.

She heard whispers in the back of her mind, taunting laughter she'd suppressed for centuries. There was a keening wail in her memory, the wrecked sobs of an immortal watching their mate's body dissolve into its element.

Tenzin hadn't waited to see Temur's blood return to the wind when she'd killed his last descendant so many centuries before, but she remembered when Stephen had died. She'd watched his body return to the water as the white strips of his burial clothes flowed away like ribbons cast into the air.

She could imagine now what that weeping vampire had felt because she had lost a mate too, experienced the wrenching pain, both physical and mental, of half your amnis dying in the body of another.

The fact that you survived it was as good as another death.

She laid his head next to his body. She would have to wrap him to give him a proper burial. His daughter would help her prepare him, but only after he appeared whole. She could feel others standing over them, watching as Stephen's body grew stiff and his daughter wept in the arms of her mate.

For the first time in Tenzin's immortal life, she understood grief.

She watched Harun and Layah flick from branch to branch, singing their song back and forth, the secret language of lovers who existed in a world of their own making. Tenzin might have built the glass walls of the garden where these birds lived, but the world that they created was their own.

What secrets did these creatures understand that she didn't? What colors did they see? What scents could they perceive? She was a prisoner of her own existence, only understanding through the senses she'd been given.

Mortal life in all its forms was brief, painful, and precious because of its brevity. Her birds' lives would pass like the flash of a wildflower in the grass, and they were all the more precious to her for it.

"Your blood will be part of this river." She bent to her mate's ear and whispered in her own language so the others would not listen. "You're not dead, Stephen. Not really. Your body will return to the water. Your tears will return to the sea." She closed her eyes and listened to the cries of her mate's beloved child.

It was one of the things that had connected them. She had told Stephen about her children because he understood.

"One day," she continued whispering, "the blood that stains this grass will fall as rain on the earth your daughter walks on. And your spirit will exist in me forever. Nothing is wasted in the end." She closed her eyes and repeated to herself, "Nothing is wasted."

Delicate flakes of snow fell on the roof of the glass house, melting at the first touch of the warm surface. The water in the air gathered on the walls, dripping down the cool glass so it looked like the walls of the garden were weeping.

The blood of Temur remembers who you were.

She knew the vampire who had attacked the house in Louisiana with a terrible, angry fire. She recognized the hate, and she remembered the rage.

She remembered the rage.

A low, vibrating anger crept into her mind, mixing with the raw grief of her mate's loss. Tenzin rocked back and forth, one hand on Stephen's cheek and the other over the place where his heart had once beat when he was human, before his life had been stolen by a ruthless vampire bent on revenge.

She would kill Lorenzo. If it was the last thing she did, she would watch the life drain from his eyes, see his body dissolve into water, and watch him become nothing.

Nothing.

Tenzin stood, watching the birds fly in circles around her as she paced back and forth in the small confines of the glass house. The air smelled of earth and water, of green, verdant life cultivated in the bitter winter of eastern North America. She'd brought plants from Yunnan and the Caribbean to fill this garden.

She'd hung orchids from Colombia in baskets along the walls and stacked rocks in the corner to make a fountain filled with water blessed by her worshippers in Tibet.

Life persisted even in darkness and cold. It cycled and turned into something new. Perhaps the water in that fountain contained elements of the mate she had lost. Perhaps the earth that grew her plants held the bodies of her children. Her mate's amnis lived in her even as she tied her life with another.

Stephen lived.

Temur lived.

And that was the truth she'd never wanted to admit.

Life persisted. In freezing winter. In fire and blood and loss.

Life persisted, and her quest to eliminate Temur's blood from the earth—the blood of those who had killed and raped and maimed—was as futile as a single snowflake falling on warm glass.

"Tenzin?" Ben tapped on the glass. "Hey. I was looking for you."

His smile was brilliant in the darkness.

Her amnis leaped in recognition, reaching out to draw him in from the cold.

"What are you doing up here?" He cracked the door open, and Layah flitted to his shoulder. "Hello, beautiful." He reached up and touched the tip of his pinky finger to Layah's curved beak. "Are you telling Tenzin your secrets?"

The ground on the riverbed was soft under Tenzin's knees as she knelt next to Stephen's body. Ancient words sprang from her, pleading prayers from a nearly forgotten part of her memory: "My mothers, guide my beloved to the tree of souls

My fathers, take his bones to build his next life

Beloved, let your soul rise to the stars

I will sing you to your next life

I will sing you to your next life

Your soul will not be lost when the mothers take you to the tree

Your body will return to build another with the fathers' help

You will not be lost if you follow my voice

I will sing you to your next life."

"What are you doing up here?" Ben asked again.

Trying to be philosophical about death when I would relentlessly hunt down anyone who made you frown. "I've been thinking about what we talked about on Penglai."

Ben blinked and his eyebrows rose. "About—"

"You told me only dead things don't grow. And that I was not dead."

Ben sat on a wooden stool by the door, and Layah flew back to the ficus tree. "Because you're not."

"And I told you that it was my right to judge Temur's descendants. That I would kill who needed to be killed if I encountered another vampire with Temur's blood."

Ben's voice was soft. "I remember."

"And I realized tonight that continuing that quest is futile. In the end, hunting down any trace of Temur's descendants—especially now—would be useless."

Ben nodded slowly. "Why?"

"I'm telling you that you are *right*." She forced the word out. "Can't you simply accept that?"

"No." He plucked at a thread on the seam of his pants. "Because I love you, and I want to know what led you to this."

She walked over and knelt beside him, slicing the thread to the seam with the edge of her fingernail so he didn't ruin his pants. "I was thinking about Stephen."

His hand lifted; then he clenched his fingers into a fist. "Your other mate."

"Who died." She sat back on her heels and looked up. "Except he didn't. His amnis lives in me. In Beatrice, his daughter. Even in Giovanni, because he is mated to Beatrice."

"In me."

"Yes." She nodded. "Our bodies and souls contain *worlds*, my Benjamin. Nothing ever truly dies. We are made of every life that came before us." She smiled. "Do you realize that in the past five hundred years, over thirty *thousand* people had to meet, mate, and keep each other alive for you to even exist?" She put her hand on his and squeezed. "Did you know that?"

Ben blinked. "What? No. That's—"

"We are *worlds*, Benjamin. Were I to hunt down every drop of Temur's blood, I would be destroying worlds." She took a slow breath and looked up to meet his eyes. "And you told me once that you didn't want me to destroy the world."

He put a hand on her cheek, stroked the skin there with his thumb. "See?" he whispered. "Only dead things don't grow, and you're the most alive person I know."

"I'm not going to hunt them again," Tenzin promised herself. "But that doesn't mean I won't protect what's mine. If you are in danger, if Chloe or Arthur or Giovanni or Beatrice or Sadia are threatened..." She shook her head. "I will still kill those who need to be killed. And I will never apologize for it."

He leaned forward and pressed his forehead to hers. "I would expect nothing less."

EPILOGUE

Seward, Alaska

B rigid sat at the old man's bedside, watching his eyes flicker behind his lids as he dreamed. She was wearing heavy sweatpants, an oversized T-shirt that smelled of her husband, and her singed head was covered in a black cap pulled over her ears.

A nurse walked into the room, checking something on a chart before she glanced at Brigid. "You the one who brought him in?"

She looked up from staring at Walter's sleeping face. "No, that was a friend of mine."

"He sleeps a lot." The nurse looked up. "But he's doing better. I think he had family visiting today."

"Good." Brigid managed to crack a smile when she thought about a baby somewhere in the south. A baby who would grow up knowing one of the toughest men she'd ever known. "That's excellent news."

"He might not wake for a while." The nurse looked at her. This was a clinic that Oleg ran; the nurse knew what Brigid was. "Might not be until daylight."

"Then I'll come back tomorrow night." She would come back as often as it took to speak to Walter herself. "Or the next."

She had time.

The nurse glanced at the angry red wound on Brigid's hand where Zasha's sword had burned her palm. "You want me to take a look at that while you're waiting?"

"It's fine." She closed her fingers around the smooth scar.

Carwyn had given her blood. That burn was as healed as it was going to heal for now. The rest was just a matter of time.

"You family too?" The nurse looked at her, clearly suspicious of the pale Irish vampire waiting at the old man's bedside.

"Not family," Brigid said. "In fact, I don't really know him that well."

"But the boss said it was okay for you to wait?"

"Yeah." She looked back at Walter's sleeping face. "I'm here to give my report."

———

New York City

TENZIN STARED at the wreckage of their penthouse. Though the majority of the rubble had already been cleaned up and their remaining belongings had been packed away in boxes in storage, it still felt like the aftermath of a battle.

She touched the edge of the scars that crawled up her neck, sliding the tips of her fingers over the smooth, swirling red marks that were evidence of the fire on Zasha's island.

Their insurance was rebuilding the top two floors of the building, including the roof garden that had been destroyed. Walls were already up, though they were bare, marked with pencil, and plaster dust was everywhere.

The basic layout would be the same. The windows and the alcove had already been built. They were adding a bathroom downstairs, along with another light-safe bedroom. The complete reconstruction would probably be done in another two months.

There was still no sign of Layah or Harun. If the little lovebirds had survived, they were not flying back.

In Tenzin's mind, she liked to imagine Harun heroically leading Layah through the storm and to the fire escape of a little grandmother in Washington Heights who would find the two birds and take them in. They would be pampered and cooed over, treated like the precious bright jewels they were.

Tenzin had made up many stories in her very long life. She decided she liked that one.

"No." Ben sat on the rebuilt steps that would lead out to the roof. "We don't need to sell it, but we should move on. At least for a while."

Tenzin had known Ben wouldn't want to stay. "Where?"

"Anywhere." He shrugged. "We've been in North America for a while. You want to be in Asia?"

She shook her head. "Politics are too complicated."

"Selfishly, I'd like to be somewhere back on the West Coast to stay near my sister since she's going to be an adult in five minutes or something," he said. "But I don't think we're very welcome in the Pacific Northwest right now."

Things in Katya's territory were definitely settled down, but there was still a lot of turmoil. She'd dug into Paulson's activities in more detail and discovered that while no one in her organization was directly involved in the hunts or Henri Paulson's silent attempt at a vampire coup, there were multiple vampires in her employ who had taken bribes to look the other way.

And there was still the issue of Oleg's creeping influence. His assistance in rounding up and identifying Paulson's shadow fleet in the Bering Sea and the North Atlantic was effective, but it was even more evidence that Katya's hold on the territory was not as secure as it had been a hundred years before.

All in all, it was an area that Ben and Tenzin wanted to avoid even if they had managed to stay above the politics. This time at least.

"The West Coast is big," Tenzin said. "And South America is an option too."

"That's still pretty far from Sadia." Ben narrowed his eyes. "What about Mexico?"

"What about it?"

"Who's the VIC in Mexico City these days? Do we know?"

"I don't know who it is right now, but it could be a relative of Ernesto's." Her eyebrows went up. "Ernesto Alvarez still likes us."

Ben nodded. "What do you say, Tiny? Want to go check out Mexico City and see what we think?"

"It's a quick flight to your aunt and uncle without being in their backyard." Tenzin nodded slowly. "Good art market," she muttered. "Nice museums."

"Tiny."

"What?" She blinked her eyes innocently. "To visit."

Ben smiled and stood up, walking over to her and taking her hand. "You never change."

"On the contrary, you make it a point to remind me nightly that I'm *evolving*." She looked around the room. "One thing that will remain unchanged is my sword collection. Which—thanks to it being metal and not canvas—was mostly undamaged by the fire."

Ben dropped her hand. "Really?"

"I'm just saying that paint and paper are less secure—"

"My library was destroyed, and it feels like you're rubbing it in." He muttered, "I'm telling Giovanni."

"I have no idea what you're talking about." She'd already been on the lookout for some new maps for him, but he didn't know that yet. "Gold, swords, and jewels are investments. That's all I'm saying."

He rolled his eyes but held out his hand. "Come on. Let's go to Gavin and Chloe's. I don't want to be here anymore."

She looked over her shoulder as they walked out onto the remains of the roof. "It will be beautiful again. You will love it here again."

"I know," he said quietly. "But right now I need to be somewhere new."

"Then let's go see our people." Tenzin took to the sky, waiting for him to catch up. "But you have to tell them we're leaving."

Cochamó Valley, Chile

CARWYN LAY in bed next to Brigid, her whole body relaxed and limp against his. She was stretched on her side, her face halfway hidden in the pillow and the scars from Alaska softened by the white silk pillow where her head was resting.

It was nearly dusk, and he'd woken in the comfort of his bedroom at their family ranch in the Cochamó Valley. Located in a remote region of Chile, it was a sprawling family compound consisting of a large ranch house, numerous smaller dwellings, human and vampire relatives of all ages.

And a lot of sheep.

They'd arrived two days before after a leisurely journey through North America, a rousing romp through Mexico City, a quick trip through Central America, and finally down to the southern continent in their new, reinforced Winnebago camper van, which was ancient, rattling, and perfect.

More perfect were the luxurious sheets and enormous featherbed in their bedroom at his daughter's massive ranch.

Brigid stirred, the first sign of life since she'd fallen into sleep that morning. She twitched, and a small spark erupted on her arm.

Carwyn reached over and snuffed it out with the heavy fire blanket he'd taken to keeping by the bed. There was another fire blanket between the sheets and the featherbed and still more blankets and a couple of fire extinguishers near the door.

Since Zasha's island, Brigid's fire had been... more present in their life. It was hard to think of it as anything other than a very excited puppy that had finally been let out of the house to play.

For the first few weeks, his mate wouldn't even let him sleep next to her and had demanded that he hollow out a cave in the ground to make sure that nothing would ignite when she was sleeping.

Deep sleep never seemed to create a problem, but Carwyn

had noticed that Brigid sparked a bit on waking. Luckily, he always woke before her, and Brigid's fire seemed to like Carwyn nearly as much as it liked Brigid.

In the years since her initial turning, Carwyn had always felt like Brigid's element was a wary ally in their corner, a weapon she carefully leashed and even more carefully guarded. Never too familiar. Never too common. Unlike the earth that he controlled, fire had always felt dangerous. Spiky and prickly, not unlike his Brigid.

But since the battle on the island, his mate had been filled with a peace that seemed to surprise her, and her fire had settled too. It was more present but less fearful. Less reactive and more a part of her nature.

There was a peace in his mate that he'd never seen before, and while none of her rough edges had disappeared, they might be just a little bit softer.

She took a deep breath and murmured his name. "Carwyn."

Carwyn smiled and traced a finger over her cheek. She turned in to his touch, her eyes flickering open, then closed again as she smiled.

"Good evening, darling girl."

"My fine man." She lifted her head and looked at him. "How long have you been awake?"

"Long enough to have a raging hard-on from looking at your arse." He planted one hand on her ample cheek.

"Such a romantic," she murmured. "Poetry just trips off your tongue."

"I know. You're such a lucky woman. Any dreams today?"

"Not a single one." She smiled. "Glorious."

Dreams had haunted her for the first few weeks, and her sleep —usually unshakable—had been restless and troubled.

She'd had visions of fire and had woken in the middle of the day screaming more than once, shaking away flames that were only in her mind. There was a bruised ache in her eyes and a haunted look.

Days passed. They left Alaska. They drove inland and spent time in the desert. She spent time with Lee, then with Natalie and Baojia. She called her friend Anne and had long sessions over video.

Carwyn knew she only needed time to heal from the battle, because every step she'd taken—every kill, every compromise—had been for the protection of the innocent.

He knew that, and eventually she'd realized it too.

Eventually he'd convinced her that while they didn't need to stop taking cases, they were due for a long and well-deserved rest.

"When we go to Bali and I keep you naked for several weeks" —he rolled her onto her back— "what food would you like me to stock up on?"

He began kissing down her body and let out a happy growl when he felt her fingers stroke through his hair. He was letting it grow, and it was getting to be more and more bearlike with every passing month. He was working toward a full reddish pelt while Brigid's hair was barely a pixie cut these days.

It suited her. He suited her.

Carwyn kissed down her body, teasing and tickling her the way he knew she loved. The only time he'd ever heard Brigid giggle was when he made her laugh in bed.

She loved him. She loved his great clumsy heart that fell in love with her, tripping over itself again and again, every time he caught a glimpse of her beautiful eyes or her pert nose. It fumbled like a clumsy oaf when her fangs dropped or her stern mouth hinted at the beginning of a smile.

She was a warrior, and he adored her. He'd spend eternity adoring her, and it wouldn't be anything but what she deserved.

Carwyn pressed a long kiss to the scar in the shape of a curled feather that had burned into the skin on her belly.

Oh, his fine woman. This soldier with the softest heart.

"I love you so much," she whispered.

He couldn't take any more. He crawled up her body, kissed her full on the mouth, and entered her, joining their bodies as if it was the first and the only and the always of what they were. It was every night they'd shared their amnis and every moment they'd made love.

He worshipped her with his body, coaxing her to climax before he flipped them over and wrung another cry of pleasure from her chest.

When he finally came, Carwyn felt the ground beneath him rock in response to the intense pleasure of her bite.

"You know." Brigid laid her head on his barrel chest and played with the fine red hair that ran from his navel to his groin. "This is why we're banished to the basement."

A belly laugh burst from him, and the ground shook with that pleasure too.

He smacked a kiss on the top of her head. "I like being in the basement."

Carwyn had dug out their room at the ranch, an annex carved into the bedrock of the valley, joined to the main house by a long tunnel that afforded him and Brigid enough privacy that they could feel like it was their own but still connected to the family.

Her voice was sleepy. "Bali is it?"

"It's warm and sunny." He wiggled his eyebrows. "I bet I can pick up a few good shirts in Bali."

"Oh, I know ya can." She smiled. "I don't think you have a neon-pink one yet. We'll have to keep an eye out."

"And aren't you the best old girl a man could have, Brigid Connor!" He put on his broadest Welsh accent. "Ooh, fy blodyn tatws."

She laughed a little bit. "What are ya calling me?"

"My *darling* little potato flower."

"You are not."

"I definitely am."

She could not contain her smile, but she shook her head and covered it with her pillow. "You insane man, why do I love ya so much?"

"How could you not?" He jumped out of bed and curled his arms to flex his biceps. "Good Lord, woman, I'm a specimen."

Her eyes were not on his biceps, and her smile only grew broader. "I can't say you're not."

"Keep looking at me like that and you'll spend all night in this bed."

"Is that supposed to be a threat?"

He jumped back into the bed, caging her with his arms and lowering his head to take her lips in a long and generous kiss.

"You delight me," he whispered. "My bride."

"Do ya think we'll ever get sick of each other?" Brigid asked. "In a hundred years? A thousand?"

"Le do thoil. Please." He scoffed. "We'll have forgotten everything we learned by then and we can just start all over."

"Sláinte! Cheers to that." She laughed, and it was the most perfect sound in the world.

It was the most perfect sound in eternity.

And it was his.

AFTERWORD

Dearest Readers,

It started with a girl who wasn't afraid of monsters, and it's ending here, under a mountain, that same girl now a powerful immortal woman in the embrace of the earth vampire who will love her for eternity.

Brigid Connor's journey has been one of the most challenging and rewarding experiences of my life.

There were a lot of doubts when I created her character. Carwyn was already a beloved character from the Elemental Mysteries series, and I knew that the expectations for his love interest would be high.

Some readers didn't *get* Brigid—at least not right away—but if you've read this far, then I think you must love her as much as I do.

She's not always an easy character to love. She can be judgmental and rigid. She has a strong sense of justice and she's hard on people, mostly herself.

And Carwyn? What else is there to say about one of the most loving, boisterous, and vibrant vampires I've ever written, except that he's wonderful. He's good. And he deserves every bit of love that readers have for him.

Despite Carwyn's age and despite the tragedies that he's experienced in his long life, he is the personification of joy. He is not a perfect character by any means, but he's a character who has always felt like home. He grabs onto life and love with both hands. He doesn't wait for the right time to find joy. He just runs toward it with his arms wide open.

What a pair they are.

The Elemental Covenant series has come to a close, but please know that Carwyn and Brigid will live on, popping into other stories as they jump around the Elemental Universe. **You may even see them in the upcoming series I'm starting later this year featuring Oleg, a vampire with a story I've been waiting years to write.**

And Ben and Tenzin? Well, there's always another treasure to find, isn't there? There's always another bright and shiny object. **Ben and Tenzin's adventures will continue.** I'm hoping to write their next book in 2025. And Tenzin's evolution—her New Year's Resolutions, as she might say—will continue too. It's been a challenge and a privilege to explore such a complicated character, and I hope you've enjoyed the ride as much as I have.

Until the next time, my friends.

Thanks for reading,
Elizabeth Hunter

HAVE YOU JOINED THE HAVEN?

Hunters' Haven is a private Facebook group for Elizabeth Hunter fans, avid readers, and lovers of fantasy fiction. Join today (don't forget to answer the questions!) and be the first to know about special sales, exclusive announcements, and new fiction.

VISIT HUNTERS' HAVEN MERCH SHOP AND
GRAB YOUR EXCLUSIVE ELEMENTAL
COVENANT "ICON TEE"

SCAN THE CODE TO CHECK OUT THIS AND OTHER
ELIZABETH HUNTER BOOK MERCHANDISE FROM
MY TEESPRING STORE!

HuntersHavenShop.com

ABOUT THE AUTHOR

ELIZABETH HUNTER is an eleven-time *USA Today* and international best-selling author of romance, contemporary fantasy, and paranormal mystery. Based in Central California and Addis Ababa, she travels extensively to write fantasy fiction exploring world mythologies, history, and the universal bonds of love, friendship, and family. She has published over forty works of fiction and sold over a million books worldwide. She is the author of the Glimmer Lake series, Love Stories on 7th and Main, the Elemental Legacy series, the Irin Chronicles, the Cambio Springs Mysteries, and other works of fiction.

ElizabethHunter.com

ALSO BY ELIZABETH HUNTER

The Elemental Mysteries

A Hidden Fire

This Same Earth

The Force of Wind

A Fall of Water

The Stars Afire

Fangs, Frost, and Folios

The Elemental World

Building From Ashes

Waterlocked

Blood and Sand

The Bronze Blade

The Scarlet Deep

A Very Proper Monster

A Stone-Kissed Sea

Valley of the Shadow

The Elemental Legacy

Shadows and Gold

Imitation and Alchemy

Omens and Artifacts

Midnight Labyrinth

Blood Apprentice

The Devil and the Dancer

Night's Reckoning

Dawn Caravan

The Bone Scroll

Pearl Sky

Tin God

The Elemental Covenant

Saint's Passage

Martyr's Promise

Paladin's Kiss

Bishop's Flight

Tin God

The Irin Chronicles

The Scribe

The Singer

The Secret

The Staff and the Blade

The Silent

The Storm

The Seeker

The Seba Segel Series

The Thirteenth Month

Child of Ashes (Summer 2025)

The Gold Flower (Summer 2026)

The Cambio Springs Series

Strange Dreams (anthology)

Shifting Dreams

Desert Bound

Waking Hearts

Dust Born

Vista de Lirio

Double Vision

Mirror Obscure

Trouble Play

Glimmer Lake

Suddenly Psychic

Semi-Psychic Life

Psychic Dreams

Moonstone Cove

Runaway Fate

Fate Actually

Fate Interrupted

Linx & Bogie Mysteries

A Ghost in the Glamour

A Bogie in the Boat

Contemporary Romance

(*Writing as Lizzy Hunter*)

The Genius and the Muse

Turning Up the Heat

7th and Main

Ink

Hooked

Grit

Sweet

Made in the USA
Coppell, TX
07 October 2024

38289637R00231